Fate's Redemption

Fate's Redemption

KEITH LEE JOHNSON

A STREBOR BOOKS INTERNATIONAL LLC PUBLICATION
DISTRIBUTED BY SIMON & SCHUSTER, INC.

Published by

Strebor Books International LLC
P.O. Box 6505
Largo, MD 20792
http://www.streborbooks.com

ISBN 1-59309-039-0
LCCN 2004118374

Distributed by Simon & Schuster, Inc.
1230 Avenue of the Americas
New York, NY 10020
1-800-223-2336

Cover Design: www.mariondesigns.com

First Printing May 2005
Manufactured and Printed in the United States

10   9   8   7   6   5   4   3   2   1

Praise for *Fate's Redemption*

"Keith Lee Johnson writes with power and vigor, navigating hot, controversial terrain with a fully charged pen."

—Tracy Price-Thompson, author of *Black Coffee, Chocolate Sangria*, and *A Woman's Worth*

"A labyrinth of thrills. From page one, Keith Lee Johnson packs on the action and never lets up. Expect a sleepless night with this read, but as you turn the last page you will have been redeemed."

—Phillip Thomas Duck, author of *Playing with Destiny*

"Keith Lee Johnson is on the fast track to becoming America's #1 suspense writer. I hate reading him while I'm working on my own books because nothing gets done until I finish the last page."

—Travis Hunter, author of *Hearts of Men, Married but Still Looking, A One Woman Man*, and *Trouble Man*

"A pulse-pounding combination of action, drama, and romance that'll grab you from the first sentence and hold you captive to the very end. Everyone needs to be reading Keith Lee Johnson."

—Brandon Massey, award-winning author of *Dark Corner* and *Thunderland*

"Keith Lee Johnson always delivers readers a striking combination of intense and action-packed enjoyment. His sinister villains instantly mesmerize, treating you to a fascinating and precarious ride; *Fate's Redemption* is no exception. With novels that are violent yet sexy, Johnson is the black folks' Sidney Sheldon."

—Cydney Rax, author of *My Daughter's Boyfriend*

Dedication

To Leonard Kress, my creative writing teacher at Owens Community College. Thanks for asking me to write this story in your class way back during the Spring Semester of 1996.

AND TO

Marcus Dixon of Rome, Georgia, an honor student who was to attend Vanderbilt University on an athletic scholarship, but was accused of "statutory rape and aggravated child molestation" by his white girlfriend.
Both were teenagers at the time of his conviction in 2003.
The conviction was overturned in January 2004.

*"The status quo sits on society like fat on cold chicken soup
and it's quite content to be what it is. Unless someone comes along
to stir things up there won't be change."*
— ABBIE HOFFMAN, 1967

*"If a man like Malcolm X could change and repudiate racism, if I myself
and other former Muslims can change, if young whites can change,
then there is hope for America."*
— ELDRIDGE CLEAVER, 1968

Prologue

Westin St. Francis Hotel
San Francisco, California
The Wise Wedding Reception
August 20, 1999

The bridesmaid blasted through the reception hall doors and ran to the groom. She was so gripped by fear that her entire body shook uncontrollably and the loud music made it difficult for the groom to hear what she was saying. The groom leaned over and the woman screamed something into his ear. Then he ran out of the hall.

The groom practically knocked the doors off their hinges when he entered the nursery, where his year-old babies wailed loudly as if they knew the gravity of the situation. He saw his wife, who was bound and gagged—her eyes bulging out of her head. Her face revealed the unimaginable fear that must have filled her mind. But the wife wasn't as afraid for herself or her husband, as she was for her two children, who lay in their crib, screaming for the affection they could only get from their mother.

A man was standing next to the wife with a silenced .9mm to her head. The hired nanny was lying in a pool of her own blood near the twin infants. The man had shot her in the face and chest when she tried to protect the children.

For a brief moment, the groom could hear the beating of his heart, which pounded in his chest like a jackhammer, threatening to explode. Having committed one murder, he knew the man had nothing to lose. He kept telling himself to stay calm, when everything in him wanted to wrestle the gun away from the man, put it in his mouth, and fire until there were no bullets left.

The man grinned. "So glad you could make it." He had a glazed, almost vacant look in his eyes. "We've got some unfinished business—you and I."

Somehow I've got to stall him. Make him think about what he's doing. "What do you want?" the groom asked in a forced calm. He looked completely relaxed, but he was mortified. *I've gotta do something before he pulls the trigger.*

"Isn't it obvious?" the man asked with a twisted grin. "I want you to watch her die. That's what I want. As you see," he continued and looked at the slain nanny, "I won't hesitate to kill, Doctor. I've killed eight others. I can still see their faces…" He seemed to be losing his grip on reality, but quickly gathered himself. "I'M NOT CRAZY!" the man shouted, then closed his eyes and took a deep breath, collecting himself again.

"I can't begin to tell you the rage I felt when I saw your wedding plans in the *Chronicle*," the man babbled on. "Here you two were getting married and moving on with your pathetic lives. And here I am with nothin'. No wife, no kids, no partner; nothin'. You two ruined my life. Now, do you really think I'm going to standby and watch you two have the best of everything? I sat in there and watched you two at that altar, looking into each other's eyes, saying your little vows like a 90's version of *Cinderella*. Well, you can forget about this fairy tale ending happily ever after."

"You don't want to kill her," the groom offered calmly, trying to maintain his composure. "I'm the one you wanted to hurt that night; not her. Please, let her and the babies go, and take me."

"Do you really think I'm going to let her go so you can be Prince Valiant? DO YOU?" the man screamed. "And don't think for a moment you can get into my head and talk your way outta this. I've been planning your deaths for too long to stop now." He pulled out another .9mm and slid it across the floor. It stopped about eight inches from the groom's feet. "Pick it up."

"Let's talk about this." The groom desperately pleaded with the man.

"That's the gun you took outta my holster that night. And this one, the one I'm holding to your pretty little wife's head, this is Sykes' gun. This way, it ends the way it was supposed to that night. Sykes would have killed you with this gun, Dr. Moretti," he told the bride. "As it stands,

2

this same gun is going to kill you." The man looked at the groom and yelled, "PICK IT UP, WILLY!"

"You expect me to be able to pick the gun up and shoot you before you kill my wife?"

"That's the deal, Willy." The man laughed. "And ya got ten seconds to try."

"What happened? Did your wife leave you while you were in prison?"

"Ten...Nine..."

The groom's mind raced. Time was dwindling. His precious bride's eyes seemed to be pleading with him to go for the gun; her muffled pleas made him even more anxious. The groom was a marksman but, with the stress of the situation, he was afraid he would accidentally shoot her instead.

"What happened to you in prison?" The groom stalled. "Were you abused? Sexually assaulted?"

"Eight...Seven...Six..."

Seeing no other way out, the groom picked up the gun as quickly as he could and squeezed the trigger...

Two years earlier...

Chapter 1: Truce

The Warehouse District
Boston, Massachusetts
August 1997

The streets in the Warehouse district were quiet enough to hear the water from an early evening rain dripping into the sewers. The city was unseasonably cool and the figures that were about to enter the district made the night air all the more chilling. After midnight, when all the warehouses were closed, the district was perfect for munitions deals, drug deals, payoffs, and murder. From the cop on the beat, to the Police Commissioner, to the mayor's office, all were getting a piece of the million dollar deals that took place in the Warehouse district.

On this particular night, Jericho Michael Wise, the leader of an elite group of former military personnel—all carrying diplomatic passports; and Cyrus King, the leader of the Jamaican Posse, were going to be there to discuss a territorial truce and a possible merger.

The limousine and a rented van were waiting for Jericho and his crew near the runway when "The Nighthawk"—Jericho's private jet—landed in Boston at 11:25 PM. Victor Marshall, third in command, took the keys from the driver and gave him five hundred dollars. Jericho got into the limo and called Sergio, his lieutenant in Boston, to make sure he had the usual fifty street soldiers on standby. The rest of the crew began loading the weapons and equipment into the van.

"How come we always gotta bring all this shit when we never use it?" Charlie fumed. "We got a fuckin' arsenal here. We got rocket launchers, grenade launchers, stinger missiles, and twenty thousand rounds of bullets.

And for what? We never use the shit. None of it. We just load and unload this heavy shit for nothin'."

"SHUT UP! And do yo' goddamn job," Victor retorted. "I'm sick of yo' belly aching every time we make a trip to the States. You know we have to be prepared for any contingency."

Victor made sure all the equipment was loaded before getting into the limo. Both vehicles left the airport, but went in two different directions. Jericho, Victor, and Cochise, the six-foot-nine Seminole, who drove the limo, went to dinner at Carmen's, a vibrant soul food restaurant with a New Orleans flavor. The van and its occupants went on to the Warehouse district.

Cyrus King was an ambitious and ruthless drug dealer from New York City. He had been taking over parts of Boston for a couple of months, and wanted to control the Warehouse district because that's where the real money was.

Jericho and Cyrus agreed to discuss their differences and to try and forestall a war. He thought he could convince Cyrus to work with him and further solidify his seat of power on the East Coast. But he didn't trust Cyrus, so he sent in a team to scout the Warehouse district and make sure there would be no surprises. If Cyrus was true to his word, Jericho would do business with him.

The team was led by Pin Tuan My-Khanh (Peen Tung Mee-Khan), Jericho's wife, closest companion, trusted bodyguard, and second in command. It was 12:35 AM when Pin led the team into the Warehouse district under the cover of darkness. They were dressed in black and green camouflage uniforms and equipped with state-of-the-art electronic surveillance equipment. They used heat scanners, motion detectors, listening devices, night vision goggles, 30-channel radios, and a super-fluous array of weapons.

Using the heat scanners and listening devices, Cyrus's men were easy to locate. One by one, Pin and the team skillfully captured all ten Jamaicans. Most of the Jamaicans weren't even aware of their presence until it was too late.

Pin took pride in her ability to extract information quickly. She lined the Jamaicans up ten across. Before asking the captured men a question, she pulled out her silenced .9mm Remington P228 Sig Sauer, and promptly executed five of them, shooting them at point-blank range right between the eyes without changing the innocent expression on her face. Just as Pin was about to shoot the sixth Jamaican, he started telling her everything she wanted to know.

The other Jamaicans yelled at the trader, trying to shut him up so Pin continued the executions, letting only the trader live for Cyrus's call. After the trader convinced Cyrus that everything was set, Pin told him he could go. When he turned to leave, she shot him in the back of the head.

At about 2:00 AM., Jericho's limo was on its way to the Warehouse district for the rendezvous when the phone rang. He was reading a copy of Niccolo Machiavelli's *The Prince* for the fifth time. Prior to being expelled from Berkeley University, Jericho had started reading the classic works of Shakespeare, Sophocles, Milton, and many others; enjoying philosophy more than any other literary work. He turned the book over and placed it on his thigh, splitting it in two. Then he picked up the phone and said, "Talk to me."

"You right. It masquerade," Pin spoke into a secure state-of-the-art cell phone, looking at the moving limousine with a pair of binoculars from the roof of one of the warehouses. She had been a citizen of the United States for about twenty years, but she still spoke broken English.

"How many?"

"Ten."

"Did they talk?"

Pin was silent. She felt insulted he questioned her effectiveness after all this time. Jericho realized he offended her with the question and quickly moved on. He thought about reminding her to make sure they were using armor-piercing bullets, but thought better of it.

"Did he check in?"

"He check in five minute ago."

"Can you see him yet?"

She moved her binoculars to the right and saw Cyrus's limo. "Yes. He approaches from east. He be here about two minute after you."

"Okay, go to channel B on the radio," Jericho instructed.

"Okay."

Only the unit knew channel B was actually channel 7. Even so, they never said anything incriminating on the phone or radio because they never knew who was listening; even though they used secure phones. *Better to be safe than locked up!* They also talked in short controlled sentences so that whoever listened couldn't figure out what they were talking about. Victor handed Jericho an electronic earpiece that served as both a listening device and a transmitter; standard CIA equipment. He said, "Eagle leader, this is Raven. How do you read?"

"Raven, this Eagle lee-dar. I read loud and clear," Pin said. Then the rest of the team acknowledged in sequence.

"Okay," Jericho continued. "Is everybody in position?" They all answered in sequence again.

"Eagle lee-dar in position."

"Eagle two in position."

"Eagle three in position."

"Eagle four in position."

"Eagle five in position."

Jericho asked, "What's the signal, Eagle leader?"

Pin answered, "When he light cigarette."

"Where is he now?"

"Just turn corner. E.T.A. 30 second."

"Get a fix immediately and hold until he gives the signal. As soon as you have a fix, let me know. Until then, maintain radio silence."

Victor waited until Jericho was finished talking to Pin, then he asked, "Gonna have to kill 'em, huh?"

"Yeah. It's a damn shame, too."

"So what was his plan?"

"When he lights his cigarette, the action is supposed to start. But we gon' reverse it on his ass."

Jericho, Victor, and Cochise sat in the limo and waited for their prey to enter the trap. A few seconds passed and they saw the headlights of Cyrus's oncoming limo. Even with the windows up, they could hear Cyrus's music. Cochise signaled the car by flashing the bright lights twice. The limo acknowledged by flashing its lights in like manner. Then both parties got out of their cars.

Victor and Cochise got out of the car first and looked around; surveying the area to make sure Cyrus wouldn't suspect anything. Then Jericho stepped out of the limo. He was five-feet, nine and a half inches tall, all muscle, granite chin, and weighed a lean one hundred sixty pounds. He was wearing a pair of black slacks, a collarless mustard-colored long-sleeve shirt, and a black leather vest that had an Oakland Raiders emblem on the back. Even though he was forty-four, he looked like he was in his mid-twenties. When he wore his wire-rimmed glasses, he looked like a college professor.

They could hear the music much clearer now. It was James Brown's "Living in America." Cyrus got out of the car, flanked by his bodyguard and three of his men. Cyrus inexplicably danced to the music and sang the chorus. He was wearing a red, white, and blue leather jacket with an American flag on the back.

As they got closer to each other, Jericho fixed his eyes on Cyrus. He could feel the murderous intent that exuded from him. Yet there was a beaming, almost angelic smile on his face. Cyrus's smile was so wide he could see the gold that covered his left canine. *He must love killin' as much as I love fightin'*, Jericho thought. As they moved closer still, he could hear Pin giving orders to the other snipers.

"What the hell are we waiting for? We could take 'em all right now," Charlie barked on the radio.

"Knock off chatter," Pin snapped. "I have Cyrus."

Then they confirmed in sequence the person each of them would kill.

"Why don't you turn that shit off?" Cochise shouted.

"What's the matter, mon? You don't like James Brown?" Cyrus teased.

"Naw, the Godfather of Soul is cool. I don't like unprofessionals," Cochise said, with a menacing snarl.

Cyrus turned around and pointed what appeared to be a remote control for the stereo system. Suddenly there was quiet again.

"So what's this deal supposed to be?" Jericho took the initiative. In his earpiece, he could hear each member of the Eagle squad say, "Ready in sequence."

"Dat's what I like about you, mon. You so direct," Cyrus said, as he moved his dreadlocks out of his face and onto his shoulders.

"Get to the fuckin' point!" Jericho snapped.

"Okay, mon," Cyrus said with that same angelic smile. "Do you mind if I smoke?"

Reaching into his pocket, Cyrus pulled out a book of matches. He struck the match with his right hand and brought his left hand around the end of the cigarette. Out of the corner of his eye, he saw his men fall to the ground in the same instant. Stunned by what had taken place, his smile vanished as he looked at the clean bullet holes in their chests. He didn't hear a shot, yet his bodyguard and three of his best men were lying dead before him with blood seeping through their shirts. He reached for his gun, but Victor and Cochise were already pointing their weapons at him. Victor went over and pulled Cyrus's gun from its holster, and put it in the front of his pants. Cyrus stood there with a confused look on his face. Then he realized Pin wasn't there.

"So where's the chink?" he wondered aloud.

Jericho said, "Come on down, Pin. Our guest of honor misses you." Then he looked at Cyrus and said, "You's a damn fool. In a few years, you would have made more money than you could have ever dreamed." His distribution network had begun in San Francisco in the early eighties and spread to the heartland and various parts of the United States. "I'm gonna give you the chance to finish what you started. But know this, even if you kill me, make no mistake, you're going to die tonight," Jericho promised Cyrus. "You don't have the vision to run this muthafucka. Now do you want it done quickly, or do you want to go out on your feet like a man?"

"Den we all die tonight," Cyrus said firmly.

Jericho's men formed a small circle around the combatants. Jericho and Cyrus stood in close proximity of each other with their hands in a defensive posture. They circled each other looking for an opening. Both men could hear the jeers Jericho's men made. One said, "Fuck 'em up, Jay." Another one said, "You 'bout tuh get yo' ass whupped, Cyrus." Cyrus moved into striking distance and swung wildly with his left hand. Jericho ducked under the blow. As the blow went over his head, he kneed Cyrus in the stomach. Cyrus grunted in pain but he was determined to continue the joust.

Angry, Cyrus swung wildly again, this time with his right. And again, Jericho ducked under the blow, and delivered another knee to his midsection. Cyrus groaned again; he was furious now. Not only was he outsmarted by Jericho, but he was also being humiliated. Cyrus screamed maniacally and charged, but Jericho dropped to one knee at the last possible second and delivered a powerful blow to the groin. Cyrus grabbed his crotch, fell to his knees, and vomited his dinner. They could see bits of shrimp, lettuce, and some sort of salad dressing that he had eaten earlier that night. He was more determined than ever to kill Jericho. He struggled to his feet. Sensing his weakness, Jericho moved in again to punish him some more. Under ordinary circumstances, he wouldn't have toyed with him but he wanted to torture him before he killed him.

Cyrus tried to jab, but Jericho slipped the punch, stepped inside again, and threw a three-punch combination to his body. The thunderous blows thudded loudly when they landed. Cyrus doubled over and spit up blood. He stood up and tried throwing punches in combination, but the constant missing drained him of any strength he had left.

Jericho moved in again, and threw a wicked right to the midsection, which made Cyrus double over again. Jericho then grabbed Cyrus's collar and kneed him in the midsection repeatedly, then let him fall to the ground.

"No more, mon," Cyrus said after that series of blows. "Just kill me and be done with it."

"I thought you Jamaicans were supposed to be tougher than this. Get up!" Jericho shouted. "I thought a bigshot wannabe like you would put up a better fight."

His taunting words gave Cyrus the will to get back up. He tried to jab him, but once again, his wild blows missed badly. Jericho slipped the jab, stepped inside and threw another three-punch combination to his mid-section and ended it with a sharp uppercut to the nose that brought Cyrus to his knees again. His blood splattered all over his face. While Cyrus was still on his knees, Jericho kicked him in the face. Then when he saw he had no more fight in him, he told Victor to give him Cyrus's gun.

Jericho stuck the gun in Cyrus's mouth and fired. As the sound of the shot echoed off the nearby buildings, they could hear the shell casing hit the ground.

Chapter 2:
Dirty Little Wars

Boston, Massachusetts
August 1997

They put Cyrus King, his bodyguards, and the men Pin had captured inside one of the warehouses into King's limo. They had to put some of them in the trunk. Just before leaving the Warehouse district, Pin thought about what happened during the operation. She was angry with Charlie for breaking radio silence.

Breaking radio silence was a flagrant breach of security. If the authorities were monitoring their frequency, he could have given away their position. The police could have figured out where they were and come. Even worse, had the police come, they might have had to shoot their way out. She decided to take care of Charlie on the spot. She walked over to him and with the friendliest of smiles, she said, "Charlie, what mean radio silence?"

Before he could answer, she slapped him with the back of her hand. Charlie's head snapped back and to the left. Her smile had distracted him just long enough to get the blow in. Then she kicked him in the groin. Charlie doubled over. He was trying to explain but Pin wouldn't have any explanations.

"What mean radio silence, Charlie?"

Then she continued the vicious beating. The other men watched in fear. They knew this was going to happen sooner or later. Pin was thorough and disciplined. They knew it was a gross breach of discipline to be talking in Jericho's ear just before they engaged the enemy. Pin kicked Charlie in the stomach again. The more he tried to explain, the more she beat him mercilessly. With every blow she delivered, she screamed, "What mean radio silence?"

Charlie rolled on the ground groaning. He was barely conscious. Pin bent down and whispered in his ear, "Can you hear me, Charlie?"

"Yeah," he groaned.

"What mean radio silence?"

"No unnecessary chatter," Charlie said in a voice riddled with pain.

Jericho didn't know what provoked her; even though he'd heard Charlie talking on the radio. Neither did Victor. They knew she probably had a good reason. Both of them looked at her, waiting on an explanation. Pin left Charlie on the ground and went over to Jericho and Victor. They all got into the limo. They always talked among themselves at times like these. There was always unity in front of the men; no matter what.

"Charlie weak link in operation."

"How?" Victor asked.

"He talk on radio during operation."

"I did call for radio silence," Jericho said, agreeing with his wife. "And he was talkin' unnecessarily."

"Yeah, and he complains too goddamn much," Victor added. "Fuck it. That's what the hell he gets for breakin' the discipline. He knows the rules of engagement."

"Let's roll," Jericho said. "Have somebody drive Cyrus's limo outta here."

"Have Charlie drive limo," Pin quickly added.

Victor got out of the limo and gave the orders to Charlie and the rest of the men. Then he got back into the limo with Pin and Jericho. Cochise pulled off and the van followed. Charlie struggled to his feet and got into Cyrus's limo. Jericho's limo had gotten several blocks away from the Warehouse district when he frowned.

"What's on yo' mind?" Victor asked.

"What do you think Cyrus meant when he said something about us all dying tonight?"

"Yeah," Victor wondered also. "That's some strange shit to be sayin'. He must have meant somethin' by it."

Suddenly, they heard a big explosion. It shook the limousine violently.

They knew instantly it was Cyrus's limo that exploded. Whipping their heads around, they could see what happened. Many of the warehouses had been completely leveled by the blast. Others were in a blaze.

Then it occurred to Jericho that Pin said to have Charlie drive the limo. He looked at her and she was sitting there peacefully filing her nails like she knew all along what was going to happen. A wicked grin covered her face. Cochise pulled the limo over. Victor got out. He could smell the C-4 in the coolness of the night air. He got back into the limo.

"I can smell C-4."

"C-4?" Jericho repeated. "Where the hell would Cyrus get C-4?"

They all looked at each other questioningly for a couple of seconds. Then it came to them all at the same time.

"Hawthorne!" they said in unison.

"Yeah, but why would Hawthorne give him C-4?" Victor asked, as though he were thinking out loud.

"To regain control. That's why," Jericho deduced.

"No wonder Cyrus was being so bold," Victor continued. "He thought by gettin' rid of us, he'd have the Agency runnin' interference for him."

In Vietnamese, Pin said, "We should be concerning ourselves with how he even knew Hawthorne. And when was he approached by him?"

"Yeah. And why was it so important to meet at two in the morning?" Jericho answered in Vietnamese. "Victor, take the van back and make sure Charlie's dead. If he's just hurt, they might turn his ass."

Victor got out of the limo and into the van. The van turned around and sped back to the blast area. They could hear sirens blaring in the distance. Time was of the essence. They had only minutes to get back to the blast, check it out, and then get out of there before being seen by the police.

"Give me your radio," Jericho told Pin.

"Nighthawk, this is Raven. Are you monitoring?"

"Raven, this is Nighthawk. That's affirmative. I say again, this is Nighthawk. I am monitoring."

"Start the engines, Nighthawk. We're comin' in hot."

"Roger, Raven. Starting engines now. What's your E.T.A.?"

"E.T.A., twenty minutes."

"Roger, Raven. Nighthawk understands twenty minutes. Out."

"Break, Break," Jericho continued. "Condor, Condor, this is Raven."

Victor answered, "Raven, this is Condor. Go ahead."

"What's the status of the situation?"

"There's nothing left."

"Roger, will meet you at the rendezvous point in twenty minutes."

"Roger, understand twenty minutes."

Jericho looked at Pin and said in Vietnamese, "We gotta figure this out. What was the plan here? What could Hawthorne get out of this?"

"Do you think he had access to a satellite?"

"Maybe. That way he has whoever comes outta this thing in one piece."

"Yeah, but did the satellite pick up everything?"

"I don't know, but we'll find out soon enough. Even if they did, it would be inadmissible in court. The CIA isn't supposed to be runnin' domestic operations. Besides, they're probably trying to get control of things; especially since the President issued a new war on drugs policy. The President's putting pressure on to stop the drugs from coming into the country. They have to make it look like they're making an effort without getting themselves indicted. Cyrus would have been easier to control so they could continue financing their dirty little wars."

"That means we've become expendable. Maybe even a liability to the Agency. This is dangerous for us. We need to get some Intel fast."

"I doubt we're expendable now that Cyrus is dead. They still need a liaison to sell weapons for them. Selling weapons is still their most profitable way to finance dictatorships. They don't want to willingly give that up."

"I agree," Pin told him. "By getting rid of the wild card, we've made ourselves viable because we can deliver. The Agency knows this. That'll buy us some time."

"Yeah, it will. But we better start making some moves of our own and secure our own future. They might try this shit again. We'll make plans when we get back to the Renegade."

The limo pulled into the airport and headed out to the runway. The van came in about two minutes later. They boarded the Nighthawk and took off for the Caymans.

Chapter 3: All Rise

Daniels, Burgess, and Franklin Law Offices
San Francisco, California
August 1997

Two weeks ago Sterling Montgomery Wise delivered his closing arguments on the Nehemiah Samuelson case. Samuelson was accused of killing his partner in order to have full control of the Liebermann Samuelson Advertising Agency. Samuelson was having financial problems and his wife was having an affair with his slain partner, making a high-profile case sensational. The case was being covered daily on Court TV and Sterling played into the media hype. He gave daily interviews and attempted, with some success, to make himself bigger than his famous client. If Sterling won, he would be able to open his own firm.

Sterling knew name recognition was everything. Winning one big nationally covered trial would make his career. But, it needed to be a case where the presumption of innocence would be laughable, one where everybody believed his client to be guilty. That way he could command the kind of retainer the partners in the firm were getting. Sterling also thought it could help him crossover into the sports agent field, which is what he really wanted to do. At today's salaries, a good negotiator could earn seven figures on one contract.

Sterling walked through the double glass doors of the Daniels, Burgess, and Franklin Law offices at 9:00 AM. As he approached his office, he heard someone say, "Monty." Recognizing the voice, he turned and saw Jesse Kennard, his father's best friend, and his boyhood friend, Nelson "Sky" Kennard. Nelson and Sterling played high school basketball together. Sky was short for Luke Skywalker. He earned the name by doing whirling dervish type slam-dunks in defenders' faces.

"Hey, Mr. Kennard."

"How you doin', son?"

"I'm doin' just fine, and yourself?"

"I can't complain."

Sterling looked at Sky and said, "What up, what up, what up," forgetting where he was. He extended his hand to greet him.

"Aw man, everythang's real cool," Sky replied.

"Y'all kids don' growed up and us ol' folk don't get to see y'all no more," Mr. Kennard said.

"Yeah, it has been a while, hasn't it? So what y'all doin' here, Sky?"

"Came to finalize the deal on the janitorial service contract."

"When do y'all start?"

"Our people start Monday. The contract doesn't officially expire until Sunday at midnight."

"I guess I'll be seeing y'all more often, huh?"

"I doubt it. We strictly suit and tie now. As a matter of fact, we gotta run. We biddin' on another building at ten."

"All right, Sky. It sho' is good to see you, man. Y'all take it easy now."

"Will do. And you do the same, hear? Catch you later, man."

The two men turned and went out the glass doors and into an open elevator. Sterling went into his office and started work on a brief.

"Excuse me, Sterling. Mr. Daniels would like to see you in his office right away," Tiffany, his personal assistant, told him over the speakerphone.

"Okay, Tiff."

Sterling walked down the hall, turned left, and went into Daniels' outer office. He saw Annabeth McMichaels, Daniels' secretary, sitting at her desk.

"Go on in, Sterling. He's expecting you," she said.

His best years of advocacy having long since left him, the gray-haired, sixty-seven-year-old Daniels was standing, facing the window. He liked to look at people's reaction to what he was saying through their reflection in the glass. He took a sip of vodka from the shot glass he had in his hand. The years of defending murderers, rapists, and criminals of all sorts had taken its toll. The lines in his forehead came all the way down to his bushy eyebrows. There was a mole on his right cheek with hair growing out of it.

"You wanted to see me, sir?"

"Yes, I do. Pour yourself a drink, Sterling."

Sterling frowned. "No thank you, sir."

He wanted to say it's too early in the goddamn morning to be drinking vodka, but restrained himself.

"You're probably wondering why I wanted to see you."

Didn't I just say that, ya drunk bastard. Sterling said, "Yes, sir. I am."

Still pretending to look out the window, Daniels took another sip of the vodka. "How long have you been with us, son?"

"Seven years, sir."

"Do you like working here?"

Sterling hesitated. He was wondering why he was asked a question like that. Then it came to him. He was about to be fired. *But why*, he thought.

"Are you firing me, sir?"

"No, you're going to turn in your resignation. It's best for you, and it's best for the firm. You just don't fit, son. I gave you every opportunity to blend in and become one of us. Don't worry; you're going to win the Samuelson case. That'll help you get started. I guess you can take the kid out of the ghetto, but you can't take the ghetto out of the kid."

There was a hint of compunction in Daniels' voice, but Sterling didn't notice. All he could focus on was being fired when he was so close to achieving his ultimate goal. "Excuse me?" Sterling frowned, obviously upset by the comment.

"I've asked you a number of times to leave that jungle talk at home. I told you it was unprofessional. It makes our clients nervous when they hear attorneys speak like street people. When clients get nervous, they tend to fire firms and take their million dollar retainers with them. We simply can't afford the defiance anymore. Frankly, I don't understand why a man of your education and experience chooses to speak in that manner."

"Excuse me, Mr. Daniels," Annabeth interrupted on the speakerphone. "Sterling, the jury's back with the verdict, and they want you in court immediately."

"Okay, thank you Annie," Sterling replied. "Sir, as you heard, I have to get to court. Can we continue this later?"

"No need. The decision's final. Don't worry; I have every confidence you'll land on your feet."

Without saying another word, Sterling left the senior partner's office. Daniels was still facing the window, watching him as he left. Just as the door closed, the first of many tears rolled down Daniels' cheek.

†††

"How the fuck he gon' tell me clients are nervous?" Sterling said aloud while sitting in his Jaguar at a traffic light. "Hell, I keep the goddamn doors open in that muthafucka! This drunkass muthafucka drinkin' vodka at nine o'clock in the goddamn mornin'! I guess the smell of vodka on the breath of the senior partner don't make they asses nervous. That's BULLSHIT! I shoulda fucked his daughter when she put the shit on the table. Now these sonofabitches wanna fire my ass? And for what? Because I spoke the language of the street in the office? Fuck all of them worthless bastards. What about Burgess's simple ass? This muthafucka got his daughter's underage best friend under his goddamn desk, suckin' his wrinkled ass dick. And Franklin's old ass can't even remember what goddamn day it is. Then his stupid ass tries to heat up a cheeseburger in the microwave and set the muthafucka on five minutes. Got all the offices smoked up and shit. Took me six goddamn months to get that smoky smell out of my office. These muthafuckas kill me with the stupid ass shit they do."

Suddenly, Sterling got the feeling that someone was staring at him. He turned to the left and a woman in a Mercedes 560 SL was looking at him with a bewildered look on her face. She tilted her sunglasses and mouthed, "Are you okay, brotha?"

Sterling laughed a little when it occurred to him how it must appear to the woman in the Mercedes. *I'm sitting in a new Jaguar yelling and swearing to myself.* He pushed the button that controlled the driver's window. The window hummed as it moved downward. The woman's window eased down and she could see Sterling through her open window. Sterling flashed his million-dollar smile and said, "I'm fine. How are you today?"

The drivers behind them blew their horns and shouted obscenities. Hearing the angry tirade, the two of them pulled off slowly still looking at each other. Sterling picked up his phone and said, "Give me a call."

"What's the number?"

"Jaguar 1." He smiled.

They both sped up and the angry drivers stopped blowing their horns. The woman picked up her phone and began looking at the alphanumeric characters on the receiver and began dialing. Seconds later, Sterling's phone rang.

"Hello."

"Hi."

"So...what's your name, you mysterious, dark and lovely lady?"

"Anita. And yours, Mr. Jaguar 1?"

"Sterling Montgomery Wise, attorney at law, at your service."

"Well, what can I do for you, Mr. Wise?"

"No need for formality. Please...call me Sterling."

"What can I do for you, Sterling?"

"I don't know. What can you do for me?" He laughed. The beauty of the mysterious lady had obliterated his anger.

"I seriously doubt I can do anything, Sterling. You see, I'm in the middle of a divorce. I'm bitter as hell. And I'm sick of you bastards treating us like fuckin' floor mats!"

Sterling thought, *Good, I can bang this and not have to worry about her hanging on when it's over. I'll be the transitional pipe.*

"I see. Well, can we at least have coffee sometime when you're feeling better?"

"If you want to put up with a bitter, vindictive, homicidal black woman— by all means."

"Is it okay for me to call you at home?"

"I don't see why the hell not. He had his bitches callin' there whenever they fuckin' felt like it. I don't see why you can't."

"Wow, you really sound pissed. Since you're so mad, why were you concerned about me, and my attitude?"

"Because it looked like you were expressing how I feel. I thought we could talk and get it out, ya know?"

"Yeah, I know. I'm quite pissed myself about some shit that just happened in the office. Hey, look here, I have to go into the courthouse now. Let me call you later on this evening, or in a couple days. I'll feel better by then and hopefully you will also. Maybe we can have dinner and go dancing. How's that sound?"

"Great. I haven't been dancing in years. My number's in the book, under Anita Saunders."

"Got it," he said and pushed the end button on the phone.

As Sterling walked into the courthouse he thought of how he could use what happened this morning with Daniels to get Assistant District Attorney, Le'sett Marie Antoinette Santiago, into bed later that evening. Santiago was a dark-skinned Puerto Rican with an exquisite body that looked as if it was curved by the finger of God. Her face was beautiful and smooth; her hair was in a bun and held together with bobby-pins; her nails were always manicured; her manner of dress was always professional and modest.

Sterling was drawn to her, but acted totally uninterested, always professional around her, looking her in the eye when he spoke to her and never even turned around to look at her ass when they passed. Santiago flirted with him throughout the trial, but he never played her game. The trial was coming to an end and now was the most opportune time to make a play for her, perhaps over dinner. Dinner between legal eagles was usually paid for by the loser. *If it doesn't work, I'll call Anita tonight. But if it does work, I won't bother calling Anita. After all, she's already admitted to being homicidal. If I see her again, I can always say I forgot her name.* Then he laughed.

As Sterling entered the building, eager reporters seeking to question him about the verdict rushed him. One such reporter asked, "What do you think the verdict is going to be?" Another asked, "How does it feel to represent murdering scum like Nehemiah Samuelson?" Then a voice he recognized said, "So what's next for attorney Wise? Will you start your own firm?"

He had known Amy Ling for several years and they had become lovers not long after they met. "Well, Amy," Sterling began after spotting the petite, but shapely Asian beauty. "What's next for me is to go into court and hear the verdict just like the rest of you." Hoping the verdict would be "not guilty," he continued, "After the verdict, I'll announce my plans for the future." Then he left them shouting questions at him that he had no intention of answering.

When he walked into the courtroom, Sterling saw Samuelson sitting nervously in his seat, Le'sett rummaging through her briefcase, and the bailiff talking in whispered tones to the stenographer. By her reactions, Sterling could tell the two of them would be getting together soon.

After spotting Sterling, the bailiff promptly went into Judge Laura Jones's chambers and told her all the attorneys were present. Then he came back and bellowed, "All rise."

Chapter 4: The Proposition

Having taken her seat on the bench, Judge Jones struck the wooden mallet on the gavel. With the exception of the gray streaks in her hair, the forty-five-year-old judge looked like she was in her early thirties. Jones kept herself physically fit by running a couple of miles each morning before she started what would normally be a grueling day on the bench, and this nationally broadcast case was draining for everyone involved. Every ruling was being debated on the court channel and other cable networks; even the style of her hair became fodder for the fashion police. She slid on her glasses, which dangled around her neck, held by a thin silver chain, adjusted the microphone, and nodded to the bailiff.

"Court is in session," the bailiff bellowed. "The Honorable Laura Jones presiding."

Judge Jones turned her attention to the jury foreman and asked, "Ladies and gentlemen of the jury, have you reached a verdict?"

"Yes, we have," the foreman said.

"Please hand it to the bailiff."

The bailiff took the verdict, and handed it to the judge. As she read the verdict to herself—chilling silence filled the courtroom. The members of the Samuelson and Liebermann families embraced each other in anticipation. Both families were praying justice would be done according to their beliefs.

Reporters positioned themselves to dash for the door as soon as the verdict was read. After reading it, Judge Jones handed the verdict back to the bailiff and said, "Will the defendant please rise?"

Sterling and Samuelson rose simultaneously. The courtroom camera focused on them and the clerk, feeding a close-up to the viewing audience. Sterling could feel Samuelson's nervous energy, which caused him to shake uncontrollably, yet it went unnoticed because everyone was looking at the clerk. Sterling put his arm around Samuelson and held him as a mother holds her child.

"Don't worry. We're going to win this thing," Sterling whispered into Samuelson's ear. But deep down, Sterling wondered. There was a lot riding on this verdict. Not only was his client's life at stake, but now, his own livelihood was on the line as well. In those precious moments, prior to the reading of the verdict, prior to the passing of the legal document from the foreman to the bailiff, to the judge, and finally to the clerk, Sterling thought about his own fate.

On the surface, Sterling appeared to be full of confidence. But now that he had lost his job, life was uncertain. Living well above his means, he was deeply in debt. He never wanted to be one of those out-of-work ambulance chasers. One nagging question filled his mind. *How would he pay for the house, the Jaguar, and the sumptuous lifestyle he led?* It was then that he began to question his proficiency as a competent advocate for Samuelson. He replayed his closing arguments in his mind, thinking of better ways to argue his points. Finally, he thought, we can appeal.

"In the matter of the people versus Samuelson," the clerk began reading, "Case number 1619JTV, we, the ladies and gentlemen of the Jury, find Nehemiah Jacob Samuelson, not guilty."

There were two immediate, but dissimilar reactions by the two families. The Samuelson family was relieved, roused, and rambunctious all at the same time. They did not take notice of, nor have any regard for, the Liebermann family and the tragic loss of their only son. The mother of the slain moaned softly at first and then the grief she felt in her spirit released itself, expressing the lamentation in her soul. She wailed aloud.

So much so, that it galvanized the entire room. The vociferous jubilation ceased as quickly as it began, causing the Samuelson family to realize that, even though they had their son back, Mrs. Liebermann would never look on her beloved son again in this present world.

The elation of the Samuelsons, and Nehemiah himself, awakened Sterling out of his stupor of self-doubt. His senses returned to him and he knew his future would indeed be secure, just as Daniels had predicted. *"Don't worry. I have every confidence you'll land on your feet."*

Sterling decided to capitalize on his triumph against all odds. As he thought of the clients he would attract, and the hefty fee he would collect, a smile emerged. A little at first, then much broader.

"Congratulations, counselor," assistant district attorney Santiago said, extending her hand—no accent. "I guess I owe you dinner, huh?"

Sterling had momentarily forgotten about her, and his plan to bed her. He stopped smiling immediately and extended his hand. "Thank you," he said, reservedly.

"What's the matter?"

"I'm going to have to take a rain check on that dinner."

"Why? What's wrong?"

"I was fired this morning. Daniels called me into his office and told me I didn't fit in, and that I should resign. He was probably trying to avoid a lawsuit." He tried to sound as pathetic as possible.

"Sterling, I'm so sorry. What are you going to do now?"

He took a deep breath and let it out slowly to show how exasperated he was. "First, I'm going to face the press. Then I'm going to go home and lie down and contemplate my future. I'll probably start my own firm now."

"After a big victory like this, you should be celebrating, not contemplating your future. I'll tell you what, let's have that dinner I owe you, and talk about what you're going to do."

Sterling smiled within. He could hardly contain himself. The plan was working perfectly. Le'sett felt sorry for him and that was exactly how he wanted her to feel. All he had to do now was reel her in. "I don't know; I kinda want to be alone tonight."

"Okay, some other time then." She turned and walked away.

Shit! You weren't supposed to say that. You're supposed to be consoling. You're supposed to insist on dinner. "Le'sett, you know, maybe I should be celebrating instead of chillin'."

"Okay, great. I'll meet you in the hall."

It occurred to Sterling that he hadn't said anything to his client—Nehemiah Samuelson. He turned to talk to him, but he was hugging his parents and friends. Samuelson, seeing that Sterling and Le'sett were finished talking, went over and hugged him. "You thought we'd lost it, didn't you?"

"Honestly. Yeah, I did," Sterling replied.

"You did a helluva job. A helluva job. Thank you for everything. If you ever need anything, anything at all, give me a call."

"Okay. I might just do that. You ready to face the press, or are you going to ease out the back?"

"Out the back. It's going to take some time for this to blow over. We're going to St. Thomas for a while. Why don't you come with us?"

"No, I can't. I was fired this morning, Nehemiah. I have to get moving on my own firm now."

"That's not right. I'll talk to Daniels personally. I'll pull my retainer if he doesn't take you back."

"No. Don't do that. My daddy always told me never to beg a man for a job. Either he wants you, or he doesn't. I live by that, Nehemiah. I'll be okay. Don't worry."

"Okay. If you change your mind, give me a call, okay?"

"Sure will. You can count on it."

The two men embraced. They had spent six months together discussing strategy and evidence. They had grown to respect and admire each other. Now it was over. They looked at each other again. Inwardly, they knew they would never see one another again, but neither said anything.

Nehemiah and his family left the courtroom. Sterling took a deep breath and entered the fray of reporters waiting just outside the courtroom. They raced to him to get his post-trial statements. Sterling walked to the podium and looked out at the throng of people, lights, and cameras. He was overwhelmed and excited by all the attention they were paying him. He'd waited a long time for this moment. Now, after all his hard work, and 13 years of practicing law, at thirty-eight, he had finally arrived. He smiled and took it all in for a moment. Then he said, "Earlier, Amy Ling of WTSF asked me what was next for Attorney Wise. Well, I am officially announcing that I will no longer be with the Daniels, Burgess, and Franklin Law offices. I resigned prior to the verdict this morning."

An eager reporter asked, "So you would have been leaving the most prestigious firm in San Francisco regardless of the verdict?"

"Yes. That's correct. Now, I'll entertain three questions only. Dan, you're first."

"Thank you," Dan said. "Attorney Wise, the most troubling question all of America wants to know is, if Nehemiah Samuelson didn't kill Liebermann, who did?"

"Well, Dan, this is real life, not *Perry Mason*, *Murder She Wrote*, or *Matlock*. Murder cases are not neatly tied up in an hour. If you look through the files in the police department, I'm quite certain you'll find a lot of cases where the perpetrator was never found. This is true not only in cases of murder, but in cases of ordinary theft. So I say to you that it isn't my job, nor is it yours to find the murderer of Jason Liebermann. Let's leave it to San Francisco's finest. Tom, you're next."

"Thank you, Attorney Wise," Tom began. He had an agitated look on his face. "Now that you've secured an acquittal, and your client cannot be tried again, in the face of overwhelming evidence, don't you think he should have been convicted?"

"Tom, you know as well as I do that you can't convict a man on circumstantial evidence. Besides, this so-called overwhelming evidence was reduced to a molehill. We shattered every witness they put on the stand. I submit that you, like most of America, got caught up in the intricate web spun by the District Attorney. If you remember, before I even became Samuelson's attorney, the DA was on television saying he expected a confession within the week. Well, sir, that statement alone demonstrates the profound arrogance in the DA's office. I think they thought Samuelson was going to tell on himself. They thought he'd plea bargain. Why else would they leak so much of the so-called evidence out before the trial even began? They never even expected this case to come to trial. When Samuelson showed the resolve to defend himself, they had to come to court with a weak case in which its foundation was steeped in guesswork and innuendo; sexual and otherwise. So, Dan," he said, as he turned slightly in his direction. "If you want to know who did it, if Nehemiah didn't, ask the DA. Peter, you have the last question."

Peter began, "You said Samuelson had the resolve to defend himself. If Samuelson didn't have the money to hire the most prestigious firm in San Francisco, wouldn't he have been convicted on the same so-called circumstantial evidence?"

"Depends on the attorney," Sterling said. Then he laughed and walked away from the podium.

✝✝✝

On his way out of the courthouse, Sterling saw Le'sett. She was absolutely stunning, and he wanted to ravish her right then and there. The combination of his victory and his desire to conquer her made his erection stiffer than usual.

"You ready?" she asked.

"Yeah."

"Sterling, can we take your Jaguar? I've always wanted to ride in one of them."

"Well, if the other attorneys knew that's all it took, they'd all go out and get one."

They both laughed.

"You're probably right. That's what so scary about men."

When they reached the Jaguar, he disarmed it, and opened the door for her. Then they left the underground garage. He pulled onto McAllister Street and saw the members of the press giving their final reports live from the steps of the Court building. His cell phone rang.

"Hello."

"One million dollars." It was a woman's voice, but he didn't know who it was. She was definitely older, but not old, he thought.

"Is this some sort of joke?" Sterling asked, a little uncomfortable now.

Le'sett looked at him, wondering what was being said. Sterling looked at her and shrugged his shoulders.

"I assure you, Mr. Wise, this is no joke," the woman on the phone continued. "This is a secure line. You may speak freely."

"Who is this? And how did you get this number?"

"This is Adrienne Bellamy. I am a woman of considerable wealth and influence. Look in your rear view mirror, Mr. Wise. Do you see the white stretch limousine?"

"Yes, I see it," he said, glancing in the mirror.

Le'sett was still bewildered by what was happening.

"Pull over and let Ms. Santiago drive. I would like to speak with you privately. I have a proposition for you. I promise you, it will be worth it."

"Okay," he said and pushed the end button. "You see that limo back there?"

Le'sett turned around. "Yes."

"That's Adrienne Bellamy. And she just offered me a million dollars."

"A million dollars!? Who is Adrienne Bellamy? And what does she want you to do for that kind of money?"

"I don't know, but I intend to find out. I can't afford not to. She knows who you are, too. She suggested you drive, and she wants me to talk to her in the limo. Do you mind driving?"

"No, I don't. Be careful."

There was genuine affection in her voice.

Sterling pulled the Jaguar over and the limousine pulled up next to his door. He got out of his car and into Bellamy's limo. Le'sett slid over to the driver's seat. Her skirt got caught momentarily on the stick.

"I swear I hate wearing women's clothing sometimes," she said aloud. Then she pulled into traffic, and got behind the limo.

Chapter 5:
The Conversation

William Marcellus Wise knew he should have skipped the Toronto trip this year. He and four of his associates attended the Annual Psychological Convention every year. If William needed an excuse, he had a great one. He was opening a drug rehabilitation clinic in October, just shy of three months from now anyway, and incredibly busy, but his associates begged him incessantly. He was planning to work on the final details of the grand opening while the quartet went to the convention but, due to their constant supplications, he had decided to go one last time. Besides, he loved Toronto, and enjoyed staying at the Westin Hotel. However, the feeling of having made a huge mistake by coming on this particular trip had plagued him all the way from Sausalito to San Francisco International Airport, during the entire flight, and even in the seclusion of his hotel suite. *What was it?*

As he entered his suite, he felt a sense of relief. Having managed to avoid his associates for a day and a half, he was glad to be in his own place to relax and be alone. It wasn't the solitude he craved; it was just good to be away from the constant questioning. After sitting on the sofa, he closed his eyes, and thought about the dismal sales of his book, *Don't Settle For Second Best*. He went to painstaking lengths to explain why people seldom find their soul mate, believing that most people settled for something less than their ideal man or woman.

William's mind was somewhere between deep thought and unconsciousness when someone knocked at the door and asked, "Dr. Wise, are you asleep?" He looked at his watch. 6:25. *Oh no!* He was supposed to meet the others in the Lighthouse restaurant at six.

"Just a minute," he called out, recognizing the soft, yet deep and relaxing voice of Dr. Terry Moretti, who spoke with a slight Southern drawl. "Yes, I did kinda doze off," he said, opening the door. "But I'm ready, let's go."

"You know who has already started drinking, so be prepared," Terry offered as they walked silently toward the elevator, which was only a few feet from his suite.

Immediately, he felt tension building in his neck and upper back. He resumed his thoughts about avoiding their questions and getting back to his suite as soon as possible.

As the elevator doors retracted, he could hear the faint sound of a cut from *Yanni Live at the Acropolis* being piped into the elevator. The music reminded him of Francis, his deceased wife. They were in Greece, that magical night of the concert, under the Parthenon.

Francis had died five years earlier of leukemia, leaving the couple childless. Every time he came to Toronto, it seemed as though something he saw or heard would transport him to another place where she was still alive—a place where her lust for life could be readily seen—a place where her ebullient smile disarmed him and made him as weak in the knees for her as Superman became when he was near kryptonite. He thought about how beautiful she was, and how they seemed to be made for each other. Francis was one of those people that everyone loved.

William first saw her at Baker Library on the Harvard University campus. From the crown of her head to the sole of her feet, Francis Dupree was indeed a specimen to behold. The five-foot-eight-inch New Orleans beauty had rich caramel skin, dark mysterious eyes, jet-black hair, well-toned thigh and calf muscles, a heart-shaped derriere that men couldn't take their eyes off of, and firm breasts that Helen of Troy would have envied. But Francis Dupree was more than a sex goddess to be lusted after; to William she was just as lovely inside as outside; she had the perfect blend of personality and beauty few women possessed. More important, she was unpretentious.

Francis Dupree refused several of William's advances, and told him their careers were more important than a romantic entanglement. She had also told him that immediate gratification was not in her plans, or her immediate future, which made him desire her all the more. Yes, Francis Dupree was a rare and spectacular jewel. Not only was she beautiful, but she was intelligent, and above all focused; she had a plan to succeed, and was determined to fulfill her vision.

In spite of William's loving memories of Francis Dupree, she wasn't exactly the way he remembered her. Yes, she was a good person and an excellent businesswoman and partner, but William had chosen to remember her strengths, and forgot her weaknesses.

The elevator doors opened, bringing him back to the present. Terry Moretti left the elevator first and William followed her. The Lighthouse restaurant was full of jovial people laughing, eating, drinking, and generally having a good time. As they walked toward their colleagues, William and Terry noticed the smirks on everyone's faces.

"What took you so long, Terry?" James Friedrickson said, grinning mischievously. He was still bitter about his divorce settlement. His scandalous wife had cheated on him and he ended up losing his house, his two children, and half his savings. James played the prankster of the group to mask his unsavory disposition, but everybody knew he was still hurting.

William and Terry ignored him, and took their seats.

Ivy Cameron, the super intelligent, but unattractive and impulsive strawberry blonde who everyone called "poison" behind her back, asked, "Dr. Wise, do you ever let your hair down?"

Here-we-go! Here come the questions again!

"Are you ready to order, sir? Or do you want a few more minutes?" the waiter asked William before he could answer Ivy's question, which he knew would lead to a conversation they really didn't want to have.

"Yes, I'm famished. I'll have the New York strip, well-done, a baked potato, salad with Thousand Island dressing, and a red sauvignon."

The waiter then took everyone's order and left.

"Is anyone going to see a Blue Jays game this year?" William asked quickly to change the subject.

"For what? They suck!" Ivy blurted out.

"They're not that bad," Bernie Beverly replied.

"Oh, yes, they are. They're dead last in their conference," Ivy reiterated.

Changing the subject is working again. They've fallen into my trap for yet another year. Now if I can just keep this up for another hour, I'll be home free.

"Dr. Wise, you have a real knack for avoiding the simplest of questions," James interrupted. "Ivy just asked you if you ever let your hair down and you nonchalantly changed the subject. We know how much you cherish your privacy, doctor, but surely, there's nothing private about letting your hair down, is there?"

William sighed in exasperation and thought, *do they ever give up?*

"See what we mean," James continued, wearing the same mischievous grin. "Why on earth would a question like that cause such consternation?"

That wasn't the question William was trying to avoid. It was the questions to come that annoyed him. Seeing the opening to evade the question again, he seized the opportunity. "We? I see. So, you all are working in concert to grill me about irrelevant matters, huh?"

"There you go again," Ivy pounced. "You're trying to put us on the defensive, when in truth you're the one being defensive."

"I'm not trying to put you on the defensive," William lied. "I'm simply trying to ascertain the relevance of letting one's hair down."

"Come on, Dr. Wise," Terry stated firmly. "We're all psychologists. If you were in our shoes, I think you'd pursue this also."

Disappointed Terry was in on the ambush, William said, "So you're part of this too, huh?"

"No, I'm not," Terry quickly answered. "This is obviously something they cooked up when I came to get you. However, I will admit that my curiosity has been seriously piqued due to your incessant avoidance."

"We've all noticed that you always avoid the simplest of questions and any psychologist worth his or her salt must make some sort of inquiry; after all, we're just trying to satisfy our curiosity. Isn't that why we became psychologists?" Ivy offered, trying hard to be congenial.

William was trapped. Now all the uneasiness he had felt made sense.

He now knew why he should not have come on this trip. The very thing he had been avoiding for years had now caught up with him and there would be no getting out of it. That much he could tell by the gleeful looks on the faces of James, Ivy, and Bernie. Sure, he could go to his suite, but they were going to be in Toronto for another day and a half. He would have to face them eventually.

After a few reflective seconds, William asked, "How long have you guys been planning this?"

"We talked about it last year, but we planned it about a week ago." Ivy reverted to her normal mercurial self.

"Well, you guys never said anything to me," Terry announced, wanting William to know she had absolutely nothing to do with the waylay.

"That's because everyone in the office knows you're in love with him. Christ, even the maintenance people know. I'm surprised you never figured it out," James revealed. Then he tried to conceal his jealousy by laughing.

But William had figured it out. He'd known about Terry's feelings for him for quite a while. He could usually sense what was going on in the minds of others; after all, he was the gifted one of the group, but he kept it to himself. So he sat there trying to look surprised and incredulous at the same time, as he did not want to embarrass her further.

Terry, 34, was very pretty and quite tall for a woman. The five-foot-eleven-inch brunette had an hourglass shape, large breasts, and a smile that could melt the coldest heart. In addition to her physical allure, she graduated near the head of her class from Stanford University. While William found her attractive, he had his reasons for not wanting to get romantically involved with her.

Terry's face reddened. She thought she had kept her love for William a secret. She tried so hard to mask her feelings, but now she knew she was only fooling herself. Terry knew how important Francis was to William. She wanted him to make the first move. Her first thoughts were to get up and run out of the restaurant, but her pride fastened her in her seat. She was furious with James for exposing her secret so callously. *How could he be so reckless?* Then it came to her like a bolt of lightning.

"Are you jealous? Is that what this is about?" Terry snapped. She looked directly into James' eyes for any opening that might reveal the truth; regardless of his answer. She could see the question, like an arrow, hit its mark. James' face wrinkled, expressing his chagrin. Sensing his vulnerability, Terry attacked him the way a shark attacks its wounded prey. "You pathetic child! You don't care about anyone's feelings but your own. Just because I won't go out with you is no reason to embarrass me. And furthermore—"

"Hold it, hold it. We're doing it again," Ivy interrupted. "I thought we were going to stick to the subject, James."

William thought it was James' idea all along. Now he knew it.

"Uh, yeah, yeah, let's not lose sight of that," James muttered, hoping to quell Terry's wrath. He knew she could reveal far more damaging secrets about him than he could ever reveal about her. He wouldn't have said anything, but the cocktails on an empty stomach, coupled with his jealousy, loosened his tongue.

"Well, doctor, what's it going to be?" Bernie Beverly queried, jumping into the fray. "I don't see what the big deal is. We just want to satisfy our curiosity where you're concerned, that's all."

Just as Bernie was finishing his statement, the waiter brought their salads and drinks, serving them from left to right, beginning with William.

"Dr. Wise, if you're thinking about changing the subject again now that we're about to eat," Ivy blurted. "We're not going to let you out of answering some of our questions this year."

William thought for a moment before saying, "I admit I have been avoiding certain questions, but that's only because I know that if I answer truthfully, my answers will make everyone uncomfortable. What if I told you guys why I don't want to talk about certain subjects? Would that suffice?"

"It depends," Ivy offered slyly.

Seeing no way out, William said, "Listen, guys," he began, "I'm certain my answers will only provoke more questions. And what would have started out as a simple question will turn into an inquisition; therefore, I will only answer your questions if we agree to finish what we start. In other words, this is the only time we discuss it, no one gets offended, no one holds a grudge, and the conversation will be of the quid pro quo variety. Agreed?"

"Agreed," Ivy answered, with youthful excitement.

"No, it must be unanimous, or no deal."

Everyone eagerly agreed, not understanding the ramifications of their conversational treaty. In their minds, this was better than what they had hoped for. They had known Dr. Wise for years, but knew very little about William Wise, the man. He didn't go to bars and drink with them after work; nor did he spend time with them away from work. And so the staff's curiosity was well founded. Now they could ask him all the questions they had always wanted to ask. They smugly sat there, never suspecting that soon they would all be turned inside out and forced to see themselves as they really were.

William picked up his fork and began eating his salad, and then asked, "Where shall we begin?"

"We can begin where we left off. Do you ever let your hair down?" Ivy quizzed, with childlike curiosity.

"Define letting down one's hair for me so we'll both have the same understanding."

"If you want me to be blunt, I'll be blunt." Ivy sighed. "Why are you always dressed to kill? I mean, here we are in a relaxed atmosphere and you're still dressed as though we were at the office."

William was wearing a double-breasted, cream-colored sports coat, black triple-pleated pants, a white shirt, and a silk cream and black tie, with a matching black and cream handkerchief.

"I'm not evading the question, and I'll answer you, but why does my attire concern you?"

"We are not in the office and we don't have any more classes until tomorrow morning, so why are you still dressed in a suit and tie?" Ivy asked, as calmly as she could.

"I dress this way because I want to be treated with respect, and to show myself to others as a man of dignity."

"Dr. Wise, we would respect you no matter how you were dressed," Ivy offered, with genuine concern.

"That's only because you all know I earned my doctorate at Harvard. Besides, I'm the boss; therefore, you're supposed to show me respect. If I were dressed in a pair of shorts and T-shirt like you, I wouldn't be respected the way I'm respected when I'm 'dressed to kill' as you say."

"Don't you think you're exaggerating a little?" Ivy asked, with a puzzled look on her face.

"No, I don't." He folded his arms. "As a matter of fact, I think what I've said thus far is an understatement. For example, which one of you has ever been in the process of leaving a mall, or the local grocery store, and as you approach your car, some woman you happened to be parked next to locks her doors?"

Feeling guilty, Ivy said, "I lock my doors no matter who comes near my car. There's a lot of nut burgers out there, ya know."

Terry said, "Yeah, that's why I lock my doors, too. It has nothing to do with race."

William picked up his fork and continued eating. He looked at Bernie and James. "Well, gentlemen, which one of you have ever experienced what I've just mentioned?"

They both remained silent for a couple of minutes and continued eating their salads while they tried to think of an appropriate answer. Then James said, "Well, doctor, you've got us there, but is everything that happens in the black community the fault of whites? I mean, don't blacks bear some responsibility for why women lock their doors when you go to your car?"

William knew questions about black people would enter the conversation sooner or later, which was why he had avoided their questions in the first place. During his collegiate years, in study groups, he was often the only black person in the group and was constantly expected to answer questions about blacks because he seemed to be the exception to "their rule" of thumb about black people. He felt his stomach churn as the adrenaline began to flow.

Then without contemplation, he said with uncharacteristic virulence,

"I knew it would come to this sooner, or later. This is the main reason why I didn't want to discuss anything personal with you. No matter what I do, where I go, or how successful I become, I still have to be an ambassador for the entire African-American community. I'm still expected to explain the intricate details of the black experience in America." With each word his voice was building to a crescendo.

"Look, you're the one that said you have to dress a certain way to be respected. That sounds like a personal indictment of white people in general. You opened the door, doctor. Don't get upset because I walked through it," James retaliated, feeling triumphant.

"Fine. You just remember I have some questions of my own. What was the question again?" He was obviously still upset by the questions due to the pronounced frown on his face.

"I asked is everything that happens in the black community the fault of white people?" James boldly repeated.

"Can you be more specific? Everything is too vague." William softened his tone, having regained his composure.

"Take black on black crime, for example. Surely that isn't the fault of whites," James stated. He tried to hide his pompous attitude by asking the question in an unassuming fashion.

"Depends on which whites you're referring to."

William knew James, like most white people who asked questions like these, was seeking exoneration from all wrongdoing of past sins committed by people of Caucasian descent, which ultimately made no sense since their argument was always the same. *Don't blame me for a past I had nothing to do with.*

"What do you mean, doctor?"

"Listen, James, you minored in history, did you not?"

"Yes, I did, but I fail to see what one has to do with the other." He had a bewildered look on his face.

"Your failure to see what one has to do with the other is the reason racism continues to flourish."

"Oh, here it comes," James said sarcastically, "the goddamned race card."

"The race card?" William questioned. "That phrase is offensive in that it presupposes that racism has been eradicated when nothing could be further from the truth and you know it."

"Okay, if you're not playing the—" He caught himself. "Just what the hell are you saying, doctor!" James blared, his voice a little louder than usual.

"I'm saying the contemporary history of a people cannot be fully comprehended without a thorough understanding of that peoples' general history, especially when it concerns the black man."

"Doctor, if you're talking about the institution of slavery, and I think you are, that was over three and a half centuries ago. How can you possibly connect today's events with what took place so many years ago?"

There was a touch of cynicism in James' voice. He had heard black people blame their plight in America on whites for years. To him, it was an old worn-out excuse and he was tired of hearing it. Slavery didn't explain black on black crime. Nor did it explain why so many black women kept having babies out of wedlock. It only explained why there was a need for the Civil Rights Movement and antidiscriminatory laws to prevent black people from being discriminated against. But the law had gone too far for far too long, and he wanted it stopped, and stopped now.

"James, you're asking a very complicated question."

"How so?"

"Because you're asking about a subject that's far deeper than it appears on the surface. I can't microwave understanding for you, James. You want me to explain an institutional problem in five minutes. That's part of the problem. A lot of whites try to understand it from their own myopic point of view. Most don't even try to really understand what one has to do with the other. It would take a considerable amount of time before you could truly understand why black on black crime goes on. It would take you even more time to understand why black on black crime is even allowed to go on.

"It would be like telling a first-grade student that Benjamin Franklin discovered electricity. Then explaining to him, in detail, the intricacies of the modern-day computer, and expecting the student to understand computers in one hour. It's not going to happen. But, if the student spent time with the computer every day and truly tried to understand how it worked, in time, the student would understand far more than he would have in one hour. The trouble is, not many white people truly want to understand. So they reject the role of slavery altogether. Without understanding the role of slavery and one hundred years of legal oppression, you'll have very little understanding of the people of which they speak."

Feeling a little insulted, James sucked his teeth and rolled his eyes. "Try me, doctor."

With a skeptical look on his face, William began, "First of all, the institution of slavery began over three and a half centuries ago; it didn't end three and a half centuries ago. If it had, your argument might carry more weight. As you well know, the Emancipation Proclamation only freed the slaves legally. The passage of the 13th and 14th amendments to the Constitution gave them quasi-citizenship a few years later. Then you have to add in over a hundred years of oppression, and the passage of more laws that didn't change anything, because the law doesn't change people. Dr. Martin Luther King Jr. was assassinated in 1968, just thirty short years ago. And you're going to tell me that in thirty years, America has evolved and gotten beyond race prejudice? Please! How old are you, James?"

"Dr. Wise, you know I'm 36 years old."

"How old were you when you earned your doctorate?"

"I earned my doctorate just after my 27th birthday. I was the youngest in my class." He beamed with pride.

"What position do you hold in our practice?"

"I'm the senior associate, second only to you, sir. Come now, you know all of this. What's the point?"

"Here's the point," he stated firmly. "If you had not graduated from high school, you would not have gotten into college; if you had not graduated from college, you would not have gotten into graduate school; if you had not graduated from graduate school, you certainly would not be the senior associate in this practice. James, you're 36 years old and everything that has happened in your life made you the man you are today, correct?"

"Correct."

"If your personal history made you who you are, then four centuries of oppression, and the present state of affairs in the black community cannot be repudiated. Things have changed for the better, sure. I'll give you that, James. But give black folk more than the thirty years since King's cold-blooded murder. If black folk are in the same position three and a half centuries from now, your argument will be much more mean-ingful. Let me ask you something, James. What's it like to be beaten so badly for picking up a book that you learn to hate knowledge, and love ignorance? What's it like to have your family broken up and sold like parts of a company, then being blamed for the breakup of the black family? What's it like to watch your father, or your mother, being beaten before your eyes, by another slave? What effect does that have on a child? Are you even aware of the fact that the white slave master used slaves to whip other slaves? The white slave master used slaves to hunt down runaway slaves. He taught the slaves to turn on each other, and hate one another because one slave had lighter skin than the other."

"Come on, doctor," James said, dismissing his conclusions, "you're not suggesting the slave master told the darker-skin blacks to hate the lighter-skin blacks, are you?"

"No, he probably didn't tell them to, but what do you expect to happen when he treats one better than the other? In our profession, we see it among siblings all the time. One is treated better, and a sibling rivalry begins. And that's only in one generation. Think of what would happen if it went on for centuries, James."

"I'm sorry, but I don't buy that."

"Well, look at the Biblical rivalry between Isaac and Ishmael. Their descendants, in the Middle East, are still fighting each other today. Now, how long ago was that?"

They all seemed to be thinking about what William had said.

Then James said, "Well, if slavery plays such a prominent role in the life of blacks, how do you explain your phenomenal success?" Then he leaned back in his chair and folded his arms. "I mean, look at you, William. You have white PhDs working for you—a black man."

William glared at James for a long uncomfortable moment, then said, "I attribute most of my success to my father because he always spoke philosophically about being black in America, and he had a great work ethic. For example, he worked two jobs so my mother could work out of our home and take care of my two brothers and me. He'd say things like, 'Not havin' is no excuse for not gettin'.' He also made me read African-American history and African-American literature, which continued the confidence-building process. My father believed very strongly in Black Nationalism. My father used to say, 'You can't make white folk accept you. You have to accept yourself.' He would constantly tell us we needed a good education to get ahead. And that we needed to be twice as good as the white man."

"Based on what you just said, the legacy of slavery had very little influence on your family," James concluded. "So why then does it affect so many others?"

"In most cases, if the father doesn't have his head on right, neither will his sons and daughters. In my opinion, some of it is biological. For example, if one or both of your parents were drunkards, you may also have a propensity to drunkenness. Furthermore, we now know that we inherit fifty to sixty percent of our personalities from our parents. If our parents have bad habits, we tend to have them. Therefore, if your parents have poor self-esteem, coupled with self-hatred, their progeny will more than likely fall into the same cycle. And I don't have to tell you how difficult it is to break that cycle. Hell, we make a pretty good living from dealing with dysfunctional family cycles."

"Yeah, but you broke it, didn't you?" James taunted.

"Uh, huh. So, since I broke it, all African-Americans should be able to break it?"

"Why not? Seems like a lot of black people are full of excuses for not achieving. For example, look at the Orientals. They haven't been here that long, yet they're running rings around other minorities."

"Perhaps if all African-Americans had my parents, maybe they would break the cycle. But realize that there are people in this world who are capable of walking on white-hot coals, and not being burned. It doesn't mean everybody can. However, if we used the same kind of mind-control techniques, we'd be able to do it also. But as far as the Asians are concerned, they're running rings around everybody, including white folk. Now, assuming what you said about Asians and other minorities is true, why do you suppose that is?"

"I'm not sure. I just know what I see."

"And that's the problem. What you see, or think you see rather, may not in fact be the case. Name one Asian, or any other minority, for that matter that is the CEO of a Fortune 500 company in the United States."

James thought for a moment, and then said, "Well, I can't at the moment, but I'm sure I could probably find one." He seemed to be mystified by William's question.

"Do you have to do any research to name a Caucasian holding the same position?"

"No, but maybe these companies couldn't find any qualified minorities for the position."

"Why not? It seems to me that a lot of white folk are full of excuses for why they don't promote minorities to executive positions. Now, let's examine what you say you see. What I think you see, as far as the Asian community is concerned, is them owning their own businesses. Is that correct?"

"Correct."

"Well, what kind of businesses do they own?"

"All kinds."

"Can you be more specific?"

Frustrated, James barked, "They own car industries, don't they?" When he had planned this conversation, he didn't think it would turn on him the way it had.

"Yeah, but the Asians who own those businesses are not the immigrants you spoke of earlier. The ones you were referring to usually own restaurants, and corner stores. Some even own clothing stores and hair-care outlets, but a lot of them are in African-American neighborhoods, catering to people who should be the owners. The lack of initiative and motivation black people exhibit has a direct correlation to the oppression they've suffered at the hands of the unscrupulous white male for centuries."

"Look, at some point, black people are going to have to forget about slavery, move on, and get over past sins!" James yelled so loud that people in the Lighthouse turned and looked at them.

Many of the patrons were already actively listening. The noise level in the restaurant was considerably lower; yet there was the same number of people. It had gotten to the point that the wives at tables closest to them were telling their husbands to keep it down so they could hear what was being said. Then the waiter returned with their dinners.

"I agree with the 'move on' part of your statement, but why should we forget about what's happened to us? Do the Jews forget about the genocide they suffered at the hands of the Nazi regime? Do the Japanese forget about Nagasaki, or Hiroshima? Do Americans forget about Pearl Harbor, Normandy, or Valley Forge? If people of other nations don't forget about what's happened to them, why in the hell should African-Americans forget?"

Feeling totally flustered, James muttered, "A lot of people are good at pointing out problems, but few have solutions. Do you have a solution to the practice of racism?"

"I don't know that I have a solution per se. In my opinion, the problem is too big for one man to solve. It will take a communal effort to make even a small dent. But we can start by acknowledging that the problem is still alive and well. Furthermore, we should stop looking at the Klu Klux Klan and the skinheads as the sole arbiters of racism. Each individual, black and white, must take a long hard look at himself for an answer to why racism continues to flourish. But we can begin with the most segregated day of the week—Sunday mornings. If preachers would simply tell their parishioners the truth as the Bible teaches, racism would be over in ten years, or less. But most preachers are too ignorant of the Bible, or too gutless to say what needs to be said. If the preacher did what he's been commissioned to do by the God he says he serves, we would not have a race problem."

"Dr. Wise," Ivy interrupted, "why do black men want white women? Is it because the white slave master took sexual liberties with black women? Is that why black men will do anything to have a white woman?"

When Ivy said this, there seemed to be a hush that saturated the restaurant. William and his colleagues were so immersed in their conversation that they didn't even notice that most of the people near their table were listening. Some of the people were hanging on to every word. It reminded one of an E. F. Hutton commercial.

"No!" William shouted. The question infuriated him. "But that's why most white women are arrogant when it comes to black men."

"Oh come now, doctor, are you going to sit there and deny that black men don't want white women?" Ivy questioned—her face flushed.

"Look, some black men date white women exclusively, but it isn't the norm. As a matter of fact, white women are usually the ones initiating the relationship, or making themselves available to black men. For proof of this, all one need do is read. The history books are replete with information that proves beyond a reasonable doubt that white women have always had secret sexual liaisons with black men."

"Excuse my French, Dr. Wise, but that's a bunch of bullshit, and you know it! Everybody knows black men have always been after white women!" Ivy roared. She seemed to be outraged that what William was saying could be true.

"Oh, I see," William said calmly, realizing he had the attention of the other restaurant patrons. "You can believe that black men have some sort of inordinate sexual desire for white women, but any evidence to the contrary angers you. Now why is that?"

"Doctor," Ivy shouted, obviously enraged, "you haven't presented any empirical evidence to support what you've said. All you've done is make unsubstantiated, inflammatory allegations!"

"I thought we all agreed not to get offended," Terry teased. She had an insincere smile on her face. She loved it when someone got the better of Ivy. The two of them have had a longstanding, but unacknowledged feud for years. Ivy thought pretty women like Terry were barriers to equality because men tended to focus on their beauty rather than intelligence. Terry, on the other hand, thought Ivy was overbearing because she had the highest IQ in the practice.

"You would stick up for him no matter what he says, wouldn't you, Ms. Secret Admirer. I guess he's right in your case, isn't he?" Ivy reviled.

"Whether I agree or disagree is irrelevant. We all agreed to not get offended," Terry told her, still smiling.

"Ivy, you're right," William interrupted. "I haven't presented any empirical evidence, but neither have you. And talk about inflammatory allegations, what do you think your comments were?"

"Doctor, the evidence is everywhere you look," Ivy's voice trembled. "I see black men with white women all the time. There's your evidence."

"Listen to what you're saying, Ivy. The black man is with the white woman. Even in our progressive time, isn't the woman usually with the man? Or at the very least, people will think a man and a woman are together. Yet when the black man has a white woman, somehow people reason he's with her, which further reduces his stature as a man."

"Doctor, that may be true, but it doesn't change the fact that you have no evidence to support your claims, does it?" Ivy grumbled.

"True, but I can tell you where to find it," William instructed. "Read *Sex and Race*, volumes one through three, by Joel A. Rogers for starters. Those books will lead you to a myriad of others."

At that point, several women whipped out pens and paper and copied down the book title as quickly as they could. They didn't believe a word of what he was saying but, just to be sure, they wanted to check it out.

"Assuming these books exist, how do you explain the fact that many, very many, black athletes and entertainers are either married to white women, or have white girlfriends?"

When Ivy said this, many of the patrons in the restaurant nodded their heads in agreement.

"I don't have to explain it. Your argument serves me far more than it serves you."

"Oh really," Ivy said skeptically. "How does it serve you better than it serves me? I'm talking about empirical evidence, doctor. Every time you see black superstars, you see them with white women. Even Michael Jackson married two of them. I've never even seen him with a black woman. Come to think of it, wasn't he running around with Brooke Shields before she got involved with that tennis player a few years ago? So you tell me, doctor, how does it serve you better than me? Use examples the way I have. I might believe you, if you do."

"You want empirical evidence? You want examples? Okay, consider what you just said, Ivy. The fact that 'many, very many black athletes and entertainers,' as you say, have white girlfriends proves white women are either attracted to black men, or it proves white women are gold diggers that are willing to do anything to get ahead. They'll even sleep with men they're not attracted to. You choose the one you prefer. White women today are only doing what their mothers and fathers have done in secret for centuries. The only difference is most of them are doing it in the open. When it comes to the black athlete and the white woman, she gets him and an opulent lifestyle. Besides, what do you expect black athletes to do when they live in, let's say, Oklahoma, or Salt Lake City, Utah, or any other city in the United States where there's a shortage of black women, and a proliferation of white women who are literally throwing themselves at them? Which one of you hasn't had sexual fantasies about black men, or black women?" This he said knowing full well the majority of people in the restaurant were white. "And if you've had fantasies," he continued, "what prevented you from getting what you desired?"

William waited for an answer, but none came. There was a deafening silence that lasted until dinner was over. Then each of them returned to their suites alone in the silence that had previously permeated the dinner table.

Chapter 6:
Decisions, Decisions, Decisions

San Francisco
August 1997

S terling observed Adrienne Bellamy with the skilled eye of a jeweler. She was blond, blue-eyed with a Nordic nose, and was wearing a black Escada suit, which was offset by a yellow vest with black velvet buttons. Her earrings were also yellow, with black pear-shaped ornaments inside. The diamond ring she wore was at least ten karats, and glittering. Her black Manolo Blahnik shoes were on the seat next to her.

Sterling sat across from her, admiring the view. She was an attractive woman who obviously kept herself in shape. He found her style in clothing to be impeccable, and the gracious tone in her voice, soothing, yet strong. In his mind, she was a well-educated woman in her late-fifties. From the way she pronounced her words, he thought she had only gone to the best private schools in America; maybe Switzerland. To him that meant not only did she have money, but it was old money. She didn't need to marry for wealth; her family was probably one of the wealthiest families in America. This was real power and influence sitting before him.

"Hello, I'm Adrienne Bellamy." She extended her hand.

"Hello."

"Can I offer you a drink?"

"No, thank you."

"Good. You're not a drinker, just as your dossier says."

"Dossier?" His eyebrow rose.

"Yes, I've had you checked out. I'm very thorough. I know everything about you. Shall I prove it?"

"Can you?" he asked, skeptical of her ability to amass information in spite of being in the visible lap of luxury.

"You were born April 18, 1958, to Brenda and Benjamin Wise. You were an A student throughout your academic career. You entered the Air Force Academy in June at the age of eighteen, in 1976. You graduated in the top ten percent of your class and went on to Law school at Georgetown University. You were assistant District Attorney before Zachary Daniels recruited you to his firm."

"Ms. Bellamy, that information has been in every newspaper from here to New York."

"How about this tidbit of information then? You are a philanderer of sorts. You have women in Denver, Chicago, and Manhattan, all well-to-do women, intelligent, beautiful. Of the three, only the Manhattan woman is white. She's a very well-respected attorney, a wife, and a mother. Her name is Chase Davenport—formerly Chase Bickford. You met Ms. Davenport at Georgetown. She's married to a doctor from a prominent upstate New York family and you've been having an affair with her for nearly fifteen years. In fact, your affair with her began before she married the doctor and you even met with her the night before her wedding." She looked at Sterling who was mortified by all the revelations. "One last fling?" She paused and waited for an answer, but he didn't respond. "You meet her every two months or so, but you haven't seen her since the Samuelson trial. Shall I continue?"

"What do you want, Ms. Bellamy?"

"I want to help you get where you want to go."

"Really? Where's that?"

"You want to be rich, Sterling. Jericho and William are much better off than you financially. You feel like you haven't lived up to your father's wishes. You are the middle child. William is the baby and gets smothered with affection. He's in Toronto as we speak, by the way. He lives in Sausalito in a house that one of your trollops helped him acquire dirt-cheap. Jericho is still your mother's favorite—even now. Even he has become an economic force, despite his feud with your father. Maybe even because of it. My sources tell me he could have been a great boxer, had your father let him fight. Now he's a drug and munitions supplier with CIA connections, living in the Cayman Islands. That, my dear Sterling, has got to make you feel like a failure to some degree, even with all of your accomplishments. I watched you and you alone this morning as the verdict was being read. Truth is, you thought you'd lost the case."

Sterling felt naked before her. She was definitely on target. But still, he felt violated by her vast knowledge of his family. *What the hell did she want?* He was more than intimidated now. Adrienne Bellamy was for real and something within him knew she was not to be toyed with. Sure, she was being nice and polite now, but Sterling knew in the minutes that she had revealed her knowledge of him and his family she could be equally destructive.

"This is all quite fascinating, Ms. Bellamy, but what do you want from me?"

"Here, take this." She handed him a silver briefcase.

Sterling opened the case and saw the million dollars she'd mentioned on the phone. He had never seen a million dollars all at one time. A chill shook his entire body. He closed the case and handed it back to her.

"I can't accept this without knowing what you want."

"So, you are not completely motivated by profit—a sincere lawyer. This is a first for me. I have a battery of lawyers in my stead. All are crooks."

"Ms. Bellamy, I've asked you a number of times what you want of me and you keep going on about other matters. I don't mean to be rude, but I want to know what you want, or let me out of here."

"First, let me tell you what I'm prepared to do for you, besides the million in cash. By the way, the million will be forwarded tax free to an offshore account of your choosing. Perhaps you'd like it to go into an account in the Caymans," she said with a devilish smile.

"Okay, what else is involved?"

"For starters, I'll send you all the business you can handle, plus set you up in the sports agent business and even get you the top pro prospects coming out of college. Isn't that what you've wanted?"

This woman is the devil himself. She offers me everything sweet to the taste.

There must be bitterness somewhere in this. All she needs is a red suit and a pitchfork.

"As you have no doubt guessed, I want you to do something that will prick your conscience. It is a simple task, really. You should have no problem pulling it off. I will be helping you from a distance. I have chosen you because you are a visible black man with a good reputation in the black community. Because of that, you'll have easier access to this woman." She gave him a picture. "This is Victoria Warren. She's my son's fiancée. As you can see, she's African-American. She's quite beautiful, don't you think?"

"Yes, she is."

"She's pregnant with his child. He cannot marry her, nor can she have his child. My son will be a Senator and the President of the United States someday. Unfortunately, in this country, a president's wife must also be white. Do you understand, now, what I'm asking you to do?"

"You think she wants him for his money?"

"No. It would be very easy to get rid of her if she did. Unfortunately she's very much in love with Sean. However, this can never be. I forbade him to see her, but he rebelled and now we have a very precarious situation. If this is found out, his political career will be over before it begins. He thinks he'll be accepted in spite of her ancestry. I know better. America is a long way from real integration. A very long way."

Sterling sat there listening intensely.

"Let me assure you, this isn't racial animus. This is practicality. I will give her five million dollars to abort the baby, and leave Sean forever. And of course, Sean must never know I did this. You may seduce her, or whatever you must do, but this relationship is over."

"Since she loves him, do you really expect her to take the money?"

"No. Not at first, but she will. I will apply pressure, and before long, she will."

"Let me get this straight. All I have to do is get this woman to have an abortion, and leave your son alone forever. And I get a million, plus perks, and she gets five million?"

"That's the deal. Do we have a bargain?"

"I need to think about it."

"No, either you will, or you won't. I need an answer right now. This kind of deal comes along once in a lifetime. A simple yes will give you everything you've ever wanted. A no could lead to bankruptcy, in spite of your mastery of the law. What's it going to be?"

"Deal," he said, and extended his hand.

"I need you to understand something, Mr. Wise. I can be a very generous woman, but do not cross me," she said, looking into his eyes. "If you do, I'll break you like a twig. Your life will start at chapter thirteen. Do we understand each other?"

"Yes, we do."

"No one is to ever know about this deal; not even your secretary, Tiffany." Bellamy picked up the phone and told the driver to pull over. The well-muscled African-American chauffeur opened the door.

"We will never see each other again. This is Winston. If you need anything, contact him and I'll make sure you get it. I'll send the money to the Caymans. They'll contact you with the account number, and answer any questions. Here's all the information you'll need on Ms. Warren. Good day, Mr. Wise."

Sterling got out of the limo. Winston handed him a card with his number on it. Then he closed the door, got in, and drove off without a word.

Le'sett drove up and Sterling got into the car with a big smile on his face and a stiff erection in his pants.

"I take it, it was a legitimate offer," Le'sett said. "And judging by that bulge in your pants, you're out of the doldrums, too." Then, she reached over the armrest and stroked his burgeoning tool. "What do you say we go to your place and take care of that tumor you've got growin' down there?"

Chapter 7:
Vision

University of California-Berkeley
March 1968

O f the three sons born to Benjamin and Brenda Wise, Jericho was the most intelligent and the biggest disappointment. Benjamin and Brenda always thought he'd be the doctor or lawyer in the family, but as fate would have it, organized crime and the life of the nocturnal was his destiny.

A born leader, Jericho had been the warlord of the Chiefs, a street gang in San Francisco. Benjamin Wise, a former world-class boxer, had taught Jericho and his two brothers, Sterling and William, the sweet science of pugilism. Boxing was as natural to Jericho as breathing was to most human beings. Nevertheless, boxing was forbidden. Benjamin had lectured his sons about the brutality of the sport and more importantly, the brutality of the boxing business. But he thought his sons should know how to defend themselves in a cruel world.

Jericho blamed his father for his strict approach to life, and for keeping him from boxing greatness. He believed that if his father had let him box, his life would have turned out differently. He loved street fighting more than life itself. In the beginning, he took his lumps like any other amateur but, before long, no one was able to defeat him. Soon, anxious spectators were betting large amounts of money on him. He was a very slick fighter with superior defensive skills, and possessed the power of a heavyweight in both hands. His ability to anticipate his opponent's punches allowed him to attack the body viciously from a variety of angles. It was street fighting that eventually landed him in jail for knocking out a police officer, who was attempting to arrest him at the tender age of eighteen.

After reviewing his high school transcripts, Judge Keenan, a black man who also had a troubled life as a youth, saw much of himself in Jericho and decided to have him take an intelligence test. The results measured his IQ at 185. Keenan saw Jericho's potential to be an asset to the black community, and thought he only needed some direction in his life. He gave Jericho the choice of leaving the gang and going to college or joining the Marine Corps, where it was a virtual certainty that he'd go to Vietnam. He chose college rather than the rigorous life of a Marine Corps grunt. Judge Keenan used his contacts at Berkeley, his alma mater, to get him a full scholarship.

But Jericho left the Chiefs in name only. He no longer wore the crimson colors of the gang. He didn't hang out with its members, or go to meetings, or participate in rumbles. Instead, he entered Berkeley during the spring semester as agreed, and was doing well. After going to a few basketball games, he saw an opportunity to make some money by booking bets. He needed a partner—a white one.

Even though the students at Berkeley were liberal in their thinking, and occasionally used marijuana, and hallucinogens, most still didn't inter-act with blacks. Therefore a white partner was essential to get Caucasians to bet with him. Jericho had remembered one of the many lectures his father drilled into his head: "If you want to make it big, you've got to get white folks to buy your product." Suddenly, this concept made sense to him. After all, the Berkeley campus was virtually white. He was only one of a few blacks on campus in 1968. He decided to ask Carlton Chadwick, a fellow student, who wanted to be his friend, ostensibly to prove he was different from other, more overtly prejudiced whites.

Carlton Chadwick was the rebellious, yet liberal son of Barrett Chadwick, an affluent banker, and a Berkeley alumnus. Carlton was being groomed to take over his father's banks in Northern California, but Barrett didn't spoil his son. He didn't give Carlton the latest sports car, a lavish apartment off campus, and unlimited money. Carlton had to work part-time to earn money for movies, pizza, ball games, and dates like his father did when he attended Berkeley.

Jericho knew Carlton wanted to make money and live well, which made him the obvious choice. He was convinced that if they were caught, nothing would happen to him because of Carlton's father's influence. More importantly, he knew the climate was such that if they tried to expel him without expelling Carlton, there would be cries of racial injustice by the NAACP. So, they started a bookie business on campus. Soon, they were making enough money to get an apartment.

If the students at Berkeley wanted drugs, Jericho thought they should buy them from him and invested their winnings from the bookie business in the drug trade. He envisioned himself as the monarch of a drug empire and used members of the Chiefs to collect debts and distribute the drugs. He didn't particularly like distributing drugs in the black community, but he believed it would eventually reach the white community where the profit margin was virtually unlimited. Besides, drugs were already in the black community long before he, or any other black man, got involved, he told himself.

The drug and bookie business was quite profitable and there seemed to be no end in sight until a couple of members of the Chiefs roughed up a freshman for unpaid debts. He called the police and they set up a sting, which eventually resulted in Jericho's and Carlton's arrests. But before they were booked, Carlton called his father, who in turn called the Mayor, who called the Chief of Police, and they were set free without anything being leaked to the local media. They continued doing business as usual until one day, in a political science class, a lecture about Malcolm X turned sour.

Jericho and Professor Sharpe, a master of disputation, were debating the merits of the Black Nationalism philosophy. Jericho believed that Malcolm X's arguments were valid, and the professor told him, "The country was better off without his kind." One word led to another and Jericho walked across the stage and hit Professor Sharpe with a left hook that sent his one hundred eighty-nine-pound body crashing to the floor.

Professor Sharpe lay unconscious and motionless in front of a silent auditorium full of students and faculty.

The board of trustees looked at each other with gleeful grins on their faces. Not one of them was concerned about Professor Sharpe's physical condition. They were glad they finally had legal grounds to expel Jericho without involving Carlton Chadwick. In less than twenty-four hours, Jericho was unceremoniously expelled from Berkeley and flung into the open arms of the war in Southeast Asia.

Chapter 8:
The Dilemma

Toronto
August 1997

He was glad it was finally over. Back in the comfort of his suite, William no longer felt the tension in his upper back and neck. All of the avoiding had grown tiresome. As he removed his clothing, without realizing it, he found himself whistling the Yanni song he'd heard earlier in the elevator. When he finished undressing, he picked up the HBO entertainment guide and noticed that *The Godfather* was going to be shown at 9:45.

He looked at his watch. 9:30. He decided to take a quick shower and to watch the epic motion picture before retiring for the night. When he stepped out of the shower, he looked at his watch again. 9:43. He grabbed a towel and rushed into the sleeping area of his suite.

When he finished toweling himself, he put on the silk pajamas Francis had given him as an anniversary present eight years earlier. They were black with a gold paisley design around the borders of the fabric. He was sitting at the edge of the bed, watching the beginning of the movie, when the phone rang.

"Hello."

"Good, you're still awake. I'll be right over," Terry Moretti said, and abruptly hung up.

"Terry, Terry," he said, but she was no longer on the phone.

What now? He took a deep breath and let it out slowly. Then he grabbed his robe and put it on as he went to the door. Terry's suite was two doors down. As soon as he reached the door, she knocked. He opened the door and put his arm across the opening, attempting to block the entrance. But she simply ducked under his arm and walked into his suite. He left the door open, and turned toward her.

"Coming here at this hour is a bad idea."

Terry nonchalantly went over to the door, and gently closed it. She then turned toward him, looked directly into his eyes, and said, "So how long have you known?"

"Known what, Terry?"

"Don't give me that! You know damn well what I'm talking about. I saw you at dinner. I saw you trying to conceal the fact that you'd known all along that I was interested in a romantic relationship with you. You can fool them with that dumb act of yours, but I saw the look on your face when James cavalierly mentioned my feelings for you. Tell me I'm wrong! Tell me I imagined it all!"

He paused for a moment while looking into her eyes. "You saw that, huh? That's pretty good. It was only for a nanosecond," he said with a smile that betrayed the ignorant veneer he'd tried to present. Then they both burst into laughter.

"Well, how long have you known?"

"From the beginning," he said, soberly.

Excited, she asked, "Why didn't you say anything, William?"

"Didn't you hear what I said during dinner?" he said, not believing his ears.

"Yes. But I still need an answer. Is it that you don't find me attractive? Or are you still in mourning?"

"It has nothing to do with your looks, Terry."

"Then it's Francis, still?" She couldn't believe he was still in love with his deceased wife after all this time.

"Francis has something to do with it, but not the way you think. Listen, I loved Francis from the depth of my soul. I judge all women by a standard she set. I know it isn't fair, but I can't help it. It's not like I'm looking to replace her. She's irreplaceable. I don't mean to sound harsh, but I know what type of woman I need in my life and you're not that woman."

"How can you say that when you haven't even given me a chance?" Terry asked, almost pleading. "There's something more, isn't there? Is it because I'm white?"

William paused for a moment or two, calculating the dangers of telling her the truth and possibly feeling the sting of a woman scorned. She could say anything when she left his suite and he was her boss. "I admit that has a lot to do with it."

"So you're against interracial relationships?"

"No, I'm not. It's simply not for me."

"So, for all that talk during dinner, you're just as prejudiced as the people you were referring to."

"Do I have to have a white woman to prove I'm not prejudiced?"

"No, but your reason for not dating someone you're attracted to because of her color speaks volumes."

"Listen, Terry, I've worked hard to put this practice together. Now it's paying off big. I'm about to open another clinic in three months. I don't need the headache of a relationship right now. Besides, relationships don't always work out. And in the current climate, a woman can scream sexual harassment, and the man has to prove he's innocent. It wasn't that long ago that Clarence Thomas had to answer allegations from Anita Hill. Even if he had harassed her, the complaint was ten years too late. The man was crucified before the entire world, and the Senate didn't prove anything. His reputation was literally destroyed. As a matter of fact, when you leave this room, all you have to say is I invited you here to discuss business, and when you arrived, I was dressed in silk pajamas. Because you're a white woman, and an attractive one at that, who do you think they're going to believe? If you wanted to, you could ruin my business right now and we haven't had a romantic encounter at all. Hell, even if I proved I did nothing wrong, my reputation would be destroyed, just as Judge Thomas' reputation was. I'd lose my business, at the very least."

"But, William, I would never do that. Given a chance, I know I could fill the void in your life."

"Sure, you could. Women do it all the time. Think of all of the people that seemed to be meant for each other. Then, the next thing you know, they're in the middle of a bitter divorce."

"So the main reason you don't want to date is because you're afraid of losing what you've worked for?"

"Yes, and there's also the stereotype Ivy alluded to at dinner."

"You mean the one about black men and white women?"

"Yes."

"So you're going to allow what other people think dictate and control your life?"

"Terry, you have no idea how much pressure I'd be under if I were to get involved with you. Once when I went back to the Community Center where I was reared, I was literally deluged by black women who think every time a black man makes it, he has to have himself a white goddess. Ms. Thang, they call her. I gave them the same arguments I gave you all tonight. And no matter what I said, they still believe the black man sells out to get the white woman. In their minds, any successful black man that dates, or marries a white woman, is a sellout; or he's having an identity crisis. It doesn't matter how attractive she is, how intelligent she is, or how compatible they may be. Her white skin is all they see. Now that I'm successful, they expect me to do the same thing."

"What about all the successful black women who make it and marry white men? I guess it's okay for Diahann Carroll, Dorothy Dandridge, Lena Horne, Josephine Baker, Diana Ross, Lynn Whitfield, Mariah Carey, Denyce Graves, Debbie Thomas, Iman, and probably a lot more that I can't think of at the moment. What do black women say about that? Do they consider them sellouts, too? Or are they simply having an identity crisis?"

Flabbergasted she could think of so many successful black women, he said, "You've obviously done your homework, but that doesn't change anything."

"Why doesn't it? Here you are telling me you owe it to black women to date and marry someone black. Yet, at the same time, black women are doing the same thing they accuse black men of doing. You don't see anything wrong with that? Isn't that like the arrogance you said white women have? It sounds like black women want it both ways. They can marry white, but black men can't."

"Honestly, I never looked at it that way. Again, I don't see how it changes anything. So successful black men and women are crossing the color line. Does that mean I should?"

"It's not like we're going to get married, or anything." She could sense that he was weakening. "It's only a date, William. Geez!"

"Even if we never marry, you're still a white woman, and I'm still a black man. And that's a powder keg with sparks flying around it."

"So let me get this straight. Even though successful black women are marrying white men in record numbers, you're still going to let them control your life?"

Feeling the pressure of the question, he said, "I guess you don't have any reservations about an interracial relationship?"

"No, I don't. I know who I am, what I want, and who I want in my life. I'm not going to let anybody control me."

"So your parents wouldn't have a problem with you dating me, huh?"

"My father would, but my mother wouldn't. My father's a lot like you, William. He talks a lot of shit, but won't back it up with his actions; says he's not prejudiced, but I'll never forget the time when my father and I were going into Blockbuster a couple of years ago. As we were going in, this black guy and his white girlfriend were coming out. My father spoke pleasantly to them, but when we got inside the store, he said, 'What is she trying to prove?' So I said, 'What if I was involved with a black man? Would you react the same way?' He said, 'But you wouldn't get involved with a black man. I didn't raise you that way.' Then he told me about Mr. Silverman, his best friend. He said the guys in the locker room at the Country Club were talking about Jennifer, Mr. Silverman's daughter. They were saying she had run off to marry a nigger. Then they started talking about how well-endowed he was and how he probably had Jennifer singing high notes every night. One day, they put an eighteen-inch, pitch-black dildo in Mr. Silverman's locker. When he opened his locker and saw the dildo standing there erect, they laughed themselves silly. After telling me that story, he said, 'That's how I know you wouldn't get involved with a black man.' Then he gently kissed my forehead and told me he loved me. That's when I realized my father would have serious problems with it. He's more concerned with his reputation than his daughter's happiness. And you aren't any different. You're more concerned with what black women think than your own happiness. How can you live that way?"

"That's just the way it is."

"What a cop-out! Are you saying you're happy being alone? Francis has been dead for five years now. Don't you get lonely, William?"

"Yes, I get lonely. Who wouldn't? But that's no reason to rush into an interracial relationship. We hardly know each other."

"Oh-come-on. We've known each other for seven years now."

"No, we've worked together for seven years. Just because we've worked together doesn't mean we know each other. Besides, do you really think it's a good idea to date someone you work with? Especially if it's your boss? Like I said earlier, what if it doesn't work out? I could lose my business if you decided to take some sort of vengeance."

Terry looked at him for a couple of seconds, shaking her head. The look on her face was one of disbelief and astonishment. "You know, William, you're an arrogant bastard. Why are you so sure you'd be the one to break things off? I'm the one who could end up disappointed. I'm the one carrying a three-year torch. I'm the one who thinks you're the man for me. What if you don't live up to my expectations? Have you considered that?"

"No, I haven't, but that's all the more reason to keep our relationship platonic. That way, I won't have to worry about my reputation, or my business. And your expectations will never become a disappointment," he said, sarcasm dripping from his lips.

"Do you really believe that two licensed psychologists who have worked together for seven years don't know each other?"

"Yes, as a matter of fact, I do."

"Yet, you knew from the beginning I was interested in a romantic relationship? How can you say you don't know me, while at the same time, know my intentions? Sounds like you're making excuses. If you don't want to date, just say so. You don't have to make up all these weak-ass excuses." Her face revealed the frustration and dejection she felt. "Tell me something. And I want the truth. If I was black, would you date me then?"

"Truthfully," he said, feeling a little jubilant. "Yes, Terry, I would."

"Are you sure about that?"

"Quite sure."

"Then tell me something. What can a black woman do for you that I can't do for you?"

The question caught him completely off guard. While he was thinking of an answer, he noticed that Terry was gloating.

Terry knew he didn't have a viable answer. She was standing there smiling from ear to ear. Sure he could eventually come up with something, but in her mind it would be another bullshit answer and he would know it. She was very pleased with herself for having thought of the question so quickly.

William couldn't think of a good answer and it bothered him to see her standing there gloating. So he flippantly said, "She can have a child that wouldn't be half-black and half-white."

Without thinking, Terry slapped him with all the strength she could garner. "You know what, William?" she said, pointing her finger in his face. "Black women are right about one thing! You don't know who you are. If you did, you wouldn't let people control your life." Then she burst into tears and ran out of his suite.

William knew he had hurt Terry deeply with his blatant apathy toward her. He knew he had humiliated her with reckless abandon. She loved him and he had rejected her and the love she proffered. He slowly walked over to the door and closed it behind her. Leaning against the door, he bowed his head in shame. It bothered him to be so cold because he was attracted to Terry. He knew she was the best woman to come along since Francis's death. She was his equal in every way. But he had a responsibility to his people, he told himself over and over again. *I cannot get involved with a white woman, and be labeled a sellout. It's better this way.* Then he walked over to the bed and sat down. He stared at the phone for a few moments and then decided to finish watching the movie.

Chapter 9: Revenge

James Friedrickson, Ivy Cameron, and Bernie Beverly had entered the first-floor lounge at 9:30. They decided to order a round of Jack Daniels and get a booth so they could privately discuss the dinner conversation.

Ivy was furious with Dr. Wise. She thought his comments about white women were outrageous. She was also angry with Terry because she wouldn't take sides during the discussion.

James was wondering if Terry was angry enough to tell Dr. Wise the things he thought she was about to tell him at the dinner table. For all he knew, she was upstairs telling him everything just to get back at him for what he had said about her. James was glad Ivy intervened when she did; otherwise it could have gotten really ugly.

Bernie wasn't angry at all. He agreed with some of what Dr. Wise said, but for the most part, he held fast to his own beliefs. He thought it was better not to argue with the man who signs his paycheck, and kept quiet.

"So what are we gonna do about this?" Ivy asked, still smoldering.

"What can we do?" James offered.

"What are we gonna do about what?" Bernie wondered.

Bernie was the youngest of the group. He was handsome, single and only twenty-eight. He was outgoing and an exceptional psychologist. He liked Dr. Wise a lot.

Ivy looked at Bernie and said, "Are you stupid, or what? What the fuck do you think we're talkin' about? We're talkin' about Dr. Wise, you idiot." Ivy's speech was slightly slurred. The earlier cocktails had begun to affect her, but she was unaware of it. All she could think of was going another round with Dr. Wise.

"There's no need to insult me!" Bernie shouted. "You shouldn't let his opinions get to you. You don't even know if what he said is the truth, yet, you call me an idiot?"

"Calm down, guys," James told them.

"You tell her to calm down," Bernie growled. "She's the one makin' an ass out of herself, not me. As a matter of fact, I want an apology."

"Apologize? To you? Don't hold your breath," Ivy quipped.

"Well, fuck you then. You fuckin' bitch!" Bernie shouted.

"Excuse me," the bartender interrupted, as he served them their drinks. "I'm going to have to ask you to keep it down. Aren't you with Dr. Wise's group from San Francisco?"

"Yeah! What of it?" Ivy snapped.

"Ma'am, if you don't keep it down, you'll be asked to leave. Please, you're disturbing the other customers."

"I'm sorry," James told him. "We didn't know we were loud enough to disturb your customers."

"Thank you, sir," the bartender said and left quietly.

James looked at Ivy and firmly stated, "Get a hold of yourself. I'm still your boss, and I'm telling you to calm down. Now!"

Ivy burst into tears the way drunks do when they've had too much to drink. "I'm sorry, I didn't mean to cause trouble," she said. "It's all Dr. Wise's fault. If he hadn't lied about white women, I wouldn't have drunk so much. I mean drank. Drunk, drank, whatever." She started laughing like a silly schoolgirl. Then she reverted to the angry woman she was before the bartender came. "We can't let him get away with it. We gotta do something," she argued. "Black men don't lust after white women! HA! The truth is a black man would rather have a white woman than watermelon. We probably taste the same to 'em." She laughed a little. "Hell, even I could get a black man if I wanted one, but I don't want one."

"What do you suggest we do? Fire him?" Bernie offered sarcastically.

"We can engage him again tomorrow at breakfast before classes start," Ivy told him.

"Do you think you'll be in any kind of shape to debate him in the morning?" James asked her. He, too, wanted another shot at him.

"I'll be fine if I get outta here now," Ivy said.

"Okay. Let's formulate our plan before we go," James said.

"I'm not sure he said anything so terrible that we should plot revenge," Bernie said. "So he said a few things that irritated us. He didn't want to talk about it. We insisted. We pushed him when he told us how it would turn out."

"That's par for the course, coming from you," Ivy snapped. "You've had your nose up his ass since he recruited you from Michigan University."

"Boy, he really fucked you up, didn't he?" Bernie shot back. "Maybe you should use your vibrator a little more often. That seems to be the only time you can be civil."

After that remark, Ivy gave Bernie the finger. Bernie said, "Stick it up your ass, and rotate it."

"Come on, guys. Let's concentrate on the task at hand. Besides, we didn't even get to the questions we wanted to ask," James said.

"Didn't we agree to talk about it one time only?" Bernie asked.

"Yeah," James said. "I've been thinking about a way to get around that and I think I've found it. Now here's what we're goin' to do . . ."

Chapter 10: Expansion

T he drug and bookie business continued despite Jericho's removal from the scene, and raked in a hefty $33,600 a month profit—a fortune at the time. Just as Jericho had predicted, drugs spread from campus to campus and were being slowly funneled into suburban America. The Chiefs were primarily responsible for collecting unpaid debts and distribution channels. Carlton Chadwick wrote Jericho detailed letters chronicling the Chiefs' activities on a monthly basis.

While in Vietnam, Jericho couldn't help noticing the rampant drug usage among the soldiers. Seeing another opportunity for profit, he formulated a plan. He would use the same formula he'd used back in the States by getting the white man involved for protection, and as a means to opening a white market. First, he needed Captain Greene, the supply officer, to agree to receive the shipments from the States. Greene had to sign for all supplies and inventory lists. Since Greene was already involved in other illegal activities, a small percentage of the take was all that was necessary to secure his cooperation.

Second, Jericho needed his Commanding Officer, Captain Drucker, who was already doing drugs. His price was a steady supply of marijuana and a percentage as well. Drucker made it possible for Jericho and others to distribute the drugs and collect money unencumbered.

Finally, Jericho needed Gunnery Sergeant Victor Marshall. Marshall would be the muscle. He had served three tours and was considered the best soldier in the platoon and knew at least a hundred different ways to kill or maim a man. After Jericho told him of how he had singlehandedly created a drug and bookie enterprise back in the States that was still vibrant in his absence, he agreed.

In late 1969, Jericho and Victor Marshall joined an elite group known as the "Hard-core Battalion." They were not, however, afforded the same luxuries as other units. They lived off the land, and became more proficient at guerrilla warfare than the North Viet Cong. They became masters of deception.

They were highly motivated men who were expertly led, and the ambush was their primary modus operandi. In other words, these guys were professional killers with state-of-the-art technology and weapons at their disposal. They worked independent of other platoons, which gave Jericho the freedom to enhance his drug business.

One night in 1972, on his last mission in Southeast Asia, Jericho's platoon ambushed a North Viet Cong guerrilla unit, killing everyone, or so they thought. But one soldier was only wounded and was about to shoot him in the back, when Pin came out of the bushes and squeezed off several rounds, killing the Cong instantly. To look at the twenty-year-old, five-foot-seven-inch Asian beauty, one would never guess she had performed scouting duties for the South Vietnamese Army, which often plunged her into the heat of battle. Jericho and Pin became eternal friends, and eventually lovers. Prior to returning to the United States, he married her.

Chapter 11:
Sterling

Toronto
August 1997

William couldn't enjoy the movie because he kept thinking about what Terry said prior to slapping him. *"Black women are right about one thing! You don't know who you are. If you did, you wouldn't let people control your life."* He found himself replaying the conversation with her over and over in his mind. Then he told himself to concentrate on the picture and let it subside. For a while it seemed to work, but eventually, he found himself replaying the question Terry asked him. *"What can a black woman do for you that I can't do for you?"* He admitted that color was the single most important thing preventing a relationship with her. *Am I just like the racists I spoke of earlier? Is she right about me?* Having despised racism all of his life, he had to rethink the matter because he appeared to be the racist. William wanted a second opinion—one he hoped would agree with his point of view. He picked up the phone and called his brother.

"Hello."

"How you doin', Sterling?"

"Hey, bro. How's To-ron-to?"

"Cool as ever. What are you doin'?"

"Watchin' Bruce Lee dust O'Hara's men."

One night, about five years ago, he brought broadcaster Amy Ling home and made wild passionate love to her. He was feeling macho, and when she fell asleep, he got up and watched *Enter the Dragon*. Ever since, he continued doing it until it became a ritual whenever he got a "fresh one."

"Got a new lady, huh?"

"Well, ya know, what can I say? They won't leave me alone. I know you didn't call me to chitchat about my love life. What's up?"

"You date all kinds of women, don't you?"

"Oh, I see. You finally found a filly, huh, Willy? 'Bout time."

"I wouldn't say that."

"Well, what would you say then?"

"I'd say I was just propositioned by one of my employees."

"Don't tell me. It was Big Bird, wasn't it?" He sounded a little frustrated. "How come the ugly ones always think they got a chance with the brothas?"

William laughed heartily. "They think it because that's who the brothas are with most of the time. But no, it wasn't Ivy."

"You mean it was the fine one?"

"Yeah, it was Terry."

Sounding more excited, he said, "Well, what happened? What did you say?"

"Well, she came bustin' in here and—"

"Don't tell me. You found a way to fuck it up, didn't you?"

"Wait a minute. It didn't happen that way."

"Just tell me this. Did you fuck her, or not?"

William laughed. "You're a trip."

"You let that get away, didn't you? Look, man, I don't mean no harm, but Francis has been dead for a long time now and—"

William interrupted, "Francis had nothing to do with it."

"Well, how did you fuck it up then?"

"It was more than one thing, all right."

"Well, what happened?"

"Hear me out before you start trippin', okay?"

"Okay."

"It all started at dinner. We were discussing some racial issues and it ended in a big debate. In the middle of the debate, James said Terry was in love with me. Terry got mad. I didn't realize it, but I had some sort of look on my face and Terry saw it. So she came bustin' in here confronting me about it. After I told her I wasn't about to cross the race line, she said, 'If I was black, would you date me?' Or some shit like that. I told her yeah. What did I say that for? Then she asked me what a black woman could do for me that she couldn't. And, honestly, I didn't have an answer. But she was so smug about it, that I said she couldn't have a child that wasn't half-black and half-white."

Sterling burst into laughter. "Then what happened?"

"Maaaaaaan, she slapped me so hard that the only thing that kept me on my feet was my pride."

Sterling laughed again. "What's the problem, bro?"

"The problem is I can't shake what she said, man. She said that I was a racist because I let color stand in my way."

"She's right."

"You know how I feel about racism."

"I know what you say about racism, but apparently, you're going to let it stand in the way of what could be a promising relationship. The woman obviously digs you if she slapped you."

"So you don't have a problem with it?"

"No. How could I? I bang 'em all. It doesn't matter to me. I think you're a fool for lettin' her get away without at least gettin' a piece. But yo' stupid ass pissed her off, and let it get away. And for what? Because she's white? Fuck that shit!"

"Hey, it's not just race, you know," William said, feeling the need to defend himself.

"If it isn't the race thing, what else is there?"

"How the hell did you pass the bar exam? Don't you realize I could lose my business if the relationship goes sour and she decides to file sexual harassment charges? Have you forgotten we're talkin' about an attractive white woman?"

"If other people in the office know she's attracted to you, I seriously doubt she would do anything like that. If I'da been in yo' shoes, I'da wore her ass out. Then she wouldn't be thinkin' about filin' charges. She'd be wondering when she was going to get another piece."

"I don't know if I wanna even get involved because of the race thing. You know how the sistas feel about the successful brothas dating white women."

"As far as the sistas are concerned, how do they feel about the successful sistas dating white men?"

"You know, Terry said the same thing. She even rattled off a long list of successful black women who married white men. I didn't even know half of 'em, but I was too embarrassed to say I didn't."

"Look, man, she's right. I get so sick of that shit! Check this out. I'm watchin' *Oprah* a few months ago and she had wild-ass Dennis Rodman on the show. So, you know Oprah, she asked him how come he only dates white women. So the wild man said he only dates white women because black women have never found him attractive. But white women have always found him attractive; even when he wasn't famous. Then the next damn day, I'm listening to the Jade Wilson show on the radio, right? What the hell are they talkin' about? Wild-ass Dennis Rodman."

"You know I used to have a crush on Jade, don't you?"

"Yeah, I know. Anyway, Jade and some sista that called in was sayin' if Dennis wanted a black woman he would find one. Then they had the nerve to say they didn't find the wild man attractive. They were confirming what the wild man had just said less then twenty-four hours earlier. My question is this: why should the wild man swim upstream? If white women find the brotha attractive, why the fuck should he go lookin' for a needle in a haystack? If I was him, I wouldn't go lookin' for any woman, black or white; especially when women are throwing themselves at me. Have you ever seen the Bulls play on T.V.? When Dennis Rodman runs out of the stadium, there's at least fifteen women lined up tryin' to get his attention, and not one of 'em is black. Fuck that shit! If the sista's don't want him, I say get who you can get. The killin' part about it is some of the women that were lined up tryin' to get his attention were fine as hell. But anyway, this black dude, on one of those Fox sci-fi shows, was on the same show, and Jade was interviewing him. But before he came on, Jade and some other sista was talkin' about how attractive the white captain of the ship was. Now how can she say a white man is attractive and not be attracted to white men? There are a lot of sistas marryin' white men, but even if they didn't, so fuckin' what! Besides, you obviously like Terry. Otherwise you wouldn't be callin' me to talk about it. I say, go for it, man. And if you don't, I'm goin' for it as soon as you get back."

They both laughed for a moment. Then William said, "Is it any different with them?"

"You mean sex?"

"Yeah. Is it different?"

"If you mean different in terms of being better, the answer's no. See, that's yo' problem. Every now and then you oughta accept some of that pussy being thrown your way. If you did, you'd know all women are different sexually."

"Thanks for the info. But I'm not exactly a virgin, thank you."

"Yeah, but you sound like one. You gotta learn how to please each one. You can't treat 'em all the same because they all got a pussy. Some women like you to squeeze their titties hard, some soft. But that's yo' job to find out what they want and give it to 'em 'til they beg you to stop."

"Sleepin' around is your thang, not mine. I'm the one-on-one type."

"That's why yo' dumb ass don't know nothin' about women."

William ignored that comment. He had learned over the years to accept Sterling as he was—raunchy mouth and all. "With all the women you see, is there any one special?"

"Yeah, several of 'em are—but none that I wanna settle down with."

"Why? You still hung up on Vanessa?"

"I don't know about being hung up. I'm waitin' for her to come to her senses, and come back to me."

"Sterling, it's been, what, two years since you left her? I don't think she's comin' back."

"Whether she comes back or not, I want someone like her. But anyway, when I think of special, I think about how good a woman is in bed. That's the only thing that separates them, as far as I'm concerned."

"I take it you'd make an exception for Vanessa, huh?"

"Hey, Vanessa had the whole package. I don't care how nice-looking she is, or how ladylike she is, if she can't take care of business in the bedroom, we won't be together long. But the ones that are good in bed, we tend to keep it goin' for a long time."

"What's the longest you've ever kept a woman?"

"I don't keep any of 'em long, relationship-wise, but as far as the sexual side of it, I've been with one for over twelve years."

"These women put up with you screwin' 'em whenever you feel like it?"

"Look, man, don't be fooled. Women ain't no different from men when it comes to sex. They want somebody to bang their ass regularly. And when they find somebody that can satisfy 'em, they tend to put up with all kinds of shit. It's not like they don't get anything out of it."

"How come you were with the one for so long?"

"I told you. Because she has it going on in the bedroom!"

"Is she black, or white?"

"She's white, but that doesn't have anything to do with it. I have a couple of black women that I've been with sexually for over nine years. They live in different parts of the country. When I'm in their town, we hook up for a session."

"Tell me about the white one. How did you meet her?"

"Her name is Chase Davenport. I met her at Georgetown when I was in law school. It's kinda funny when I think about it. There she was sittin' across the room when our eyes meet. I knew what was on her mind right then and there. She wanted to fuck me. At least, that's what I thought. It had been a while since I had some. Besides, she was cute. Anyway, it was our last year of law school and she was gettin' ready to marry an intern who had graduated a year earlier. She seemed like a shy girl, so I thought I'd give her the fuck of her life and keep the stereotype updated; ya know what I'm sayin'." He laughed. "So, ya know, I was gettin' my swerve on like a muthafucka, and when she started cummin', I really started rockin' her, right. Figured I'd finish her off like I do everybody else. That's the secret to keepin' a woman, Will. Ya gotta fuck the shit out of her. Then they won't leave yo' ass alone. Anyway, I was seriously gettin' my swerve on, right, then she started doing Kegels on me."

"Kegels, huh?"

"Yeah. You know. That's when a woman controls the muscles in her pussy. And I'm tellin' you, man, it felt like she was blowin' me! I kid you not!"

"I know what Kegels are. I do sex therapy in addition to my counseling sessions. Or have you forgotten?"

"What the hell ever. You sho' know how to fuck up a good story. Anyway, she started talkin' shit to me in my ear. Sayin' shit like, 'I want it to be good to you. Is it?' I don't know why, but I found myself sayin' yeah, baby, yeah. And for some reason, her talkin' made it all the better. I finally had to get a hold of myself because the shit started feeling too good, ya know what I mean? I didn't wanna end up being pussy-whupped. See, once a woman pussy-whups you, she loses respect for you. Anyway, we both thought that would be the only time, but we couldn't seem to stop makin' arrangements to see each other. We even did it the night before she got married, thinkin' that would be the last time, but it wasn't. To be honest with you, bro, I didn't want to give the shit up either. That's why I haven't. But anyway, she decided to go through with the marriage. Now they have two kids and live in the Upper Eastside of Manhattan. I hope the kids don't grow up to be rich brats like their rich daddy. I still see her from time to time. She flies me there first-class and—"

"Hold on. Somebody's at the door."

William slid his feet into his slippers. Then he walked to the door and opened it. Terry had returned.

"I need to apologize, William," she said sincerely.

"Come on in. I'm on the phone talking to Sterling, my brother."

"That's okay. I can talk to you later." Not wanting to appear pushy twice in one day, she started to leave. She didn't really want to leave though. She just wanted him to think she was willing to leave.

"No. We need to talk now. Come on in and have a seat. I'll be with you in a second."

Terry entered the suite. She felt a little apprehensive because she didn't know what to expect; especially after what had happened the last time she came into his suite. Although she was wearing the same outfit that she'd worn to dinner, somehow, she looked and smelled better than before. She was wearing a silk cream blouse that wrapped around her waist and tied on the side, black slacks, and a pair of black Coach mules. Her hair was pulled back and tied with a black scrunchie that held her hair in place. White pearl drop earrings dangled from her ears.

William walked back into the sleeping area of his suite and picked up the phone. "I'm back, but I gotta go. I have company."

"Is it Terry?" Sterling asked, almost as if he was asking only to confirm his suspicion.

"Yeah, it's her."

"I knew she'd come back. Don't fuck it up this time."

"Okay. I'll talk to you later."

"Let me know what happened. Bye. Oh, hey man, remind me to tell you about the shit that went down today at the office."

"Is it serious?"

"Yeah, man. Real serious."

"Can you tell me what it's about right quick?"

"Hey, I know you gotta go and get yo' sex thang on, but uh, let me say this. I think it's time for me to go solo. I'll tell you the rest tomorrow, all right?"

"So you're going to start your own firm, huh? It's about time. You sure you don't want to talk about it now. I can talk to her tomorrow."

"Naw, man. Go on and straighten out your problems with Terry. I'm cool with the shit."

"All right, bro. I'll talk to you later."

"Hey, Will, make her hit the high note." Sterling laughed uproariously.

William laughed along with his brother. Then, in between his laughter, he said, "You's a real trip. You know that, don't you?"

"Yeah, man, I know. Later."

"Bye," William said and hung up the phone. Then he shook his head and laughed a little more.

Chapter 12: The Vampire Files

Renegade Hotel & Casino
Grand Cayman Islands
August 1997

Jericho's limousine pulled into the underground parking garage of the Renegade Hotel and Casino. They had changed their clothes on the plane. Instead of fatigues, Pin was now wearing a red formal evening gown that had a halter top, and Jericho was wearing a black Armani tuxedo with a red cummerbund and bow tie made of the same material as Pin's gown. Victor and the other men were wearing black tuxedos with black bow ties and cummerbunds. From the bulletproof glass-enclosed elevator ascending to the penthouse, they could see people at the gaming tables and slots.

A woman hit the jackpot on a slot machine. Lights were flashing, and the bells were ringing loudly as the woman jumped up and down while repeatedly shouting, "I won fifty thousand dollars!" Although Jericho didn't like the idea of losing fifty grand, he knew her winning in the crowded casino would make the other suckers think they could win also. He would have the money back in a matter of hours.

Jimmy, the floor manager, picked up a house phone and dialed the private elevator when he spotted Jericho and the crew.

Cochise answered. "Yeah."

"Carlton Chadwick is here," Jimmy said. "He wants to see the boss right away. He's in the high stakes poker lounge."

"Okay," Cochise said, and hung up the phone. He looked at Jericho. "It's Chadwick. He wants to see you in the lounge."

Jericho asked, "Did he say why?"

"No."

"Okay. Go up and check the mail. We're gettin' off here to see what Carlton wants. See what shipments are due. Ain't no tellin' what Hawthorne's up to. He could've had the FBI seize our shipments and made himself look good in the process. I want everybody from New York to San Francisco on alert. I don't want any goddamn mistakes. The man who fucks this up will answer to me personally."

Jericho, Pin, and Victor got off the elevator and approached a suite that had "The Poker Lounge" engraved in calligrapher type stencil on the double doors. The guard opened the doors and they entered the smoke-filled room. Sandy, the waitress, greeted them. She was wearing a toga similar to those worn by the waitresses at Caesar's Palace in Las Vegas. Her white tunic was wrapped tightly around her taut body and revealed lots of her large breasts.

"Can I get you anything, sir?" Sandy said to Jericho.

Jericho shook his head and they continued back into the lounge where several poker games were going on. He spotted Chadwick playing with a couple of sheiks, wearing turbans and expensive business suits; a man wearing a Stetson and a leather, brownish yellow vest; and a former Prime Minister of Monaco. All of them were chewing on expensive, sweet-smelling cigars from Cuba. There appeared to be more than two million dollars and what looked to be a deed of some sort pushed into the center of the table. The Prime Minister and the two sheiks apparently folded. They were just waiting to see who would win the pot.

"Will ya take an IOU?" the man wearing the Stetson asked.

"How much we talkin' here, partner?" Carlton said, speaking with a mock Texas twang.

Jericho turned to Sandy and whispered, "What's that paper worth?"

"That's the deed to a string of cathouses on the outskirts of Vegas," she told him. "Whorehouses are legal there, ya know?"

"How much are they worth?" Victor asked.

"I don't know," Sandy answered. "I just know they started with some businessman from New York. The sheik wearing the gray suit won it from him. Then the Texan won it from the sheik, who really didn't want it in the first place."

"Three million dollars. Or is that too rich for your San Franciscan blood?" the Texan asked Carlton Chadwick.

"It's too much for an IOU, but I'll accept a wire transfer," Carlton countered.

The Texan looked at the dealer. "Can I use the phone?"

The dealer looked at Jericho. He nodded to the dealer. The dealer went into the next room and when he returned, he had a white telephone that read "Renegade Hotel" on the receiver. He plugged it into the wall nearest to the table and handed it to the Texan.

The Texan made a call and assured Carlton the wire transfer would be downstairs in the lobby within the hour.

Carlton smiled. "Well, why don't we wait until the money arrives?"

"Why? You don't trust me?"

"Hell no, I don't trust you. Not for that kind of money."

"I'll make good on it, Carlton, if you win," Jericho chimed in. "I want to see who wins this now."

"Thank you, fella," the Texan said to Jericho. "I owe you."

"Yes you do, fella," Jericho said sarcastically. "If you lose, don't even think about trying to run outta here without that wire transfer."

The Texan looked at Jericho sternly. He wasn't used to people being so frank with him. Victor flashed his pearly white teeth at the Texan. His bald head glistened when the light in the room hit it. The Texan thought to himself, *whoever this nigger is, he has balls and money to back it up*. He got the feeling that it wasn't bravado either. He smiled at Jericho, then tipped his Stetson to him the way cowboys do in the movies.

The Texan turned back to Carlton and said, "Chadwick, I raise you three million dollars."

"I call you, Tex," Carlton said, and pushed the appropriate amount of chips in the center of the table. "What do you have?"

"A straight club flush," the Texan said, and placed the five, six, seven, eight, and nine of clubs on the table slowly. He didn't bother looking at the cards as he turned them over. He stared at Carlton the entire time. Then he re-lit his cigar in triumph.

Carlton shook his head and waited until the Texan reached for the pot. Then he slowly turned over four aces and a joker. He looked at the Texan and laughed a sinister laugh. "Looks like you lose, fella," Carlton mocked in that same Texan voice. The Texan stopped reaching for the pot. The people in the room breathed again.

"Hope you got three million dollars, fella," Victor growled.

The Texan started to stand. Victor went over to him and placed his hand on his shoulder, squeezing a little to get his attention.

"What's the rush?" Victor asked, still showing his pearly whites.

"Why, I've never welshed on a bet in my life," the Texan said loudly. "I don't intend to start now."

"Did I say you was welshin' on a bet, mister?" Victor asked him.

"No, but you implied that I would."

"I implied nothin', mister. But, you try tuh get up again, and I'm gonna apply some pressure to this here shoulder of yours, ya hear?"

The Texan kinda slumped back into his chair. "Can I at least have a drink?"

"Sandy," Jericho said, "get the man a drink. Carlton, I think we have some business to discuss. Am I right, or what?"

The phone rang and the dealer answered it. "It's for you, sir," the dealer said to Jericho.

Jericho looked at Pin and she took the call. He put his arm around Carlton and they walked out of the lounge together. When they entered the corridor, Carlton was about to tell Jericho why he had come to the Renegade.

Jericho put his forefinger over his upper and lower lips. "Shhhhhhhhh, let's wait until we get to the penthouse. The place is bug-proof."

Moments later, they got off the elevator, where a tall halo-like electronic apparatus was positioned that they had to walk through to get to the penthouse. It was state-of-the-art scanning equipment specifically designed to pick up hidden microphones and surveillance devices. They walked through the halo and entered the penthouse. Then they walked down six steps and into the sunken living room.

"Can I get you a drink, Carlton?"

"I'll have bourbon on the rocks."

"We've come a long way since our bookie days at Berkeley, haven't we?"

"Yes, we have. But I think it's time to sever the umbilical cord."

"Why?" Jericho handed him his drink. "You want more money, right?"

"No, that isn't it at all. The IRS, the FBI, the Secret Service, or the CIA has been going through our computer files. And they made sure I knew about it."

"How do you know?" Jericho asked him with a serious look on his face.

"For about three months now, I've noticed things were being moved in my house and my office. Little, insignificant things were being moved. Like the nameplate on my desk. I could see how the wood looked different there than the rest of the desk."

Jericho sucked his teeth. "The janitors could have done that, Carlton. You're paranoid."

"That's what I thought, too. But, yesterday, I got a call from a man named Hawthorne." He took a swallow of the bourbon. Jericho raised an eyebrow the moment he heard the name. "He told me he wanted to meet me and that he could make any problems I might be having with things being moved in my office and at my home go away."

"Go on. Did you meet with this man?"

"Yes, I did. He gave me what he called the Vampire Files. I think some stuff was missing."

"Yeah, I can tell you what's missing. He showed you enough to scare you, but not enough about him, or the Agency, to expose himself to his superiors."

"The Agency? You mean, this is a CIA Operation you're involved with?"

"We're involved with, Carlton." He was pointing his forefinger back and forth from himself to Carlton. "We're in this together. You and me. We. Us. This is in the plural vernacular."

"Well, I want out," Carlton demanded, and gulped his bourbon. His hands were shaking now.

"Out? There is no out! You're going to ride this roller coaster all the way, babe. All the way. Daddy can't get yo' ass outta this shit, either. You're in it neck deep. Now, what was in them files?"

"Everything. They've got us all. They know about me, you, and the other bankers."

Pin and Victor walked into the penthouse. "The three million just arrived," Victor told Jericho. "Hawthorne's here with our old buddy Captain Greene, and some anal-retentive brotha. He wants to meet. He says he knows Chadwick's here and there's no point in tryin' to hide him."

"Show the man in."

Carlton finished off his drink. "Let me have another bourbon."

Pin left to escort Hawthorne and his men to the penthouse. Jericho picked up the phone and called Cochise. "What did you find out?"

"I've been in chat rooms since we got here," Cochise said. "I've talked to most of our people and there's no sign of trouble."

"Hmm. Maybe we can contain this shit at the top. Let's find out what Hawthorne wants. Come to the penthouse."

"On my way."

Pin came back with Hawthorne and his men. Cochise came in immediately after them.

"Shall we go to the conference room, gentlemen?" Victor asked, and extended his arm in the direction of the room.

They all went into the conference room and sat in cushioned black leather swivel chairs at the table. Hawthorne and his men sat on one side. Jericho and the crew, including Carlton, sat on the other side. Captain Greene had grown a goatee since his Vietnam days, which made him look tougher. He sat quietly and stroked his goatee repeatedly.

It was Captain Greene who had introduced Hawthorne and Jericho in late 1979. The CIA needed to raise money to arm a faction of the Islamic Fundamentalist to fight against Iran during the hostage siege. They sold Jericho confiscated cocaine at a reduced rate, which he turned into crack and made nearly a billion dollars. Shortly after, Hawthorne used Jericho's crew to safeguard the weapons they sold to foreign governments to stunt the growth of communism in the Middle East. Jericho learned the arms trade and went into business for himself. He discovered he could make more money selling arms to warring countries around the globe than he could selling crack. He set up bank accounts in twelve different countries and used the wiring service to move his money around.

"What's this all about, Hawthorne?" Jericho asked.

"What's this all about?" Hawthorne repeated sarcastically. "This is about power. This is about who has it and who doesn't. In case you're confused, the people on this side of the table have it. The people over there have none. Zero. Zilch. Nada. Do you understand? We're corralling you, son. No more of this maverick renegade shit you been pullin'. Now get this. I'm the only thing standing between you and life imprisonment without the possibility."

Jericho laughed. "You seem to forget I'm on British soil."

"You seem to forget the President's up for reelection. You've also forgotten he appointed Nora Clayter to the Executive Director chair of the Agency. She has a hard-on for cleaning up the Agency and putting a stop to our dirty little wars. I can have all of your asses extradited in less than twenty-four hours."

"Quit sellin' wolf tickets and get on with it," Jericho said, clasping his fingers together.

"You don't seem to understand the gravity of the situation, son. You've forgotten that I made you. ME! Now, I'm going to break you. I've got your balls in a vise and I'm about to squeeze. We know everything. We know about you, too, Chadwick. We know about all the bankers also. We don't mind the munitions, but the drugs have got to go—until we need them again. It was a good scheme while it lasted. It was smart to have Chadwick here recruit twelve of his banker friends, none of whom know each other, and each of them recruit twelve, using the same formula, until you covered a significant portion of the country. And you had us running interference for you. But all of that is over. Unless…"

"Finally," Jericho said. "No more bullshit. Unless what?"

"Unless we get rid of Clayter. Some overzealous agent with access to the Vampire Files gave them to her and now you're on her number one hit list. All of you. Now, either she goes, or you go. We want her to go. Hell, we've been runnin' the Agency this way for better than fifty years. She thinks she can bring her prissy ass in here and change things."

"We wouldn't want a little law and order, now would we, Hawthorne?" Victor said sarcastically.

"So what you're saying is, it's to our mutual best interests to get rid of Clayter," Jericho concluded.

"That's right. But we gotta move on this right away."

"Is that why you had Cyrus try and kill me with C-4?"

"Like I said, we needed to corral you. He had no idea how big this thing of ours is. He settled for peanuts. We would have killed two birds with one stone, you might say. It wasn't personal."

"Don't tell me," Victor snarled. "It was business, right?"

"Shut up!" Hawthorne snapped.

"Why don't you come over here and shut me up?" He had a menacing frown on his face. He never liked Hawthorne and this was as good a time as any to express himself.

"As you were, Sergeant," Jericho told Victor.

Victor regained his composure.

"Gentlemen," Jericho continued, "let's put our differences aside and work together to resolve the Clayter problem."

"As I was saying," Hawthorne began again, "we would have gotten rid of you and stopped a lot of drugs from entering the suburbs. We would have given Clayter what she wanted. She would have more than likely been satisfied and we could continue on as usual. All of that changed when you got rid of the Jamaican."

"Where the fuck you get off talkin' about gettin' rid of us!" Victor yelled.

Hawthorne stared at Victor. He wanted to kill him but restrained himself.

"You feelin' froggy. Leap yo' ugly ass on over here so I can fuck yo' ass up," Victor told him. Then he looked at Captain Greene, who was also staring at him. "What? You want some of this? I'll fuck you up, too. You think by growin' that goatee you scarin' somebody? I'll bounce yo' ass off the ceiling, then toss yo' ass out the window."

Pin laughed. She didn't like any of them either. If she had her way, none of them would leave the hotel alive.

"Can we get back to business, please?" the anal-retentive black agent asked, breaking the tension.

"Has she seen the videotape from the satellite yet?" Jericho asked. He had learned from the Berkeley incident to remain cool when others have lost theirs. Since he'd gotten older, he was more contemplative than reactive.

"Figured it out, huh? No matter," Hawthorne conceded. "She won't see it until Monday morning. So you need to rectify the situation by then."

"I'm going to need more time. Can't you stall her a while?"

"I can try. How long we talkin'?"

"At least a week. Then we're back to business as usual."

"No. Not business as usual. You're out of the drug business. You're strictly munitions as of right now, deal?"

"Deal. But I'm going to need her file first. You know, to know her movements. As you know, women are hard targets because they're unpredictable. So I need to know where she goes and how often. Stuff like that."

"I thought you would." He tossed a folder on the table. It slid over to Jericho.

Jericho opened the file and began reading. Then he said, "Pin will see you to the door."

They all stood up. Jericho and Hawthorne shook hands. Then Hawthorne and his men left with Pin. Jericho and his men sat down. They waited until Pin returned.

"We're dead, as far as Hawthorne is concerned," Jericho told them. "It's just a matter of time now. He wants us to get her out of the way of his private profiteering. We're going to cool out on the drugs as planned, for now. We find out what Clayter knows first. I don't think she knows anything. If she did, she'd know about the videotape from the satellite by now. If she really had a hard-on for us, she would have personally supervised the operation. I don't think she knows who we are at all. The question now becomes why does he want her killed? But assuming Hawthorne is tellin' the truth, we take her and Hawthorne out the same night and blame it on the Islamic Fundamentalist Movement."

They all nodded their heads.

"I don't want any part of killing people," Carlton said.

"Don't worry, Chadwick." Victor smiled. "I'll do Hawthorne and Greene m'self."

"You better get somethin' through your head, Carlton," Jericho said firmly. "They'll have you doing whatever they want, if we don't stop them first. Do you understand?"

"Yes, but I don't want to know about it."

"Okay, gentlemen, we've got a week to settle this once and for all. I want somebody on Hawthorne. I want to know where he is at all times. Carlton, you go on back to San Francisco. He'll be watching you, so carry on as usual. We'll take care of the rest."

Chapter 13: Voir Dire

When Sterling hung up the phone, it occurred to him that he hadn't told William about winning the Samuelson case. He was about to call his Toronto hotel but decided to tell him later, rather than interrupt what was happening between him and Terry. He started watching the movie again as he sat on the sofa clipping his toenails in the nude. Bruce Lee was in the basement of the palace fighting Hahn's men. He was trying to open the elevator doors when he found himself surrounded.

At that moment, Le'sett came out of the bedroom wearing one of his Georgetown sweaters. The sweater came down to mid-thigh on her, but it came down to his waist on his six-foot-two-and-a-half-inch frame. She walked right in front of the TV screen waving the last Trojan in the air. Sterling snaked his head, attempting to see the action. Le'sett was in the mood for another round of hot sex and she would have it. She slowly began pulling the sweatshirt up, exposing her vagina.

Seeing this erotic display, Sterling felt himself beginning to stiffen again. With the sweatshirt off and tossed on the floor, he could see her brown erect nipples. He looked at her body as she stood before him. He wanted her again.

Le'sett lowered her eyes—Sterling was throbbing. She walked over to where he was sitting, and slid the Trojan on. Then she straddled him, guiding his thick tool to the entrance of her furry kitten and slid down onto him with relative ease. She liked the way he felt inside her. The toe-nail clipper fell to the floor.

As she moved up and down on him, he licked her left nipple while caressing the right. She moaned softly at first, but as the intense pleasure she felt built, she could no longer contain what she felt. Her moaning grew louder and louder. The deep penetration drove her wild as her movements became rapid and uncontrolled. She finally wrapped both arms around his head, pulling him deeply into her bosom. She pumped faster and harder. Her moans filled the room. Finally, her pleasure over-whelmed her and she released her passion. The orgasm was so powerful that her vagina involuntarily gripped and released him over and over.

Sterling stood with Le'sett still impaled on him. He kissed her hard as he walked to the bedroom. His lust for her ever-growing, he laid her on the bed and without mercy, he thrust himself inside as hard and as fast as he could.

She could feel the deepness of his hardness and the pleasure she received from his pelvis touching her clitoris. "It's been so long," she repeated in subdued tones.

"Daddy doing you good?" Sterling asked her. He had heard Glynn Turman say it in the movie, *J.D.'s Revenge*. This was something he even-tually asked all of his women. It always amazed him when they answered.

"Yes! Oh yes, daddy!" she screamed.

Although he enjoyed sex with her, it was his ego he wanted to satisfy now. He loved making women climax. So he kept plunging himself inside her. Sometimes in circular motions, other times up and down.

She thought he would never stop. So she placed one hand around his thick back and with the other, she grabbed his ass and pulled him tightly. Then with all the force she had, she met each of his thrusts with her own. Sterling began moaning in her ear. Hearing this, she pumped faster than he wanted her to. She could feel him losing control. He pumped faster and harder until he was moving only a little. She no longer felt his hard-ness. He withdrew himself and lay on his back panting. Le'sett laid her head on his chest and watched his stomach move up and down rapidly.

"So when are you going to tell me about the mysterious Ms. Bellamy?"

Still panting, he said, "I believe that would fall under attorney-client privilege, counselor."

"So she gave you a million dollar retainer for nothing?"

"Are you deaf? Didn't I just say, in a polite way I might add, none of your business?"

She laughed. "Well, a girl has to try."

"On the other hand," Sterling continued, "if you were to join my firm, you'd be privy to everything she said."

"Are you asking me to become your partner?"

"Just like a woman. I said join MY firm and you inexplicably heard, partner." He laughed while simultaneously shaking his head.

"You want me to join your firm, huh?"

"Yes, I do. You're an excellent attorney. You just need a few tips from me and you'll be right up there with the best of them."

"What tips are you referring to, counselor?" she asked him, looking flirtatiously into his eyes. She had her arms crossed on his chest with her chin squarely on her hands.

"Tips cost. What are you willing to pay?" he asked playfully.

"I just gave you all you could handle. Now you want me to give more for some of your cunning and knowledge? Or is it your wisdom I'm buying? Oh, I know, you want oral gratification. Is that it?"

"Hey, who am I to turn down a little head?" He laughed. "No, I'm only kidding. The thing that it will cost us is we can never do this again. There are two kinds of women I don't sleep with. The ones working for me, like Tiffany's fine ass. And the ones I work for, like Ms. Bellamy, who I know is good in bed."

"How do you know she's good in bed?"

"It was something about the chauffeur. He was a little too nonchalant. I don't know for sure what it was, but there's something there."

"So you think he's doing more than driving Miss Daisy, huh?"

"Uh-huh."

"Well if that's all it's going to cost me, I accept."

"No, I'm serious about that. Sex in the office is nothing but trouble. You still have to see the person and work in close proximity when it's over. Tempers flare often and we're in a business where our clients depend on us for their lives and livelihood. Those are the rules I have, and live by. That's why I don't have those problems. I could never sleep with a woman I'm working with. You know my reputation. I might want to sleep with your secretary, your friend, or your sister. I'm just like that. Even if you put up with it, if we're in the same office, and it got out that I'm doing it with other women in the office, you'd look like an idiot, or they'd think they have pull with me and disrespect you. Either way, you've got a volatile situation in what's supposed to be a business-like atmosphere. Understand?"

"Yes, I understand. But I wouldn't put up with it." She frowned.

"Why not?"

"Why not? Would it be okay if I did the same?"

"Yes, I wouldn't care. Who you sleep with is your business and vice versa." There was a serious tone in his voice.

"You wouldn't think I'm a whore for doing so?"

"No. Why would I, when I'm doing the same?"

"That's a very progressive attitude, counselor."

"Yes, it is. The shit is overdue though, don't you think?"

"Yes, I do."

"Tell me the truth then," he said, looking at her.

"Okay."

"Haven't you ever seen a good-looking man that you just wanted to fuck? I'm not saying going through the routine of dating and playing the dumb shit. You know, the cat and mouse game. When in fact, you just wanna get laid. No romance, just steamy hot sex?"

"Yes, of course. Why do you think I'm here with you? You don't think this was your idea, do you?"

"Yes and no." He looked a little confused.

"Typical male. You think you got me here by being charming. Don't get me wrong. You are charming and handsome and a good lay, but this was my idea, not yours. Well, partly yours, but I wanted you first," she gloated.

"Really?"

"Really. I knew you wanted me, too, a little while after the trial began."

"How did you know?"

"How, is going to cost you."

"Let me guess. It's going to cost me the tips, right?"

"Right."

"Okay, you first."

"No. You first."

"What? You don't trust me?" He couldn't keep from grinning.

"No, I don't."

"You know I could like you, girl." He climbed on top of her.

"Don't even try it, all right? I already got what I came for. I don't need any more."

"Yeah, but what if I do?"

"Fine. Just know you're still going to tell me first, or no deal."

He laughed. "Okay. Tell me something, counselor." He rolled onto his back again. "Why do you think you lost a case that everybody thought you should have won easily?"

"You put on a better case than the state?"

"True. Besides that, why did you lose the case?"

"Because you're a better attorney?"

"True, again. Besides all of that, why did you lose the case? Perhaps I should ask you this. When did you lose the case? Now, that should help you out."

"When the jury came back with a not guilty verdict." She laughed. "Seriously, I don't know what you're getting at. I put on an excellent case. My opening statement was good, and my closing statement was flawless."

"Do you really think my opening and closing arguments were that much better than yours? The only thing different from the prosecution's opening and closing and the defense's opening and closing is that the defense says whatever the prosecution says is not true. Not much more. Do you agree?"

"Yes, but I'm lost as to where you're going with this. Just spit it out."

"Part of being a top-notch attorney is learning from those who are better than you. What have you learned from this case?"

"I learned that he, who has the money, usually gets away with murder." She laughed again.

"True. But remember I used to be an assistant DA, too. I would not have lost this case. You did. And you didn't lose because I was better than you. You lost because I knew something you didn't. That's all there is to it."

"Okay, fine. What do you know that I don't, counselor."

"You still don't know how you lost this case, do you?"

"No, and I'm starting not to give a damn. Now are you going to tell me, or not?"

"Le'sett, listen. When I was a child, me and my brothers and my mom and dad would sit around the kitchen table during dinner discussing things. I was about eight. My baby brother, Will, was six and my older brother was sixteen. Anyway, my father would be talking about things that most adults don't even discuss. He'd talk about philosophy, poetry, etc. My father isn't educated. Well, not formally educated. Anyway, he'd ask us questions that made us think. He wouldn't accept 'I don't know' for an answer. When you gave him an answer, he'd ask you questions about your answer, which forced you to think even more. I felt like such an idiot during these discussions. I think we all did. Anyway, I finally did say what you just said. I said, 'Dad, why don't you just tell me what you're talking about?' He looked at me with his steel eyes. I could tell he was mad because I had given up the search for wisdom, knowledge, and understanding. Anyway, he said, 'Sterling, whatever you do, never, ever forget that the light burns brighter when you turn it on yourself.' I was confused as hell. I remember sitting there thinking, what does that have to do with the question you asked. But I nodded my head and continued eating. Still confused, I wondered if other children had similar fathers who spoke in such ambiguous terms."

"Ambiguous? That's a huge word for an eight-year-old, don't you think?"

"Ha, Ha. You know what I mean. Anyway, it wasn't until years later that I fully understood what he was talking about. I was watching a Bugs Bunny cartoon and one of the characters was thinking of a way to trap the other and a picture of a light bulb illuminated over his head. Then it came to me that he was talking about ideas and how important it was to figure things out for yourself, because then you truly understand. And this understanding becomes philosophical the more you think about it.

"Soon, what is difficult to understand becomes simple. In other words, complexity and simplicity are one and the same. A rudimentary understanding of simple things leads to a full understanding of the same. This, in turn, leads to a rudimentary understanding of complex things. And a rudimentary understanding of complex things leads to a full understanding of the same. Finally, simplicity and complexity become cyclical,"

"What?" she said, with a confused look on her face.

Sterling laughed. "You should see your face right now. I'm sure that's the same look I had on my face when my father tried to explain himself to me."

Le'sett had the same confused look on her face. "Why don't you just tell me what you're talking about? What does complexity and simplicity have to do with you winning today?"

"Everything, Le'sett, my sweet, everything. I'm so grateful to my father for forcing me to think about things. It helps me succeed where many have failed."

"Excuse me, Mr. Plato—Mr. Socrates or whoever the hell you think you are, but could you just answer the damn question, please? Shit... I almost don't wanna know the answer, the way you keep philosophizing."

"Okay, okay."

For the first time, Sterling understood how his father had felt when he tried to get them to understand what he was talking about. "You lost this case during voir dire."

"How do you figure that?"

"How many peremptory strikes did you have?"

"Thirty, same as you."

"No, I had sixty peremptory strikes; you had none. I used your strikes, too. Why do you think I argued with Judge Jones so strenuously for thirty strikes?" He paused for a moment. "So I could get the jury I wanted. A jury that would listen and believe what I told them. You used your strikes when I wanted you to. I used psychology, in other words. I made you think I wanted people I didn't and you'd strike them every time. Then I argued you didn't have cause and used weak arguments that would allow the juror you thought I didn't want to stay."

"Didn't you run the risk of alienating yourself with the jurors?"

"Yeah, but it was a minor risk. Why do you think I always said nice things about them the entire time I argued against them? I'd say how intelligent they were and so forth. If you remember, I'd say a man was handsome. Or I'd say a woman was pretty. If they weren't physically appealing, I'd say something about their dress, their manners, their smile, or anything that made them feel good about themselves. People love to be flattered—especially women. A woman can be smart as hell and still feel intellectually inadequate most of the time. That's why y'all hate to be called stupid; especially by a man."

"Now that I agree with. There's something about being called stupid that pisses me off; even though I know I'm not. If a woman calls me stupid, I tell her a thing or two. If it's a man, I read his ass the riot act."

"Voir dire is the most important part of the trial. I know I'm going to win most of the time before opening statements. My philosophy is to win the trial before it even begins. If you come with me, you will also. You have to use what works according to your personality. Understand?"

"Not really. However, I'm willing to learn."

"So are you going to come in with me, or not?"

"I don't know yet. I haven't had a lover for some time now. I may need to use you from time to time. Even though you have an atypical attitude about women and sexual freedom, most people don't. I have to worry about my reputation. That's all a woman has. Once she loses her reputation sexually, men and women lose respect for her. In this line of work, respect is everything. You understand what I'm saying, Sterling?"

"Yeah, you wanna fuck me when the mood hits you." Le'sett hit him playfully and laughed. "Well, am I right?"

"Yes, but I wouldn't put it that crudely. I trust you to keep this our little secret, okay?"

"Okay. Now tell me about you choosing me, or whatever you said earlier."

"Sterling, you're a very attractive man. However, it isn't just your looks that attract women. It's your whole persona."

"What do you mean?"

"I mean, you carry yourself well. You don't run with the gang. You don't kiss and tell. Every time I hear about you and some woman, it's never a guy telling me. It's always the woman herself. Or I overhear her telling another woman. Most men can't wait to get back to the office and tell everybody about the conquest. You don't do that."

"Okay. So how did you choose me though?"

"I've had my eye on you for some time. When we were in court, I'd flirt with you, but you didn't respond. That's one of my techniques in court. You know how men generally think with their dicks. My philosophy is if you're thinking about getting me into bed, you might miss a crucial objection. And if you do, I'll really pour it on then. You wouldn't respond at all. I got suspicious because I'm an attractive woman and I knew you weren't a homosexual. So either you weren't interested or you were playing hard. I began to speculate as to why you would play hard because I knew it wasn't me. At least that's what a girl tells herself. So I thought, he must be playing the not interested game. The one when you pretend not to notice a woman when you really do in order to make her more interested in you."

"I know it well."

"I thought that's what you were doing, but I wasn't sure. When you came into court this morning with that puppy dog face, I wanted to cheer you up. Then, after you had won the case, and I was ready to pay off, you said no. I walked away hoping you'd come after me. When you did, I knew it was a game."

"So you wanted this all along then, huh?"

"Yes. Don't you feel stupid?"

"Yeah, kinda. I knew I had played the role too long."

Beep! Beep! Beep! He grabbed his pager off the nightstand and looked at the number that flashed. It read 537-4246. It was Jericho's way of saying come online. The number was spurious. Each number corresponded to the letters of his name sequentially.

"Who is it? One of your women?" Le'sett asked playfully.

"No. It's my brother, Jericho. He's in the Caymans and he wants me to come online."

"I need to shower and get outta here anyway."

"I'll be in my office down the hall. Let me know before you leave, okay?"

"Okay," she said, then went into the adjacent bathroom.

As he left the room, he could hear the toilet flush. Then he heard water splashing in the tub.

Chapter 14: Let's Talk About It

Toronto
August 1997

William walked back into the living room area of his suite. Terry was sitting on the sofa with her legs crossed. She was moving the crossed leg back and forth nervously.

"Can I get you anything, Terry?"

"No thank you, I'm fine."

"Are you sure?"

"Positive."

He sat in the matching lounge chair next to her. "You're probably wondering why I wanted to talk to you." Before she could say anything, he continued, "Terry, I owe you an apology. What I said earlier, you know, about having children that weren't half-black and half-white. That was out of line. Can you forgive me?"

"Yes," she said with an inviting smile that lit up the room. Then she uncrossed her legs, and leaned forward. "I need to apologize, too. I shouldn't have slapped you, William. I can't believe I did that. I'm one of those women that's always saying men shouldn't hit a woman for any reason. Must be that Italian blood in me. Do you accept my apology?"

"Of course, I do. I had it coming. Don't worry about it. I won't tell if you won't."

Terry looked at William as though she expected him to say something more. Silence filled the room as they stared at each other for what seemed like five minutes, but only about three seconds had actually elapsed. Then they both looked away. He wanted to talk to her about what she had mentioned earlier, but he was nervous, and he felt a little tongue-tied.

"Is there something more you wanted to say, William?" Terry sensed his nervousness and thought she could help him say what was on his mind. For a moment she thought he wasn't going to say anything.

Then finally, he said, "Terry, we need to talk about our earlier conversation."

"Okay. Let's talk about it."

"Well…" He coughed to clear his throat. "Excuse me," he said politely. "This is really difficult for me, so be patient with me, okay?"

"Take your time," she said, trying to conceal her excitement.

"Well, I thought about what you said. You know, as far as me not knowing who I am. I couldn't get it out of my mind, so I called my brother and told him what happened. When I finished telling him, he pretty much raked me over the coals for not jumping at the chance to be with you. Before I say anything more, tell me something. What do you want from me?"

Terry grinned. "Everything."

"Why? I mean, you can have any man you want. Why me?"

"Because I admire you, William. I think you have an inner strength most men would give their right arm for. You started out with nothing and built a business practically on your own. You're very intelligent and extremely well-read. You're sensitive to the needs and feelings of others. You're handsome and single. But the most important thing I admire about you, William, is the love you had for Francis. These days, it's difficult to find a man who can commit to one woman the way you did with her. I know women throw themselves at you because you're successful, which is one of the many reasons why Roger and I split. As you know, we were already having problems, but when he started seeing other women, I left him. Does that answer your question?"

William concealed his emotions, but inwardly it made him feel good to hear her talk about him so affectionately. He wanted to smile, but maintained his composure and sat there with a stalwart look on his face.

"Yes, but are you sure this isn't some sort of black fantasy?"

"No, William. It isn't a black fantasy. I've already fulfilled that fantasy. Just kidding," she quickly added. "But I admit, I'm curious."

"Are you sure you want to get involved in an interracial relationship, because I'm not. I think you have many of the same qualities you say I have, but I'm not sure I want to deal with all of the scrutiny we'll be subjected to. Before you told me I was being racist for allowing color to get in the way, I wouldn't have even considered myself a closet racist. When I thought about it, and after I talked to my brother, I had to face the facts. You were right about me. I guess what I'm saying is, if we cross that bridge, you're going to have to be really patient with me."

Terry could no longer contain herself and bubbled over with excitement. "Does that mean what I think it means?"

"Yes, it does. But there are strings attached."

"Strings?"

"Let's keep this between you and me. I think it would be imprudent to tell everybody about this too soon. Plus, the people at the office will start treating you differently the moment they find out. You'll no longer be one of them. They'll think you're a spy for me. When you walk into a room they're already in, they'll stop talking and leave. When it comes to rewards, perks, benefits, etc., they'll think you're only getting yours because of your relationship with me."

"You're right. It's one thing to know I'm attracted to you and quite another to know we've decided to see each other. We'll keep it between you and me. But—"

He interrupted her before she could finish. "Tell me something. Who is Denyce Graves?"

"She's an opera singer."

"So you like opera?"

"Not particularly."

"Then how did you know who she was? As a matter of fact, how were you able to rattle off so many names so quickly? I was telling my brother I didn't know half the people you named."

"That's what I was about to tell you before you interrupted me, William. I didn't want to tell you like this, but if we're going to see each other, I'd better tell you the whole truth."

"Yeah, that would be best."

"Do you remember when I said I saw a certain look on your face at dinner?"

"Yes. How could I forget?"

"Well, the truth is I didn't see anything. I bluffed you. I was going to confront you on this trip no matter what, but the dinner conversation was a godsend. I knew you would be more relaxed since you got all that stuff off your chest. So I came over and confronted you."

"That doesn't explain how you knew about those black women."

"I'm getting there. The truth is your secretary, Jeannine, told me about them. She gave me a copy of an *Ebony* magazine article that featured interracial couples and had me memorize their names so I could defeat your arguments. You know how difficult it is to win an argument with you. Look at what happened to James's plan. You weren't even prepared and yet you mopped the floor with them."

He laughed. "Damn. Is everybody working an angle on me? First, the conspiracy at dinner; now this. Was Sterling in on it, too?"

"No. That was his own doing, which proves this was meant to be. Call it fate. Call it providence. Call it anything you like, but things couldn't have worked out any better."

"How did Jeannine know I was attracted to you? I never said anything to her about it."

"Before we left, she came into my office and told me she knew you were attracted to me because she'd seen you watching me when you thought nobody was looking. She said you'd never say anything to me because black women disapprove. Then she told me what your arguments were going to be before you made them. Jeannine knows you really well, William. She knew practically everything you were going to say before you said it. So I was prepared for you. She even told me not to ask if I could come over. She said if I asked, you'd think of some lame excuse to put me off. Jeannine really cares about you. Besides, the fact that she advised me as to how to talk about us proves that not all black women are against black men dating white women. I hope you're not upset with her. Personally, I think she did us both a favor."

"No, I'm not upset with her. Well, it's getting late. I think we both need to get some sleep."

"Speak for yourself. Now that we've finally gotten this out in the open, I feel as though I could talk to you all night. But if you wanna get in bed, that's fine also. Where do I change?" she asked with a mischievous grin.

"I've always enjoyed your sense of humor."

"I'm only half-kidding. But if you want me to stay, I will."

"Naw, I need my sleep. Besides, I know Ivy and James aren't gonna leave well enough alone. They'll find some way to bring it all up again."

"What makes you say that?"

"Just a feeling I have. If I had listened to my feelings before we left, I never would have come on this trip. I had a feeling something bad would happen, but I ignored it. I don't usually do that. For some stupid reason, I let them talk me into coming."

"See, it's fate! If you had listened to your intuition, we wouldn't have had this wonderful conversation."

"That's true. We both may live to regret that I didn't listen to my intuition before it's all said and done."

"You sure you don't want me to stay with you tonight?"

William stared at her for a few seconds and then said, "If you want to give this relationship a real chance, you'd better discipline yourself."

"Are you saying you want to date each other exclusively?"

"Yes. I don't bed hop. That's dangerous as hell these days. Besides, I'm not seeing anybody right now, are you?"

"No, I'm not. Nobody serious anyway. Okay, it's just you and me then."

They both stood and walked to the door.

"Do you know why I hired you, Terry?"

The question surprised her and curiosity lines surfaced on her forehead. "No, William, I don't. I thought I did, but apparently I was wrong."

"During the interview, when I asked you what you thought the most important aspect of an employer-employee relationship was, you said 'loyalty.' That's what settled it for me. Don't get me wrong; your credentials were impeccable, but I'm more impressed with a person's loyalty than anything else. Believe it or not, you and Jeannine are the only people working for me that gave that answer. The point is, I knew you were special when I hired you. I thought you oughta know that."

"Thanks, it's good to know we're starting our relationship off on a good note, William."

He opened the door for Terry and she stepped into the hall. "Oh, and Terry, don't call me William around the others. It will give them the wrong impression." Terry mimicked zipping her lips, locking them, and throwing away the key. "See ya in the morning for breakfast at the Regatta. Good night, Terry."

"Okay. Good night." She turned and walked down the polychromatic corridor. When she heard the door close, she screamed, "Yes!" But no audible sound could be heard.

Chapter 15:
You Need a Vacation

San Francisco
August 1997

S terling walked into his office, sat down at his desk, and pushed the power button on his Power Mac 4400. Moments later the contents of the hard drive were visible. He double-clicked the America Online icon and typed in his password. Before long, he heard his internal modem initializing. The America Online software went through a series of checks before he heard, "Welcome! You've got mail!" Seconds later, his buddy list was visible and he could see Renegade, Jericho's screen-name, on his buddy list. He clicked the locate button, which let him know that Jericho was in a private room.

Why would you tell me to come online if you were in a private room? Sterling decided to check his mail until Jericho came out of the room. While holding down the command key, he pressed the letter R and his mailbox came up, which contained three letters, one from each of his girlfriends. Cynthia's letter was first.

"Congratulations, babe. I knew you could do it. Give me a call so we can get together and celebrate. Love, Cynthia."

The next letter was from Crystal. Her letter read: "Congratulations, Sweetheart. You know he did it. LOL (laughing out loud)!! Why don't you come to Chicago so I can work you over? I know you need some by now. LOL!! You go, boy. Love, Crystal."

The final letter was from Chase. Her letter read: "Congratulations, Sterling. You're almost as good as me. It wouldn't have taken me six months to win the case with the flimsy evidence they had, but you keep practicing. LOL! Hey, I missed you. I'm wondering, now that you have time, why don't you come to New York for a week, or so? I haven't been laid in six months. At least not the way I like it anyway. Just this morning, I was thinking about our escapades that last year of law school. We had some wild times, didn't we? I never thought we'd still be seeing each other after all these years. I want you inside me as I type. I'm getting wet just thinking about you being deep inside me. Did that make you hard? I hope so; that way you'll understand what it's like to wait six months for you. Gotta run. I'm due in court this afternoon. Do try and come here. Love, Chase. P. S. My mouth is hot, too. I know how you like head so I thought I'd entice you a bit more than Cynthia, and Crystal. I'm sure they're trying to get you to Denver and Chicago. I know you're hard now. Bye."

He felt himself starting to rise again after Chase's final comments. Just as he began to consider their offers, Jericho sent him an instant message.

Renegade: How long you been on? And don't use my real name either.

Jaguar 1: 10 min. I know not to. You say that shit every time. Give me some credit.

Renegade: OK. Congrats, little bro.

Jaguar 1: Thx, big bro.

Renegade: You need a vacation. Come down here for a while.

Jaguar 1: Maybe later. I just got three intriguing offers from three lovely ladies and I don't know who to choose. I might have to get all three of them together and make a sandwich and shit. LOL!

Renegade: I need you to answer some legal questions for me. Come on down. I'll send the jet for you.

Jaguar 1: What kind of questions?

Renegade: Legal questions, I said!

Jaguar 1: What's in it for me? LOL!

Renegade: LOL my ass. Are you comin' or not?

Jaguar 1: I just got finished cumin'. LOL. Yeah, bro, I'll be there.

Renegade: Good. When can you leave?

Jaguar 1: Is tomorrow too soon?

Renegade: No, that's fine.

Jaguar 1: It'll be about four days before I get there though. I need to stop in Denver, Chicago, and then Manhattan.

Renegade: LOL, you a trip. You still wit that white girl in New York?

Jaguar 1: Yeah. Best head in the continental United States. LOL

Renegade: LOL

Jaguar 1: Guess what?

Renegade: What?

Jaguar 1: Will finally found a woman.

Renegade: Bout time

Jaguar 1: Guess what else?

Renegade: What?

Jaguar 1: She's white. LOL. I wish I could see your face right now.

Renegade: You bullshitin'.

Jaguar 1: Naw, I'm straight up.

Renegade: How she look??????????????????

Jaguar 1: You guessed it. She's blowed. She got a grill that would stop a Mack truck. I'm talkin fucked for life here. LOL

Renegade: We gotta put a stop to it.

Jaguar 1: Why? You never say anything about Chase. Why say something about Terry?

Renegade: U and Will are 2 different people. U fuck white women but I know yo' ass ain't gon marry 1. Will is different from us. He'll end up married to the bitch. I just can't see my baby bro with a WW. And an ugly 1 at that.

Jaguar 1: I was just bullshitin. She's not ugly. She's fine as hell. And she got an ass on her, too.

Renegade: Well that makes it a little better. But what about his money? You know how them white bitches are. Look at the Juice (OJ Simpson) now. He ain't got shit now, fuckin' with them bitches. They want that dick, then they take yo goddamn money. I'm tellin you now, if he ends up with her, and she tries to take his money, I'll kill her ass. Hey, did you see Chris Rock bring the pain? LOL

Jaguar 1: Yeah, I saw Rock. But Terry's different from most women.

Renegade: How u know? Did you fuck her 2?

Jaguar 1: LOL. Naw, man. But I would. You would, too. The girl got it goin' on in a big way. I think she's alright. She doesn't fun off at the mouth.

Jaguar 1: fun = run

"Hey, baby," Le'sett interrupted. She was standing in the doorway of his office. "I'm getting ready to go."

"Okay, just a second," Sterling said. "Let me tell my brother to hold on."

Jaguar 1: brb

"Let me walk you to the door," Sterling said.

"Have you forgotten I rode with you over here?"

"Oh yeah, I forgot. Let me tell my brother I'll catch him later."

"Don't worry about it. I called a cab on my cell phone. He's out front. I had to mess with you a little bit," she told him.

"Well, I can see you to the door then."

"That's okay. I'll find my way out." Then she blew him a kiss and flicked him a Susan B. Anthony. "There's your tip, babe. You were great." She laughed.

Sterling caught the coin and said, "I think it was worth more than a dollar." Le'sett didn't respond. He heard the front door close and then he turned back to the computer.

Jaguar 1: Sorry about that.

Renegade: Don't make it a habit.

Jaguar 1: Now where were we?

Renegade: Do you really want to stop in all those places?

Jaguar 1: Yes.

Renegade: Do you have any idea how much that's goin' to cost?

Jaguar 1: My counsel has gone up considerably since this morning. LOL

Renegade: U ain't bullshitin

Jaguar 1: What time should I be ready?

Renegade: A limo will be at yo place at 8 AM sharp.

Jaguar 1: I'll be ready.

Renegade: OK. I will see you in a few days then.

Jaguar 1: Later, bro, and thanks

Renegade: No problem.

Jaguar 1: By the way, what were you doing in that private room?

Renegade: Running my business.

Jaguar 1: Okay, I'll leave it alone.

Renegade: Good. Now bye.

Jaguar 1: Bye.

Jaguar 1: Oh yeah.

Renegade: Oh yeah, what?

Jaguar 1: Do you know a rich WW name Adrienne Bellamy?

Renegade: Naw. Why?

Jaguar 1: 'Cause she knows you.

Renegade: How you know her?

Jaguar 1: Met her this mornin'. She knows about yo' business, too. Just thought you should know.

Renegade: Really? The night is full of surprises. I'll have her checked out and let you know when you get here. I'll have that Terry woman checked out 2. Last name?

Jaguar 1: Moretti, I think. She's from back East some place.

Renegade: I'll find out all there is to know about her. You'd be surprised how much info you can get on people.

Jaguar 1: Really?

Renegade: Yea, really. I'll know when and where she was born. Her financial statement, address, account #'s, access #'s, everything.

Jaguar 1: Bellamy must know some of the same people then.

Renegade: She must.

Jaguar 1: Okay, later.

Renegade: Later.

Sterling hit the command key and the letter Q. A few seconds later he heard the America online software say, "Goodbye!" Then he picked up the phone and called Cynthia.

Chapter 16: Heartache

S terling got into the white stretch limousine at 8 o'clock sharp. As they rode down the street, Sterling admired his brother's taste, and sense of style. Jericho sent him a stretch limo similar to Adrienne Bellamy's. He wondered if it was the same limousine service. Then he assumed she owned hers. He looked around the luxurious automobile and shook his head. "Must be nice," he said aloud.

He picked up his briefcase and opened it. He decided to get started on the Bellamy case. He looked at the picture of Victoria Warren. She reminded him of Vanessa Wright, his former live-in lover. Not only did they have the same initials, both women were exceptionally good-looking. It was Victoria's innocence in this sordid affair that reminded him of how he'd lost Vanessa.

Vanessa knew of Sterling's philandering ways when she met him. She didn't try to change him; she accepted him as he was. Vanessa's mother told her that sleeping around was something men did and it was best for everybody to accept a man as he is. "Otherwise, you'll only frustrate yourself trying to change him." Vanessa took her mother's advice, but added a few stipulations. She told Sterling she realized he liked to run around, and while she didn't like it, she knew how he was. She also told him she didn't want to know about it, and to be discreet. She made him promise to wear a latex condom. She told him she didn't want any of his women calling their house and above all, she didn't want him sleeping with any of her friends. She promised him she would leave him and never return if he ever disrespected her by bringing another woman into their house—into their bed. Sterling willingly agreed to her terms and had every intention of keeping them.

But, one day, Brandy, Vanessa's best friend, came over to the house when Vanessa was downtown at a Mary Kay convention. Brandy was wearing a spandex bicycle suit and shades. When he opened the door, he knew he shouldn't let her in, but he had gotten a serious erection just looking at her in the doorway. Besides, he knew why she was there, and so did she.

Brandy sat in her car, waiting for Vanessa to leave. Although they had been friends since they were teenagers, she simply had to have Sterling at least once. That's what she told herself. This was going to be a one-time thing. What Vanessa didn't know wouldn't hurt her. After all, she never meant to hurt her. She would bed Sterling, see if he was as good as Vanessa claimed, and be done with him. When Vanessa got into her car and pulled off, Brandy got out her car and rang Sterling's doorbell.

Brandy had flirted with Sterling for over a year, and he had ignored her advances. He loved Vanessa. He wanted her to be his wife, and to have his children. But, when Sterling saw Brandy in that tight bicycle suit, when he saw those vivacious curves, he looked at his watch and thought: *I got about three hours to bang this HO and get her the hell outta here before Vanessa comes home.* He decided he wouldn't take any chances and would only let her stay an hour.

He pulled her into the house and closed the door, kissing her deeply. Her back was against the door. She wrapped her arms around him and pulled him tightly to her. He squeezed her ass and caressed her firm breasts. She stopped him and peeled off that bicycle suit and stood before him completed naked. His mind whispered, "Don't do this to Vanessa. It isn't worth it." Sterling was about to stop. But when Brandy realized he was going to stop and send her away, she dropped to her knees, pulled out his tool and took him into her mouth.

After that, Sterling was powerless to stop himself. He said, "Fuck it. I tried to do right." He picked Brandy up and laid her on the couch.

Moments later he was inside her, pumping her as hard as his lust demanded. Brandy had one leg draped over the couch and the other one on the floor. As Sterling plunged ever deeper, she babbled indistinguishable words and moaned uncontrollably. Then they heard a key being inserted into the lock.

Shit, Sterling thought. He knew he was caught and there was nothing he could do to prevent it, so he pumped faster, attempting to climax before Vanessa entered their residence. *If I'm gonna get caught, I'm at least gonna bust a nutt.* In the distance, he heard Vanessa saying to her Mary Kay friends, "I'm so sorry about this. The makeup kits are in the bedroom. It's right this way. It won't take long."

Sterling pulled himself out of Brandy. He was about to put his underwear on, but thought, *why bother?* It was going to be embarrassing enough without him falling on his face trying to put them on. Brandy got as far as slipping the spandex over her feet when Vanessa and her friends walked past the living room.

Vanessa gasped. She stood there with her mouth wide open. She didn't say anything. She looked at her best friend from childhood and her man acting like irresponsible teenagers. Vanessa focused on Sterling. She looked down at his glistening tool. Semen was dripping on the emerald carpet.

"We better go," one of Vanessa's friends said.

"Yeah, you better," Vanessa agreed. She was still staring at Sterling. "You don't need me there. Y'all can handle that while I handle this."

Vanessa and her friends went into the bedroom and got the makeup kits. Then her friends left quietly. By the time Vanessa entered the living room again, Sterling and Brandy were dressed, looking and no doubt feeling guiltier than Adam and Eve. Brandy was about to say she was sorry.

Vanessa put up her right hand like a police officer directing traffic and yelled, "GET OUT, BITCH!"

"Vanessa," Brandy began, "let me explain."

"Save that shit for somebody who cares," Vanessa snapped. "I don't wanna hear that 'it just happened' shit either. NOW GET THE HELL OUT BEFORE I KICK YO' ASS UP IN HERE!"

Brandy ran out the house. Vanessa turned to Sterling and said, "I told you what would happen if you ever did this in our home, didn't I?"

"Yes, you did, baby, but let me explain," he pleaded.

"Explain what! How are you going to explain this shit, Sterling?"

"I didn't know she was coming over here, baby," he said, desperately. "I swear I didn't."

Vanessa laughed sardonically at the stupidity of that statement. Then she said, "And you think that makes a difference?"

"I just want you to know I didn't plan this shit. I'm sorry."

"Sorry? You goddamn right you're sorry! I told you I didn't want this in my house, didn't I? I told you no friends, didn't I? And I told you to wear a latex condom, didn't I? It's bad enough that I'm not woman enough for you. I've tried everything to make you happy. I cook and clean for you. Have you ever come home to a messy house? Have you ever come home and I didn't have something for you to eat? I bathed you and fed you your food! I did all that freaky shit in bed you wanted me to do! I even put up with Ms. Manhattan! So tell me why you think so little of me? That's all I wanna know."

Sterling stood there thinking of an answer, but none came to him. He didn't blame her. She was right. But instead of throwing himself on the floor and begging her forgiveness, he allowed his pride to direct his path.

"Look goddammit! You know how I am! Either deal wit' it, or get out!"

"Fine," she said with uncharacteristic calm. "I'll have my things picked up next week." Then she walked away.

"You'll be back!" he shouted as she went out the door.

As soon as he heard the door slam shut, the voice said, "Go after her now, or you'll never see her again." He wanted to go after her, but again, he allowed his pride to direct his path. That was two years ago, and Vanessa still refused to see, or talk to him. His eyes watered every time he thought about it.

The limousine pulled into the airport and headed out to the runway. The driver stopped the car near the plane and got out. He opened the door for Sterling. Then he got the garment bag out of the trunk and handed it to him.

"Have a good flight, sir," the driver said politely.

"Thank you. I'm sure I will."

Sterling picked up his briefcase and boarded the jet. He saw a very attractive black woman wearing a captain's uniform.

"Welcome aboard, Mr. Wise. I'm Captain St. John. Make yourself comfortable. We're ready to take off."

"Hello, I'm Tina, your flight attendant. I'll be serving you breakfast as soon as we're airborne. If you need anything, anything at all, I'll be at your service."

When she turned around to take her seat, Sterling checked out her ass. It was round with plenty of padding. Tina sat in a seat directly across from him. She opened her legs—she wasn't wearing panties. They looked at each other as the plane taxied. Moments later, he could feel the engines surge as the plane began picking up speed. He could hear the rumbling sound the tires made as the plane moved across the cemented pavement. Then he felt the nose of the plane lift up. Shortly after that, he heard the landing gear retracting.

When the plane leveled off, Tina went into the pantry to get breakfast. Captain St. John came out of the cockpit and said, "I'm sorry to have to tell you this, but we will be going directly to the Cayman Islands. I know you thought we were going to Denver, Chicago, and Manhattan, but your brother paid us to take you straight to the Caymans. You can use the phone to make any necessary calls."

"Why the change in plans?"

"I don't know, sir."

Now Sterling understood why Tina was being so friendly. *It won't be a total loss*, he thought. Tina brought out breakfast and sat beside him and smiled. It was the kind of smile that promised more if he wanted it. She picked up his fork and began feeding him. He picked up the phone and called Cynthia.

"Hello."

"I got bad news, baby," he said between mouthfuls.

Chapter 17:
Let's Get Out in the Open

Toronto
August 1997

William's alarm rang at 6 AM, but he was already awake. His biological clock automatically awakened him at 5:50, no matter what time he fell asleep. Occasionally, he was able to go back to sleep, but most of the time he was up for the day. While at Harvard, he forced himself to get up at 5:50 every morning so he could go out and run five miles before breakfast. But this particular morning, he had woken up at 5 AM and the conversation he'd had with Terry was on his mind.

William had always found her attractive, but he was wondering if he'd made a mistake agreeing to get involved with her. Although her arguments were persuasive, he was unsure how it would work in the office. He realized that if he dated Terry, there was always the possibility he could end up married to her. Then he remembered the words that his father had repeated over and over again.

'Son, be careful who you date because the woman you date will one day be your wife. Make sure you like her and she likes you. Notice I said like, not love. Love can be a tricky thing. Talk to her early in the relationship. Find out what things you have in common. The more things you have in common, the better. And above all, stay out of the bedroom. Nothin' can ruin a relationship faster. Sex will make you think you in love when you're not. But if you talk enough, eventually you'll disagree. And then you know if you can live with her, or not. Folk today think they can know somebody by living with them first, but they're putting the

cart before the horse. They don't realize they're getting emotionally attached to the person and that makes them think they're in love too, but they're not.'

William used to get tired of hearing his father's speeches about life, but in time, he came to depend on his father's advice. It took some time, but he discovered that his father was right about most things. He decided he needed to talk to Terry again to make sure she knew what they were getting into. Then he got out of bed and took a shower.

William walked down the corridor to the elevator. He pushed the down button and it illuminated. Seconds later the elevator doors opened. There were several couples on already. Some of the couples smiled and some didn't. At first, he didn't think much of it. But as the elevator filled with people, these occurrences continued. The elevator finally reached the first floor, and everyone got off. On the way to the Regatta restaurant, he saw Diego, the desk clerk, flagging him down. Once he knew he had his attention, he signaled him to come over to the front desk.

"Will, what happened last night upstairs in the Lighthouse?"

"What do you mean?"

"The hotel has been buzzing since I got here this morning."

"Buzzing about what?"

"That debate or whatever happened last night."

"Really? I knew some people were listening but I had no idea…"

"So what happened?"

"It was just a simple disagreement on some racial issues, nothing more."

"That's not what Eddie, the bartender, said."

"What did he say?"

"He said some of your party was so upset last night that they were arguing with each other in the lounge. He had to put a stop to it because they were disturbing the other customers. After they left, some of his other customers were talking about it, too."

"Thanks for the info. I gotta go. I'll talk to you later."

"Okay. See ya later."

As he walked into the Regatta, William thought about the occurrences on the elevator. Now it all made sense. *Were people really discussing what was said?*

"How many?" the hostess asked.

"Five."

"Smoking? Or non-smoking?"

"Non."

"Follow me."

He followed the hostess to a booth near the atrium. He could see the green plants and an assortment of flowers. The yellow daffodils stood out more than anything else. The hostess placed five menus on the table.

"Your waiter will be with you shortly. Can I get you anything to drink? Coffee, tea, water…"

"Just a glass of ice water for now."

"I'll bring it right out."

He opened his briefcase to see what time the first class would begin.

"Here you are," the hostess said enthusiastically as she sat the ice water on the table. Then she disappeared before he had a chance to thank her.

↑↑↑

Terry was the first of three children born to Dyan and Douglas Moretti, two liberal-minded Democrats, who believed strongly in the goals of the Civil Rights Movement. That's why it had confused Terry to hear her father talk that way in the video store. She had wanted to confront him about his obvious inconsistency, but she thought better of it. Terry knew that if she was right, and her relationship with William worked out, she would have to confront him.

Terry was twelve when her father accepted an executive position with Seagreens Liquors and Wines, based in New Haven, Connecticut. The move was all of a sudden and Terry had trouble adjusting. Her father encouraged her to play sports. Taking his advice, she went out for the track team and she became a long distance runner. Soon, she began watching sports with her dad every weekend, solidifying their bond. Sometimes, he'd take her to football and basketball games. By the time she was fifteen, Douglas had taught her how to shoot a pistol. She was an expert now, and owned a nine-millimeter Baretta. On Saturday afternoons, she practiced at the Marin County Gun Club in San Francisco.

After showering, Terry came out of the bathroom wearing the towel she'd dried herself with, and another wrapped tightly around her head. She walked over to the dresser and turned on her portable compact disc player. She'd brought several of her favorite CDs with her. *The Best of the Dramatics* was in the carousel. She was a child of the sixties and her taste in music reflected that era. She liked modern music also, but felt much of it left a lot to be desired.

In her mind, the music of the late sixties and early seventies was better because the artists didn't rely on sexual innuendo. The artists of the sixties and seventies were more substantive and romantic. With the exception of Luther Vandross, Lionel Ritchie, and Kenny "Babyface" Edmonds, few other writers and singers had the talent to maintain her attention. She still enjoyed Smokey Robinson, Marvin Gaye, the O'Jays, the Spinners, and the Temptations. To her, their music and lyrics transcended time.

She pushed the play button, and opened a drawer that contained her intimate apparel, and pulled out a black lace bra and matching panties. She swayed rhythmically to the music, and sang the chorus as she slid into her panties. Then she let the towel drop to the floor. She put on her bra and hooked it in the front, and took out a new pair of pantyhose. She decided to wear her favorite Jones New York olive-green, knee-length skirt suit, with a pink camisole with lace trim underneath, and a pair of olive-green slingbacks. Then she went into the bathroom and put on some Clinique mauve lipstick, and sprayed on some Design perfume as a finishing touch. She turned the music off, picked up her briefcase, and left the suite. She saw Bernie, James, and Ivy heading toward the elevator and caught up with them.

†††

William was still reading the seminar schedule when Terry and the others arrived. They all said, "Good morning," and sat down. William looked at

Ivy. She was wearing a dark pair of Foster Grant sunglasses. The first word that came to mind was "hangover." The expression on Ivy's face made him think her panties were cutting her. Terry was attempting to be inconspicuous. She didn't want to give away their secret. Bernie was reading the sports section of a *USA Today* newspaper.

"Have you ordered yet?" James asked.

"No," William said, "I decided to wait on you guys. It was the least I could do, since I kept you all waiting for me last night."

"What looks good?" Terry asked.

"Jesus, Terry," Ivy blurted out. "They're serving breakfast for heaven's sake. They serve the same things. Eggs, bacon, sausage, toast, juice, et cetera."

Terry stared at Ivy for a few seconds—frowning. Ivy's superiority complex always angered her. "You oughta leave the Jack Daniels alone," Terry told her. "It's hard enough to put up with you when you're sober, let alone when you're hung over. Or is it that time of the month?"

Bernie laughed under his breath.

"I'm thinking about having the buffet," William said, ignoring the combatants.

Then one by one, Terry, James, and Bernie, said, "Yeah, me too."

Ivy said, "I'll just have a cup of coffee."

The waiter came over. "Are you ready to order?"

"Four buffets and a cup of coffee," William said, looking at Ivy.

"Regular, or decaf?"

"Decaf," Ivy said.

"The plates are at the beginning of the line," the waiter said. "Help yourselves."

After returning to the table, William said, "Do you guys remember which classes you're going to attend?"

They all nodded and continued eating. The sound of plates scraping when their forks touched them filled the air. In between mouthfuls, he'd hear, "Ummm, this is really good. How's the French toast? Great."

Bernie took a swallow of his apple juice and resumed reading the sports section and then let out an agitated, "Humph."

"Humph what?" Ivy asked.

"Oh nothing," Bernie answered.

"I hate when people do that." James frowned. "You know we're all interested, now that you won't say."

"Well, if you must know? The Bulls are gonna give Michael Jordan a one-year, thirty-five million dollar contract," Bernie grumbled.

William and Terry looked at each other briefly to acknowledge that they were thinking the same thing. This was the bait to start the whole thing all over again, but William wasn't going for it. He wasn't going to respond.

"Thirty-five million dollars! To play basketball?" Ivy repeated, pretending to be agitated.

"That's ridiculous!" James continued the farce.

"Sports figures are probably the most overpaid people on the planet," Bernie announced.

So that's the plan. They're working together now, William thought. Terry continued eating her breakfast, unmoved. She looked at William and wondered what he was going to do.

"Dr. Wise, do you think athletes are worth all that money?" Bernie asked.

They all looked at him, but he put another forkful of food in his mouth and didn't say anything. They were sure he heard the question, so they waited in eager anticipation. Even Terry wanted to hear his answer, but she pretended to be uninterested.

William put another forkful of food in his mouth, and didn't even bother to lift his head to look at them. With his head still tilted, he said, "Thought we made an agreement." Then he continued eating.

"You said we had to finish what we started, and we never finished. So based on your own words, we have to keep talking until we're finished," Ivy blurted out with venom. Even though her head was killing her, it made her feel good to draw first blood.

Terry looked at William. The look on her face said, "They've got a point," but she didn't say anything, and continued eating. William finished what was left of his breakfast, put his fork down, looked directly at James and said, "It's difficult to have an intelligent conversation with disingenuous people."

"What do you mean?" James asked, attempting to sound sincere.

"This whole charade. You guys must think I'm stupid. Let's get it out in the open. You guys want to ask me questions about black people in spite of how I feel about being some sort of spokesman for the entire African-American community. Let's at least be honest about that."

James lowered his eyes, revealing his guilt. When William looked at Ivy and Bernie, they diverted their eyes also.

After a couple of moments of silence, James asked, "Well, don't you have questions about white people?"

"Actually, I don't."

"We've been trying to get to know you, but you're so secretive we had to concoct this plan just to get to know you," James replied.

"There you go again. Can't you at least be honest when you've been caught with your hand in the cookie jar? If you were trying to get to know me, you would not be asking me questions about black people. You'd be asking me questions about me. Now get this. If you want to talk, let's talk. If we continue this, I expect you to say what's really on your mind. In other words, quit pussyfooting around and no more bullshit! If you guys can't be honest, there's no point in continuing the conversation."

"Don't you think you could be opening a can of worms if people say what they really think?" Terry asked, concerned as to where the conversation could go if there were no restrictions.

"Open 'em then. That's the problem. When people are precluded from saying how they really feel, nothing gets accomplished. They keep dancing around the issues, speaking in dubious terms, and getting nowhere. Then when they get home, or among their own, they openly say what they really think to people who have heard their speeches a million times. Either we go all the way, or it ends right here and right now! Now what's it going to be?"

James knew this would be the last opportunity to discuss the issues that troubled him. He was unsure if he wanted to hear the truth, as William saw it. He looked at Ivy and Bernie. They both nodded. Then he reluctantly said, "All right then. We'll be honest from here on out."

"Don't forget I also said I could ask you guys questions." They all nodded in agreement. "I'll defer my questions until this evening."

"What questions?" James asked.

"It can wait. Don't worry about it. Now to your question, Bernie. I believe you wanted to know if I thought athletes were worth all that money. Is that correct?"

Bernie nodded his head.

"How much do you earn a year?"

"A hundred thousand dollars."

"You earn two to three times as much as the average family. Do you think you're worth what you get paid?"

"Yes."

"Why do you think you're worth that kind of money?"

"Well, at the risk of coming off as an arrogant bastard, I'm very good at what I do."

"Do you know how much money I earn?"

"No sir, I don't."

"Why not?"

"Because you're the boss. I'm only an associate."

"But if you make a hundred thousand, I must make significantly more than an associate, don't you think?"

"Yes, sir."

"And so it is in the NBA. If they can afford to pay the athletes millions of dollars, how much are the owners making? Before Michael Jordan went to the Chicago Bulls, did you ever see them on national television?"

"No, sir, I didn't."

"Now you see them a couple of times a week, right?"

"Right."

"Did you know the Chicago Bulls sell more paraphernalia than any other NBA franchise?"

"No, sir."

"Do you remember when Michael Jordan came out of retirement wearing number 45?"

"Yes, I do."

"Did you know sports stores around the country were selling his number by the tens of thousands? Isn't he entitled to profit from the market he's created for himself?"

"Well, when you put it that way, yeah."

"Now here's the problem with what you asked about the athletes' salaries. It seems to be okay that professional golfers, professional tennis players, and any other white-dominated profession, make money hand over fist. Who questions Jack Nicholson's, Demi Moore's, Michelle Pfeiffer's, Julia Roberts', or Tom Cruise's multimillion-dollar salaries? These people get paid millions of dollars each year because they generate hundreds of millions of dollars each year. But if a black man is earning millions of dollars on the gridiron, or on the basketball court, or on the baseball diamond, somehow he's not worth the millions of dollars he generates. This is the ultimate double standard, don't you think?"

"Yeah, but some of these guys are fresh outta college. How can you say they generate millions?"

"Never said they did. However, some of them do."

"Like who?"

"Like Shaquille O'Neal."

"So you think Shaq was worth all that money coming outta college?"

"Yeah. And I'll tell you why. He was one of only a handful of players in any profession that was an instant sensation from the time he left college and entered the pro game. Tiger Woods did the same thing when he left Stanford. Other than players like that, I have to agree with you. But let's not ignore the fact that a lot of people are just flat-out jealous. That's all it is. And, in my opinion, what it comes down to is intelligence. That's the bottom line.

"Athletes are known more for their brawn, not their brains. And so, many whites feel like they're somehow being cheated because they have a college education. What they don't realize is that the sporting business is like any other business, in that the owners can only earn what the networks are willing to pay. If the networks are willing to pay so much money to televise a game, why shouldn't the players, who are responsible for the bottom line, get their piece of the pie?"

"Yeah, but what about the fans?" Ivy asked. "They have to pay more every time a player decides to hold out for more money. Don't you think a player under contract should negotiate after his contract has expired?"

"Certainly he should wait, but at the same time, the owners should recognize that a particular athlete isn't being paid what he's worth. The intelligent owners do. Look at the 49ers organization, for example. Do you think they won four Super Bowl trophies because they refused to pay their players their worth? And as far as the fans go, what about the people who go to movies? Don't they pay a lot more because movie stars want more money? Sly Stallone and Jim Carrey are making twenty million a picture right now. Demi Moore was paid twelve and half million for a striptease comedy. Now, are any of them worth that kind of money?"

"No," Ivy said.

"Well, why didn't you guys mention them instead of talking about how much the athletes make? Acting doesn't require a degree either. You just have to be good, or appeal to a large audience. Look at it this way. If we grossed a billion dollars this year, wouldn't you all want your share, considering I needed you in order to earn that kind of money?" They all nodded their heads. "I didn't start this business strictly for altruistic reasons. Nor did I hire you because I felt sorry for you.

"I hired you because you were the best people available at the time." He looked at his watch. "Listen, we're going to have to finish this later. If we don't leave now, we'll be late for our classes." William raised his hand to get the attention of the waiter, and gave him his American Express card. Wanting to avoid another scene just in case the conversation got ugly again, he said, "Let's have dinner in my suite tonight and discuss the rest of your questions."

After the waiter returned the card, they left the restaurant and headed toward the elevators. When the doors opened, he told Terry and Bernie to go ahead. "I need to speak with Ivy and James." Terry and Bernie got in the elevator and the doors closed.

"Ivy, you should go upstairs and lie down until you feel better."

"I'll be okay."

"That's not a request."

"Okay," she agreed, sensing his anger. She pushed the up button and waited for the elevator to return.

"James, I need to talk to you privately."

"Sure."

"Diego," William said to the desk clerk, "can I get into the safety deposit room for a few minutes?"

"But you didn't sign for a key," Diego reminded him.

"Uh, this is kinda personal. Do you mind?"

"Sure, no problem."

Diego opened the safety deposit room for James and William. Then he left them alone in the room.

"What's bothering you, James?"

"What do you mean? Nothing's bothering me."

"So what the hell happened in the lounge last night?"

"Nothing much. Ivy had a little too much to drink. That's all."

"If that's all, how come the bartender had to come over to your table and talk to you about it?"

"Well, Ivy did get a little loud."

"I expect more outta you, James. You're the senior associate. You should have taken control."

"I did, after the fact. I'm sorry. It won't happen again."

"Fine. But that isn't the only thing bothering you, I'm sure."

James assumed Terry had told William the things he had been saying behind his back.

"Listen, I didn't mean any of those things I said to Terry about you being lucky to even get into Harvard. She's right, I'm a little jealous. I know you earned your degree just like I earned mine. It's just that since my divorce, my life has been turned upside down. It isn't fair for a woman to sleep around and still end up with everything. The house. The car. The kids and the bank account. What can a man do? I mean, shit! She was fucking the guy in my goddamn bed!" He paused for a second and appeared to be thinking about what he'd said. Then continued, "Ya know what's really fucked up about Sharon getting the house?

"She's still fucking the guy in my goddamn bed! When I pick up my kids for the weekend, they tell me their mother spends a lot a time in the bedroom with Darren. They say they can't get to sleep some nights because of all the noises their mother makes. I tried to date Terry, but she wouldn't go out with me. She didn't say anything, but I started noticing she seemed to be more interested in you. I got frustrated; that's all. It was like, every woman I wanted, wanted a man that wasn't me. I'm sorry about all of this."

"For the record, Terry didn't tell me anything." Surprise registered on James' face. "I can understand how you feel about what your ex-wife is doing to you, but you're going to have to pull yourself together. It's my reputation on the line, not yours. I've been coming to this convention for years and I've always stayed at this hotel. There have never been any problems with any of the people associated with me. These people know me, James."

James stood there with his head bowed. "Yes, sir."

Then William continued the tongue-lashing. "You need to move on with your life. Sharon has. If you need some time off, say so. But what happened last night in the lounge better not happen again. Do we understand each other?"

"Yes, sir. I understand. It won't happen again."

"I need to be able to depend on you, James." William softened his tone. "I was going to surprise you all Monday morning, but I'll tell you now. Keep this to yourself. I want it to be a surprise to the others. I'm going to promote all of you and put you in charge of the other offices. You'll have your own staff and everything. Of course that means raises and benefits. Maybe this promotion will help alleviate some of your financial problems. Now…can I count on you, or not?"

"Yes, you can." James grinned. The weight of the world was lifted from his shoulders. That was the funny thing about William. One minute he could be giving you the tongue-lashing of your life; the next minute he could be as soothing as ice cream to a sore throat. The two men shook hands and then went to their classes.

Chapter 18: Rendezvous

Villiam entered his suite and tossed his briefcase on the sofa. He left the last lecture of the day early and wanted to shower and change before his guests came over for more Q & A. In some small way, he was looking forward to tonight's exchanges, but still felt a little uneasy about the whole thing. As he walked toward the sleeping area, he saw the red message light flashing on his phone. He assumed it was Sterling calling to find out what happened with Terry the previous night.

His brother was like a woman sometimes, he thought. Sterling always wanted the details of a story. He had a network of friends, most of whom were women, who supplied him with all sorts of valuable information. It was Sterling who, through an ex-girlfriend who worked in real estate, provided him the information to get his new home in Sausalito. Sterling's personal motto was, "Don't buy anything until you check with me first. I might know somebody who can get it for you cheap."

Sterling had a people-person personality and he used it to get whatever he wanted—especially from women. He managed to maintain good relationships with them; even after they were no longer a couple. Sterling was more than a lothario. He was uppity in that he would not date any woman who didn't make a certain amount of money—not for long anyway. All of the women he dated were professionals who made a substantial income. That way if he ever married and then divorced, he wouldn't lose much because she would have as much as him.

William picked up the phone and pushed the play button and the LED continued flashing, but he couldn't hear the message. He pushed the button again and again, but still nothing. He decided to report the phone problem to the front desk. He listened for the dial tone, and pushed six for the front desk. Nothing happened. Confused, he decided to use the phone in the bedroom to report the trouble. He went into the bedroom, and lifted the receiver and was about to push six to report the problem when it occurred to him that he had a message.

He pushed the play button and listened. The message began playing and he heard Terry's cheerful voice saying, "Hi, William!" Then she cleared her throat. "Excuse me. I mean, Dr. Wise." She laughed. "I bet you didn't expect it would be me leaving you a message, huh? Anyway, earlier this morning I was thinking about what we talked about last night while I was listening to some music. The song I was listening to and your personality just seemed to go together. So please listen to it, okay?" He sat on the bed and the music started. He recognized the tune immediately. It was "Whatcha See Is Whatcha Get" by the Dramatics.

He smiled as he listened to the song. He felt affection for her at that moment he had previously denied. The words of the song were so appropriate to the whole weekend, he thought.

At the end of the song, Terry said, "William, I really mean these words. Maybe we can talk about it later on tonight, okay? See you later, bye." He dialed her room number to leave her a thank you message.

"Hello," Terry said. She was just about to take a shower and had a towel wrapped tightly around her head and another one covering her torso.

"What are you doing there?"

"I'm staying here for the weekend, you silly man, you," she said in such a way that he could tell she was smiling. She had an alluring way of disarming him. He liked that about her and felt more relaxed with her now than at any other time.

"Well, I guess that was a stupid question. I was calling to thank you for the song. I've always liked that song and it was right on time, given all that's happened since we arrived. You know what I mean?"

"Yes, I do," she said softly, sensing he was letting go of his personal prejudices at that moment and seeing her as an individual; probably for the first time. She knew he wasn't a racist, but he needed to recognize some things about himself. "So can we talk later?"

"Yeah, we can talk later. I was calling to leave you a message telling you how much I liked the song and that we could and should talk. I thought about some things this morning and—"

"You haven't changed your mind?" she interrupted, obviously disappointed, sounding as if a powerful vacuum had sucked out the joy she was experiencing.

"No, I haven't. But there are some things we need to discuss right away."

"What things?" She wanted to be prepared to argue whatever issue he could bring up. She thought they finished any arguments he had. This would be something new. Something she wouldn't have the benefit of being prepared for as she had been the previous night.

"I'll talk to you about it then, okay?"

"Well, can't you give me a hint?"

"Yes, Terry, I could. But, if I did, you'd want to talk right now and get it settled. And there's no way we'd finish before dinner. I just think it would be better to wait until after dinner, and talk face to face, okay?"

"So you want a rendezvous, huh?" she said in a charming and unmistakably sexual way.

"You might say that, but not a *rendezvous* rendezvous, okay?"

"Okay," she said nervously, having no idea of what to make of what was about to unfold.

"I'll see you in about half an hour or so. Oh, and thanks again for the song. Bye." He hung up.

Terry sat there holding the phone. She was wondering what he had to talk about that was so important it needed to be discussed right away. *He hasn't changed his mind, so it couldn't be too bad.* She hung up the phone and took a shower.

Chapter 19: I Need a Lawyer

Renegade Hotel & Casino
Grand Cayman Islands
August 1997

The limousine driver opened the door for Sterling and he stepped out of the climate-controlled vehicle and into the blazing heat. Sweat began to accumulate on his forehead. Seneca, the doorman, grabbed his bags.

"How long will you be staying this time, Mr. Wise?"

"I don't know, Seneca. It depends. This is a spur of the moment sort of trip."

The two men walked into the Renegade. Sterling felt the cool air dry the sweat on his forehead like a sponge. He saw his smile before he saw Jimmy, who Sterling wanted to avoid because Jimmy would run his mouth nonstop, asking stupid questions and then answering the very questions he asked. But Jimmy had a gift; he could remember your name even if he only met you one time, which was why he was the floor manager and official greeter.

"Sterling." Jimmy smiled. "It's been a long time."

"Yeah, I've been busy." *Don't start runnin' yo' mouth, muthafucka!*

"Yeah, I know. I watched as much of the trial as I could. So tell me, did he do it, or not?"

"Hell, I don't know. The man said he didn't, and he paid the firm a lot of dough to make sure the jury believed he didn't."

Jimmy laughed. "So he did it; he just isn't going to jail for it, right?"

With a dumbfounded look on his face, Sterling barked, "Are you deaf? I said I don't know. It's not my job to know if he did it. My job is to aggressively defend. Now do you understand that shit, muthafucka?"

"Okay, Okay. Don't get your drawls in your crack. I just asked."

Sterling frowned. "Well, listen to my answers the next time you ask me a question."

"Same ol' sharp-tongued Sterling," Jimmy mumbled.

'*Same ol' simple ass Jimmy*,' Sterling wanted to say, but he knew it would lead to another set of stupid questions. "So, where's my brother?"

"He's in the gym working out with Pin in the penthouse."

"Okay." He handed Seneca a ten-dollar bill. "Take my bags to my room."

"Sure thing, Sterling."

"Do you want me to take you to the penthouse, Sterling?" Jimmy asked.

"No. I know the way."

"Okay. Enjoy your stay at the Renegade."

"I'm sure I will."

Jimmy turned and started walking away. Sterling could tell that he had hurt his feelings.

"Jimmy," Sterling called out. Jimmy turned around. "Look man, I'm sorry for being flippant. It's just that I've had to answer that question for six months. I'm tired of the implication of the question. You understand?"

"Yeah." His smile returned. "Don't worry about it. Have a good time while you're here."

Sterling watched Jimmy as he walked to the hotel entrance. A black woman with a French accent and a large diamond on her finger walked in. Jimmy recognized her. "Angelique, it's so good to see you again. How long has it been?" Sterling laughed a little and entered the glass-enclosed elevator. As it ascended, he looked at Jimmy. He was still talking to the woman. They were both smiling at each other.

The elevator doors opened and Sterling saw Cochise standing near the French doors of the penthouse waiting for him to exit the elevator.

"What up, Chise?"

"Same ol' same ol'. The boss is in the gym working out with Pin. He doesn't like people watching 'em work out, but I guess he won't mind you comin' in."

"He better not; especially since he sent for me."

"Go on in then."

"Okay."

He walked down the stairs into the living room and then through a series of hallways. He admired the decor of the penthouse as he walked, occasionally stopping at a painting that captured his attention. Then he moved along until he finally reached the gym. He could hear the sound of a body being slammed on the canvas. Sterling laughed a little to himself, and wondered who was getting the worst of the workout.

He opened the double doors and walked in and looked up onto the canvas, where Jericho and Pin were dressed in black uniforms with elastic in the hem of the slacks. Both of them were sweating. They were engaging in some kind of martial art, Sterling thought.

Their hands and feet were padded with what looked like red boxing gloves, but he could see their fingers were not covered. Both of them were going through a series of swift moves and counter moves. He stood there and watched them for a few moments to see who would end up on the canvas first. He'd seen Jericho fight before, but never at this level.

Jericho finally got a punch through Pin's defense. The blow caused her to drop to one knee. But she spun around in a sweeping motion, keeping her right leg straight. Her leg hit Jericho's ankle and he fell hard on his back. There was a loud thud. They were both on their feet again in a defensive posture. Sterling sat down. *This is getting good*, he thought. Jericho attempted to punch Pin again, but she intercepted the blow and flipped Jericho over her back. Jericho bounced back up and attacked again. And again, Pin flipped him over her shoulder. Each time he hit the canvas, there was a loud thud.

Jericho got up and attacked again. Pin intercepted the blow and was about to flip him, but this time when Pin grabbed his arm and positioned herself to toss him, Jericho raised his arm up, which forced Pin to raise her arm, exposing her side. He then chopped her in the ribs and when she doubled over, he bent her backwards over his knee. Pin screamed in pain. Jericho looked at her in that awkward position and said, "I bet you would've been happy to flip me all day if I didn't put a stop to it, huh? Now say I love you, so we can end this."

Pin shook her head. Jericho applied more pressure and she screamed again. "Give it up. You can't get outta this shit. I can break your back in this position."

"NO!" Pin shouted. Then she swung her feet in the same direction as her body was being forced to go and kicked Jericho in the side of the head. He let her go immediately. Then she faked a kick to his leg, but kicked him in the head. Jericho staggered a little from the force of the blow. While he was staggering, Pin ran toward him and took him down with a scissors move around the waist. She kicked him in the stomach and let him up. Jericho jumped up as quickly as he could. Pin attempted to kick him in the head again, but Jericho sidestepped the blow and hit her in the same leg she'd tried to kick him with. She fell to the floor and held her leg for a second. She got up quickly, but her leg was a little numb. Jericho moved in to finish her, but the bell, which was set to ring after three minutes, rang and they both stopped immediately and bowed to each other.

Sterling applauded. "I think you've met your match, Jerry. No wonder you don't want anybody in here when you two spar."

"Shut up, Sterling. You just wish you could last this long in the ring with me."

"Don't tempt me. You'd be surprised how well I'd do."

"Step yo' ass on up here then. If you're worried about your clothes, I have some spare uniforms. Yo' ass'll be out in less than a minute."

Sterling laughed. "Yeah, and I'll sue yo' ass, too."

"I bet you would."

"So why'd you haul my ass all the way down here? You know I was plannin' to meet my women."

"Sorry, but this couldn't wait. Didn't you like Tina?"

"The flight attendant? Yeah, she was cool."

"She's not a flight attendant. She's a madam."

"What? Are you serious?"

"Hell yeah, I'm serious. One of my business partners won a string of cathouses in Nevada. He asked me to run 'em for him. I said no at first, but when I thought about it, the shit had great moneymaking potential. I came up with a few ideas to bring the call girl business into the twentieth century, thanks to Heidi Fleiss. I'll tell you about it as soon as we shower, okay?"

"Okay, but tell me why you wanted me here so quickly."

"Because I need a lawyer."

"Okay. Let me call Tiffany and have her fax you a receipt to make it official."

"All right. We'll meet you in the conference room in an hour, or so."

"Why so long?"

"'Cause, we got business of our own to take care of."

"Oh, so you fuck my shit up, and then you get you some while I wait in the conference room?"

"You can still have Tina," Jericho said, laughing, as they went into the shower.

Chapter 20:
Dreams Do Come True

Renegade Hotel
August 1997

Sterling walked back down the hallway and realized he didn't know where the conference room was. The penthouse was huge, encompassing the entire top floor of the hotel. He started opening doors randomly; some doors were locked and others were accessible. He opened another door, and saw a room full of men sitting in front of personal computers. From the looks of things, they were all in chat rooms on an online service. Then it occurred to him this is what Jericho must have been doing when he paged him.

"Can I help you, Sterling?" Cochise asked.

"Yeah. I'm looking for the conference room."

"I'll take you there."

"Thanks."

"No problem."

They left the room and closed the door behind them.

"So where's Victor?" Sterling asked.

"Victor's on a special assignment right now."

"Special assignment, huh?"

"Yeah, real special. Here's the room." Cochise pushed the door open for Sterling.

"I need access to a phone. Is there one in there?"

"Yeah. A fax machine also, if you need one."

"Yeah, as a matter of fact I do."

"I figured you would. The boss says you're the new lawyer."

"Yeah, but what's this all about, Cochise?"

"You'll find out soon enough. Now, is there anything else I can do for you?"

"No, I'm fine now."

"Okay, if you need anything else, don't be wanderin' around the penthouse and shit. The boss doesn't like that shit. Just push the button that says Cochise and I'll get whatever you need, okay?"

"Okay."

Cochise turned around and walked back toward the computer room. Sterling went into the conference room, sat in the first leather chair he saw, picked up the phone and dialed Tiffany's house.

"Hello."

"Hey, Tiff, this is Sterling. How you doin'?"

"Where are you? I haven't seen or heard from you since the verdict."

"I'm in the Caymans."

"The Cayman Islands?"

"Yep. I told you my brother owns a hotel down here, didn't I?"

"No, you didn't. I didn't know Will owned a hotel."

"No, not Will. Jericho."

"Well, Sterling, you never talk about him. So how am I supposed to know who you're talking about?"

"Yeah, you're right. Well, my oldest brother owns the Renegade Hotel and Casino down here. You really ought to see the place where I'm staying. It's got everything. He chartered me a jet down here and everything."

"Awwwwwww, I'm jealous. You could have taken me with you."

"Now you know how I feel about that. I like things the way they are between you and me. We don't need the hanky-panky, right?"

"Need it? No. Want it? Maybe."

They laughed.

"Listen, I called because I need you to fax a receipt for one dollar to this number. Make it out to Jericho Michael Wise, okay?"

"Okay."

"I need you to do it right away, okay?"

"Okay. But you should know that a woman named Adrienne Bellamy had all of our stuff moved to the top floor of the building."

"You're shittin' me. When did they move us?"

"Right after you left the office Friday. Everything was already set up. I didn't even have to move our files; they moved them for us. I was working out of that office Friday and we've gotten calls already. I thought you knew all about it until you told me you were in the Caymans."

"Naw, I didn't know anything about the move. I know Ms. Bellamy. And I knew we were moving, but I had no idea we were moving so quickly."

"So you didn't authorize the move?"

"No, but it's cool. Don't even sweat it."

"Good, because my office is the shit. As a matter of fact, our offices put Daniels, Burgess, and Franklin to shame. You gotta see it. We've got state-of-the-art everything. We've got the latest computers, fax machines, cell phones, and a brand-new telephone system complete with voice mail, and everything. The place is so nice. I wouldn't mind packing my bags and moving in. I mean the place is nice. Your office is huge. You've got a view of San Francisco and Oakland. And get this...the place even has a master bedroom in it. Does this woman know you, or what? Or are you banging her brains out?"

Sterling laughed. "Yes and no."

"Yes and no what?"

"Yes, she apparently knows me. And no, I'm not bangin' her. And apparently you know me, too."

"Yes, I know you."

"Then you know what my next question is, right?"

In unison, they said, "Did Vanessa call?"

"No, she didn't. It's been a couple of years now. I think she would have called by now, but it isn't any of my business, right?"

"Right."

"So what does Ms. Bellamy want, if you're not bangin' her?"

Jericho and Pin walked in the room. Sterling looked at his watch and mouthed, "That was quick." Then he covered up the transmitter and laughed.

"She wants us to handle a delicate case for her. The good news is I'm going into the sports agent business."

"I know. Lucius Rhames, the star guard for USC, called and said he wanted you to be his agent after the season. He's coming out early."

"Really!?"

"He's not the only one calling."

"Who else?"

"I don't have their names in front of me, but there were about six football players, three or four basketball players, and one baseball player."

"What positions do they play? Please tell me we have some quarterbacks, and seven-foot-tall centers who can play."

"Well, I don't know what they look like, Sterling. I only know they called. You'll have to look them over when you get back in town."

"Do we have any other cases?"

"Yes, the phone has been ringin' off the hook. I don't know what you promised this Bellamy woman, but you better deliver. She certainly has."

"Yeah, she has, hasn't she? Well, look, I gotta run now. But for right now, go to the office and get their numbers and tell all the college boys we're taking them as clients. Let them know where I am, and that I'll be back within the week."

"Sterling, I have a date tonight. Can't it wait until tomorrow morning?"

"Hell naw, it can't wait. This is business. We can't afford to let them get away. You know Daniels fired me Friday, don't you?"

"No, they said you quit."

"I didn't quit. Daniels told me I didn't fit in."

"Oh, really? Well, he's telling everyone you quit to start your own firm."

"When did he say that?"

"Right after you left the office. Then he had the nerve to act like he was hurt."

"He's going to be hurt for real later. Fax me everything you have on the clients and what they want us to do. Include Kym Daniels' phone number."

Tiffany laughed. "You…Dog."

"Hey, I don't work there anymore." Sterling laughed. "Daughters and desperate housewives are no longer off limits."

"You are a real trip."

"Yeah, I know." He laughed again. "I'll catch you later, Tiff."

"Bye."

Sterling thought, *Dreams do come true*, and hung up the phone. He looked at Jericho and Pin. They were sitting in the conference room chairs quietly listening to his conversation.

"Sounds like you really trust Tiffany."

"Yeah, I do. But not nearly as much as you trust Pin."

"Pin is exceptional."

"Yeah, so is Vanessa."

"You think she's ever comin' back?"

"One day, I hope. But anyway, what do you need a lawyer for? And what is this call girl crap?"

"First of all, the call girl business is anything but crap. It's quite lucrative; especially the way I'm going to run it. Second, I need you to take care of my last will and testament."

Sterling frowned. "Why are you thinking about a will now, Jerry? You worried about something?"

"We're getting ready to make a serious move. This move could upset a lot of people. It's us, or them. I'd rather it be them. But, I can't guarantee that. So I need you to take care of my money, just in case."

"What's going on, Jerry?"

"You don't need to know, little brother. You know all you need to. If I told you much more than that, you could be killed also. The only reason I know you and the family will be safe is my enemies know I operate on a need to know basis, understand?"

"Yeah. I understand. When do you want to get started?"

"Immediately."

"Okay, I'll have Tiffany fax the paperwork here also. Now, what's this about Tina being a madam and you running cathouses and shit?"

"I told you about one of my business associates winning a string of 'em in Nevada, right?"

"Right."

"Well, this business partner can't afford to be caught in, or have any ties to the business because he's a banker."

"Hmm. A banker, huh?"

"Hell yeah, man. Ain't no way you can clean large quantities of money without a banker being involved."

Anxious, Sterling asked, "Who? What bank?"

"You're my lawyer now, right? That means I can tell you this shit and you have to keep the shit to yourself, right?"

"Right. As soon as Tiffany sends the receipt, it'll be official. That means you can tell me anything."

"Well, I'll tell you about this, but not the move we're making. Being a lawyer won't save ya ass if the move goes bad, understand?"

Sterling nodded.

"Okay, are you familiar with Chadwick International?"

"Yeah, the whole family banks there."

"I know. Do you remember when they went international?"

"About ten years ago, I think. Why?"

"Because we ran so much money through there that we had to start sending money overseas. I've got twelve bank accounts in twelve countries. And each account has well over twenty million dollars in it. My biggest account is right here in Cayman International Bank. I have over seventy million dollars there."

Sterling's mind started churning. He was trying to figure out how much he had. "Let's see. You have twenty million, in twelve banks, right?"

"No. I have over twenty million in eleven banks and over seventy million here."

"Okay, so that's twenty times twelve plus seventy, right?"

"Right."

Sterling started calculating the figures in his mind again. "So you've got over three hundred million dollars?"

"Yep. Collecting twenty percent interest."

"Who are you gonna leave all that money to?"

"You, if you want it. Just promise me you'll help Mom and Dad out, or anybody else in the family, if they need it."

"Of course I'll do it. That goes without saying. But shit, I'm in the wrong business. How did you get so much money, man?"

"Well, you have to remember, I've been in business for over twenty years. You also have to take in account that I don't pay taxes on anything but the money I make here at the casino. And there's a lot of money to be made selling arms. A whole lot. That's where the real money is. People wanting to wipe each other off the face of the earth. Men have been at war since Cain killed Abel. They're willin' to pay big-time money to do it, too. I'll tell you who I'd like to have for clients, but can't get 'em."

"Who?"

"The Israelis. Now they spend some serious money."

"Who do you sell to then?"

"A lot of Israel's enemies. I was also selling to the Serbs, before the United States stepped in. America can't stay there forever. And when we pull out, they'll be fightin' again. And I'll be supplyin' 'em again."

"Well what about this cathouse?"

"I'm trying a different approach based on demographics. There are far more women than men, right?"

"Right."

"So no matter what, some women are going to go without. And when you consider women gaining more and more power, soon they'll be doing the same things men do. Actually, I got the idea from *The Autobiography of Malcolm X*. You remember the part about the white lesbian who started a call service for white women who wanted black paramours?"

"Yeah. Who can forget that shit?"

"If women were doing it back then, they'll do it again today. So I'm taking her idea to another level. She had three apartments; I'm buying the apartment building itself. That way I own everything from the door-man to the apartment manager to the maintenance man. I'm starting in Los Angeles, Chicago, and New York."

"And you really think this will take off?"

"Hell yeah. And the shit'll be safer, too. You know how women keep secrets and shit. See a man can't keep his mouth shut. How you think they caught the madam in Beverly Hills? I bet some man was runnin' his mouth, and got her caught. Women, on the other hand, have to keep the shit on the downlow, understand?"

"Yeah," Sterling said, shaking his head. "You be comin' up with some shit, don't you? If it works, you're going to mess my game up."

"I got news for you, brotha. The shit is already workin'. What do you think the escort service is about?"

"Good point," Sterling said. Then he picked up the phone and called Tiffany again. "Tiff, when you fax me that other stuff, fax me will and last testament forms, too."

Chapter 21: The Conversation II

Toronto
August 1997

William looked at his watch when he heard someone knocking on his hotel room door. It was six o'clock sharp. He opened the door and each associate walked into the suite single file. As usual, James led the group and was followed by Ivy, Bernie, and Terry. They all entered with a pleasant smile and a friendly greeting, but Ivy was carrying a briefcase. Her reading glasses were around her neck, and connected by a thin silver chain.

Since Ivy had the day off to recuperate from last night's fiasco, he knew tonight would be different. As far as debates go, Ivy was a woman to be reckoned with when she was prepared. This would be a bloody and perhaps vicious battle.

William thought about what Terry had said at breakfast about having no boundaries and was now having second thoughts. That's when he decided that if Ivy was right on something, he would agree quickly and move on, preferring to do battle with her only when she was vulnerable, or just plain wrong on a given issue. He wasn't worried about James or Bernie because James was too much of a coward to say what he really thought and Bernie was a laid-back, easygoing kind of guy.

Ivy was strong-willed and spoke without emotion during the many debates he had witnessed—silencing those who disagreed with her each time. He thought it would give him an advantage if he knew what she wanted to talk about before she actually had the opportunity to catch him off guard. He would wait on her to ask her question first, and then ask his.

William told them which room to go in and instructed them to make themselves at home. "Our dinner should be here in a moment," he said. As Terry passed him, she winked her eye, smiled, and mouthed, "I'll talk to you later, handsome." He returned her smile and shook his head much like he did the previous night after having gotten off the phone with Sterling. He could smell her perfume, even though she was in the next room with the others.

Room service arrived almost immediately and William opened the door to let the waiter in. He was a tall, thin, dark man from Somalia—very polite. The waiter had a professional manner about him that made everyone pay attention as he worked. William tipped and thanked him. After the waiter left, quiet consumed the room. It was like arriving at a four-way stop with three other cars, all of which were waiting for the other to be the aggressor.

Finally, Ivy, in a brisk tone, began, "Dr. Wise, you know why we're here. Let's get started, before you think of some excuse to kick us out."

Terry and Ivy stared at each other for a brief moment. The animosity was still boiling from the morning's exchange between the two rivals. Terry wanted to call her an uncouth and disrespectful bitch, but remained quiet.

Ivy stared at Terry, waiting for her to say something so she could rip her for the comment she made at breakfast. The remarkable thing about Ivy's disposition was that she was cool, calm, and collected. She was ready for William this time, and Terry too, if she stuck her nose where it didn't belong.

Bernie watched the two women, waiting for an eruption. He found their little spats quite humorous. They were an endless source of amusement for him.

"Yeah, we might as well start. That's why we're here," James added and sighed.

"Dr. Wise," Ivy began, "Yesterday, you talked about how the past influences the present. You mentioned something about leaving the mall and some woman locking her doors when you approached your vehicle. Is that correct?"

William thought, *I knew I could count on her to tip me off as to where she wanted to go.* He smiled inwardly, but presented an uncompromising stare. After chewing a mouthful of salad, he said, "Correct. But isn't it my turn to ask you all questions? This morning at breakfast you reminded me that we never finished. So let's begin with my last question to you all. Which of you haven't had sexual fantasies about black men, or black women? And if you've had them, what prevented you from getting what you desired?"

The room was suddenly quiet again. Each of them looked to the other to see who would speak first. Terry folded her arms and leaned back in her chair. She couldn't wait. They had no doubt teased her behind her back for the past three years, she thought. Now it was their turn to deal with the issue.

James bowed his head the way children do when they don't know the answer to the teacher's question.

Seeing this, William decided to ask him first. If he wasn't prepared, he'd get the truth and not a packaged answer that would alleviate his guilt and annul the truth of what he believed. "So what about you, James?"

James looked dumbfounded. He felt like it was a question he couldn't answer without being vilified as a racist. *If I tell the truth, I'll be called a racist. And if I lie, I'll never get the chance to ask the questions I want to ask.* He concocted this plan to restart the conversation, but it never crossed his mind that William would bring up the last questions he'd asked them.

"Well," James began. "Sure, I've seen black women that were attractive. And to be frank, yes, I would have liked to have had sex with them. Who hasn't at least thought about it? I'm not saying I would actually do anything about it, but I have considered it."

Shit! William hadn't counted on him telling the truth. He hoped he would lie so he could end it all just as quickly as it began. He couldn't believe he actually admitted it. He knew all the men in his offices lusted after Jeannine, and she was a daily topic of conversation at the water cooler when Jonathan, her fiancé, wasn't around. He hoped he could spring this knowledge on him, drive a few points home and end the conversation at the same time. But James' honesty forced him to go in another direction. William was about to ask a follow-up question when James began to volunteer information.

"But I said I would be honest and I will. So here goes. I wouldn't want my daughters dating someone outside of our race."

Everybody looked at James with quizzical looks on their collective faces. Bernie thought, *damn, the man asked you to be honest, not to divulge personal shit like that.*

Terry laughed under her breath a little and thought, *here—we—go. It's going to get wild now.*

Ivy was thinking of her response to the question. She would be honest as well, but she would deliver her answers with much more explanation. In her mind, James was walking through a mine field. At any moment he'd step on one and be blown away by William's commentary.

James offered William the break he hoped for. He knew there was more to it than what he said, but he couldn't have imagined an opening like this. "May I ask why you wouldn't? Your daughter, I mean, in terms of dating?"

"I understand the frustration black people must feel, but I wouldn't—"

"I'm asking you about your daughter, sir. Not the frustrations of black people." Besides, William thought, *how could you possibly know our frustrations?*

"You mean why I wouldn't want my daughters to date outside my race?"

"Yes. That's something I think we should pursue."

"Well, it just doesn't sit well with me. I can't explain it, really. This may sound patronizing, but one of my best friends is a black man who dates only white women. That doesn't bother me, but if it was my daughter, it would."

"I bet he's not an athlete either," Ivy added, feeling vindicated. She was trying to hold back her glee, but couldn't.

Bernie chuckled a little under his breath.

Terry looked at her, thinking, *what a bitch*.

William frowned. "What do you mean by that?"

"I don't want my daughters dating anyone outside our race, period."

"But James, don't you see there's something deeply rooted in what you're saying. One of your best friends is a black man who dates white women exclusively, and it doesn't bother you? Yet, if it's one of your daughters, it would?"

Terry was in total disbelief. She kept a straight face, revealing none of her inner feelings. It had been less than twenty-four hours since she and William had their conversation about this issue. And now William was championing the very issues she had brought to his attention. *This year's Toronto trip was definitely fate.* At that moment, she wanted him more than ever because she saw he was willing to change once he realized he was wrong.

William's willingness to change was something she hadn't experienced with men before now—not even with her father. In her mind, a woman could be right about something and a man would deny it to his dying day, especially if they were traveling by car. Inwardly, she was glad and relieved at the same time. Now she knew only good things were going to happen when she spoke to him later.

In the meantime, James responded to William's question. "I know that it's wrong. But, believe me, I'm not raising my children to be negative towards other races."

"Tell me something, James. How can you say that when you harbor negative feelings toward black men? Are you able to suppress these feelings when you're around your children?"

"I try."

"How old are your daughters?"

"They aren't even teenagers yet. So it won't be an issue for several years."

"Okay, fine. What about when they're of age? What are you going to tell them then? Treat everybody the same, but whatever you do, don't fall in love with a black man? If so, aren't you teaching your daughters to think negatively of black men at the very least?"

"I honestly don't think I am."

The room was quiet for a moment. It seemed as though everyone except James understood the point being made, and wanted to move on.

"James, when do you think it begins? At what age?"

"Isn't it a natural desire to want to be around your own kind? And what is racism anyway?" James asked, perplexed by the questions.

"Racism is systematic discrimination based on the belief that some races are by nature inferior, or superior," William answered.

"Yeah, but racism like that is fostered by hate groups and it's taught. I don't think I'm superior to any other race, but I do believe certain races have certain characteristics that could be considered superior."

When James said this, Terry wanted to slap him for not only saying it, but for believing it. She leaned back in her chair, folded her arms again, and shook her head in disbelief.

Bernie was biting his bottom lip, trying to keep from laughing.

He just stepped on a mine, Ivy thought.

"James, are you not systematically discriminating against black men simply because they're black?"

"No, I'm not. I don't look at a black man and immediately think he deals crack or that I'm better than he is because I'm white. I said I wouldn't like it, but then times can change."

"Then why would you not want your daughter to marry a black man she loves. The fact that you wouldn't like it speaks volumes, don't you think?" William briefly looked at Terry when he said that and then continued. "Please don't be offended, James, but that's exactly what you're saying in the matter of interracial dating, or marriage."

"Yes, it does say that. But I was raised that way. And I'm not saying I'm better than a black man because I wouldn't want my daughter to marry one. That doesn't make it right, but that's how I was raised. Can't you understand that? People can't change how they were raised overnight. I'm trying to be as honest as I can about the issue, okay?"

"Okay, but what if he's a decent, hardworking American, such as yourself, and loves her as his own body. Would you still be against the union?"

"No. I think I might be able to accept it, but it would take a lot of time. I just think all species have a natural tendency to want to be around their own kind."

"See, that's what I mean, James. The fact that this man could be a successful doctor or lawyer means nothing to you. Isn't that what most men want for their female offspring? Besides, I'm not disputing the Natural Selection Theory; I'm disputing your reluctance to accept your daughter's choice of a mate."

"I see what you mean. Because I wouldn't like it, does that make me a bad person?"

"Not altogether bad, but it does reveal who you are, deep down in places where most of us don't want to look. It's very difficult to remove the scales, as it were, from our eyes, and see ourselves as we truly are."

William looked at Bernie. "What about you?"

"Well," Bernie began, "yeah, I'd date a black woman; especially if it was Jeannine. Could you put a good word in for me?" Then he laughed and continued eating his dinner.

William looked at Ivy. But before he could ask the question she started speaking.

"Well, let me say this," she began, with her characteristic haughtiness, "I found out that the books you talked about last night do exist. I can only assume that what you say is in them is also true. Personally, I don't find black men attractive. And, doctor, I don't care what you say; I'm not racist for saying so either."

"Oh bullshit, Ivy," Terry blurted out, no longer able to keep quiet.

Ivy looked at her and calmly said, "Just because you have a jungle fever thing for Dr. Wise, doesn't mean we all do." Ivy was satisfied the comment did the damage previously calculated.

Terry looked at her and rolled her eyes. She realized if she responded, she might slip up and say something about her new relationship with William.

"You mean to tell me, you haven't seen any black men you found attractive? None?" William asked, not believing a word of what Ivy was saying.

"No, I haven't. And I don't care what some book says either. Personally, I prefer white men. Besides, why even cross the color line when you know people won't accept it?"

Sensing Ivy had revealed more than she planned, William repeated his original statement, "You mean to tell me, you haven't seen any black men you found attractive?" Then he added, "Or are you concerned with societal and familial rejection?"

"To be honest, I think both are a factor in my decision not to date black men."

"I thought you just said you didn't find them attractive."

"Well, Denzel Washington and Wesley Snipes aren't bad-looking."

"So you do find some black men attractive then?"

"Some, not all. Very few."

"So if one of the few wanted to date you, would you date him?"

Bernie had been trying to hold his laughter since Ivy said she didn't find black men attractive. Now he had to laugh because Ivy hadn't had a man in the three years he'd known her. In his mind, she couldn't afford to turn anybody down, black or white. But more importantly, she wasn't attractive, nor did she have the personality to be choosy. So he just laughed a little. Then, he laughed a little more until finally, Terry and James laughed also.

William wanted to laugh, but it would have been too cruel. So he held it back as best he could, and never even smiled.

"Well, it's true," Ivy told them. "I would date Denzel Washington."

They laughed louder and louder. William looked at them with stern disapproval in his eyes and they got the message. Soon the laughter subsided.

"So, Ivy, you said personal attraction, and societal and familial pressures are your reasons for not dating black men. Which one is the major factor?"

"I would say my personal attraction."

"Okay. What if you are attracted? What then?"

"Then he would have to have the kind of attributes that would make it worth the trouble of being involved with him, I guess," she admitted.

"So, we're right back at the beginning then."

"What do you mean, back at the beginning? I've answered the question twice now. What more do you want from me?"

"I want the truth."

"Are you saying I'm lying?"

"Perhaps, but not intentionally. I believe the truth has yet to surface where you're concerned."

"Well, what is the truth as you see it, doctor? Since my answers aren't true, or aren't good enough for you. You tell me. Since you know everything there is to know!"

"I think you spoke the truth when you mentioned crossing the color line. I also think societal pressure and perhaps familial repudiation are the main factors with you. The fact that you find Denzel Washington attractive says a lot, really. As my brother Sterling says, 'If you find one attractive, you find two, and if two, a thousand.' Therefore, there must be something else. I think it is your familial connection. But that's just my opinion."

"Well, you're entitled to your opinion like the rest of us. Now can we get on with some of the more weighty matters, please? We've been honest. Now it's your turn, doctor."

Content that he had made his point, William agreed, "Sure. Let's move on then. What would you like to ask me?"

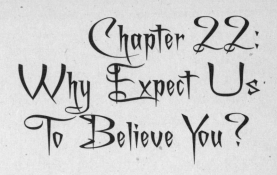
Chapter 22: Why Expect Us To Believe You?

Toronto
August 1997

Now that they had answered his questions, they were eager to question him about some of their concerns. Ivy picked up her briefcase, opened it, and took out some papers. She put on her glasses, and began to organize them. As she looked them over, she seemed to be collecting her thoughts. James was wondering if he should just come out with his questions, but didn't know how to do it without sounding racist. The tension began to mount as they looked at one another.

"So what would you like me to try and answer, James?"

James was about to ask a question, but hesitated. During James's brief moment of reflection, Ivy said, "I think I should be first. I had already begun when you wanted your question answered. It's only fair I continue."

James looked at Ivy. "It looks like you have a lot to talk about there. I only have one question, maybe two, and some follow-up questions. Let me ask mine first and then you can have the rest of the time, okay?"

Ivy frowned. She was anxious to get into the debate with William. She took four Advil capsules to take care of her throbbing head and had used her day off to dial into the San Francisco Library Computer system so she could research the books William mentioned on her laptop. After learning the books did exist, she began researching other facts to support her arguments. When she felt she had enough ammunition, she had the information faxed to the hotel.

"Dr. Wise, how much time do we have to discuss this?" Ivy asked, looking at her watch.

"I'd really like to get this done tonight. So, however long it takes."

Terry looked concerned. *This could take forever*, she thought. She wondered if he would still want to talk to her after debating with them all night. William and Terry looked at one another for a brief moment, which went unnoticed by the others. She looked into his eyes and he into hers. Then she knew they would still talk later. Feeling at ease, she continued eating her salad.

"In that case, go ahead then, James," Ivy said.

"Okay," James said, looking at William. "I really don't know how to begin this. It's kind of like the interracial dating thing, you know? I don't want to come off as a racist."

"Just say whatever's on your mind," William said. He hated when James was so mealy mouthed. He could understand why Sharon left him and why Terry wouldn't date him. He was a good psychologist and business manager, but the man didn't have any balls.

"Earlier, I said I can understand the frustrations black people feel. For example, when the cops beat Rodney King to a pulp and the jury found them not guilty. If I were black, I'd be angry also. So I can understand them feeling negated by our system of justice. Now, having said that, why do black people burn their own neighborhoods?"

William looked at James and, from the look on his face, he believed James already had his own answer to this question. It was a question William had seen discussed several times on talk shows, CNN, and *Nightline*. On those shows, the white people who asked the question usually had an opinion already. It was an opinion they usually believed, and it always amazed him when they asked the question. He, however, believed this was simply a way to call black people stupid without calling them stupid.

"Do you really want to know, James, or do you simply want me to confirm your preconceived notions?"

"I don't have any preconceived—" James stopped short, realizing he was about to lie again and then continued. "Look, all I'm saying is this. When OJ was acquitted, you didn't see any white people burning their own neighborhoods, so why do black people burn theirs when they get shafted? I mean, I think OJ did it and so does most of America, but WE didn't riot. Nor did WE burn down our neighborhoods. So again, I renew my question. Why do black people burn down theirs?"

There was a sanctimonious tone in his voice that William found irritating. Nevertheless there was truth in what James was saying. William, however, felt as though he was being asked to justify the wrongdoings of the few, and not the good of the many. He decided to query James to see what he really thought about the issue. It was difficult for William to hide how he felt at that moment.

His eyes narrowed and became more penetrating than usual. They had all seen this look before because they had all been the recipients of his anger in the past. He ran a tight ship. Tardiness and unprofessionalism of any kind was not tolerated. However, he did make exceptions for Jeannine. He also made exceptions for Terry and Ivy's personal feud. He never yelled at them, but he spoke in such a way that they knew he was angry.

The group waited for him to answer. Finally, he began, "Tell me something, James. Why do you suppose some blacks burn their neighborhoods and whites don't?"

James frowned. Tiny beads of sweat began to surface on his ever-balding head. He was irritated because William expected answers to his questions, yet he would answer their questions with questions. Feeling a little frustrated, James growled, "Why can't you just answer the question sometimes? Why do you have to always question everything someone says to you? It's a real simple question. Could you just answer it, please?"

"First, keep in mind that I don't want to be questioned either. Second, given what's taken place this weekend, I think your motives should be questioned. And third, the question is simple, but the answer is far more complicated. So, could you answer my question? Or do we end this now?"

"Excuse me, Dr. Wise, but if James doesn't answer, does that mean I don't get to ask my questions?"

"That's exactly what it means, Ivy."

"James, don't you screw this up for me. Answer the question," Ivy demanded and glared at James in such a way that one would think she was going to kill him if he didn't.

James took in a deep breath, and let it out the way teenagers do when they think their parents are making a federal case out of a minor issue. Having allowed his frustration to get the better of him, he blurted out, "Because it's common sense not to burn your own homes; no matter how angry you are. Don't get me wrong. Again, as I said earlier, I can understand the frustration they must have felt, but come on, burning down your own neighborhood! That's stupid!" Realizing he might have stepped over the line, he quickly added, "I'm not saying black people are stupid. I happen to believe people can do stupid things and not be stupid."

Bernie laughed out loud and said, "That's ridiculous. How can you have one without the other?"

James looked at Bernie. "I don't think there's anybody in this room who hasn't done something stupid in their lives. Yet, everyone in this room has above-average intelligence. Therefore, in my opinion, you can have one without the other."

Terry added, "Yes, I agree. God knows, I've made some stupid decisions in my life, and I wasn't frustrated when I made them either."

"Humph," Ivy mumbled. "Doesn't surprise me in the least. Your reasoning skills leave a lot to be desired. I would expect more of the latter than the former from you."

Terry was fed up with Ivy's constant insults. She looked at her and quickly assessed how much damage she could do and realized she could exploit her self-consciousness about her looks. Ivy's eyebrows were painted on because they never grew back when she shaved them off for some unknown reason. "Well, I would expect you to paint your eyebrows on straight since they won't grow back."

James and Bernie laughed and so did William, but not out loud.

Ivy felt herself getting angry by the comment. She wanted to maintain her cool for William. She decided she'd get her later for this latest outburst.

William had grown weary of their juvenile exchanges and decided he would talk to them in private later. Then he asked, "Are there any other possibilities, James?"

"I don't know, why don't you tell me? I really want to know; I'm not a bleeding heart liberal, but I do want to know."

"Let me ask you this then. What would you say if the same stupid people came to your neighborhood and burned it down; would that make more sense?"

"No, it wouldn't. What I'm saying is, why burn down any neighborhood? What did it solve?"

"That's the point, James; why did they?"

"I really don't know."

"If you don't know, why are you making sweeping judgments and indictments?"

"Are you saying that these people shouldn't be judged and jailed for what they did?"

"No, I'm not. Certainly they should be judged and jailed. Here you are asking me why they burn their neighborhoods down while simultaneously patting yourself on the back for having what you call the 'common sense' not to burn down yours. Let me be clear on one thing before I go any further. I am not justifying the burning of neighborhoods, yours or ours.

"First, understand something. Not only do they not own most of what they burned, but they don't live in Sausalito, or even where you all live. Second, understand that the black folk who live near you didn't burn their homes either. Now why is that?" He paused for a moment to let them reflect on what he just said and then continued. "Listen, most of the people who burned the neighborhood after the King verdict were criminals and should be locked up. What you ought to be asking yourself is why was it allowed to go on for so long? Why didn't the police go in and stop it? Isn't that what we pay them to do? Isn't that a dereliction of duty? Aren't they supposed to serve and protect? Who were they serving and protecting by not going in there and stopping it?" He paused. "Themselves, in particular, and white people in general. Every police officer swears to give his life to protect the innocent. Not one of them said, 'Except when there's a riot in a black neighborhood.'

"Third, understand this. It is a long-established, albeit unspoken, truth that as long as black folk are harming themselves, no harm, or very little jail time, will come to them. That's why many turn to black on black crime.

That way they can vent their frustrations on the white men who own their neighborhoods. Besides, when people are enraged, for whatever reason, they tend to riot or turn on themselves. For example, if you look at just about any group who has been exploited for years, you'll see that they turned on each other also. Why? Because the authorities allowed it. Just think, what if the rioters sat down and reasoned it out? What if they decided to do a Denmark Vessey or a Nat Turner in Sausalito?"

They all looked at him in wonder, having no idea who these men were. As William was finishing his statement, Terry said, "The telephone is ringing. Would you like me to answer it?" He looked at her and nodded his head.

William continued speaking. "Do you really think they would have been allowed to do what they did? HELL NO! The police would have gone in and shot to kill, and rightly so, as the law of the land makes provision for using deadly force in those situations. So the question is beyond why do they do it, but rather, why are they even allowed to do it?"

Terry left the dinner table and took her salad with her, eating as she walked over to the phone. She picked up the receiver. "Hello." But she could still hear the phone ringing. She realized the phone she was holding wasn't working, and decided to get the phone in the bedroom. The others were so engrossed in the conversation that they didn't notice she had left the room.

As Terry approached the phone in the bedroom, she put more salad in her mouth and decided to wait until she swallowed before greeting whoever was on the other end. She picked up the phone while she was still chewing and placed it to her ear without saying a word and heard someone talking before she even said hello.

"So did you get yo' dick wet? I bet you tried to break yo' dick off up in her, didn't you?" The man laughed.

She quickly deduced that it was Sterling. She sat on the bed, ate her salad, and listened as he continued talking.

"Yeah, I know you did. Don't even bother denying the shit. The poor woman's pussy is probably worn out. She's probably walkin' funny, too."

Terry laughed, but not out loud. She continued eating and listening. "So did she hit the high note, or what?" He continued and laughed again. "I bet yo' ass was ridin' her like the stallion she is. Did you break the pussy in right?" He laughed again. Terry did, too. "Will?" Silence. Sterling began wondering if he had the right room. "Will?" he repeated.

Terry realized he wasn't going to say anything more until he knew who he was talking to. So she said, "Hello."

Shit! "Is this William Wise's suite?" he asked, tentatively.

"Uh, yes it is."

"Is this the maid?" he asked with desperation in his voice.

"Guess again." Terry was relishing the moment and wished she could see his face. Then she'd have a better idea of what must be going through his mind at that instant.

Feeling guilty and like an idiot at the same time, he said, "Do you normally answer other people's phones and listen to other people's calls?" His voice had a charming tone to it when he spoke to her.

"Does that normally work?"

"What do you mean?" Sterling asked.

"Turning the situation around and turning on the charm when you're dead wrong, and caught." She laughed.

"Yes, it does." He laughed with her. "You have a lot of nerve."

"Yes, I do have nerve, don't I?"

"Sorry about that. You're not offended, I hope."

"No, I'm not. I think the whole thing was funny."

"Okay, good. Is Will there?"

"Yes, but he's in the middle of a debate. You want me to get him?"

"No, that's okay. He's kickin' ass, isn't he? You know, he wanted to be an attorney like me, but didn't like either side. That's why he went into psychology. But I'm sure you know all of this, right?"

"Actually, no, I didn't."

"Oh, okay. Well, listen, tell him Sterling called, okay?"

"Sure, no problem."

"You take it easy. Bye."

"I will and you do the same. Bye now." She hung up the phone.

"Well, let me ask you this," James was saying as Terry returned to the room. "Do you have a problem with whites forming their own organizations, like other people do?"

"It depends on what they're organizing for."

"I don't want to sound like a racist because I'm not, but I have a friend who's a police officer and he tells me black police officers have an organization called NOBLE. This stands for National Organization of Black Law Enforcement Officers. Its name alone shows a bias towards black law enforcement officers. Now, if white officers attempted to start a similar organization, they would be labeled as racist. Do you see the double standard?"

"Yes, I do. But why do they have a black-only organization? For that matter, why do women form women-only groups, et cetera?"

"That's my point. Why do they? There are women-only health clubs. If I tried to join them, I wouldn't be admitted. However, if I started a men-only health club, I would have to admit women if they wanted to join."

"Again, why do they have these exclusive groups? Why would women want to join them?"

"I guess my main point is, if certain groups want exclusive clubs and they aren't committing illegal activities, what's the harm?"

"First tell me, why you think the groups that you've named want exclusivity?"

"Like I said earlier, there's a natural tendency to be with your own kind."

"I disagree with that premise. Shall I opine?"

"Please do."

"For centuries, blacks have been ostracized and labeled by white males; so much so that they could not trust them to do the right thing, so they had to do right themselves by themselves. And that goes triple for women. If you read world history, you'll find what I'm telling you is not only true in the western hemisphere, it is true throughout the world. But with respect to America, this has gone on for so long it is difficult, if not impossible, for many blacks to trust whites, and more specifically white men.

"It's difficult because they're the ones with all the power and authority to dictate and control the lives of the masses. This is undeniable and even the concept is nocuous to them without power. This is one of the reasons why America never ever trusted the Russians. This is why America sought to bring down the Soviet Union, or defeat their way of life. America signed several treaties with them, and we are taught that the Russians broke them all. The strange thing about it is, didn't America do the same thing to the so-called Indian?

"If white males in authority don't trust white leaders of other countries due to the many examples of broken promises, why expect women and blacks to accept that, suddenly in the latter part of the twentieth century, white men have changed? Why expect us to believe that now they want total equality when all we've ever gotten from them is more and more civil rights legislation that cannot be enforced? That is nothing more than a broken treaty, even though it is the law. And so, the real question is why do blacks and women still feel alienated? Not why do they have exclusive health clubs and the like."

Chapter 23: The Content of Their Character

Toronto
August 1997

I vy was finding it difficult to stay angry with William because he'd stood up for women moments ago. Being a Wellesley graduate and a staunch feminist, she couldn't help but love his eloquent dissertation. She had always found him articulate and handsome, but would never admit it. In fact, she was unaware of it herself until now. She always found intelligence sexually alluring. Maybe there was something to what he was saying about familial and societal rejection, she thought. She didn't know for sure what it was, but something in her had changed, and changed permanently. Whatever it was, however, it wouldn't deter her from her mission to set him straight on a few things.

"I take it, it's my turn now," Ivy announced as she rearranged her papers.

"Okay, Ivy, what's your question? And how many do you have?" he asked, looking at his watch.

"One or two." She looked at her watch. "It's not even ten o'clock yet. You said we were going to finish tonight." She was feeling cheated after all the work she had done earlier that day.

"I said we will finish and we will, okay?"

Ivy smiled for the first time that evening. She didn't seem to be so nerdy at that moment. She actually had a nice smile, William thought.

"Okay," Ivy began. "Last night, you said the past influences the present. You mentioned something about leaving the mall and some woman locking her doors when you approached your vehicle, right?"

"Right and I stand by that."

"Okay then." She picked up her papers, and put on her glasses. "Are you aware that twenty-five percent of black males from the ages of twenty through twenty-nine are either in jail or under law enforcement supervision?" William was about to respond, but Ivy cut him off. "Hold on. I'm not finished with the data. Let me have my say now and you can have the floor when I'm done, okay?"

She said this in such a respectful and humble way that Bernie and James looked at each other in amazement, wondering if this was the same person who only hours ago wanted revenge in the worst possible way?

"Okay, Ivy, I'll wait until you're done. Just a second, let me get a pen and some paper to write your points down, okay?"

"Sure, go ahead."

William grabbed the hotel note pad near the phone and began writing.

"Do you have the first point?" Ivy asked him.

William picked up on her change in attitude and decided to see just how serious the change was. "You know, Ivy, you have a really nice smile. I wish you'd smile more often."

"You really think so?" Her smile was much broader now.

"Yes, I do."

"Thank you." Then Ivy began again. "Did you know that blacks in urban areas constitute less than thirty percent of the population, yet they are convicted for sixty percent of the crime? Fifty percent of black households are headed by women. Fifty percent of the births in black communities are out of wedlock. Almost fifty percent of black high school students drop out and the remaining fifty percent have poor reading and writing skills, making them less marketable and less competent for jobs. Now, when we compare white high school students to black, we find that almost twenty percent drop out and forty percent go on to college while less than twenty percent of blacks go on to further educate themselves. Sixty-one percent of the forty percent of whites go on to graduate from college, while only thirty-five percent of blacks graduate. Then we have the drug problem. As you know, drug use, especially crack cocaine, is way out of control in the black community. I can go on and on."

Her words lingered in the air. They waited for him to answer. But his head was still bowed as he was still writing down what she said.

"Okay, what's the point?" he asked when he looked up. "Or do you have more data?"

"What's the point?" she said incredulously. "Did you or did you not say the present is influenced by the past?"

"Yes, I did."

"Well, don't you see? This is glaring evidence."

"Evidence of what?"

"Are you playing dumb, or what?" There was no disrespect in her voice. She really didn't understand why he couldn't get her point.

"No, I'm not playing dumb. Spell it out for me."

"Well if all of this is true, shouldn't women lock their doors when they see a black man approaching their car? It's better to be safe than sorry, don't you think?"

"Certainly it's better to be safe than sorry. But you didn't know those statistics yesterday. And you certainly didn't know them when you locked your doors, did you?"

"No, I didn't. But hey, I watch the news. Almost every night there's some black guy being arrested for something. And it isn't just the local news. It's also in the national news. So should I just ignore what I've seen on an almost daily basis? In my opinion, it is those past events that affect my present attitude when I'm in my car...especially at night. I think it's stupid for me not to lock my doors in that situation."

"You make great points, Ivy. And one can certainly see why you would lock your doors. However, I have to question why the local and national news find it necessary to continue showing this stuff on television."

"Oh come on, doctor!" James practically bolted out of his seat. "Black men are committing sixty percent of the crime. Are you suggesting it's the media's fault? Besides, didn't Dr. King say we ought to judge people by the content of their character?"

"Yes, he did, and I'm not saying it's the media's fault. I'm simply questioning why they continuously show it on television. Listen, I'm not attempting to justify the crimes that black men commit. I'm only trying to get you to see why they commit them. As far as the evening news is concerned, I would like to know why you think they're always showing this stuff."

"I don't know. It's news, I guess."

They all had a look of agreement on their faces.

"Yeah, but if black men are indeed committing sixty percent of the crime, at some point, it becomes redundant and ceases to be news, doesn't it? For example, when the Menendez trial was going full speed, even it took a back seat to the OJ trial. The point again is this. Since this is so prevalent, why continue to show it on the news? In my opinion, all this type of journalism does is push us further and further apart. It also makes decent white people think negatively of black people, and treat us accordingly."

"I don't think negatively of blacks in general," Ivy told him.

"Maybe you don't, Ivy. But what do you expect to happen to the masses when their collective minds are bombarded with negative images of black people, and black men specifically? Isn't that what America did during World War II with its newsreels? Without those newsreels, which showed negative images of the Japanese, I wonder if America would have been able to get away with having her own version of concentration camps." He paused for a moment to let it sink in and then continued. "Now, back to the numbers. What the numbers don't tell you is, even though sixty percent of the crime is committed by black men, it's usually the same ones over and over again. The vast majority of us are law-abiding citizens, but you never hear about us. All you see is the hoodlums who should be in jail. This is why I question the motives of the media when they show it on television so often."

"So you think we should have tougher laws?" James asked.

"No, I don't. We should enforce the ones we have, period. No more of this early out stuff. The judges and the whole legal system should be held accountable for letting hoodlums back out on the street to continue terrorizing neighborhoods that would otherwise be decent places to live. 'You did the crime, now do the time,' my father always said."

"I agree with that."

Then they all nodded in agreement.

"Anything more? Or are we done?"

"Yes, a couple more," Ivy continued. "Do you still think slavery plays an active role in crime today?"

"Yes, I do. I do not believe slavery causes black people to commit crimes. I do think, however, that the legacy of that abominable institution has far-reaching effects and we are still feeling those ripples today. And don't think for a moment that my Harvard education somehow insulates me from what the masses of African-Americans feel. Don't think for a moment that my blood doesn't boil every time I'm stopped by the police simply for being black in an exclusive community.

"I feel the mental anguish of my fathers and mothers when I see the injustices committed by judges and juries, and the legal system itself, in the matter of race. I carry the blood of slaves in my veins, just like other blacks. And while I will never know what they suffered, I see and feel what they have bequeathed by proxy. And you see it as well. You see it every time you turn on your televisions. You see what slavery, discrimination, and oppression does to a people, and their posterity."

"But Dr. Wise," Ivy began. "What about the many doctors, lawyers, inventors, and scientists of every genre?"

"What about them?"

"I think it goes back to what James said last night. Some people are just making excuses for why they fail. For example, I read today that as early as 1790, there were black property owners in the South." She shuffled her papers again. And when she found the article she was looking for, she added, "In Tennessee, where it was illegal for a slave to practice medicine, some slave they called Dr. Jack was practicing and had great success, even though he had to give much of his money to his master. The article went on to say that when his owner died, he set up a practice in Nashville and his white patients were so pleased with his services they petitioned the State Legislature to repeal the Act of 1831 that prohibited slaves from practicing medicine."

William was about to respond when Ivy said, "Wait, there's more. Are you aware of the many slave entrepreneurships? One slave woman ran two businesses at the same time. One was a coffee shop. The other was a secondhand store. Some guy named Robert Gordon purchased his freedom and moved to Cincinnati where he invested fifteen thousand dollars in a coal yard and a private dock on the waterfront. When his white competitors tried to run him out of business through price-cutting and fixing, he hired light-skinned blacks who could probably pass for white to buy their coal and fill his own orders.

"How about this one," Ivy continued reading. "In Charles Town, a couple of slaves, unbeknownst to their master, hired themselves out at night, and on the weekends. This sort of thing was going on so much that the term quasi-free Negroes came into being, according to the article. And what about Harriet Beecher Stowe, who wrote *Uncle Tom's Cabin* in 1850. According to my research, she sold a half million copies and was the first female to earn a living as a writer. Finally, doctor, wasn't it Frederick Douglass who said, 'Learn trades or starve?' This is what I meant yesterday about empirical evidence. Now, what do you say to these many examples, doctor?"

"First, let me commend you on your fine research. But I respond the same way I did last night. The successes of a few, and believe me, they are few, does not annul the disadvantages of being black in white America. Yeah, you'll always be able to point to a success here and a success there. However, until white America becomes more like the citizenry of Tennessee in the 1830s, America's racial problems will not go away. In fact, they'll increase. It's funny how the successes you quoted from the past resemble the few successes today. For example, when we consider the world of entertainment, including sports, film, and television, people think black folk are now in the mainstream of society, and we are not. I want to be clear about that. Just because Michael Jackson, Michael Jordan, Bill Cosby, Oprah Winfrey, and Denzel Washington have great success, this, in no way, is indicative of what's really going on."

"Well, Affirmative Action is not a viable answer to the problem, doctor," James forced himself to say. "Or are you for it?"

"No, and yes. Listen, as I said earlier, should black folk trust white folk to do the right thing, when at every turn, we find they aren't doing the right thing?"

"Again, do you have empirical evidence to support what you say?" Ivy asked.

"Yes, I do."

"Well, let's hear it."

"Okay. Let's begin with Texaco. The executives were calling black people niggers and black jelly beans. Then you have the verdict of the video-taped beating of Rodney King, and only God knows what else. All of this is symptomatic of a deeper problem."

"Hey, King wasn't a model citizen," Bernie added. "Every time you turn around, he was breaking the law."

"So what, Bernie? It isn't LAPD's job to exact punishment. Their job is to apprehend and detain until trial. The court was to decide his punishment for any laws he broke, not the LAPD. But see, you're only proving my point."

"Back to the Texaco thing," Terry interrupted. "I don't know for sure, but the man who turned the company executives in was probably white. If so, doesn't it say something about change?"

"Certainly it does. But what it doesn't say is how long this stuff goes on undetected, and how many other companies do the same. And don't sit there and tell me white folk don't know this stuff is going on. It wasn't until the one guy at Texaco was fired that he revealed the truth. My point is this, guys. Until white folk are willing to lay down their lives for what's right, and justice for all, *there will be no real changes*."

"What do you mean, lay down our lives?" Bernie queried.

"I mean, be willing to blow the whistle before you get fired. I mean, be willing to sacrifice yourself for the sake of justice and what's right, knowing full well you could lose a job that paid in excess of two hundred grand a year; knowing your wife or husband could leave you for doing the right thing; knowing your children will have to leave private elite school systems because you did the right thing. I mean, blowing the whistle on anyone who doesn't.

"And until that mystical day comes, we'll have racial problems in America, because people aren't willing to do the right thing on a massive scale. Most whites are for doing the right thing, as long as somebody else does it. Or as long as it doesn't cost them anything. The strange thing about it is we tell children they should do the right thing when most adults don't have the courage of their own convictions. So who's going to do all of that? You, James?"

James didn't say anything.

"What about you, Bernie?"

Bernie was quiet also.

"That's what I thought. Now if that's all, it's late."

When they stood to leave, William said, "Dr. Moretti and Dr. Cameron, I need to speak with you two for a moment."

They all looked at each other. Whenever he addressed them by their surnames and titles, it meant an ass-chewing session was about to commence. Bernie laughed to himself. He wished he could be there to witness it.

"We'll be in the lounge, guys." James smiled.

"Have a seat, ladies," William commanded.

The two women sat down, knowing what was about to happen and why. They looked at one another as though it was the other's fault.

"The bullshit stops right here and right now!" William barked. "I don't give a damn if you two never get along, but the name calling and the unnecessary confrontations will end right now, or I'll accept both of your resignations! I should have put a stop to this a long time ago. And I take responsibility for that. But dammit, you two will conduct yourselves like professionals from here on out! You don't have to like each other to get along. Am I making myself clear?"

They both looked at each other and nodded.

"Okay then. That's all."

Knowing they had just been dismissed, the two women quietly left the suite without a word.

Chapter 24:
The Bell of Truth

Toronto
August 1997

William was about to pick up the phone to call Terry's suite when it rang. "Hello."

"Do you have anything pleasant to say to me tonight? Or do you want to chew off the other half of my ass?"

"Hi, Terry, I was just about to call you and ask you to come back so we can talk. I can see you're not upset about the ass-chewing I just gave you."

"No, I'm not. And I know why you did it, too."

"Really? Why?"

"I'll tell you when I get there. Do you mind if I bring some music? I have an oldies but goodies tape I'd like you to listen to."

"Sure. Bring it. I'm sure it'll be something I like, judging by what I heard earlier."

"Okay, I'm on my way. Bye."

A moment later, Terry knocked on the door.

"Where can I plug this in? Oh, yeah. Sterling called earlier."

"Okay, I'll call him later. There's a socket on the wall by the wet bar. See it?"

"Yeah."

"So why do you *think* I chewed you guys out?" he said, putting emphasis on the word "think."

"It's not so much why. It's more like *when* you chose to do it." She pushed the play button on the cassette player.

He wondered if she really knew. "Explain."

She sat on the sofa and crossed her legs. "You would have been content to let me and Ivy argue and cut each other up well into the turn of the century, as long as it served you." Al Green's "How Can You Mend a Broken Heart?" was playing in the background. "Do you like this song?"

"Yes. It's always been a favorite of mine. Please, finish what you were saying."

"Like I told you last night, William, you can fool them with your little dumb act. But I know you. You only put a stop to it because you no longer had anything to hide. You've been saying what you've wanted to say the last two days. Now the bickering is not only annoying, it now serves no purpose for you. Am I right, or what?"

"Yes, you are," he said, unable to keep from laughing. He looked deep into her eyes. "I guess you do know me better than I thought."

"We know each other, darlin'," she said, her Southern accent more pronounced.

"Okay. I guess you're right about that, too. I think there are some things you need to know and understand. That's why I wanted to talk to you tonight before we go any further with this…this…relationship. This isn't easy to say, so please don't interrupt me. Wait until I'm done, okay?"

"Okay."

"Okay." He took a deep breath, the way people do when they're about to say something unpleasant. "This morning, when I woke up, I was thinking about our arrangement. I thought about some things my father had told me about dating women. He told me a thousand times, if he told me once, that I should be careful who I date because the woman I date will one day be my wife."

"Really? How insightful of him." She grinned.

"Isn't it though? Anyway, I heard him, but didn't hear him, ya know?" Terry nodded.

"Even when I was dating Francis, the truth of what he was saying didn't ring true until this morning. Now, I know what I'm about to say is going to sound a bit premature, but you really need to hear this, okay?"

"Okay."

She had an idea of what he was about to say and found it difficult not to jump in there and say, *I'm sure I want to be with you. I've thought it through and I'm more than sure about you*, but didn't say a word.

"Listen…remember that long list of attributes you rattled off last night?"

"Yes."

"Well, I realize now that you meet a lot of those requirements. You're dependable and loyal, respectful and sincere with me. I don't want to go through the whole list again, and that's the kind of woman I want in my life. To have and to hold. To be there with and for me; and I, for her. To share our lives, and be together. To agree and disagree. But love each other through it all. To have commonality. This is very important to me. I never thought, nor dreamed, I would see, let alone, want this from you. But you have most, if not all, that I seek and desire in my woman of choice. How can I ignore the similarities? It could be providence or fate as you mentioned last night. But it can no longer be ignored like a bother-some undisciplined child.

"No, it must be looked at and examined thoroughly and evaluated for what it's worth. You also mentioned your looks last night. Let me say that I find you very attractive; however, I hasten to point out that although beauty is a desirable quality, it takes a back seat to what I think of the right woman. Let's be honest; physical beauty is good for sexual attraction. But it fades, and fades quickly. When I consider what a person is, and my compatibility with such a person, I find that sexual desire is tremendously heightened. I need a woman who can both talk and listen—a woman who can debate, and think critically; a woman who can love me outside the bedroom as passionately as she loves me inside the bedroom.

"Let's face it, Terry, sex only lasts so long, but the time we spend together outside the bedroom is far more important. In fact, it determines the intensity of our lovemaking. And if we can't communicate in the intellectual, the emotional, and the spiritual realm, how can we expect sexual love to make up for that which makes us human? This is obvious, but animals have sex, too. To me, sex is the culmination of the intellectual, emotional, and spiritual relationship. It is the icing, not the cake. Therefore, my woman of choice must be more than good-looking. She must be all I desire her to be without me trying to change her. And I must be all she desires without her trying to change me.

"What I'm talking about here is mutual and full acceptance of each other's faults and strengths; our likes and dislikes. But above all, truth as it is, not as we would like it to be. I know all of this seems sudden and strange, but you do have an attraction I find seductive. Today, I found myself questioning last night's decision. I was thinking, you know, like, what the hell have I gotten into? Is there something there worth pursuing? Or is it purely sexual in nature? What about all the obstacles? What about the race issue? Can we ignore the cultural differences? What about how we'll be received? Can we simply say people will be people and go on with it? What if it works out? What is the ultimate end—marriage, or what? Then I thought where will we live? Who will our friends be when we get there? Will our families support us?"

"I know, William, and I've thought about it a lot. I can't answer those questions and neither can you. All I know is, I've wanted this moment for a long time and now that it's finally here, I don't want to lose it. Marriage is a long way off, but I'm not opposed to it. Since we're being totally honest, let me tell you how I feel and what I want from you, my man of choice. I want all that you are. I want your heart in the palm of my hand. I want you to give it to me unreservedly and without regret, or remorse. I want you to lose yourself in my love and not have a second thought about it. I want you to free yourself of all the burdens that afflict you and embrace my love and be forever freed from doubt."

She stopped for a second and thought about what she had just said. William looked at her. He was floored by her poetic prose and the delivery with which she spoke. Not only did it sound good to his ears, but it touched his heart as well. Terry went to the table where the phone was and jotted down what she said. She, too, was amazed.

Surprised by what she was doing, he asked, "You write poetry, huh?"

"Yes, when I'm in the mood. But sometimes things in my heart come out of my mouth already in poetic form. At those moments, I have to write them down before I lose them forever. If I could remember all the things I've said, I'd have a book of poems by now."

"You know, you have a beautiful smile."

"Thank you." Her smile broadened. "Here, I made a copy for you. Memorize it and know my words are who I am. And if you hide them in your heart, I will be there also."

They looked into each other's eyes and for a moment, they were lost in what was transpiring between them. He wanted to kiss her, but restrained himself.

"Okay, I'll memorize it, but I need to tell you a few other things as well. Assuming we go as far as marriage..." He hesitated, then continued on. "Look, I'm only bringing all this up now because you're 34 and I don't want you to waste time with me when you could find someone else and live happily ever after."

"What does my age have to do with anything?" She looked confused.

"I mean your biological clock is ticking. I don't mean to sound insensitive, but let's say we find out two or three years from now it won't work out for whatever reasons. You'll be 36 or 37 by then. You will have lost valuable time. And to me, that's a tremendous risk, considering the interracial thing, ya know?"

"I'll tell you what. You let me worry about my biological clock and the risk I'm taking, okay?"

"Okay. Fine. But I have some other things for you to consider. Realize that if we go all the way, get married I mean, your children will be considered black in spite of you being white. Once you have my child, you might as well be black yourself. If I, God forbid, die, or we end up in divorce court, you should know going in that most white men will not marry you with a black child. So unless you plan on sleeping around with white men, you'll more than likely be stuck with dating black men from now on."

"I know the child will be considered black, but I disagree with the last part. I think all men are looking for a good woman. In other words, I think I'll be okay, if you die on me, William."

"So you've really thought about this, huh?"

"Yes, I have. I'm not saying I don't believe the things you say. It's just that I know what I want, and that's you, darlin'."

"Well, don't speak your mind, Terry." He laughed.

"Is it going to be a problem? Speaking my mind, I mean?"

"No. I don't trust anyone who never stands up for anything. You never know where they stand, ya know?"

"Yes. And I totally agree. This is going to sound bad, but I would trust Ivy before I'd trust James. And she and I don't even get along. But at least I know where she stands."

The phone rang.

"Excuse me a second. It's probably Sterling." As he walked to the phone, Heatwave's "Always and Forever" began playing. "I really like your choice in music." He picked up the receiver and put one finger in the air. "Hello."

"Is this Will Wise's suite?" Sterling asked.

"Yeah, man. You know my voice."

"What the fuck you doin' lettin' her answer yo' goddamn phone? I told you to fuck her, but apparently she fucked you. Probably got yo' ass tossin' salad and everythang else."

William laughed. "Naw, I don't toss salads, bro. I see you saw Chris Rock's special, too, huh?"

"Yeah, you know I did. He had me rollin'. It was the truth though. Don't try to change the subject either. She's probably there right now, telling you everything I said, huh?"

"Yeah, she's here. What did you do?"

"She didn't tell you?"

"No. What did you do?"

"Look, man, I thought it was you on the phone so I was talkin' a little shit, thinkin' I was talking to you. I was just riding you a little about your thing with her. But she didn't say anything? Wow! Hey, bro, she might be a keeper. Most women don't know how to keep their goddamn mouth shut. Well, I'll let you go. I just wanted to tell you a couple of things that happened yesterday. Oh yeah, I talked to Jerry last night. He invited me to the Cayman Islands for a while. He sent a jet for me."

"Tell 'em I said hi, and he didn't have to invite me."

"Okay. Well, aren't you going to congratulate me?"

"You won it?"

"Yeah."

"Wow. You know he did it."

"The jury said he didn't. And I know nothing of the kind."

"Yeah, right."

"Anyway, Daniels fired me yesterday. Told me he wanted me to resign because I don't fit in. Muthafucka had the nerve to tell me he could take the kid out of the ghetto, but he couldn't take the ghetto out of the kid. Pissed—me—off."

"What did he mean by that?" He looked at Terry and mouthed, "Just a second."

She mouthed, "Take your time."

"You know Sky, right? Well, he and his dad were in the office when I came in yesterday. We were shootin' the shit and the next thing I know Daniels called me on the carpet about some shit I said."

"Oh, you were talkin' street?"

"Yeah. I forgot for a moment. That ain't no reason to fire a brotha."

"Hey, man, you should have known better. You know the language. Speak it when you're in the office."

"I know. The shit just pissed me off, ya know?"

"Yeah, but the good thing is, it forces you to get out on your own. You should have been gone a long time ago. Every time a big case comes along, they give it to you. That should have been your clue."

"Well, I got a case with a heavy retainer already, man. I'll rap with you about it later. So did she hit the high note, or what?" Sterling laughed.

"I didn't do anything." Will said, concealing what they were talking about.

"Damn, ain't that fluid backin' up in you? You need to let that shit out before you explode."

Will's laughter burst out uncontrollably. "Sterling, let me catch you later."

"Okay. Talk to you when I get home. Bye, bro."

"All right, later, man."

As he walked back over to the sofa, he thought, *Wow, that's the second time she could have told me some gossip, and didn't.* For the first time in a long time, he felt he had finally found someone he had a lot in common with—someone who knew him, and someone whom he respected and wanted to know much better. The two of them listened to music and talked until the rays of the sun began shining into the suite.

The time had flown by and neither of them was ready to stop talking. They looked into each other's eyes and knew without saying a word that this was a relationship to be cherished. He looked at her wide mouth and then back into her hazel eyes. He wanted her and she wanted him.

"You know we have to check out soon," he said softly.

"Yes. I know," she said, still staring into his eyes, hoping the inevitable would happen here—now.

Their heads involuntarily moved closer, tilting to the side and they kissed; gently at first, but more passionately when she opened her mouth. They embraced and their breathing increased. She could feel the rapid beat of his heart pounding feverishly in his chest. The sudden ringing of the phone startled him and he pulled away, feeling like a teenager being caught on his parents' couch.

"What's wrong?"

"Nothing. We should start preparing to leave," he told her, as he walked to the phone.

Disappointed, Terry remained on the couch and composed herself. She thought about what was about to happen and wondered when a more opportune time would come. She could feel the moisture between her legs the heat of the moment had brought to bare and wanted him inside her, but knew there would be another time.

"Hello."

"Is anything wrong, Willy?" his mother asked him. "I woke up a moment ago and you were on my mind."

"Hi, Mama," he said, looking at Terry. His mother always seemed to know things in advance. She never knew exactly what was going on, but she always knew something. She could sense things in people, and she had passed the gift on to him. "No, Mama. Everything is fine. How are you and Daddy doin'?"

"We're just fine. Are you sure nothing's wrong? I don't wake up in the middle of the night for nothin'."

He looked at his watch. It was seven in Toronto, making it four in San Francisco. He shook his head and wondered how she always knew.

"I'm sure, Mama. Nothing's wrong. I'll be home later today. Go on back to sleep now, hear?"

"Okay. You know I have to check on y'all when I wake up like this. Last time I had to call you this early was when you met Francis. You haven't met any of those French girls up there in Canada, have you?" She laughed.

Shit! He shook his head and looked at Terry, who was wondering what was going on. He laughed nervously with his mother. "Mama, you're always trying to put me with somebody."

"Okay, then. I'll see you when you come home. Bye," she said and hung up the phone. Then she shook her husband. "Benny! Benny! Willy found himself a woman and he likes her. Grandchildren! Finally! Lord knows I've been patient." She smiled to herself and went back to sleep.

William hung up the phone and said with distinct sobriety, "My mother knows about us. She doesn't know who you are, but she knows you're here and that we've been here all night."

"What? How?" Terry wondered, stunned by what had just happened.

"My mother knows things without knowing. Believe me, she knows and she's telling my dad as we speak."

"Is that so terrible?"

"Terry, this is painfully obvious, but my mother is a black woman."

"So she'll have a problem with it, huh?"

"Yes, a serious problem. She's telling dad right now about the grand-children that she's wanted for years. See, Francis and I didn't have any. Sterling doesn't either. And Jericho is another story altogether. I'll tell you about him later."

"Are you sure she knows?"

"Take my word for it. She knows. She even made it obvious by mentioning the time she called me in college when Francis and I got together. She knew then, too."

"Hmm." Her eyes beamed. *If his mother was right about Francis, she could be right about me, too.* The whole idea intrigued her. Now she was happy James's slip of the tongue had occurred. *Fate!*

"Hmm, what?"

"Oh, nothing. Well, I better pack." She smiled, unplugging the portable stereo.

"Yeah, me too."

He held her hand as he walked her to the door. Then he kissed her hand and then her lips.

"See you in a couple of hours," she said, and left.

He closed the door behind her and leaned his back against it. Then he shouted, "SHIT! THIS IS FUCKED UP!"

Chapter 25: Home Again

W illiam was awakened by the captain's voice over the public address system of the plane. "United Flight 932 will arrive on schedule. We will start our descent in a moment. It's a cool 73 degrees in San Francisco. The time is 12:30 Pacific. We hope you enjoyed our in-flight movies. The crew of Flight 932 thanks you for flying with us today."

William looked at his watch. 3:25 PM. In his haste to pack, he forgot to change his watch to Pacific Time. He slept during much of the flight. The last thing he remembered was watching the beginning of a Ron Howard film, *Ransom*. He hoped sleeping on the plane would offset any jet lag he might suffer later. He took a deep breath and stretched—glad to be home again. He was looking forward to having the rest of the day to do as he pleased, and later sleeping in his own bed.

The captain said, "Please remain seated until we come to a complete stop."

This was the moment he hated about flying—the mad dash to get off the plane. Every time he flew, he could count on a rush to the door, which meant there would be a long line. *Why can't the people in the back realize it's easier to let the people in the front off first? If people would just do things in order, it would go much smoother.* Nevertheless, he stood up and got in line like the rest of the impatient people behind him. Terry was five rows up from him. When Jeannine booked the tickets, he had her make sure the staff never sat together. She scattered their seats so they wouldn't know he was avoiding them. That way, he could have a little peace on the way to and from Toronto.

Terry looked back at him and smiled.

William returned her smile and then caught himself. He wondered if the rest of the gang were paying attention to them. *What if they called her room last night?* This was the one time he hoped they were too busy drinking. He finally exited the plane and was on his way to the baggage claim area, where Terry was picking up her luggage.

"How did you sleep on the long flight home?" she asked him.

"Slept the entire trip. I tried to stay awake so I could watch *Ransom*."

"How 'bout I rent it and swing by your place later?"

"Naw, that's okay. I don't want to see it that badly. But you can swing by anyway. You can see the house. We can grill some steaks and talk. You play chess?"

"Yes, I do. And I'd love to see your place, William."

The rest of the gang finally arrived. They looked like they'd been up all night drinking. They grabbed their bags and made their way to the exit. When they exited the terminal, Ivy said, "Are you going to need a ride, Dr. Wise?"

"No, I have a friend picking me up. Thanks anyway." He took out his cell phone and called Cleveland Thomas, his best friend. He hated calling his house because he didn't like his wife.

"Hello."

"Hi, Cheryl. This is Will. Is Cleve there?"

"No," she said gruffly. "He left a half-hour ago."

"A half-hour. He should be here by now."

"Hey, that's yo' friend for you."

"Okay, bye."

Sharon, James's ex-wife, pulled up in a Ford Expedition with his kids. He was surprised to see her there. They hadn't gotten along at all since the divorce.

"I wonder what the hell she wants now," James grumbled. "Probably some blood. She's got everything else."

Bernie laughed. "That's why I'm never ever getting married. Who needs that shit?" Then he laughed again.

James walked over to see what she wanted. They all watched to see what would happen. After a few minutes, James came back over to the gang with a broad smile on his face and said, "She wants me to come home. So I won't need a ride, Ivy." He picked up his luggage and practically ran back to the vehicle and left with Sharon.

Ivy said to Bernie, "I guess it's just you and me."

"Looks that way," Bernie said, and they left.

"I wonder what that's about," William said, referring to Sharon and James with mixed emotions.

Terry said, "I don't know. Maybe they're going to try and work it out."

"I hope she's serious this time."

"Do you think you'll need a ride?"

"I don't think so. I'm going to call the Jeep. Hopefully he's on his way."

"Okay, I'll get my car. If he isn't coming, or something happened, I'll give you a ride home."

"Okay."

William dialed his Jeep. Cleve answered. "I'm pulling in now. Keep ya pants on. I knew yo' ass would be callin'." Then he laughed.

"HA HA. Just get up here. I'm ready to go home."

The Jeep pulled up minutes later. Terry pulled up in her candy-apple red Mitsubishi 3000GT seconds later. She got out of the car just as William approached the Jeep.

"Hey, would you like to meet my best friend?" he asked her.

"Sure."

Cleveland hit the power button and the window slid down. They looked into the Jeep together. Terry gasped. William stood there with his mouth wide open. He couldn't believe what he was seeing. Cleveland had a thick patch of gauze over his right eye and more gauze wrapped around his head holding the gauze over his eye in place.

Cleveland smiled. "What's the matter? Ain't you ever seen a patch covering somebody's eye before?"

Terry thought, *What the hell happened to you?*

Having no idea what to say, William simply introduced them.

"Cleve, this is Dr. Terry Moretti, one of my associates. Dr. Moretti, this is Cleveland Thomas, my best friend."

"Pleased to meet you," Terry said. She reached into the Jeep to shake Cleveland's hand.

"Hi, Terry. So you and Will are an item, huh?"

William curled his lips and rolled his eyes.

Terry didn't know what to say so she didn't say anything.

"You have to excuse Cleve. Sometimes he shoots his mouth off when he should be quiet. That's probably why he's got that patch over his eye."

"Aw, that's cold, man. You didn't have to go there."

"I'll be right back," William told his best friend of over twenty years. "I'm going to walk her to her car."

"What time do you think you'll be coming over?" William asked Terry when they reached her car.

"What time would you like me to?"

"How about two or two-thirty? Is that too early?"

"No. That's fine. I'll see you then."

Terry got into the Mitsubishi and sped away. The tires screeched as she turned the corner. William walked back to the Jeep and got in.

Cleve looked at William, then said, "Don't say shit about my eye either," and drove off.

"You know I'm going to say something. Why do you put up with her? And I don't want to hear nothin' about her givin' great head either. I'm serious, Cleve. One day she's going to kill you. Or you're going to end up in jail for killing her."

Cleve had heard this so many times that he knew what his best friend was going to say long before he uttered the words. But Cleve had no intentions of leaving Cheryl—ever. He was seriously whipped, and he didn't care. He loved Cheryl; no matter what she did in a fit of anger. Besides, she was always sorry afterwards and showed her contrition by giving him a blow job.

"So you bangin' that or what?"

"No."

"Well, she's fine as hell for a white woman. Shit, I'd bang her—often. I was checkin' out that ass when you walked her back to her car. Ain't often you see a white girl with an ass on her. Sweet ass—sculptured ass. Shit, I wouldn't mind squeezing that ass m'self. So how come you didn't get with her? She didn't offer it, or what? You know what they say about them white girls."

"No, Cleve. What do they say?"

"You know how freaky they are. She probably woulda wore yo' ass out anyway. When's the last time you had a piece?"

"Don't change the subject, Cleve."

"Look who's talkin'. Look who's talkin'. Every year you come home from your little Toronto trip braggin' 'bout how you got over on 'em again by changin' the subject. I'm surprised you haven't started ringin' my ears with it yet. So how did you do it this time?"

"It didn't work this time."

"What? They got hip to yo' ass, huh? It was just a matter of time. So what happened?"

"You're not slick, Cleve. You tell me what happened between you and Cheryl first." Will laughed. "You're trying my stuff on me, but it won't work. So what precipitated it this time?"

"Precipitated? Hey, bro, you wit' me now. Just talk normal. Precipitated," he repeated again, shaking his head. "All you had to say was, 'What happened?' But no, you have to get all technical and shit. Next thing ya know, you'll have my ass on a couch somewhere askin' me some shit like, 'So when did realize you hated your father?'" He was speaking with a British accent when he said this.

Will laughed. He loved Cleve's sense of humor.

"So, Cleve, my main man, my ace boon coon, soul brotha like no other, what went down at yo' crib with that bitch of yours? Is that better?"

Both men laughed uproariously.

"That's mo' like it. So does she play spades?"

"I don't know."

"Well, ask her. You need a new partner so Cheryl and I can kick y'alls asses."

"I doubt that. But what happened, man?"

"Hey, I wanna stop at Mickey D's. I wanna show you somethin'. Plus, I wanna know if you'll go in on a business venture with me."

"Cleve, I'm ready to go home. I've had a very trying weekend and I'm going to have to fight that Golden Gate traffic as it is. Besides we just passed a McDonald's a little while ago."

"Naw, man. I wanna go to one in the 'hood. I wanna show you somethin'."

"Show me what?"

"You know Scott Tyler, right?"

"Yeah. And…?"

"You know he owns three McDonald's, right?"

"WILL YOU GET ON WITH IT?"

"Okay, okay. Shit. You don't have to bite my head off."

"Naw, I'll leave that up to Cheryl."

They laughed again.

"Tyler is lettin' his business run down. You should see what's going on in there. You go to the drive-thru and sixty percent of the time, the order's wrong. And if you go inside, the employees act like they're doin' you a fuckin' favor for taking your order."

"Yeah, I know that. So?"

"So, I want you to help me take it over."

"How am I supposed to do that? If that's the only reason you're stopping, don't bother."

"I was thinkin' maybe Jericho can help me out. He helped Alicia Harris get her salon out of hock. Now she's got three of 'em."

"Yeah, but Alicia is a gifted hairstylist. She just lacked the business acumen to run it successfully. You, on the other hand, know next to nothing about business."

"Did I ever tell you how proud I am of you, man? I look at you today and I look at myself. I wonder how come some of you didn't rub off on me after all this time. I work at a job I can't stand. I try to get ahead and find myself fallin' further behind. I can't win. I went to the bank the other day; tried to get a loan. Turned me down flat. The white man won't give a brotha a chance, ya know."

"Listen to you. You just said how proud you were of me. Where do you think I got my loan? From the white man, that's where. I didn't get it the first time I tried either. I went up and down the coast before going back to the original banker and he took a chance on me. Now my loans are all paid back. Cleve, you know I love you, brotha, but look, if I had to go through all of that, and I have a PhD from Harvard of all places, what makes you think you can do it on a high school diploma from a substandard inner city school? To be honest, Cleve, if I were a banker, I wouldn't give you a loan either. It's bad business to give hundreds of thousands of dollars to people of any color who have no expertise in business."

The Jeep stopped in front of Cleve's house. He turned the ignition off. They sat in the Jeep and continued talking.

"Well, I may not have a PhD from Harvard, but I have goals. I'd like to live in Sausalito, too, or Muir Woods for that matter. I remember when we were kids and we'd take the ferry over and ride our bikes through the neighborhoods. We would say how one day we were going to live there. Well you did it, man. I wanna do it, too. Don't think I'm jealous of you either. Your success is my success. If white folk blame me and label me every time one brotha does something wrong, I can take some credit from every brotha that does it the right way. You know what I'm sayin'?"

"Yeah, Cleve, I understand. But look here, it's not too late. Why don't you go back to school and take some management courses. Who knows? You may even like going to school. You might want to get a degree in business. I'll tell you what. You get back in school. Get a degree in business. And I'll go in with you. How about that?"

"I'll think about it."

"See that's what I mean, brotha. You'll think about it. You just said you had goals. Do you expect manna from heaven? You have to make up your mind, brotha. That's one reason why the banker wouldn't even consider backing you. Then you wanna blame him when you should prepare yourself first. Then see the banker."

"I see what you're sayin', but I get tired of seeing foreigners come over here right off the boat, and openin' stores and shit in our neighborhood. Ya know?"

"Yes, I know. And something needs to be done about that, but in the meantime, make up your mind, okay?"

"Okay. I'll catch you later," Cleve told him and got out of the Jeep. Will slid into the driver's seat and started the engine. He pushed the passenger window button and it retracted.

"Hey, Cleve, are you going to tell me what happened?"

"Don't forget to ask your girlfriend if she knows how to play spades!" Cleve yelled back to him and entered his house. Will put the Jeep in drive and headed home.

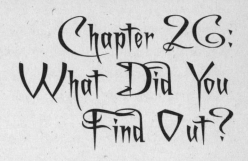

Chapter 26:
What Did You
Find Out?

Langley, Virginia
August 1997

Victor Marshall followed CIA Executive Director Nora Clayter as she drove her blue and white Volkswagen Jetta at speeds exceeding 80 mph from Langley to Sandbridge, Virginia, where she met Stan Moore at a beach house on Sandfiddler Road for a romantic weekend. Moore was waiting for Clayter, who arrived a little before noon. They ravaged each other immediately, showered and sunbathed for an hour before having lunch at Margie & Ray's Crabhouse, where they ate scallops, shrimp, crab cakes, and perch.

Victor sat at a table near the amorous couple, and ate buttered crab legs, catfish, hushpuppies, and a salad. He listened to them plan a trip to the Maritime Center. Later, they were going to have a quiet dinner on the deck of the beach house. As far as Victor could tell, Clayter had no idea who Jericho was. None of it made any sense to him. Her cell phone never rang—if she brought it. And if the cell had been turned off, why even bring it? *For a roadside emergency?*

If Clayter was really after Jericho and the crew, wouldn't she require updates? Would she be on a weekend romp now, when the CIA supposedly had the crew under surveillance? And if the crew was under surveillance, wouldn't they know that Victor, a known killer, was back in the States, following their executive director, and sitting two tables away from her? Maybe she knew about Hawthorne's personal enterprise. Maybe he was telling the truth about her making changes in the Agency and wanted her out. Maybe that's why it was so easy to get close to her, Victor deduced.

Later, when Victor followed Nora Clayter and Stan Moore to the National Maritime Center in Norfolk, Virginia, he spotted Captain Greene and his partner following him. That's when he decided to find out what was really going on. He lost Greene and his partner in the center, knowing they would split up to try and find him. When they did, he went to the parking lot and waited for one of them to make sure his car was still in the lot.

After about ten minutes, he was about to go back inside when he saw Greene coming. He ducked behind some cars, and watched to see if anyone was around. No one was. He snuck up behind Greene and hit him in the back of the head with a blackjack and tossed him in the trunk of his car. He gagged him and duct-taped his hands and feet. Then he waited for Greene's partner, and did the same thing to him.

†††

Jericho was sitting in the conference room reading the information he was being faxed about Adrienne Bellamy. He had gotten a call from Sydney Drew, a contact in the States telling him the information was on its way. Each page contained specific background information on Bellamy and how she came into so much money. Then he read an item that shocked him. He picked up the phone and called Sterling's room.

"Hello."

"I got the info on, Bellamy. You might wanna take a look."

"On my way."

Jericho read several more pages of the information about Bellamy while he waited for Sterling. Then he picked up the phone and called Pin in the computer room.

"Still no sign of trouble?" Jericho asked in Vietnamese.

"No sign at all," Pin said in the same tongue. "I think you're right about Hawthorne. It's all a set-up to kill the woman, I'll bet. She must be onto him, or something. We have to kill him."

"I agree." Sterling walked into the room and sat down at one of the chairs across from Jericho. "But keep monitoring the situation just to be safe." Then he hung up the phone.

"Check this out." Jericho slid the papers across the table.

Sterling picked them up and began reading. Then he looked up at Jericho with a confused look on his face and said, "She's black?"

"Umm-hmm."

"There must be some mistake. The woman I saw is white. No question about it."

"She's passing for white, you mean. Look at the birth certificate. Her mama's black and her daddy's white. How much you wanna bet her mama was real light-skinned?"

"You think her husband knew?" Sterling asked.

"Probably. But I bet no one else knows. Maybe that's the real reason she wants the Warren girl outta the way."

"Maybe. It really doesn't matter. I signed on to do a job and I'm going to do my part. The decision is up to the girl, not me."

"You don't have to do this, bro. You can work for me. I know just as many celebrities as she does. Believe it or not, the Chiefs are still running the bookie operations. So I still have contacts on campuses across the country."

"Naw, bro. Like I said, I made a deal. Besides, she's done her part. Tiffany tells me we're already in business. I'm going to have to get back and start soon."

"A woman like that ain't nobody to play wit'. You best do what you said, or get out of it now. How far do you think she'll go if she even thinks somebody knows her secret? And if it got out that she's black, what would that do to her circle of friends and her influence? People will look at her differently. A woman like her will do anything to keep the truth from surfacing. Last thing she wants is for her 'tainted' past to get out."

"That's true. But her being black doesn't change anything. I'm going to carry out the agreement."

"Okay, bro. It's yo' call."

The phone rang.

Jericho answered. "Yeah."

"Hey, man, it was all a set-up," Victor told Jericho. He was calling from Hawthorne's home in Langley, Virginia, where he had used plastic zip-lock straps to secure the men to chairs. As he spoke into the receiver, he kept his silenced pistol pointed at the men.

"Thought so."

"The woman doesn't know anything about us."

"You've confirmed this?"

"Hawthorne wouldn't talk, but Green, being the pussy he's always been, goatee and all, gave it all up. Set a new record for spillin' his worthless guts. Guess what else?"

"What?"

"They don't have a tape. No visuals whatsoever. They don't even have access to satellites no more. Clayter cut 'em off. Hawthorne is on suspension. If something happens to Clayter, it all goes away. I think we oughta end this shit now while we can."

"Do it."

Victor squeezed the trigger and his gun hissed three times; bullets entered the heads of the men. "Leave the woman out of it, right?" Victor asked calmly.

"Right."

"I'll have our friend at the funeral parlor cremate the bodies and dispose of them."

"Come on back to the Renegade," Jericho said and hung up the phone. Sterling was still reading about Adrienne Bellamy. He seemed to be intrigued by her financial statement. "You sure you won't change your mind?"

"Yeah, I'm sure, Jerry. She seems to have her hand in everything. She's got part ownership in several sports franchises. She owns the fourth largest television network, three newspapers, and a shipyard. She has stocks in the major film studios in Hollywood and Culver City. She's even got stock in four of the top ten sneaker makers. It goes on and on."

"That's why you don't wanna fuck with this bitch. You can bet she knows how to fuck people over." He paused for a second. "You ever find out how she knows you?"

"Naw, not yet. I can only assume she saw me on television, like most of the country."

"Don't count on it. A woman like her wouldn't have to find you that way. There's more going on than she's lettin' you know."

"Probably. But in the meantime, I'm going to Manhattan for a day, or so. Then I have some pressing business in Chicago and Denver."

Chapter 29:
Getting to Know You

San Francisco
August 1997

T he vestiges of Anita Baker's "Body and Soul" could be heard through the cracked window when the Mitsubishi pulled into the circular driveway. Terry looked at herself once more in the vanity mirror. She was wearing a long-sleeved, cream-colored, beaded tunic. In order to show off her shape, she decided to wear her favorite pair of hip-hugger jeans along with a pair of brown sandals that had beads across the band similar to the ones in her blouse.

She grabbed the bottle of red wine and exited the car. As she approached the house, the high, massive columns and the high, dramatic arches of his white brick home captured her attention. A path of small palm trees, shrubs, assorted flowers, and nightlights led to the entrance of the impressive hideaway in the hills. She smelled the Pacific Ocean and wondered if there was a view of the bay.

A sequence of chimes rang out and reminded her of the fairy tales she'd listened to when she was a child, after pressing the doorbell. As she waited for William to answer the door, she took a deep breath and wondered what it would be like to live there with him. After three years of waiting for him to make the first move, she couldn't believe she was actually on his doorstep.

William opened one of the French doors, which were made of oval-shaped glass encased in navy blue oak. "Come in," he said, smiling.

Terry stepped into the foyer and with a brief glance, she looked at him from head to toe, paying particular attention to the black and cream cardigan he was wearing, the matching black slacks, and loafers. "Here," she said, handing him the wine.

"Thank you. That was thoughtful. I hope you're hungry."

"I'm starved," she said. "I haven't eaten since dinner yesterday."

"Good. I hope you enjoy it."

They walked into the spacious island kitchen and then through the patio doors, stepping onto the deck. Terry smelled the burning charcoal and felt a slight breeze that caused her hair to move. The view was breathtaking. She could see a picturesque view of downtown San Francisco, the Golden Gate Bridge, and Fisherman's Wharf. As she continued taking in the view, she watched one of the Red and White Fleet cruisers dock at Pier 41, while a Blue and Gold Fleet cruiser was departing Pier 39.

They walked past the glass-enclosed sunroom just off the kitchen and Terry sat down in one of the patio chairs. William threw the steaks on the fire and heard the searing sound of T-bones broiling.

"You like football, Terry?"

"Love it."

"Who do you like—the Niners or the Raiders?

"The Niners, of course. I guess you like the Raiders, huh?"

"I like them both, actually."

"Okay, but who do you like when they play each other?"

"Then I like the Raiders. Everybody in my family likes the Raiders, except my mom. She likes the Niners, too. Jerry Rice is her favorite player. She doesn't like the Raiders because of how they beat the Chargers twenty years ago, or so. You remember that play when they cheated by fumbling the ball forward and fell on it in the end zone? Every time they play, you can count on her to bring it up. We just laugh. It was so long ago, but she keeps talking about it like it happened yesterday."

Terry observed the boyish look on William's face when he spoke about his mother. She could tell he loved and respected her, but also wondered if his mother would pose as much of a problem as he'd said when they were in Toronto.

"Anyway," he continued, "they're playing each other in a preseason game at five o'clock on ESPN. You wanna watch it after our chess match?"

"Sure, if you don't mind me cheering on the Niners."

"I don't mind, but don't you think the Niners are a different team without Ricky Watters?" He wanted to see if she was a casual fan or if she really knew the game.

"Yes. Definitely. He made the team move with his pass-catching skills out of the backfield. You know, the Niners have always had a good running game to go with their passing attack. And since Ricky left, we haven't been the same. I remember when we had Wendell Tyler and Roger Craig. Most people don't realize this, but it's the running game that makes the West Coast offense what it is. I didn't realize it myself until they didn't have it anymore. Jerry Rice is going to get his, but they need a versatile runningback, too. When we get one, you'll see just how awesome we can be. Especially when our defense is playing well."

Satisfied she had a firm grasp of the game, he asked, "So how do you like your steak?"

"Well done, please."

"Yeah, me too."

Terry asked, "So are we going to have dinner out here, or what?"

"Do you want to have it out here?"

"Yes. I think this view is absolutely fabulous."

"Thank you. Sterling is the one who found this house for me."

"Really? Tell me about it."

"Terry, my brother is a lady's man. Women love him for some reason."

"Are you jealous?"

"No, not at all. I love my brother. I didn't mean to come off that way. I just meant if it weren't for him, I wouldn't have this place."

"Good, because I can see why women love him. He's funny."

"Yeah, he told me you guys had a little talk the other day. He wouldn't tell me what happened, but he thinks a lot of you though. You impressed him by not telling me what he said to you on the phone. So what happened? What did he say?"

"Do you really want to know?"

"Yeah, why not?"

"Are you sure?"

"Yes. Just let me get some plates and silverware from the kitchen." He turned the steaks over and then went into the kitchen.

"Well, you don't sound sure to me," she called out.

William returned to the patio. "Are you going to tell me or what?"

"Okay, okay. Keep your pants on, Geez. First, tell me how he got you this house."

Terry was smiling broadly, which he found incredibly alluring, and equally disarming.

"Like I said, Sterling's a lady's man. When Francis died, I couldn't live in our home anymore. It was just weird living there and expecting her to come home or be there waiting for me when I got there. I found myself talking to her, then realizing that she was no longer alive. It was a hard adjustment for me. I finally moved back home with my mom and dad. About three months later, Sterling told me one of his friends, as he calls them, had the perfect house for me. So I came out to see it. The woman who owned the place told me her husband died in his plane on the way home from a neurologists' convention in Seattle. This was their dream house and she couldn't bear to live here without him. When I told her about my loss, we hit it off. We had coffee and talked at length about our deceased spouses. By the time we finished talking, she made me a great deal on the house, and here I am."

"Wow! That's great!" Then she realized how that must have sounded. "I didn't mean it the way it sounded. I meant you were able to get this really nice place at a reduced rate—I didn't mean that either," she said, feeling like a complete idiot.

"I understand. Why don't you tell me about your conversation with my brother now?"

"Okay. Here goes," she said, relieved he understood what she was trying to say but couldn't quite put into words. "I go into the bedroom of your suite because the phone doesn't work in the room we were having dinner in, remember?"

"Yeah, I remember."

"So, as I'm walking into the other room, I'm eating my salad and when I pick up the phone, I hear Sterling already talking."

"What was he saying?"

"I don't know what he said before I put the phone to my ear, but the first thing I heard him say was, 'So did you get your dick wet?'"

She was looking right at him to see how he would react before telling all. That way she would know if she could tell him everything without fear of him getting angry, or jealous. She knew how men were when it came down to women and what they expected of them. She wanted to see if he was different from most, and he was. William laughed uproariously when she finished.

"He didn't even wait for an answer. He just kept on talking and talking."

"Sounds just like him, too. Just like him," he said and paused for a moment. "What else did he say?"

"I can't remember everything, but I do remember him saying, 'I bet you broke your dick off in her.' Then he said something about me hitting the high note. That's when I had to laugh myself. Oh, I almost forgot. He said, 'I bet you rode her like the stallion she is.'"

William laughed again. "So then what happened?"

"At some point during his chiding you, he realized you hadn't said a word and he called your name a couple of times. I decided to have a little fun myself. Eventually, I said hello, and he asked me if I was the maid. He knew I wasn't the maid. He was just hoping, probably praying that it wasn't me. So I said, guess again. Then he had the nerve to try and blame me for what he was saying about us. But I have to admit what he was saying about us sounded good."

William pulled the steaks from the grill and placed them on their plates. "Just a second." He went into the kitchen and brought out a tossed salad along with baked potato skins with cheese, chives, and real bacon bits. "Would you like some sour cream?"

"Yes, please."

"Okay, I'll get it."

William returned with the sour cream and sat across from her and they began eating.

"Umm," she said involuntarily. "This is so good. I can only think of one thing that would make this meal perfect."

"And what would that be?" he said, feeling slightly insulted the meal wasn't already perfect.

"The meal would be absolutely perfect if I could have a glass of red wine. Know where I can get some?"

"Oh, I'm sorry." He bounced his palm off the side of his head. "I completely forgot about the wine you brought." He returned a few moments later with two chilled wineglasses. He poured a glass for her and one for himself. Then he sat down and resumed eating. "Terry," he said, looking at her. "About what happened at the hotel this morning...I don't think it's a good idea to sleep together too soon."

"Is that why you think I came here?" She was frowning as she spoke.

But William thought her anger only enhanced her natural beauty.

"I didn't mean to insult you. I just thought...after what you said about Sterling's remarks..."

"You are so arrogant. Just because I accepted your invitation to dinner doesn't mean I want to spread my legs for you."

"I'm sorry. I just thought that since you thought that what Sterling said sounded good, you wanted it to happen tonight."

She folded her arms. "Oh, really?"

"Let's skip it. I made a mistake and I'm sorry."

"You sure did!" She rolled her eyes. "You invited me, remember?"

"Yeah, I remember, but that was after you had invited yourself, remember?"

"I remember wanting to watch a film with you. What's wrong with that?"

"Nothing. You—"

"You assumed because of one little kiss that I was willing to give myself to you. Men! Do you really think you're that irresistible?"

"Why don't we drop it?"

"Yeah, let's."

The two of them ate their meals quietly for a few minutes; both of them wanted to know what the other was thinking as the intensity of the moment abated itself. Neither of them knew what to expect next.

William took a sip of his wine and said, "Maybe I jumped to the wrong conclusion, Terry. Do you want to put this behind us or what?"

"Maybe I shouldn't have called you arrogant either."

"I forgive you for the second time on the arrogant thing."

"And I forgive you for jumping to the wrong conclusions a second time."

"We're still going to play a game of chess, aren't we?"

"Yeah. You think you've got a chance?"

"Who's being arrogant now, Terry?"

"Hey, it ain't arrogance if you can do it." She grinned and her Southern accent came alive again.

"That's true."

When they finished their meal, Terry helped him clear the table. William rinsed the dishes and put them into the dishwasher.

"So are you ready for the game of chess?"

"Yes," she said. "Are you ready for the beating I'm about to give you?"

Terry had a pugnacious way about her and William found it intriguing. It was something about the way she looked when she was ready for a fight. She had a combativeness about her that made him want to conqueror her sexually. He felt the desire to kiss her inviting mouth, but resisted the urge to do so.

"My chess set is in the den. Follow me."

They left the kitchen and walked past the dining and living rooms and walked down a hallway. The den was the last door on the left, just before the master bedroom.

"What's in there?" Terry asked, pointing at the double doors.

"That's where I sleep."

"Oh. Can I see it without you thinking I wanna spend the night?" She grinned wickedly.

"Yeah, you can see it and I promise I won't think you want to spend the night."

They both laughed. He opened the double doors and gestured for her to go in. She was immediately impressed with the décor and the cleanliness, but didn't say anything. She walked into the sitting area of the room and looked out the picture window. It provided the same view as the patio. Then she went into the bathroom.

"This is the only room on this end of the house."

"Nice," she said, looking at the large glass-enclosed shower. The color scheme was navy blue and white. There were matching fixtures, rugs, and towels. She walked over to the sunken tub and looked out the retractable skylight. She wondered what it would be like to take a hot bath at night when the stars were out. "What's in here? Linen?" she asked, referring to the door just left of the entrance.

"No, that's a closet."

She opened the door, turned on the light, and walked in. It reminded her of the closet the character Richard Gere had in the film *American Gigolo*. The closet was divided by three walls. Suits were on one wall with shoes underneath on a rack. A myriad of shirts, slacks, ties, and sweaters filled the other two walls.

Grinning, Terry asked, "You know you're going to have to move your stuff to the other bedroom closets when I move in, don't you?"

William looked at her as if to say, "Puh-lease."

They left the master bedroom and entered the den. A small chandelier hung over the antique chess set and its accompanying table. The pieces were a replica of the Greek and Roman gods.

Looking around the den, Terry thought the room would more appropriately be described as a library from a period in American history, when reading was a leading form of entertainment. The bookshelves were ceiling high, and made of beautifully crafted cherrywood, complete with leather-bound books.

The desk was against the wall with a personal computer on it, which seemed to be out of place in a room reminiscent of the early 1900s. A brass-framed, custom-crafted mirror hung right above the desk. Through the mirror, Terry could see books on the other side of the room. Her eyes full of wonder, she walked around the den looking at the books, recognizing a set of leather-bound Britannica's and the Great Books of the Western World, which consisted of famous philosophers such as Locke, Pascal, Copernicus, Hume, Hobbes, and Kant. There were books of poetry and literature. Some of the authors were Emily Dickinson, Maya Angelou, Langston Hughes, Stephen Crane, William Faulkner, Nathaniel Hawthorne, Alice Walker, Ernest Hemingway, Nikki Giovanni, James Patterson, Jackie Collins, and Eric Jerome Dickey.

Terry continued walking around the den, looking at the books when she spotted all three volumes of *Sex and Race*. She remembered William referring to these books during that first heated debate in Toronto. Intrigued by what obscure knowledge their pages contained, she picked up volume one and began reading the table of contents.

"I thought we came in here to play chess," William said, smiling.

She smiled back at him. "I want to look at some of this and see if you know what the hell you're talking about."

They walked over to the chess table; Terry was still reading the table of contents as she walked and then she sat down.

"If you're looking for your ancestry, you should read chapter fifteen. I believe it's page one fifty-one."

She continued reading the table of contents and discovered that the chapter he suggested was titled "Miscegenation in Spain, Portugal, and Italy." Terry said, "And what makes you think I'm interested in that chapter?"

William moved the queen's pawn two spaces forward. "You have Italian blood, don't you?"

"Yeah...so what?"

"Terry," he said, laughing a little, "the book is appropriately named *Sex and Race*. What do you think is in the books? Considering the names of the chapters, why wouldn't you be interested in your ancestry?"

She thought for a moment. "Okay, you have a point. So what's wrong with wanting to know what it says?"

"Nothing, I was just trying to help you get the information you wanted."

"No, you weren't. You wanted me to read that chapter, didn't you?"

"Did you want to read that chapter, or not?" He had a smirk on his face.

"Yeah, but why do you want me to read it? You know that it says something about Italians being black, don't you? You seem to relish the idea of me reading that chapter." She felt sure of herself.

"So what if I am? It's funny to me. White people don't know that most of 'em have black blood in their veins. I like watching their reactions when I tell them they do." Then he laughed. "You should see their faces when I tell them. I get one of two reactions. One, they immediately reject the information, apparently because it says that they're black also. Or two, they are infuriated by it, which lets me know how they feel about black people; regardless of their standard clichés about how there are good people and bad people in all races. So I watch them as the conversation progresses and slowly they began to contemplate the possibilities of me being correct. They usually have an expression on their faces, which leads me to believe that deep down, they know I'm telling them a truth they don't want to deal with. Then they want to know how I know this information. So I ask them if they would like to read the books. And without fail, they all say 'no.' That's when I know they know I'm telling them the truth and they no longer want to talk about it. Your move."

Terry moved the Roman Eagle pawn of King Jupiter forward two spaces and then turned to page one fifty-one and began reading. The page basically said that Spain and Portugal were Negroid. "This doesn't say anything about Italians being black."

"Turn to page one sixty-two," William said and moved Queen Aphrodite out four spaces. "Your move."

Terry quickly flipped to page one sixty-two and learned that the African Moors dominated parts of Italy and had even captured Sicily in 878 A.D.

"Your move," William said again.

Terry looked at the board momentarily. The history of her ancestors was so mind-boggling that she had no idea the game would be over in two moves. She moved Diana, the queen's knight, two spaces up and to the right. Then she began reading again.

William was counting on her to keep reading so he could checkmate her in four moves. As far as he was concerned, she ran her mouth about beating him so it would serve her right to lose in four moves. He let her read for about ten minutes without interruption, hoping she would be anxious to move again and wouldn't bother looking at his position. Finally, he moved Poseidon, the King's bishop, into position. He waited another ten minutes as Terry was reading rapidly now—the pages ruffled loudly as she turned them.

"Your move," he told her.

"Okay," she said mechanically. Without looking, she moved Diana up two spaces and to the left.

"Checkmate," he said calmly.

"Okay," Terry said almost inaudibly. Her lackadaisical response to defeat stole the joy of beating her in four moves. Terry kept on reading—completely unmoved.

"Again?"

"Huh?" she said and then looked at him. "I'm sorry. Do you mind if we play again another time. This is so interesting."

"You want to take it with you?"

"Could I?" she asked enthusiastically.

"Just make sure you bring it back."

"No problem."

"It's almost five. The game will be starting in a few minutes anyway."

"Okay." Terry grabbed the other two volumes and they went into the family room.

✝✝✝

It was half-time and Terry really hadn't paid any attention to the game. She read almost the entire time. Occasionally, she'd looked up and then she'd start reading again, fascinated by the book and now she understood why William had gotten so upset about Ivy's comments concerning black men and white women. What she found more appealing was that there were three volumes dedicated to the subject of race-mixing.

"Terry, do you want to call it an evening so you can read?"

"I'm sorry, William. I don't mean to be rude, but this is so fascinating."

"It is, isn't it?"

"Yes. Would you mind if I took off?"

"No, it's okay."

"Are you sure?"

"Yeah, it's not a problem. The game is kind of boring now anyway. They've taken the starters out. Just promise me you'll talk to me about the books when you're done, okay?"

"I promise. I'm a fast reader. We can discuss them in a couple of weeks."

William walked her to the door and kissed her. As he watched her walk to her car, it occurred to him that he'd forgotten to ask her if she played spades. "Hey!" he yelled out. Terry turned around. "Cleve wanted me to ask you if you play spades. Do you?"

"Yes, as a matter of fact, I do."

"He wants to get together with him and Cheryl to play. Would you like to?"

"Sure, anything for you, darlin'." She flashed her smile.

"Well, I hope you play spades better than you play chess."

"I let you win in four moves to boost your ego."

"Yeah, right. Anyway, they cheat so I'll have to show you all of their signals so we'll have the advantage, okay?"

"You sly dog, you," she said, still smiling. Then she turned and started for her car again. When she got into the car, she saw the overnight bag she had brought with her, just in case she ended up staying the night. She thought about the earlier argument with William and laughed as she backed out of the driveway.

Chapter 28: How About Lunch?

The next day, William was sitting behind his desk trying to find the words to make his mother accept his decision to date Terry. A number of different scenarios entered his mind—all of them miserable failures. He knew she'd say, "Well, you haven't been seeing her that long. She's white. Why can't you find a black woman?" He thought about all the black women he'd dated since Francis's death; most of them were nice women from his mother's church, who wanted to marry him before he even picked them up.

William was ready to move on with his life, but he wanted a woman who was more like himself—a woman who had similar interests and a personality that meshed with his. The key to a marriage or any other relationship was compatibility, he believed. Any relationship lacking those essential ingredients would lead to disaster; no matter how nice the woman was or how beautiful. In Terry, he'd found a charming, congenial woman with intelligence that matched his own. She was also strong with a mind of her own and he liked that.

William wondered if Francis would approve and decided she probably would. On her deathbed, she told him to find another who he could be content with and have lots of children. "Be patient and look around," she said. "The right woman will be an asset. She will help you continue what you've built on your own. She'll be good for you and help you live again. The wrong woman will be a liability. She'll be a nuisance and she'll cause you much heartache. Wait a while, is all I ask. You'll know her when she comes to you." When he remembered her words, it reminded him of what they had together. He missed her at that moment. *She was so unselfish*, he thought.

William knew an interoffice romance would eventually cause some serious problems with the staff, and decided to remove himself from the environment to alleviate any conflicts of interests from the onset during their Monday morning colloquy. He promised James he'd announce the promotions this morning, but he'd add a little something extra, too.

He heard Jeannine come in. She turned the radio on and sat at her desk. He buzzed her on the speaker and said, "Jeannine, could you come in here for a second before you get too busy?"

Surprised he was there before her, she walked in and asked, "What are you doing here? How did your weekend go?"

Jeannine was wearing a French vanilla, ribbed, three-quarter-length sleeve sweater with a ballet neck and a black twill skirt. The outfit showed off her vivacious curves. She wore her hair up, which unveiled her queen-like African features. Her skin was dark, smooth, and flawless. An effervescent smile emerged as she was expecting good news.

He could tell she was anxious to find out what happened with Terry. "You're looking especially nice today."

"You like." She turned around the way models do on a runway.

"Jonathan is a lucky man."

"He sure is."

"You crazy, girl." He laughed. "Listen, I want you to start packing our things; we're moving to the new building today. When everyone arrives, let me know. I'll make the announcement. Get my dad on the phone, will you?" There was a bit of apprehension in his voice.

"What's wrong? Did the Toronto trip go sour?"

William knew what she meant and decided to put her at ease, as he trusted her far more than the others. He gave the Valedictorian speech as a senior, and was the guest speaker at every graduation since he'd moved back to the bay area. After his speech at her graduation, she came up to him and they talked. She was obviously intelligent, and her enthusiasm was infectious. He hired her on the spot.

"Jeannine, I want you to know I appreciate what you did for Terry and me. I hope it works out, but I still have my doubts. That's one reason why we're moving outta here today, instead of October as planned."

"So it worked out between you then, huh?"

"Well, we're going to try this thing and see. Honestly, I think it has potential, but like I said, I have my doubts."

"Why, because she's white?"

"That, and my position in the community. I'm considered a leader for black causes and I want to be taken seriously. You can understand that, can't you?"

"Yeah, but at some point, you have to think about yourself, and what's good for you. You know what I'm sayin'?"

"Yes, I do. But tell me this. Would you date a white guy?"

"You mean if Jonathan and I weren't together? Maybe. It depends on the white man, I guess. Let me put it to you this way. If I were in your shoes, and a man, any man, black, white, red, or green, cared for me the way Dr. Moretti cares for you, yes, definitely, without a doubt."

"So, you wouldn't feel beholden to the community at all?"

"Yes, I would, but I'd be willing to deal with the race thing if he was worth the trouble."

"You serious?"

"Yes, I'm very serious." She sat down in one of the two leather chairs positioned in front of his desk. She leaned forward and rested her head on the palm of her right hand. "I wouldn't have helped her, if I didn't think she was good for you. Besides, there have been plenty of black women before me who have done the same. Like Mildred Loving. You know who she was, right?"

"Yes, she was the woman who married the white man down South somewhere and the Supreme Court ended up striking down the laws making interracial marriages a crime."

"Well, it isn't just her. It's a lot of them. I was tellin' Dr. Moretti about all the black women I had read about in *Ebony* magazine, of all places. I made her memorize them, in fact."

"Yeah, tell me about it."

"Worked, huh?" She grinned.

"Let me put it this way. We've decided to see each other secretly for a while and we'll see from there. Back to the white man thing. Guess who likes you?"

"Dr. Beverly," she said, without hesitation.

He was just about to ask her how she knew when Jeannine seemed to be reading his mind. "A woman always knows. He's cute enough. I might have given him a shot, if I didn't have Jonathan. You know Dr. Cameron likes Jonathan, don't you?"

"Ivy? Really? You should have heard her up in Toronto, talking about how she didn't find black men attractive."

"Hey, any time a white woman says she's not attracted to black men specifically, she is. She may not be aware of it, but she is. If she gets involved with one, she ends up going off the deep end. I mean, this kind of white woman falls hard for a brotha when she realizes color doesn't make a difference."

"Not to change the subject, but you knew Francis pretty well. Do you think she would approve of Terry?"

"As a woman, definitely. But I'm sure she'd be concerned about some of the same things you are."

"So you think she would have been okay with me seeing her?"

"I don't know, but considering how long you've been looking, or at least waiting for the right one, I think she would be happy you two made that move. She liked Terry. You know that, don't you?"

"Yeah, I know."

"If you want to know the truth about it, I think it was out of respect for Francis that Dr. Moretti didn't pounce on you as soon as she and her doggish-ass husband broke up. He actually tried to get with me while they were still married. He'd come over to my desk with that 'I wanna fuck you' look in his eyes, knowing full well I was with Jonathan."

"That's sexual harassment. How come you never said anything about it?"

"Because I didn't need to. After I told him about himself, he quit coming around. That's all any real woman has to do. They don't need to be filin' these sexual harassment charges all the time. All they need to do, most of the time anyway, is stand up to these horny men, and they'll back off."

They could hear the staff assembling in the conference room. William wondered if Jonathan had made it there yet. He wanted to speak with him. "Speaking of Jonathan, I want him to take one of the five offices now. He's ready. He's been working with me in group sessions anyway. They know him and they're comfortable with him. What do you think?"

"He'll be excited. Remember when he first came in here?"

"Yeah, I remember."

"He was pitiful, wasn't he?"

"Sure was. He came in here talking about he wanted a job like mine. I remember asking him what he was willing to do to get a job like this. And he said, 'Whatever I have to. I'll go to school for a couple of years like you, then I can have an office like this and drive a car like yours.' It was all I could do to keep from falling out of my chair."

"Yeah, but look at my baby now." Her eyes were full of hope and expectations. "All he has left is his dissertation, and he's done. He'll have a job and we can get married. I remember him trying to take me out and he didn't have a slug in his pocket."

They both laughed.

William said, "He has come a long way, hasn't he?"

"Yes, he has."

"I think you had a lot to do with his success."

"Dr. Wise, any good woman will have that kind of effect on a man."

"I agree. Well, look, I think everybody's here now, or should be. Get my dad on the phone and tell them I'll be right in."

"Okay."

Jeannine was about to leave when William started speaking again. "Oh, yeah. Then get Terry on the phone for me. And don't forget to keep our little secret."

"You know I wouldn't say anything, Dr. Wise. And I'm glad you're going to give the relationship a chance."

Jeannine left the office and moments later, he heard her on the speaker-phone saying, "Your dad is on line one." He picked up the phone.

"Hi, Dad."

"How you doin', son? Life treatin' you well?"

"I'm doing well, Dad, and you?"

"Just fine."

"Mom okay?"

"Yeah, she's fine. She had a closing this morning on one of her properties in Oakland."

"Do you have any plans this afternoon? Say around twelve?"

"Besides driving my cab? Nothin'. Why?"

"What time is your lunch break then?

"I can take lunch any time I want, but you know I don't normally take lunch breaks because there are so many tourists and they tip good."

"I understand, but can you carve out an hour for me?"

"Where we goin'?"

"How about the Cannery?"

"Are you going let me order what I want? You know your mother don't want me eating ribs too often."

"Excuse me, Dr. Wise," Jeannine interrupted. "Dr. Moretti is holding on line two for you."

"Okay, thanks," he said, covering up the transmitter. "When's the last time you had ribs?" The leather crackled when he leaned back in the chair.

"Fourth of July. But you know Labor Day is coming in a week or so."

"I won't tell if you don't, but it won't be an all-you–can-eat rib-off either, okay?"

"Okay. In that case, let's go to Mr. Big Stuff's. They have a better view of the bay."

"Okay, Dad, I'll meet you there."

"Okay, son. Bye."

"Bye, Dad."

"Terry?" he said after pushing line two.

"Yes, William. And how are you this morning?"

"Just fine. Listen, I'm wondering if you'd like to meet my dad this afternoon."

"This is kind of sudden, don't you think?"

"Yes, it is, but I would like you to meet him anyway. I thought about this last night after you left. Remember when my mother called me when we were in Toronto?"

"Uh-huh. Just as things were getting hot and heavy. I was wondering when they were going to get hot and heavy again." There was a sexy tone in her voice.

"In due season. Let's take our time, baby."

"Do you realize your voice sounds sexy as hell?"

"Yep. But back to my mom though."

"Okay, you tease."

"Anyway, since my mom called Toronto, I know she can't wait to ask me about you. I think if my dad met you first, it could all go a little easier. I'm sure if anyone will support us, besides Sterling and Jeannine, he will."

"Are you sure you want to do this now?"

"Do you have a problem with it?" Her question gave him a momentary uneasiness. "Are you having second thoughts?"

"No. It's just that I thought you wanted to keep it a secret, is all."

"I told you, my mom knows already, which means he knows already. In a couple of days, she'll be asking about you. I can tell you now that she's thinking about the wedding already. Me meeting someone and having children is very important to her. I need to let him meet you now, and I'll talk to her later, okay?"

"You don't have to convince me to meet your dad, William. I'd love to. I was simply thinking about what we agreed to, is all."

"Okay, so meet me at Mr. Big Stuff's at Fisherman's Wharf at about 12:30, or so. My dad has to leave and get back to work so try not to be late, okay?"

"Sure, no problem. I have a two o'clock appointment anyway."

"If you get there early, get a table or something until I call you over."

"Will do, big boy." It was her best impression of Mae West.

"Okay, I'll meet you in the conference room and I'd work on the Mae West impression if I were you. Bye," he said and hung up the phone.

Terry could hear him laughing right before the line disconnected.

††††

William walked into the conference room and sat at the head of the table. "I have good news. Today will be my last day at this office. As a matter of fact, I won't be at any of the offices for a couple of months. As you all know, I plan to open the substance abuse clinic the first part of November and I will be leaving anyway. But due to some recent commitments..." He looked at Jeannine and Terry briefly; they were both looking at each other with tiny smirks on their faces. "... I've decided to move on now. That means Dr. Fredrickson, Dr. Moretti, Dr. Cameron, Dr. Beverly, and Dr. Jonathan Darling will be running the five offices."

"I'm not a doctor yet," Jonathan was quick to point out.

"We have no doubt that you'll make it though," Ivy assured him. She always liked Jonathan. He was the one person who genuinely got along with her.

"Absolutely no doubt at all," William added. "Each of you will manage an office with your own staff. That means no more floating. The clients will come to one office." They applauded. "Choice of offices will be by seniority. That means James has first choice. Then Terry, Ivy, and Bernie. Jonathan, you get whatever's left. There will be raises and benefits to go with the added responsibility. I will, however, continue one-on-one therapy here in Sausalito."

They all applauded again and murmured among themselves with big smiles on their faces.

"All of you will be reporting to James from here on out. James will be reporting to me. If there are any problems, talk to James first, then come to me. I expect the best from you and I expect you to support James's decisions. And anyone who doesn't will be in serious trouble."

They all laughed.

"If there are no questions, we're done."

All the doctors came over and thanked him personally for their promotions. The other members of his staff began talking to each other as they left the conference room. Jonathan waited until everyone left. Then he went over to him to shake his hand. William pulled him to his chest, and they hugged each other for a second or two, and then stepped back.

"I'm proud of you, Jonathan."

"Thank you for the opportunity. I appreciate the confidence you've shown in me. I won't let you down."

"I know you won't. If, and when there's a problem, take it to James. Don't come runnin' to me first. You understand what I'm tellin' you?"

"Yeah, I understand. You don't want me to take advantage of our relationship as black men, right?"

"Right. You still have a lot to prove. I believe you can do this; otherwise, I wouldn't have given you the opportunity. Remember what I told you when we first met years ago. It is the same thing my father told me and something black people have believed for decades."

"I know. I have to be twice as good as them."

"That's right. Take pride in what you're doing and it will work out. That means you're going to have to stay later and get here earlier than everyone else. Then you'll gain their respect."

"I understand. And I won't let you down."

"You better not. Now get to work."

"Yes, sir." Jonathan saluted.

†††

William had gotten to Mr. Big Stuff's fifteen minutes early and ordered ribs for himself and his father. It was a brisk 70 degrees and windy. He was looking out the window at the spectacular view of the San Francisco Bay. From where he was sitting, he could see the Golden Gate Bridge and Alcatraz. There was a group of tourists just about to enter the fabled prison. He took a big swallow of his ice water and looked toward the entrance for his dad. Moments later he saw him. He was wearing a pair of black slacks, a gray turtleneck sweater, and a Raiders cap. With the exception of some scar tissue over his eyes, lifelong mementos from Alverez Sanchez, he looked good to be sixty-four years old. He was cleanshaven and he had a touch of gray around his temple and in his moustache.

"Did you see the Raiders beat up on the Niners last night, son?"

"Yeah, I saw it."

"Your mother was mad as all get out. She kept screamin' at the TV, 'Put Jerry in. Put Jerry in.' I laughed so hard, I almost busted my gut listening to her scream. Like they would actually put him in for a preseason game."

"Sounds like you guys still have fun together."

"We do. So did you order already?"

"Yeah. I was wondering when you were going to get around to that."

"You know how I love me some ribs." He laughed a little. "So what did you want to talk about? Your new girlfriend?" He had a serious look on his face. His father knew this meeting was about something important. William showed no signs of surprise. He knew his mother had briefed him, just like he told Terry. "Yeah, your mother woke me up all excited about some girl you met. I figured that's what this is about. I figured something else out, too."

"What's that, Dad?"

"Since you called me for lunch and you're going to let me have some ribs, there must be a problem with the girl. She must be white, or somethin'. You know how we've been hoping you'd find someone since Francis's death. If your mother wakes up like that, she must be right on it. So, am I right? Is she white? You know it doesn't make any difference to me, son."

"Yeah, dad, she's white."

"I knew it," he said, with a youthful jocularity that seemed to stem from the knowledge of being right. "Now for the big question. How she look?"

"Does it matter, Dad?"

"Yes, it does. You remember when you were a teenager and we had this discussion, don't you?"

"I knew you were going to bring that up."

"Can I gloat just a little then?"

"Do you have to?"

"Yep. Because I told you when you got older you might meet some white woman that you like. And you said you didn't find white women attractive and you couldn't see yourself dating one, let alone marrying one, remember?"

The waitress brought their lunches. They thanked her and began eating.

"Yes, I remember, but that was a long time ago," he said after taking a swallow of his tea.

"So, how she look?"

"She's attractive."

"One to ten?"

"Eight, maybe nine."

"Well, that's good. At least she's not a dog. You know how I hate that. It makes us all look bad when a black man grabs the first white woman that'll have him. Now that that's outta the way, what do you want to talk about?"

"You remember telling me to be careful who I date because I could end up married to her?" His father nodded, then took a bite of his ribs. "Well, I live by those words when it comes to women. That's why it's taken me so long to find someone that I would even consider marrying. I mean, it's like you said, if you date her, you could marry her. So I wanted you to know she was white first. I knew I could count on your support, if no one else's in the family. Well, you and Sterling of course, and probably Karen."

"You like her a lot already, huh?"

"Yes, we kinda hit it off as soon as she convinced me that the only reason I didn't date her was because she's white. You know, I've been working with her for seven years now."

"Son, you don't have to convince me. The fact that you asked me to come here for this says it all. It's your mother you have to worry about. When she woke me up the other night, all she could talk about was the grandchildren. She was so happy." He laughed. "Considerin' that she knows you have a girl now, this is going to be real interestin'." He pulled out his bottle of hot sauce and shook out about ten drops of the tangy liquid into his barbecue sauce. Then he took another bite of his ribs, and washed it down with several swallows of his lemonade.

"Dad!" William said, raising his voice.

"What? It needs some flavor, that's all."

"Hot sauce wasn't a part of our agreement. Does Mom know you carry that around with you?"

"What's bothering you about the woman, son?" his father asked, to avoid the question.

"Nothing's bothering me about her. She's all right. I like her a lot. I guess I've been in denial for sometime now. But, I'm concerned about my status in the black community. I want to be taken serious when I fight for black causes. I want to continue speaking at NAACP dinners and any other black functions. But I feel like if I do, I can't take her. Which means I'd be hiding her and I don't want to do that forever. Just until I'm sure this relationship is going somewhere. I don't need the headache in the interim. But, assuming it flourishes, I can't keep her in the closet forever. You know what I mean?"

"Uh-huh." He finished off the bone he was working on. "But, son, that's a life choice you're going to have to make. You can't make people accept you and her being together. You have to do that. And if you can't do that, you need to leave it alone. If you don't, you'll end up hurtin' that woman. I can only assume she's crazy about you, if she had to convince you her color was the only thing standin' in the way. She must have spunk. I like her already. So how long has this been going on?"

"Two days."

"Two days!! Is that all?!"

"Yes. Two days."

"Two days ago is when your mother woke me up at four in the mornin'." Then he thought for a moment. "Hmm. Your mother must have ESP. This is going to be real interestin' when she finds out that the mother of her grandchildren is white. Well, who is this woman? Someone you work with or what?"

"Yeah. I told you she works with me."

"Good. At least you know her as a person and that's always good. You ain't sleeping with her, are you? You know that confuses things, don't you?"

"No, I'm not sleeping with her. And, yes, I know it confuses things. I listen to you, Dad. The older I get, the more sense you make."

Will saw Terry come in and take a seat. He looked at his watch; it was twelve-thirty. He liked her punctuality.

"Well, it's about time you realized that." His father smiled.

"Would you like to meet her then?"

"Yeah. When?"

"Right now."

"Is she here?" his father said, looking around the restaurant.

"Yes, she's here. I'll tell you what, Dad, you pick one since you're so caught up on the looks thing."

"Okay," his father said, still looking around the restaurant.

After a few seconds, he said, "The woman over there in the lavender business suit, right?"

Will looked at the woman. And he'd done it. He'd picked Terry out in a crowd.

"Right. Sitting alone gave it away, didn't it?"

"That, and her making an effort not to look this way. I saw her when she came in. You looked at her and your eyes brightened."

"So what do you think?"

"I don't know. I have to talk to her first."

"No, Dad, I mean in the looks department. Does she pass inspection, or not?"

"Yes, but I still want to talk to her."

"Okay."

He raised his hand to get her attention. Then he waved her over. Terry walked over to the table. She smiled at Mr. Wise as she took her seat. She looked into his face, studying every line. She was looking for the resemblance, but there wasn't much. She saw the scar tissue over his eyes and wondered if he ever boxed professionally.

Mr. Wise looked at Terry's face, and saw the natural color in it. Her lips were thicker than the average white person. He wondered about her pedigree.

"How y'all doing today?" Terry asked.

"Terry, this is my dad. Dad, this is Dr. Terry Moretti."

"Pleased to meet you, Mr. Wise." She extended her hand.

"Pleased to meet you, too. We doin' just fine, and ya' self?"

"I'm doin' fine, too. And what about you?" she said, directing the comment to William.

"I'm great, now that I'm going to be working at the clinic from now on."

Mr. Wise said, "So you decided to move out of your office already, huh? That's good. It could cause problems with other people working for you. So y'all serious already, huh?"

Will continued eating quietly. He was waiting on Terry to respond, but she didn't know how to respond to the question without coming off like a desperate woman who couldn't find a man. So she said, "Well, Mr. Wise, I've liked your son for three years now. But we just decided to get together this past weekend in Toronto. I don't know if that makes us serious though."

"Three years, huh? If that ain't serious, I don't know what is," Mr. Wise said.

"Good point. Let me put it another way then. We've decided to see each other exclusively and William wanted you to know I wasn't a black woman."

"Good answer," Mr. Wise said. "So do you go into all of your relationships with that philosophy in mind?"

"What philosophy would that be, Mr. Wise?"

"Terry," Will began, "I forgot to tell you that my father is huge on philosophical discussions. Be careful."

"I see," she said. "So is that where you get it from?"

"Yeah. At our house, we had philosophical discussions all the time. And my dad wouldn't allow 'I don't know' answers, like parents do today. He forced us to think about what we were doing and to evaluate things in terms of what could happen down the road. So, I'm telling you, if you get into a discussion with him, it could turn into a cross examination of your philosophical ideology of life itself."

His father laughed. "I'll take it easy on her, son. Was I really that bad?"

"Worse," he said. "First you'd ask us questions that you knew we didn't know. Then you made sure that question was on our young minds until we went to bed. Then you had a story to tell about every single issue you discussed, complete with a myriad of examples. You'd go on and on and on."

They all laughed.

"It worked didn't it, son? You're a thinker now, ain't you?"

"That he is," Terry agreed. "It's part of his charm. I find intelligence very attractive."

Mr. Wise said, "Uh-huh. So…you from the South, huh?"

"That I am."

William suddenly felt uncomfortable when he noticed that people were now staring at them. He could only speculate as to why they were suddenly paying attention to them. *It was because a tall, good-looking Italian woman was now sitting with two black men.* There were a couple of black women sitting to his immediate right. The one with her back to him turned around and looked at them. She shook her head in disgust. Then she turned around and said something to the other black woman, and they both laughed. He couldn't help but feel as though they were discussing him. The waitress came over and said, "Is everything okay?"

"Can I get a refill of lemonade please?" Mr. Wise asked. "And could you put a lot of ice in it. As a matter of fact, if it's not too much trouble, fill the glass with ice, then pour the lemonade over the ice, okay?"

"No, problem. Can I get you anything, ma'am?"

"No, I'm fine."

The waitress left.

"Where 'bout in the South you from?"

"Good ol' Biloxi, Mississippi. Our house wasn't far from Gulf Port. Do you know where that is?"

"Sure do. Sterling, my other son, had a case down there once. When he came back, he said they grow white women differently down there, and from what I can see, he was right."

Terry laughed. "Thank you."

The waitress returned with the lemonade and said, "Is that enough ice for you?"

"Yeah, that's just the way I like it. Thank you."

"You're welcome," she said. Then she placed the check on the table and cheerfully said, "Have a good day."

"Oh, okay. So where did you get that tan from?"

"Here—we—go." Will laughed.

Mr. Wise laughed also.

"What's so funny?" Terry asked.

"You'll see," William told her.

"Oh, y'all must be laughing about how I got my tan, huh?" She smiled. "Well, it isn't a tan actually."

"We know," they said in unison and laughed a little more.

"I guess I'd have pale skin and look more Nordic had the African Moors not invaded Sicily and taken her from the Normans, huh?" She joined the laughter.

With a confused frown on his face, his father asked soberly, "How did you know that?"

"I let her borrow some of my books, Dad."

Will watched the two black women get up and leave. He wondered if they could hear their discussion. They went to the cashier and then they looked back at him. They shook their heads again. William wondered if this was just the beginning, or the worst of it.

"And you read them, huh? Hmm." Suddenly, he was serious. "So what are your thoughts about what you've read?" He was gearing up for a debate with her. Depending on what she said, he would ask her more questions.

"What are you asking me, Mr. Wise?"

"I'm asking you if you believe what you've read."

"Yes, I do. I have Cherokee, Italian and Irish blood lines."

"What I'm asking you is do you believe that black Africans mixed their blood with white women centuries ago?"

"Yes."

"So you believe Italians, or Sicilians, or whatever, have African blood in them?"

"Yes. Why not?"

He frowned. "Why do you believe something as incredible as that?"

"Well, present company excluded, in my opinion, men, once they invade a country, can't wait to invade the women; no matter what color they are. And since white men did it in good ol' Mississippi and all the other slave states, who am I to say the black Africans were any different? Now, I hope I haven't offended you, Mr. Wise."

William and his father looked at each other. His father smiled at him, giving his approval without saying a word. He knew it would be a lot easier now if things got serious.

"Impressive...very impressive. What do you think about the one-drop rule, given what you just said?"

She thought for a moment, and then said, "Honestly, I think it's an ugly and stupid rule that absolves white men of their responsibilities to the children they sired then, and the ones they sire now. It robs the children of their collective heritage. I mean, if we subscribe to the Out Of Africa Theory, or even believe the Biblical account of man's beginning, it's difficult to argue that white people were here first.

"But, ya know, I think I should have been taught more about other cultures in grade school, or at home. Don't hate me for saying this, but when I first read some of this stuff, I rejected it. I thought about it all last night and when I put it together with what I'd learned in Cultural Anthropology, Biology, Physiology, and just the fact that you can't get black people from white people, but you can get white people from black people, it made sense to me. It angered me when I realized this information had been kept from me. Maybe that's why racism goes on so much. The things I learned in school can make white people have a superiority complex because we think we invented everything. For example, how did the African Moors get to Europe and Sicily without ships if they didn't build them? Did they swim over or what? It's little things like that. I don't know, but if more people knew this stuff, maybe the races could get along better. I don't know. What do y'all think?"

"I think she's a diamond in the rough, son," Mr. Wise said. Then he looked at Terry again. "Can you cook? Do you like professional sports? You know, football, basketball, boxing. That's what he likes."

"Yes, I can cook. And yes, I like sports. I was a long distance runner at Stanford and I also high-jumped."

"Here's a boxing question for you. Who's the greatest boxer of all time?"

"What do I get if I get it right?" she asked playfully.

"You get nothing, but if you miss it, you're out," he quipped. "Naw, I'm just kiddin' wit' cha. I think you're okay."

"Okay, do you want to know pound for pound, or do you want to know who the greatest heavyweight was?"

"So you do know something about the boxing game. Okay, I'm looking for the pound for pound best boxer."

"In that case, it would be Sugar Ray Robinson," she said.

Surprised she knew, he asked, "How did you know that?"

"Because Ali said so. If he says Sugar Ray Robinson's the best pound for pound, who am I to argue with him?"

"Last question. You know my wife had a premonition about you two the other night, so I have to ask, when's the wedding?"

They all laughed for a moment.

"Dad, it's only been two days."

"I know, but it'll happen if you both are strong enough. Besides, you've been workin' together a long time. You know if you like somebody's ways, or not. Plus, you'll be shootin' blanks by the time you find somebody, if you don't get married soon. And that'll kill your mother. That is, if she don't have a heart attack when she finds out about you, Terry."

"I know. William told me how black women feel."

"Well, as long as y'all know it won't be easy," he told them. He looked at his watch; it was almost one o'clock. "If there's nothin' else, there's a lot of money to be made driving folk around to the sights. So I gotta go get it."

"Yeah, I have a two o'clock appointment, too."

"Okay, we can go. Thanks for coming, Dad."

"No problem, son. It was my pleasure. Glad you finally found somebody. Terry, I hope to see you again soon. You good people. I like the way you think."

"Thank you. It was a pleasure meeting you also."

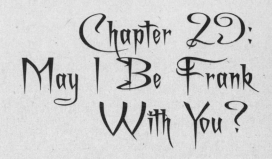

Chapter 29:
May I Be Frank
With You?

San Francisco
August 1997

S terling walked into his new office at about ten in the morning. He was immediately taken in by the lavish outer office, and wondered what his office would be like. He saw Tiffany sitting at her circular desk with the phone to her ear, and remembered what she had told him about the offices when he was in the Caymans. He expected the best, but what he saw exceeded his expectations. He walked up to Tiffany's desk. She raised a finger and mouthed, "It's Kym Daniels. Do you want to take this?" He shook his head and mouthed, "Take a message." Tiffany nodded her head and Sterling walked into his office.

The moment he walked in, he felt like a child in a candy store. His office was in the corner of the building with two views, just as Tiffany had told him. He walked over to his desk and sat down in the huge leather chair, which seemed to absorb him. He could hear the air escape the cushions when he sat down. He swiveled around and looked out the window at the Golden Gate Bridge. Then he swiveled the other way and looked at the Bay Bridge. He couldn't help smiling. *I finally made it!* He swiveled around again and saw two doors, wondering which one was the bedroom.

He walked over to the first door and opened it. It led to the elevator. *This is going to be great!* Then he opened the other door and saw the bedroom. It also had a view. It was like a small one-room apartment, or hotel room, complete with all the comforts of home. He wondered who he'd have in there first. The way he felt at the moment, he thought of suspending his rule against sleeping with Tiffany and bringing her in there to try it out first. Then he laughed to himself.

Suddenly, he heard beeping and Tiffany's voice, "Sterling?"

He looked around the room. He saw a red light on the telephone, which was on the nightstand next to the bed. He went over to the phone.

"Yeah?"

"It's nice, isn't it?"

"Yeah, it sure is."

"I would come in there and break the bed in for you, but Kym Daniels is on her way up."

"What?"

"Yeah, I told her you'd be in any second. She said she had some important information you might need. Do you want me to stall her, or what?"

"No, I was going to call her anyway. Let her in and hold all my calls."

She laughed. "I guess I'll have to wait my turn in there, huh?"

"I guess."

†††

"Sterling, Ms. Daniels is here," Tiffany's voice rang out through the intercom.

"Send her in."

A few seconds later, Kym walked into the office. She was five feet six and weighed about a hundred-ten pounds. She was wearing a plum jacket and skirt, a white collarless blouse, and plum pumps. Her shoulder-length hair was permed and looked wild with curls, yet controlled. Their eyes met and instantly they both knew what was on each other's mind. The only question was when, and where?

Sterling smiled. "Have a seat, Kym."

Kym was a woman who'd had everything. No one denied her anything. She was used to controlling men and Sterling was the ultimate challenge. Not only did he turn her down, but he was black. And black men had always wanted her, and tried to get her in bed. She sat down and looked into his eyes, having every intention of sleeping with him.

"May I be frank with you, Sterling?"

"Always, Kym."

"I know why you finally called me after all this time."

"You think so, huh?"

"I know so. And as much as I'd like to think you finally came to your senses after all these years of making me wait, I know you really want to get back at my father for firing you."

Sterling couldn't help but laugh.

"Can you deny it?" She smiled.

"To a degree, yes. Look, Kym, I'm not going to bullshit you. Yes, there is a measure of revenge, but I've always found you attractive. You know that, right?"

"Yes, I know that."

"Then you also know I'm not looking for anything serious either, right?"

"We'll see about that. You don't mind if I try to lasso you, do you?"

"Only if you don't have some sort of metamorphosis that turns you into Glenn Close, and shit." He laughed. "You know, get fatal on me."

Kym laughed. "I won't promise you anything, but I'll try not to. But don't you get crazy either if you enjoy it more than you think, okay?"

"You don't even have to worry about it. Now, what was the important information you had to tell me?"

Kym's expression changed. She looked serious now. He knew what he was about to hear would be the truth. People always looked a certain way when they told the truth, he thought.

"You're probably going to have a hard time believing this, but my father didn't fire you, Sterling."

Agitated, he said, "You're right. I am having a hard time believing that; especially when I was in his office when he did it."

"Well, okay, he did fire you. But he didn't want to. It hurt him to have to do it. Didn't you notice he was drinking vodka? You know he wouldn't be drinking at that hour unless something was bothering him."

"If it hurt him so much, why did he do it?"

"Because Adrienne Bellamy told him to." She could tell he knew who she was by the way his eyebrows furrowed. "So you know who she is, huh?"

"Yes, I know her. She's the one who set me up with this office and everything you see in here."

"I guess it's true then."

"What's that?"

"She buys everything and everyone."

Kym knew she shouldn't have said that, but she couldn't help herself. It just came out of her mouth.

Sterling stared at her for a second, or two. "So you think she bought me? Is that it, Kym?"

"Well, if she didn't, why would she supply you with such an elaborate office in the same building ten floors up from my father's offices?"

Sterling stood to his feet and looked out the window. He was considering what Jericho had told him while he was in the Caymans. *What's going on? What does Bellamy really want?*

"Who was here before you, Sterling? Did she simply pick up the phone and have whoever was here move out?"

"Kym, I don't know what's going on. All I know for sure is that I was fired on the greatest day of my life by a man who I thought was a friend and mentor. Then the next thing I know, Adrienne Bellamy calls me and offers me the world. Now, you're telling me she orchestrated the entire thing? For what reason?"

"I don't know. Only you know why she hired you. What does she have you doing for her?"

"I can't tell you that, Kym, but I appreciate the information. I can handle it from here."

Kym walked up behind him and whispered in his ear, "I guess you're not in the mood now, huh?"

Sterling was quiet. He was still thinking about Adrienne Bellamy. He decided they needed to talk again. Kym, still standing behind him, reached around and massaged his tool. She could feel him stiffening. He turned around, and they embraced in a deep, passionate kiss. Then he pulled away and picked up the phone.

"Tiffany, set up a meeting with Ms. Bellamy. Don't accept no for an answer and hold all my calls for the next couple of hours."

Tiffany laughed loudly. "Okay."

Then Sterling turned back to Kym and kissed her again.

Chapter 30: The Meeting

Three days had passed since Tiffany contacted Winston, Adrienne Bellamy's driver, who then called Adrienne in Sun City, Africa, and told her it was of vital importance that she fly back to the States immediately to meet with Sterling about the Warren case. Shortly after Tiffany left the office, Adrienne and her driver entered the outer office.

Sterling, still in his office looking over the Warren file, heard the door open and close. He thought it was Tiffany coming back to get her keys, or something. He didn't expect Adrienne to show up for another hour, or so.

Sterling looked up when he heard his door open. Adrienne and Winston walked in. Winston was wearing the traditional chauffeur's uniform, but Adrienne was dressed in a red, double-breasted tweed pantsuit. It was hard for him to believe that this blond, blue-eyed, white woman was black. He looked at her nose and her lips. They were distinctly Caucasoid.

Sterling could tell she was angry by the scowl on her face, but it didn't intimidate him. Instead of standing up to greet her, Sterling remained seated, leaned back and narrowed his eyes so she would know he was angry also.

When Adrienne looked at him, she could see there was something different about him. She wasn't sure what it was, but it had the feel of quiet assurance, and it made her nervous. She wondered if he knew her secret, but she couldn't let him think she was worried, so she said, "This had better be important, Mr. Wise."

"Oh, it is, Adrienne," Sterling said forcefully.

Adrienne knew Sterling knew something. They weren't on a first-name basis. She knew he wouldn't take those kinds of liberties without having an ace up his sleeve.

"As a matter of fact," Sterling continued, "you might wanna have Winston wait in the outer office."

Now, Adrienne was sure he knew she was black. *But how?* Then it occurred to her that Jericho must have found out and told him.

"There are no secrets between Winston and me."

So I was right. He is ridin' Miss Daisy. Sterling wanted to laugh, but knew it was inappropriate. "Please, have a seat."

Adrienne and Winston sat in chairs in front of his desk.

"What is this all about, Mr. Wise?"

"You tell me, Adrienne. You're the puppet master."

"My compliments to Jericho. He's quite thorough."

Sterling didn't say anything. He just looked at her with total disdain in his eyes.

Adrienne could see how he felt about her. She'd seen that look many times when she was a child growing up in Harlem. She remembered how dark-skinned blacks like Sterling often hated her for looking white, but being black, while others envied her because she had the best of both worlds and could go places they couldn't. She remembered how black men wanted her because they thought she was white.

Adrienne said, "I've seen that look before."

"What look?"

"Don't be coy, Mr. Wise," she said, in a quiet, soft, inviting tone. "You think I'm what they call a sellout, do you not?"

"What?"

"Ignorance doesn't become you. You know what I mean. An Uncle Tom, a wannabe white bitch. You know the clichés."

"It's not so much that you're hiding who you are," he said and leaned forward. "It's the fact that you don't want your son to marry a black woman when he himself is black, as was your mama. Or did you call her mother like the white folks?"

"Touché," she said, finally able to unwind now that her truth was known. "And yes, my mama, as I called her, was black, as you know. But you've forgotten what I told you the day I picked you. My problem with Victoria Warren has nothing to do with racial animus. It's practicality. You and I both know that sex between white men and black women is something reserved for bordellos and streetwalkers. It isn't winked at anymore—not if the man is going to sit in the seat of power. It's one thing to be rich and have a black wife, and quite another to run for president and have a black wife.

"You've got to understand that many of the people who run for office on the Democratic platform are the very ones who use the racial slurs. They're the people who make speeches lamenting the conditions of blacks, while privately they couldn't care less. Most of them know that if the condition of blacks change for the better, they have virtually no chance of being in office again.

"They know most blacks, when voting, only care about jobs, and keeping Affirmative Action alive. So they cast their lots with the Democratic Party, even though they totally disagree with much of their liberal rhetoric. They're nothing more than sharks feeding on the flesh of black people, who have not taken a serious look at all the issues on the table. You should hear them at dinner parties, and fundraisers, and board meetings. I'm the proverbial fly on the wall, you might say. Yet people like you, look at me, and judge me, and say absolutely nothing while many of the so-called black leaders are selling their own people down the river, while they live high on the hog."

Sarcastically, Sterling said, "And you're going to wave your magic wand and put a stop to the exploitation? Is that it?"

"I am putting a stop to it," she said, matter of factly. "But behind the scenes. I have to remain anonymous."

"How are you doing that?"

"Ten years from now, you'll see more integrated commercials than you've ever seen in your life. When Americans see these commercials day after day after day, attitudes will change. Changing hearts and minds is something no law can ever do. Television can—given enough time. At first there will be resistance to this. But, as the commercials continue to be shown, race will slowly become a thing of the past, ushering in an America worthy of the ideals of our Constitution." She paused to let her words sink in. "You probably think the only reason I set you up in your own practice is to get rid of Ms. Warren, right?"

"I suppose you were simply being benevolent, huh?"

"To a degree, yes. But think, my dear Sterling. Couldn't I have chosen practically any attorney to do this? I chose you."

"Why?"

"Because you were in the right place, at the right time. You had just won the Samuelson case. I had recently found out about the pregnancy. The Warren family will listen to you when you reason with them. Some other attorney may not have the opening you created for yourself. Besides, you were ready to go on your own. You don't need a prestigious firm anymore. Black people have to own businesses to effect change. As long as they're working for white people, they will be powerless. Trust me, when you own, you have influence. You can back whatever government officials you want."

"In other words, he who has the gold makes the rules."

"Exactly," she said, her confidence returning. "Having said that, what difference will it make if one black woman has an abortion so I can gain the White House in a few years?"

Sterling was thinking about what she said. It made sense to him. *Why not? The choice would still be Ms. Warren's.* He looked at Winston. He nodded.

"Well, what's it going to be, Sterling? I've set it all up for you. They need the money right now. Both parents have been fired from their jobs and she's lost her scholarship on fraud charges. I own the mortgage on their house and they will be homeless soon. All you have to do is ride in on a white horse and save the day. All will be restored with one phone call from me. Close this deal for me and all you have now will be yours. It's up to you."

Sterling thought for a moment and said, "Deal. It makes no difference to me. But if you get the White House, do the right thing."

"Good." She smiled. *If you only knew how close to death you really are.*

"My plane is waiting to take me back to Sun City. If you need anything, call Winston." She stood up, and extended her hand. "I bid you adieu."

When they left his office, Sterling looked out the window at the limousine. He saw them leave the building, get into the limo, and drive off. Then he opened the Warren file and found her parents' phone number. He picked up the phone and dialed the house. A man answered.

"Mr. Warren?"

"Yes?"

"Attorney Wise here. I understand you're having severe financial difficulties and I think I can alleviate them."

Chapter 31:
Now Let's Play
Some Spades

Months passed and William and Terry's relationship blossomed. Late at night, they spent countless hours talking on the phone, discussing everything from religion to politics. During those long discussions, he realized she was right when she said they knew each other well. They were more compatible than he could have hoped. All he needed now was time—time to lay aside the doubts of it not working— time to decide if he would be willing to deal with the consequences of dating her openly, or even marrying her.

One day, after finishing up some financial matters at the Bank of America, he went up to the 52nd floor to have some of the Carnelian Room's award-winning cuisine. He was finishing his dessert and enjoying the stunning, 360-degree panoramic views of San Francisco when he noticed an interracial couple about to leave the restaurant. The woman was white, around five-nine with sandy brown hair, and weighed about two hundred pounds, give or take ten pounds. The man was black, same height as her, and a little on the chunky side.

As they left the restaurant, everyone stared at them. One black woman shook her head in a manner that bespoke the rejection she felt at that moment and probably the rejection many black women feel when they see a white woman with a black man. Perhaps she would not have felt so bad had the woman looked more like Cindy Crawford.

The couple seemed to be impervious to the attention people of both races paid them. They seemed undaunted by a society that talks out of both sides of its mouth. He wanted to be more like the couple he'd seen, but he knew he wasn't there yet, and it bothered him. Terry knew this, but kept it to herself because she promised to be patient. The only place they'd been out together was the Marin County Gun Club.

Terry took Will, as she now called him, to the club and was teaching him to shoot her .9mm Baretta. It had taken him some time to learn to squeeze the trigger instead of pulling it. Terry told him he had seen too many Clint Eastwood movies. Soon he was hitting the target. It wasn't long before he purchased his own weapon. He practiced when he could and was on his way to becoming an expert like Terry.

Normally when they went to the club, they'd go to the indoor range, shoot for a while, then go back to his place and eat and talk, or whatever. But this time, Terry suggested they go to the clubhouse for a late evening lunch. His first thought was to say "no" but he could tell she really wanted to start getting out. The members of the club usually treated him well, until they saw him with her.

Several men were friendly at first, then Terry would come out of the women's restroom, or they'd enter the gun club together. The men were not aware of it, but their expressions changed immediately. He could tell by the looks on their faces that they were thinking he was the typical successful black man who'd made it and now had to have the ultimate prize. Before they saw Terry, they would talk to him openly about his profession, his political beliefs, and his time at Harvard. It was nice to feel accepted, but because of his relationship with her, he knew it wouldn't last, and it generally didn't.

They walked into the clubhouse and were seated immediately. Right away, people began staring. Their reactions served as a reminder to what he'd witnessed at the Carnelian Room and any time there was an interracial couple in the vicinity of disapproving, or curious eyes.

Terry could see he was uncomfortable and said, "What's wrong, Will?"

"Nothing."

"Will, I know something's bothering you. Please…tell me what it is."

"It doesn't bother you that people are staring at us every time we come to the club?"

She looked around the room and said with her infectious smile, "Darlin', those women are just staring because you're so handsome, is all."

"I suppose the men are staring at you because you're so good-looking, huh?"

"Of course," she said, with a devilish grin that disarmed him as usual. "Tell ya what. We can make our order to go. I'm starting to get my cramps anyway. You know how bad they can be. Remember the time Ivy and I had that huge argument last year when my cramps were real bad? I can usually tolerate her, but with my cramps the way they were, I didn't care anymore. I simply had to tell her a thing, or two."

Will laughed. "Do you have your Midol with you?"

"No, I don't. But they're not too bad yet."

"Okay. But let's eat here if you can make it through lunch."

"You mean it," she beamed.

"Yeah, I mean it. We gotta start getting out sooner, or later. I know you prefer it to be sooner."

"Good. It's about time," she said. "It's about time for some other things, too."

Terry wasn't aware of it, but she had a way of saying things or making facial expressions that gave him a stiff erection. They stared at each other for a couple of seconds and then the waitress came to take their order.

"Are you ready to order? Or do you need a few more minutes?"

"I'm ready. Are you?"

"No, not just yet."

"I'll come back in a few minutes. Okay?"

"Okay."

The waitress left. Will could still feel the daggers coming from every direction in the restaurant. He wondered if he'd ever get over this feeling of being watched. When he looked at the people, they'd look away. He decided to keep staring at them to see what they'd do. Eventually, they would look again and he'd be staring at them. Finally, they stopped looking.

"What are you looking at, Will?"

"It's not important. Hey, order me the grilled chicken salad. I'll be right back. I have to go to the little boy's room."

"Okay."

Will left and the waitress returned. Terry felt the pain increasing, but she wasn't about to ruin their first "real" lunch together.

"Are you ready now, ma'am?"

"Yes."

As soon as the waitress left, one of the men who gawked at her from across the room came over and introduced himself. He looked to be in his early thirties. He was very well-dressed and polite, but Terry knew why he came over to the table—at least she thought she knew. She quickly deduced that if he were really being nice, he would want to meet them both. If that were the case, she thought he would have waited until Will came back. He was sitting near the restrooms so he had to notice Will going in there, she thought.

He handed her his card, and she looked at it. His name was Dr. Andrew Manning—plastic surgeon. Another pain shot through her.

"So what can I do for you—" She looked at the card again. "Andy?"

"I was thinking more along the lines of what I could do for you," he said with a charming grin.

"Do I look like I need plastic surgery?!" she snapped.

People whipped their heads around to see what was going on. Will came out of the restroom just in time to see the action. Dr. Manning looked around the restaurant nervously, forcing himself to smile, but was thoroughly embarrassed.

"I didn't mean to offend you," he apologized.

Terry wasn't through with him. She would finish the castration. "You didn't, huh? Okay. Let's cut to the chase. How big is it?"

The clubhouse guests were still watching the exchange. Will was nearing their table.

"Excuse me?" Dr. Manning frowned.

"You heard me. How-big-is-your-dick? Because I'm telling you now, if you don't have at least nine inches, you can forget about it. Did you see the man sitting here a minute ago? That's what he has. Soooooooo?"

Terry could hear the couple in the next booth laughing.

Will came back just in time to hear her mention penis size. He could see how angry Terry was and wondered how much of her attitude stemmed from her pain.

Feeling totally humiliated, Manning turned around and left. He almost bumped into Will on the way back to his booth.

Will said, "What brought that on?"

"Can you believe that guy? He had a lot of nerve, coming over here trying that shit. I bet he won't try that again."

"I bet he won't either. But what brought that on?"

"I wanted to kick him in the balls without kicking him in the balls, you might say. You know how men are about their dicks. Most of them think they're smaller than what they really are, and they have a complex about it. And you know what they say about black men. I knew it would humble him real quick. Do you mind if we take our lunch with us? My cramps are getting unbearable. I need to lie down before Cleve and Cheryl come over."

"Okay. Do you want to cancel the card game then?"

"No. I'll be okay. I know you've been looking forward to this."

"It's no big deal. We can play cards another night."

"No, let's play. I'll be okay. Really."

"Okay, I'll tell you their signals on the way to my place. Then you can lie down for a couple of hours before they get there."

The waitress brought out their lunch.

"I'm sorry, but could you pack this up? We've decided to take it with us."

"No problem," the waitress said.

†††

The faint voices she heard coming through the half-opened double doors of the master suite awakened her out of her deep slumber. She figured Cleve and Cheryl were there already and Will didn't want to wake her. Although she had been lying on Will's bed for several hours, it had only been a half-hour since she'd fallen asleep. She was lying on her stomach diagonally with her head near the foot of the bed. Her bare arms and hands felt the delicate texture of his burgundy and gray king-sized comforter as she rolled over onto her back. Paying no attention to the voices in the distance, she stared at the ceiling for a moment and contemplated her relationship to Will.

She wondered what sex would be like with him, and allowed her mind to wander further into the sexual realm of her love for him. She thought of the softness of his lips and the way they felt when he pressed them against hers. His kisses filled her with desire and fostered a sense of security that made her feel absolutely safe from harm. She went into the bathroom to freshen up. Looking in the mirror, she wondered what the evening had in store. *How will Cheryl respond to me?* she wondered as she gargled mouthwash.

"I'll just be my normal charming self," she said aloud after spitting. She took a deep breath, blew it out, and then left the bedroom. As she got closer to the family room, she could hear Randy Crawford's "Street Life" playing softly in the background.

"I'm serious, Cheryl," Will was saying. "Whether you like her or not, don't be trippin' up in here. And don't y'all embarrass me either."

"I'll treat her the way she treats me," Cheryl retorted, snaking her neck. "If she comes in here actin' like Miss High and Mighty, we gon' have a problem. Y'all hear me? I will not be talked down to by her or no-body-else. And if you wanna put me outta yo' house…that's fine with me. But I'm not havin' that patronizin' shit they do. I'm tellin' you now, if she starts some shit, it's gon' be on."

Cleve frowned. "Do you always have to be so goddamned obnoxious? I can't take you no place without you actin' like a fool!"

"Well, you know what you can do," Cheryl snapped. "If you can't deal wit' it, find you somebody else."

Terry listened for a second longer and decided to go back to the bedroom and shut the door loud enough for them to know she was on her way. She approached the family room and she could hear them talking in hushed tones now. When she walked into the room, she saw them playing three-man spades.

Will put his cards down, walked over to her, and took her hand. He brought her over to the card table and introduced her to Cheryl, who extended her hand. Terry took her hand and they both smiled nervously.

Both women felt awkward and uncomfortable and wondered what the other was thinking at that moment.

Cheryl was five feet two inches tall with short black wavy hair. She had a cute round face, small breasts, big hips, and a round chiseled ass.

"So how long have y'all been here?" Terry asked.

"'Bout fifteen or twenty minutes," Cleve replied. "Will called and said to come an hour later because you was havin' menstrual cramps and shit."

"Cleve!!" Will snapped. He couldn't believe Cleve would say that to her. Terry looked embarrassingly at Will.

"That's yo' friend," Cheryl said as though she was denying their marital status.

"What's the big deal?" Cleve continued. "So she cramped up a little. A lot of women get cramps before they have they period. So what! Now, let's play some spades."

Chapter 32: Why Can't We Be Friends?

Terry seemed to take Cleve's off-color comment in stride and took her seat at the card table across from Will. She looked around the table and saw no refreshments. After Cleve's comments, she thought a glass of white wine would mellow her out.

Cheryl collected the cards and shuffled them as she began the optical autopsy of Terry. The cards made a fluttering sound when she bridged her hands. She looked at Terry with the skill of a medical examiner. *She's pretty. Nice figure. Better-looking than the average white woman I see brothas with.*

Cheryl didn't trust white women because they seemed to be so uppity. To her, they came off like they were better than black women. She also hated the idea of everything being geared toward white women. Almost all of the models were tall, slender white women, with long necks. She felt left out. There was no representation of black women who looked like her—women who were more voluptuous than slender—women who actually had thighs and a round ass. Every time she went to the store, it was a struggle to find something as simple as a pair of jeans without having to buy the next size up. Everything was about the almighty white goddess and she was sick of it.

"I'm sorry I wasn't awake when y'all got here," Terry told their guests. "I wanted to greet you and show you some Southern hospitality, which Will obviously has forgotten. I'm going to have a glass of wine. Can I get anybody anything?"

"I haven't forgotten anything, baby," Will said. "They're not guests. They've been here before. They know where everything is."

Isaac Hayes' "Walk On By" was playing in the background. The sound of the Kenwood speakers were so crisp that they could hear him take deep breathes before he bellowed his deep tenor voice.

"Now that's what I'm talkin' 'bout," Cleve said. "Some Southern hospitality. We ain't seen no hospitality up in here since Francis died."

"Cleve!" Cheryl shouted.

"What?" Cleve wondered with a confused look on his face.

Will looked at Cleve and shook his head. Cheryl looked at Terry. The two women made a momentary connection. She knew Cleve's faux pas cut Terry a bit. Not a lot, but enough for it to be visible to another woman. Terry was attempting to break new ground and while Cheryl didn't like the idea of her being white and with a well-to-do black man, she understood.

"You have to excuse my ignorant ass husband sometimes," Cheryl said. "He means well. He just doesn't have a clue sometimes."

"It's not a problem. Can I get anybody anything?"

"Yeah," Cleve said. "I'll have a Mocha Cappuccino Espresso Ristretto." Then he laughed. "I just like the way that shit sounds."

"If you don't mind," Cheryl said, "I'll have an Ethiopian Harrar, please."

"Let me help you out, baby," Will offered.

Walking behind Terry, Will watched her ass sway from side to side. They could hear Cheryl saying, "Why don't you think before you open yo' goddamn mouth?!"

Terry opened the refrigerator door and bent over to take out the relish tray she prepared before they went to the Gun Club. Will walked up behind her and pressed himself up against her. She felt his hardness and stood up. She turned around and grabbed his bulging crotch. Still holding him firmly, she looked into his eyes and said with a sexy grin, "Don't start something unless you're willing to finish it. Now, are you going to do something with this, or what?"

"Maybe I do plan on doing something tonight. Who knows?" He smiled.

"You are such a tease." She squeezed him a little and let him go. "Just in case you want to, I won't start until tomorrow, or the next day."

Will took her into his powerful arms and kissed her thick soft lips gently. He could feel her large breasts pressing against his chest. Terry opened her mouth and relaxed her tongue and Will took it into his mouth. She grabbed his ass, holding one cheek in each hand. Then, starting at the base, she licked all the way up his neck as though she were licking an ice cream cone. With her left hand, she pulled his head down to hers and kissed him hard. She could feel his erection right above her pelvis.

"HEY! WHAT Y'ALL DOIN' IN THERE!" Cleve shouted.

They reluctantly pulled away and looked wantonly into each other's eyes. Will took a deep breath and let it out slowly.

"Umm," Will moaned, still looking at her with lustful eyes.

Terry knew she had gotten to him. She had teased him the way he'd teased her so many times.

"How does it feel?" she asked him.

She turned around and took out the relish tray and vegetable dip and then she walked back into the family room. Will was still in the kitchen, unzipping his pants and repositioning his tool downward so as to not attract attention to it. He could hear Terry saying, "We'll bring the drinks right out. Enjoy."

"Y'all want us to leave?" Cleve asked playfully.

"Eventually," Terry told him. "We are consenting adults." Then she winked at them and went back into the kitchen.

"How you doin', big boy?" Terry asked, looking at Will as he zipped up his pants. "You got him under control now?"

Will washed his hands and finished Cleve's espresso and Cheryl's Ethiopian Harrar. The exotic African blend filled the kitchen as he poured it into the cup.

"Bring it on in, brotha; it's hummin' from here." Cheryl sounded desperate to taste the imported beverage.

Will walked into the family room with Cheryl's coffee, Cleve's espresso, and his Colombian Supremo on a tray. Cheryl lifted the cup to her nose and inhaled. Then she took a sip of the coffee and swallowed slowly, savoring the dry, unmistakably winy flavor. She was in heaven.

Terry came out of the kitchen with a chilled, tall, thin glass of white wine. She took her seat opposite Will again and took a sip.

"So what are the rules?" Terry asked.

"No talking across the board," Cheryl explained. "So no helping her, Will. After biddin', you can move the bid up, but you can't move it down. If you bid ten, and get it, you get two hundred points. If you don't get it, you're only minus a hundred. You can go blind sevens anytime. Do you know what I mean by blind, Terry?"

"No."

"A blind seven is when you bid seven books before the hand is actually dealt," Cleve explained. "If you get it, you get one hundred and seventy points. If you don't—"

"You're minus seventy," Terry finished the sentence.

"Right," Cheryl confirmed.

"What about nils? We are playing with nils, right?" Will asked.

"Yeah," Cleve confirmed. "Nils are worth a hundred."

"A nil is when your hand is pitiful and you don't think you can make a book," Will explained. "One partner can bid a nil, but the other partner can make as many books as he wants. But, if the partner that bid the nil gets one book, they are automatically minus one hundred points, understand?"

"Got it," Terry said. "Can we French deal?"

"NO!" they all shouted in unison.

Terry took another sip of her wine, and said, "Okay, just checking."

Cheryl took a swallow of her coffee and began dealing. The first card went to Terry, then to Cleve, then to Will, and finally to herself.

Terry looked at Will. He tilted his head toward Cleve. Cleve's free hand had its two middle fingers curled under, indicating he had the big joker, the little Joker, and the queen of spades. Terry looked at Will, acknowledging that she knew. Then they looked at Cheryl's free hand.

Cheryl was tapping it three times lightly at regular intervals indicating that she only had three spades. Will and Terry looked at each other again. They knew Cheryl and Cleve had at least six spades.

"So what do y'all bid?" Cheryl asked.

Will picked up the pencil. "How many you got, baby?"

Terry looked at her hand again. She had the ace of hearts, the ace of diamonds, the king of clubs, and two small spades.

"Three," she told him.

"Now, is that two, possibly three? Or is that three, possibly four?" Will asked her.

"Hold the hell on," Cheryl interrupted. "Didn't we say no talkin' across the board?"

"I was just checking to see if we wanted to move the bid up," Will explained.

"That's bullshit," Cheryl snapped. "You know goddamn well that was a signal to count the possibles from now on."

"Well, if it wasn't a signal, it is now." Will laughed. "Did you get that, baby?"

"Got it, darlin'," Terry said, and took another sip of her wine.

"Y'all a trip." Cleve laughed.

"So what y'all gon' bid?" Cheryl repeated. Then she picked up a celery stick and dipped it. The celery crunched loudly as she ate.

"Hmm. Three, huh? Okay, we'll go six." Will wrote it down.

"I've got five. How many you got?" Cleve asked Cheryl.

"Three."

"Shit, that's eight," Cleve concluded. "Let's set their asses!"

Will thought, *Damn! Cleve or Cheryl must be cutting something early.*

"Well, let's go seven and be safe," Cheryl cautioned. "If we set 'em, we set 'em. If not, we don't get set."

"Okay," Cleve yielded. "Give us seven."

Will wrote it down. Terry drank the remainder of the wine in her glass.

"It's on you, Terry," Cheryl said.

Terry played the ace of diamonds and Will collected the book. Then she played the ace of hearts, followed by the king of hearts. Cleve cut the king with the two of spades. He used a lot of wrist action when he played it. When the card landed on top of the king, it sounded like someone being slapped in the face

"That wasn't one of your three, was it, Terry?" Cleve laughed. "Y'all 'bout to take a sweet ass whoopin'." Cheryl collected the book.

Will looked at Terry. "I forgot to tell you. They talk a lot of shit when they play."

Cleve played the ten of diamonds. Will played the jack. Then Cheryl popped the king down with the same furor as Cleve did when he cut Terry's king of hearts.

"That wasn't one of your three, was it, Will?" Cheryl laughed.

"Play cards and shut the hell up!" Will growled.

Terry was relaxing comfortably in her chair, taking in all of the self-aggrandizing. She wondered if she would cause them to lose the game and foster more ridicule. She decided to have another glass of wine, and put her hand down. "Excuse me a sec. I'm going to have another glass."

"Okay," Cheryl said, and swallowed down the last of her coffee.

Terry returned a few seconds later. Cheryl played the nine of clubs. Terry had the two of clubs and the king of clubs. Cleve looked at her and showed her the ace of clubs. He was smiling. Terry played the two. Cleve popped the queen of clubs down hard. Then he played the ace of clubs and drew out Terry's king.

"Y'all through," Cleve told Will, laughing hard. "You know that, don't you?"

Cleve and Cheryl laughed and gave each other high-fives across the table. Terry felt responsible for the lost hand. They weren't going to get their six books. They weren't even going to get five books now. Cleve was cutting hearts and Cheryl was cutting clubs.

"Y'all in the crossfire." Cheryl laughed.

Terry took a swallow of her wine. Cleve and Cheryl were having an uproarious time. Every few seconds, they'd hear one of them popping a card and laughing.

"Don't worry about it, baby," Will consoled. "It's just one hand."

"It may be one hand," Cleve taunted, "but we're going to beat that ass until the cows come home."

"Cleve," Terry began. "Will tells me you work at the main post office."

"Yeah. I work there," he admitted, and popped another card.

"Didn't they have a shooting down there last year?" Terry asked.

"You tryin' to distract me?" Cleve wondered. "Well, it won't work." Smack! He smashed another card on the table.

"No, I'm interested in why so many shootings take place in one organiza- tion," Terry told him. She was starting to get a buzz from the wine. "I know it happens in other places, too, but it seems to happen more frequently at the post offices around the country. Why do you suppose that is?"

"Don't get him started on that damn post office," Cheryl warned.

Will laughed and decided to have some tuna salad and Townhouse crackers. He went into the kitchen and took the bright yellow Tupperware bowl out of the refrigerator. Then he got the crackers out of the cabinet.

"Why not?" Terry wondered aloud and shuffled the deck.

"Because he won't know when to shut up," Cheryl replied.

"Oh, now I'm really interested." Terry smiled.

She dealt a fresh hand and hoped she and Will would fare better, but they were set again. This time, Cheryl and Cleve bid a ten and ended up running a Boston. They had lost the game in only two hands. It was a mercy killing.

"Y'all wanna play another, or just surrender now?" Cleve mocked.

"Y'all got lucky," Will said, with a mouth full of tuna.

"Does anyone mind if I play my music program?" Terry asked.

"What kind of music?" Cheryl wanted to know.

"Yeah." Cleve frowned. "We don't want to hear none of that loud ass heavy metal and shit."

"No country either," Cheryl objected.

"Okay," Terry smiled. "Hand me the remote control, darlin'."

Will handed it to her and promptly popped another cracker with tuna on it into his mouth.

Terry pushed the letters T. M., and the number one. They could hear the compact disc changer making a lot of mechanical sounds as it searched for the program. Moments later they heard Chic's "Good Times."

"Hey!" Cheryl said excitedly and popped her fingers to the rhythm. "I haven't heard this in a long time." She sang the chorus and moved her body to the beat.

"So, Cleve, are you going to tell me what happened at the post office, or not?" Terry repeated.

With a mouth full of tuna and crackers, Cleve mumbled, "Yeah, I'll tell you." He dealt a new hand. "Do you want the long version, or the short version?" Cleve asked, straightening out his hand.

Terry looked at his hands to see what trump cards he had. "The long version," she told him. "I want all the details."

He tapped his thumb four times. Cheryl was showing the pinky finger only, indicating that she had the queen of spades. Will and Terry looked at each other with optimism. They were both thinking this might be a good time to set Cleve and Cheryl; especially since they were beaten so quickly by them. Terry thought they might be a little more relaxed, and hopefully, overconfident. She decided to lowball them.

"I have one, possibly two, darlin'."

"I have five," Will said, "but let's play it safe and go five."

"Let's go the seven, Cheryl."

"How many do you have?"

"Three or four."

"I have three or four, too."

"Let's go that eight, babe."

"I said three, possibly four."

"I know."

"You gon' have to get 'em if they cut early."

"Now hold on," Will said, interrupting them. "I thought you said no talking across the board."

"Okay," Cheryl said. "You right. Give us eight."

Terry and Will looked at each other, believing their plan had worked. Now all they needed was six books.

"Skin Tight" by the Ohio Players was playing now.

Cheryl was even more into this song; it reminded of her junior high school days.

Will played the jack of clubs. Cheryl played the queen and Terry played the ace. Then she came back with the king of clubs. Will played off with one of his three diamonds. He only had the jack of clubs in that suit.

"So what happened down there, Cleve?" Terry repeated.

"There's this black dude we called brothaman," Cleve began. "Brothaman was quiet. He didn't bother nobody, but the white people down there liked to fuck with brothaman. Why? I don't know. Everybody thought he was militant and shit. He was always readin' or carryin' a book with him. He was the kinda brotha white people didn't like."

"Did the white people dislike him because he was black, or was he a trip?" Terry asked.

Terry played the ten of clubs and Cleve played a heart because he knew that Will was cutting also. Will played off, knowing Cheryl couldn't beat the ten, or Cleve had reneged. Either way, they would win this book.

"Hell, I don't know, but they was always fuckin' wit' him about how smart he was," Cleve continued. "He was a college man, like ya boy Will and shit. I guess they didn't like him because he wasn't like some of the brothas down there."

Terry played the four of diamonds and Cleve popped the ace down on top of it. Will played his last diamond.

"How are the other brothers, Cleve?" Terry asked.

"Most of them are good people, but uneducated, like m'self," Cleve told her. "The problem is some of them are just plain stupid. Some of the white ones are just as stupid, if not stupider." He laughed. "Is that a word?" he said and laughed again. "Anyway, they would say shit about him, but not directly to him. Just around him so he could hear the shit. You know how cowards are."

Cleve played the king of diamonds and Will popped down the four of spades. It made the same popping sound that Cleve and Cheryl made with their cards. Then Will started drawing out their spades. He started with the big joker, then the little joker. He got Cheryl to play her only trump, the queen. He played the eight of spades, hoping Terry had the king. She did.

"Ooh!" Will shouted. "Y'all set this time."

"Why don't you pay attention to what the hell you doin'?" Cheryl shouted. "I told yo' dumb ass not to bid that eight."

"Don't let the shit go to yo' head," Cleve warned. "It's one hand, brotha."

They stopped Cheryl and Cleve from making their eight books and that's all that mattered to him. Then he looked at Cheryl and said, "Y'all through now." Then he and Terry slapped high-fives across the table.

"Are you going to finish the story, Cleve?" Terry asked.

Will shuffled the cards and started dealing them.

"So anyway," Cleve began again. "The atmosphere on the LSM was getting thick. It was hot and people had short fuses and shit."

"What's a LSM?" Terry asked.

"It's the letter-sorter machine. It goes sixty miles an hour. I know it seems fast, but it's slow once you learn how to do it. Anyway, one of the mechanics said something to him. Brothaman got fired up. Next thing I know, they was up in each other's face. Yellin' at the top of their lungs and shit."

"So it was a fight that brought this tragedy about, huh?" Terry concluded.

"Yellin' is not a fight," Cheryl explained. "That's what white people call arguing. See, if you black, you ain't fightin' unless you throwin' blows."

Will resisted the urge to say, "You outta know," by popping more tuna and crackers in his mouth.

"I'm going to get another glass of wine, but I want you to tell me the rest of this story, Cleve. Can I get you another cup of coffee, Cheryl?" Terry asked.

"Yes, please."

"What about you, Cleve?"

"Naw, I'm all right."

Terry got up to get the wine and coffee. Will said, "What about me?"

"You live here. You can get your own," she said, playfully.

"Trouble in paradise?" Cleve joked.

Will followed Terry into the kitchen.

"Cleve, let's leave after this game," Cheryl whispered. "I think they want to be alone. We can play again another time."

"Okay."

Terry and Will came back into the family room.

"Hey, man," Cleve said. "We gon' get up outta here after this game."

Disappointed, Terry said, "So soon? This is only our second game." She looked at her watch. "It's only nine-thirty. Stay a bit longer, if you can. Can you?"

"Yeah, we can." Cheryl smiled. She was having a better time than she thought she'd have.

Terry was obviously feeling good now. Whatever pain she was experiencing earlier had completely subsided.

Cheryl was dealing now.

"Please finish your story, Cleve," Terry urged. "Did they start fighting right there?"

"Naw, they didn't fight there. But that's only because it's a felony to hit a postal employee while they're on the clock. Otherwise, people would be fightin' more often."

"What do you mean?" Terry asked.

"They can be fired for fighting," Cheryl added. "It's about the only thing they fire people for down there. Unless, of course, you steal something. According to Cleve, the place is a total trip."

"So what happened, Cleve?" Terry asked, anxious to hear the rest of the story.

"They decided to settle their differences on their lunch break outside the gates. Needless to say, everybody brought their lunches outside the gate to watch instead of going into the break area. To make a long story short, Brothaman beat the shit out of the mechanic. The shit was funny to me. We must have talked about that shit for three months. It still cracks me up, just thinkin' about it."

"So the mechanic shot the place up because he lost a fight to Brotherman?" Terry asked.

"He didn't just lose, Terry." Cleve laughed. "Brothaman reshaped his goddamn head. But no, it wasn't over the first fight. It was over the second fight."

"The mechanic wanted to fight again?" Terry asked incredulously.

"Not really. He left Brothaman alone after the beating he took. Everybody left Brothaman alone after that shit. That's why the shit was funny for so long. People that used to talk all that shit started goin' the other way when they saw him coming." Cleve laughed again. "Come to find out later, Brothaman was fuckin' his wife. His wife calls in sick and so did Brothaman. Nobody suspected they was fuckin'. The mechanic goes home early and finds Brothaman wearin' the shit out. Another fight broke out and Brothaman kicked his ass again. Homeboy flipped after that shit and went off. Killed his wife, and then came to work the next day looking for Brothaman. He just came in shootin' indiscriminately and shit. The sad part about it is, Brothaman called in sick again. Fifteen people died for nothin'. Then when SWAT got there, he shot himself."

"Were you scared?" Terry asked.

"Hell yeah," Cleve admitted. "The kinda environment that management allows causes this kind of shit to happen. When the argument happened, there were three managers there and not one of 'em did anything to stop it. One of 'em even left the scene like she didn't see it. The other two were men and they stood there and watched like spectators and shit, just waiting for one of 'em to hit the other so they could fire both their asses. They should have stopped it and maybe they ass would be alive today."

"You mean the managers were among the fifteen?" Terry asked.

"Yep. That's some ironic shit, ain't it? They were a party to their own deaths. Kinda poetic to me though. Hopefully, them muthafuckas will learn somthin' from this shit. It's crazy as hell down there still though."

"The people seem a bit extreme at the post office," Terry pointed out. "Now are you going to get a gun and shoot me for saying that?"

"Funny you should say that because the shit just crossed my mind," Cleve joked. They all laughed. "I could tell you all kinds of shit about the post office. Like the time one of the managers was havin' an affair with another manager. They broke up and she comes in and shoots up his car. Then there was the time I caught some jungle fever going on in one of the closets in the basement of the building."

"See, what did I tell you?" Cheryl interrupted. "He doesn't know how to stop. We ain't even playing cards no more. We're just listening to his post office stories."

"Do y'all mind the stories?" Cleve asked.

"No," Terry encouraged him. "I always wondered what was going on that people got shot all the time."

"Well, I've heard these stories a thousand times," Cheryl said. "I get sick of 'em after a while."

"Let me finish this one, then we can play some more, okay?"

"Okay."

"So anyway, I came out the bathroom and I'm walkin' past the closet and I hear some moanin' and shit. You know how you can't believe what you heard, so you listen all the more?"

"Uh-huh." Terry nodded.

"It's quiet down there, for the most part. I go by the door and I hear the moanin' again. I start laughing to myself, then I snatch open the door real fast so they won't have a chance to pull they drawls up. One of the janitors had his boss bent over the sink with her dress up and her drawls down around her ankles. Now, Terry, you'd expect the brotha to stop and pull his pants up, or somethin', right? Not this brotha. He kept bangin' her. She was trying to get him to stop 'cause she heard me open the door. This brotha had the nerve to turn around and say, 'Hey, man, close the door.'"

They all rolled. Even Cheryl laughed after hearing it again.

"So what did you do, Cleve?" Terry laughed.

"I closed the door. Who am I to keep a brotha from gettin' a nut? I wouldn't do it there, but, I mean, shit, if that's the only place he could get her."

As they laughed, they could hear "Why Can't We Be Friends?" They all caught the groove and resumed playing cards.

"I love this song," Terry told them.

"Me, too," Cleve said. "Loop that shit."

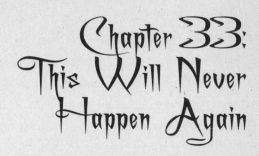

Chapter 33:
This Will Never
Happen Again

Key West
October 1988

Jericho and the crew were in town to trade fifteen million dollars' worth of weapons and ammunition for uncut cocaine that had just arrived from Honduras by way of the Dominican Republic. The cocaine was being used to raise money to buy arms for the Contras who were at war with the Sandinistas. Hawthorne, a CIA control officer, recruited Jericho and his crew as operatives for the Agency. It was supposed to be a simple exchange, but Jericho was set up by a DEA agent named Manny Trinidad, who was deep undercover in Manuel Zepeda's drug cartel.

The DC-4 cargo plane landed at Key West Airport and taxied to the hanger, where Jericho and the crew waited with the weapons. They were supposed to unload the drugs and put the guns on board. The plane would be refueled and leave the coast of Florida for the Nicaraguan border as soon as the exchange was made. After they unloaded crate after crate of cocaine, Jericho opened up a bag from a crate, tasted a little, smiled, and spit it on the ground. Then he looked at Manny and nodded, telling him he would accept the shipment.

"Load the plane," Jericho ordered.

Suddenly, DEA agents swarmed into the hanger, wearing helmets, combat boots, flack jackets, and carrying automatic weapons. "FREEZE! NOBODY MOVE! DEA! FACE DOWN ON THE GROUND! EVERYBODY! NOW!"

Jericho turned around and looked at Manny Trinidad, who was pointing a .9mm in his face. He raised his hands and Manny took Jericho's weapon and stuck it in the front of his pants.

"Turn around and put your hands behind your back," Manny said calmly.

Jericho just stared at him, completely surprised by the betrayal. The other DEA agents were still screaming at Jericho's crew, but no one moved, even with automatic weapons in their faces. They were waiting for orders from their unquestioned leader, who was still staring at Manny Trinidad like he was in a hypnotic trance.

"Tell them to lay down, man," Manny said. "You have no chance of escape."

Jericho turned around, put his hands behind his back, and with a single nod, told his crew to surrender.

Two hours later, Hawthorne and several of his agents walked into the police chief's office, flashed their badges, and took Jericho, his crew, the weapons, and the drugs back to the hangar, where the plane was refueled and ready to take off. Shortly after the DC-4 took off, Jericho and the crew boarded a chartered executive jet and left the country.

As soon as the jet leveled off, Jericho held a meeting at the conference table to discuss his new plan. With both elbows on the table, his fingers in steeple formation, he said, "This will never happen again. We cannot rely on Hawthorne to be there to get us out if one of his people turns out to be DEA, ATF, NSA, or what the hell ever! From this moment forward, we will be armed to the teeth, just like them, ready for anything. We will secure the area where we do our exchanges. In other words, we're going to be responsible for our own security. One day, when Hawthorne doesn't need, or want us anymore, he may decide not to show up, leaving us to fend for ourselves."

In Vietnamese, Pin said, "That's going to cost a fortune, but it will be money well spent. We're also going to need more men to cover our asses if we ever have to shoot our way out."

Jericho looked at his wife and said, "From now on security is your responsibility. Recruit as many men as you need, spend as much as you need to spend, but we can't afford to be taken down by anybody. If word gets out, other crews will try and move in on us."

Chapter 34:
Morning After

San Francisco
November 1997

I t was a little after one in the morning and they were no longer playing cards. The music was loud and the atmosphere, festive. They were
all drinking wine now and feeling light-headed. They sang the chorus
of Funkadelic's "Knee Deep" and danced until they worked up a sweat.
Then a series of Mariah Carey songs came on. Instead of bobbing their
heads, and hunching their shoulders, they began to sing along and sway
their bodies from side to side.

But Terry drank six tall glasses of wine and had a serious buzz and
seemed to be feeling the lyrics as she sang them to Will. The words made
what she felt for Will come alive. When she heard the beginning of
"Music Box," excitedly she said, "This is my song, y'all! This is my song!"
Her Southern accent was much more alive when she spoke, but was almost
non-existent when she sang. She hummed the beginning along with
Mariah. In her mind, she actually sounded like her. "I just love the way
she sings."

"Mariah is bad," Cheryl agreed. "But can't nobody do it like Whitney
Houston. The girl can blow."

Cleve laughed. "I guess we'll have to ask Bobby about that."

Cheryl hit him playfully. "You know what I mean, boy. But seriously,
once she sings a song, you might as well break that bad boy because the
song doesn't sound right no more. Shit, I can't stand to hear the National
Anthem now. As a matter fact, it ought to be the law from now on, at

every game, at every ceremony that requires the National Anthem to be played; Whitney ought to sing that bad boy. And if anybody even attempts to sing it, they oughta be arrested and sent to jail for life."

"I hear you," Will said.

"Y'all want to see me do my Mariah Carey impression?" Terry asked them.

"Yeah," they answered enthusiastically.

"Too bad I don't have a mike."

"What about the empty coat stand over there in the corner?" Cleve suggested.

"Yeah, that'll do," Terry said, walking over to the coat stand. She placed it in front of the stereo.

They clapped their hands and whistled as though they were at a real concert.

Terry—glassy-eyed—grabbed her imitation mike and said, "Thank you. I love you, too. Will one of you fast forward to 'Forever' for me? She bowed her head and waited for the music to play. The acoustic guitar began. "Hold it. Stop the music, darlin'," Terry told Will. The music stopped. "I'm dedicating this song to my man. I love you, Will," she spoke into her mike.

Then she bowed her head again. Will pushed the play button and the acoustic guitar began again. With her head still bowed, she began humming the song along with Mariah. When the words began, she lifted her head on cue. Her lips were in perfect sync with her idol. She had sung the song so many times that the mime came naturally. She moved her arms to add emphasis at certain points in the song. She pointed at Will every time she said "you" and pointed to herself when she said "I." Sometimes she would cross her arms as though she was holding Will in them. At other times, she would raise her arms and lower them slowly. When she held a note, she'd tilt her head back. A vein could be seen when she did this, which made the mime look authentic.

She finished the number by holding a long note and pointing at Will. The performance was very dramatic, and it moved him. Not only did it turn him on sexually, it stirred his emotions—emotions he had long since left behind. But it was more than the performance; it was a time of letting go of the past and embracing the present. He had finally made up his mind. There would be no more priming the pump. Tonight he would give himself to her, both mentally and physically. He was sure now. Terry Moretti was the one—his woman of choice.

Terry came back to the table and kissed Will. He pulled her to himself and hugged her with emotion. Although she'd felt his embrace many times, this embrace was altogether different. She felt what she interpreted as his love. For the first time she understood why an infant dies if it doesn't feel its mother's loving touch. She sat on his lap and relaxed. She could sense he was letting go of the past. She believed he would withhold nothing from her now.

"Do a Whitney Houston song for me, Cheryl," Cleve said.

"I can't do that, Cleve."

"Yes you can, Cheryl." Will encouraged. "Just let yourself go for once."

"Just let myself go? Look who's talkin'. The master of control. I'll tell you what. I'll do a Whitney song, if you two do my favorite Luther Vandross song."

"What's your favorite Luther song?" Terry asked.

"I like three of them. I like 'There's Nothing Better Than Love,' 'So Amazing,' and 'Any Love.' Y'all can choose the one y'all wanna do. Which Whitney song do you want me to do, Cleve? 'I Will Always Love You?'"

"Naw. I want you to do 'All the Man I Need.'"

"Yeah, Cheryl," Terry said. "I like that one, too."

Cheryl went up to the mike and bowed her head as the intro music came on. Like Terry, she lifted her head on cue and sang. Cheryl was actually singing and she sounded good. She sung to Cleve and he took it all in. They hadn't had this much fun together in years. In those moments that Cheryl sung to Cleve, she remembered why she married him. It was something about the words and the melody. Perhaps it was the distant, but ever present piano that caused her to feel the words. Her eyes began to fill with tears, but none fell. When she finished the song, she said,

"Cleve, I know I don't act like it, but I love you, boy." Then she cried.

Cleve hugged her. "I love you, too. There could never be another to take your place."

"Awwwww." Terry smiled as the couple kissed.

Will picked up the remote control and began programming the CD player with all of Cheryl's requests. After listening to Cheryl speak that way to his best friend, he was glad to do something to make her happy. He didn't think he would ever hear her speak lovingly to him again.

Will and Cleve went up to the mike. Terry pushed the play button. Cleve began Luther's first verse and Will did Gregory Hines' part. They did the chorus together, and the women loved it.

†††

It was approaching two hours past midnight. The wood crackled as it burned in the fireplace. The lights were low, giving the room a romantic ambience, and they were still slow dancing, still singing softly to each other on that spontaneous and magical night.

Will hadn't been this happy in years and wanted the night to go on forever. He held Terry tight, inhaling her intoxicating perfume, and pressing his stiff tool against her soft body.

"Hey, Will," Cleve called out.

"Yeah, man. What is it?" His head was leaning against Terry's as they danced in circles around the room.

"We're gonna get outta here, bro."

"Okay. We'll see y'all to the door."

He took Terry by the hand and they walked Cleve and Cheryl to the front door.

"I really had a nice time," Cheryl told Terry.

"Can I talk to you for a second, Will?" Cleve asked.

"Yeah...we'll be right back, ladies."

The two men left the women standing at the door.

"I had a good time, too, Cheryl," Terry said. "I hope we can do it again sometime."

"That would be nice. Y'all let us know when and we'll be here."

"Will do. I hope it's soon.

Will and Cleve could hear the women talking in the distance as they walked over to Cleve's car.

"So what's up, man?"

"How long we been friends, Will?"

"Long time, bro. A long time."

"Look, man, this doesn't have nothin' to do with Terry. I like her. She cool and shit. She needs to learn how to speak English though. Did you hear her in there? 'So what did Brotherman do," he said, mimicking her. "She sounds so white."

The two men laughed together. "So what's this all about, Cleve?"

"Are the police still stopping you from time to time?"

"Yeah. But not as much as before."

"The only reason I'm sayin' somethin' about it is because I see you gettin' serious about her." Will frowned. "Hey, I'm just looking out for you, bro. If they don't like you living out here, what do you think they're gonna do when they see her with you? You know white people still pissed about that O. J. shit. All I'm sayin' is be careful, man. It's a shame I even have to say this shit, but, hey, you know the deal."

They heard Cheryl coming toward the car.

"You ready, Cleve?"

"Yeah, baby, let's go." Cleve said. "You think about what I said, Will."

"Okay, man. And you think about getting back in school."

"Been thinkin' about it."

"Bye, Will," Cheryl said.

"Bye, Cheryl."

Will walked into the house, and closed the door. He touched the appropriate keys to turn on the alarm and went into the family room expecting to see Terry waiting, but she wasn't. *She must be in the bedroom waiting*. He opened the double doors to the master suite and walked in. An orange-yellowish light glowed from the burning log in the fireplace. He went into the bathroom and she wasn't there either. Just as he turned around, Terry was standing right behind him.

"Looking for me?" She yawned.

"What do you think?"

Then they embraced in a deep, passionate kiss. They could hear the roar of the Pacific as the waves crashed against the shores. The wood crackled as it burned. Will undressed Terry feverishly. He pulled her 49ers jersey over her head and looked at her breasts, which were being held in place by a black satin bra. He unhooked her bra and took the left nipple into his mouth. She moaned. Hurriedly, he led her to the bed.

While he took off her jeans, she finished taking off her bra. Terry was wearing black satin panties. He kissed her chest gently and moved down to her breasts, licking both nipples delicately and then took one into his mouth. She moaned again. He kissed her stomach and moved further downward, positioning himself between her long elegant legs. He kissed her knees, then her inner thighs. He could see her pad and it occurred to him that she might have started her period.

"Are you sure it's okay?" he asked.

Terry didn't say anything.

"You sure it's okay?" he repeated.

She didn't answer. Her stomach was moving up and down slowly. He could hear a purring sound, which couldn't really be called snoring, but it was.

"I'll-be-damned," he said.

†††

Will opened his eyes and instinctively knew it was 5:50 AM. The orange yellowish glow that filled the room was no more and the roar of the Pacific was non-existent. Terry slept in his arms as though she were in a cocoon. He could still hear her purr-like snore. Every so often, she would move her hands across his bare chest. As he stared at the ceiling, he contemplated his future and knew Terry would be a big part of it. It was time to tell his mother.

Will talked to her several times about the mystery lady, as his mother called her, but she still didn't know Terry was white. He knew she would be really upset; especially since she was the one who called his suite back in August. He remembered the way she sounded on the phone, the excitement in her voice. It no longer mattered to him how she always knew things about him and his brothers. The only thing that mattered now was that he had fallen for Terry, and she would be his wife sometime soon. Suddenly it occurred to him that his mother's call could be used to end any argument she had.

How many times had she been right about the things she told him? She could tell you about a person and what they would do in a given situation. She would tell him which of his friends he could trust, and which ones would leave him to fight alone. She could have been a psychologist, he thought. He had learned to trust his instincts because of her, and would use that as his argument. Content he had found the perfect argument, he drifted back to sleep, thanking God for such wonderful parents.

10 AM. Terry opened her eyes. The first thing she saw was Will's swarthy chest, and the mane thereon. She took a deep breath and sighed lovingly. She kissed his neck gently and wondered what had happened that night. Slowly, it started coming to her. She remembered the card game, the singing, the slow dancing, and coming into the bedroom. *Did we do it?* She could feel moisture in her panties and she realized she needed to change pads. She hoped nothing happened because she wanted to remember the first time they made love.

She rolled out of bed, and then looked back at Will to see if her sudden movements had awakened him. They hadn't. She picked up her bra and put it on. Then she picked up her jeans and her 49ers jersey and went into the family room to get her purse. She went into the bathroom and came out wearing the jeans and jersey. She decided to get the overnight bag she had brought with her so many times, but had never needed until now. When she opened the door, the alarm sounded.

"Shit," she said, and quickly hit the numbers to shut it off. She hoped it didn't wake Will.

Having silenced the alarm, she went out the door and approached the passenger side of the car. She grabbed the hunter green bag. It had her initials on both sides between the nylon web handles.

Awakened by the alarm, Will got out of bed. He put on the black and gold silk robe and matching underwear that Francis had given him. He was looking out the window at Terry. When he saw her coming back in, he went to the door to meet her.

"Good morning," he said when she walked in.

"Hi," she said enthusiastically. "How you doin' this mornin'?"

"Are you generally this vibrant in the morning?"

"Depends on who I wake up with. I don't know, maybe you just have that kinda affect on me."

"Uh-huh. I'll try and remember that. You want some breakfast?"

"Sure do. You're making it, right?"

"Right. Unless you want to make it?"

"No, but I promise to make it next time, darlin'."

"I'll hold you to it. But, uh, we've some serious talking to do, okay?"

"Okay. Let me clean up first, all right?"

"Okay. I'll be in the kitchen."

"I won't be long, darlin'."

Terry returned to the kitchen. She walked up behind him and wrapped her arms around his waist and laid her head on his back.

"You were wonderful last night," she told him.

"So were you."

Disappointed, she said, "So we did it and I missed it all?"

"No, nothing happened. Something was about to happen and you fell asleep."

"I'm so sorry, darlin'."

"So am I."

"Well, we're going to have to wait for a few days now."

"So you started, huh?"

"Yep. Sorry."

"Okay."

She could tell he was disappointed.

"You mad?"

"No, but I was looking forward to it though. And I'm going to be busy as hell next week at the clinic."

"What about next weekend then? Just before Thanksgiving. We could drive to Napa Valley and get a hotel, or something."

"You paying?" he asked playfully.

"Yeah, I think I can swing it."

"Sounds good to me."

"What can I do to help you with breakfast, darlin'?"

"Stir the grits."

"Oh, you're making me grits? My mother used to make me grits."

Will poured the eggs into the hot skillet and then broke the bacon into smaller pieces and put them into the eggs.

"Ummm. Everything smells wonderful, Will."

He thanked her and put four pieces of bread into the toaster.

"I think the grits are ready, darlin'."

He looked at them.

"Yeah, they are. Do you mind setting the table?"

"Not at all. What did you want to talk to me about?"

"It's time to talk to my mother about us."

Chapter 35:
Fifty Years

Will and Terry ate breakfast in the glass-enclosed sun porch. The sun was shining in an azure sky; yachts navigated the Pacific on a breezy day. The intermittent wind gusts caused the tree branches to sway, but according to the thermometer, it was a comfortable eighty degrees on the porch.

"So have you given any thought to what you're going to say to your mom?"

"I don't know how I'm going to start the conversation, but I'm going to lay it all on the table."

In between a mouthful of grits and the bacon-cheese omelet, she said, "How do you think she's going to react?"

"She's going to be pissed."

"So your mother's racist, huh?"

"No. I wouldn't say racist."

"So then my father isn't racist either then, right?"

Will took a swallow of his apple juice. Terry stopped eating, folded her arms, and sat there looking at him as though she was demanding an answer.

"Don't look at me like that."

"Like what? How am I looking at you, Will?"

"You know how you're looking, Terry."

"No, I don't. Why don't you tell me?"

Will put a forkful of omelet into his mouth and mumbled, "Like you're going to keep staring at me until you get an answer, or something."

"Don't evade the issue, Will. I'm willing to admit my dad has racist's views. Why can't you do the same?"

"Terry, we aren't having this conversation."

"Typical," she said, and started eating again. "Can I say just one more thing about this?"

"No, you can't."

"Ya know, Will, you're quick to point out white racism, but when it comes to a black person's racist views, you tend to clam up and become evasive."

"Are you through?"

"And let me say another thing. Any time you refuse to acknowledge black racist views, when it's obvious, you endorse white racism by default."

"How eloquent," he said sarcastically. "But you just remember that it is the white man who started it all—not blacks. In other words, he who hates another without cause has no complaint when the object of his hatred returns his hatred to him."

"So what you're saying is, since the white man hated the black man first, the black man has a right to hate him back, right?"

"Right."

"Okay then, if we follow that logic, then the black man should only hate he that hates him, right?"

Will finished off the rest of his breakfast and washed it down with the remainder of his apple juice and took his plate to the sink.

Terry folded her arms again. "Are you going to answer me?"

"No."

"Why not?"

"Because you said you only had one more thing to say. And that was a thousand paragraphs ago."

Terry laughed. "That ain't why. The reason you don't want to discuss it is because you fell into your own shit. I called you on it and now you don't want to talk about it."

"Are you through now?"

"Quite through. But let me say one more thing."

"Let you? What the hell you mean, let? Yo' ass just keeps talkin' and talkin'. You say you only have one more thing to say and then you keep right on runnin' off at the mouth. Let me say one more thing. Let me say one more thing," he said, mocking her with a pseudo Southern accent.

"Are you going to let me say one more thing, or not?"

"Is this going to be it? Nothing else. This is the sum total, right? I mean, this is the end of your little dissertation. No more memos and no more—"

"Yo' ass just keeps on talkin' and talkin'," she said, mocking him in a semi-baritone voice.

Will turned around and looked at her. She was sitting there looking at him with her wide smile. Then they both burst into laughter. He went over to the table to pick up her plate.

"Hey," she said when he came to the table.

"What?"

"Kiss me."

He bent down to kiss her. She opened her mouth and slipped him her warm tongue. He felt himself stiffening and she stroked his hard penis.

"You want me to take care of this for you?" Before he had a chance to answer, she pulled out his penis and took it into her mouth. Will moaned. Then he realized they could possibly be seen through the glass. He withdrew himself. "What's wrong?"

"People can see. There's probably some voyeur out there with a telescope getting an eyeful as we speak."

"Oh." She gasped. "I completely forgot about that. I'll wait for you in the boudoir."

†††

It was almost 12:30 when Will turned on the 26-inch Sony Trinitron, positioned against the wall near the foot of the bed. Announcers James Brown, Terry Bradshaw, Howie Long, and Chris Collingsworth were doing the Fox pregame show. Bradshaw was building up the game between the San Francisco 49ers and the Oakland Raiders, addressing the preseason game between the two Bay City rivals, a game the Raiders won, and how the Raiders would be playing a different 49ers team. James Brown was saying the two teams should play each other more often, considering their close proximity. He went on to talk about how Cleveland played Cincinnati twice a year and they were hundreds of miles away. Then he said, "I think this is a rivalry the fans want to see."

Will and Terry were still lying in bed cuddling. They were quietly watching the pregame show. Will had his left arm around her. He liked the feel of her next to him. He felt comfortable with her there.

Terry was watching the TV, but couldn't really hear what was being said. Her mind was on her future with Will. She wanted what they had to go on forever. She daydreamed of a big wedding and a long honeymoon away from everything and everyone. She wondered how many kids they would have together, and what they'd name them. *What if he isn't as serious about me as I am about him?* She decided to find out.

"Will, were you serious about telling your mother about us today?"

"Yes." He kissed her forehead. "Why do you ask?"

"I don't want to rush things, but it tells me this is going somewhere, you know what I mean?" She looked at him.

"I think so." His eyes were still transfixed on the television screen.

"Are you listening to me, darlin'?" she said, still looking at him.

"Umm, Hmm."

"What do I mean then?"

"You want to know if I feel what you feel." He stopped looking at the television, and looked at her. "And if I've envisioned a life with you and if I want to have children with you. I thought about all of that stuff the day after you came bustin' into my suite in Toronto. I'm not saying I envisioned everything then. I just thought about whether or not I would go that far. So I do understand you completely."

Terry stretched her long neck upward and kissed him. Then she rubbed her hand across his chest. Will resumed watching the Fox pregame show. The players were running out onto the field just before they went to commercial.

"So have you thought about it lately? You know…a life together?"

"Yes, I think about it a lot."

"And?"

"And I think we need more time and I kinda like things as they are."

"So you would be content to leave things as they are?"

"No. I want to have children. I'm thirty-six and I'll be thirty-seven in

February. Like my dad said, I'll be shooting blanks soon." They laughed. The game was back on. The 49ers had just kicked off.

"But seriously, I don't think it'll take a long time to move forward. It's not like I don't know you and—GO! GO! GO!" he shouted as Napoleon Kaufman found a seam up the middle of the field and broke to the outside and into the end zone for a Raiders touchdown. "I know my mother is sick now," he said, still excited about the ninety-seven-yard scamper. "I think I'll call her and tease her. Then I'll ask her to come out here for coffee so I can tell her about us." He picked up the phone on the nightstand and dialed his parents' home. His father answered.

"Hello?"

"Hi, Dad. Did you see that run?"

"Yeah, we saw it. Your mother didn't want to see, but it happened so fast, there was nothing she could do but sit there and watch it."

They laughed. He could hear his mother ask his dad who was on the phone.

"It's Willy."

His mother said, "Tell 'em don't get too excited. It's only one play."

"Did you hear that, son?"

"Yeah, I heard her. Hey, Dad, can you and Mom come out today?"

"Hold on. Willy wants to know if we can come out today. Do you want to?"

"It's about time. Gimme that phone."

As she walked to the phone, Jerry Rice caught a five-yard pass and eluded three would-be tacklers. He was running between the hash marks all alone for an eighty-yard 49er touchdown.

"What did I tell y'all, huh? What did I tell y'all?" he heard his mother saying. She was closer to the phone now. "Don't get too excited. Ain't that what I said?"

"Like you said," his father replied, "It's only one play."

"Willy. Don't be callin' here to gloat, boy. Did you see what Jerry just did to your little Raiders secondary? A man among boys," she said, laughing. "A man among boys."

"Whatever. We got the ball now."

"Yeah, it's going to be three and out. Watch."

Almost as soon as she said that, Napoleon Kaufman fumbled the ball after a twenty-three-yard run. Ken Norton picked the ball up and ran into the end zone for another 49er touchdown. Brenda cleared her throat.

"You were saying? Napoleon can't even hold onto the ball. He got his little touchdown and now look at 'em. Now fumble the ball again and see what happens."

"It's still the first quarter, Mom."

"I know. That's the beauty of it. We've got three more quarters to explain to James Brown why we don't play more often. It's a mismatch. That's why." Then she laughed triumphantly.

Will put his hand over the phone and said to Terry, "My mother's a trip. She's over there going off about that little touchdown."

"Well, at least she likes the Niners," Terry whispered.

"So are you guys coming out here, or what?"

"Why? You want us to meet somebody?"

"Maybe. I don't know if she can make it today, but I'd like to talk to you about her in person."

Terry looked at him with a puzzled look on her face, thinking, *I'm here right now, Mrs. Wise. I'm in bed with him.* But she continued watching the game and listening to the conversation.

"You like her a lot, don't you?"

"Yes. I like her a whole bunch."

"You know you've been sayin' that since you were about four years old. I remember when your daddy and I took you to Fisherman's Wharf for the first time, and bought you some cotton candy. That's the first time you ever said that. You remember?"

"Yeah, I remember."

"I'm glad. I knew when I woke up that night three months ago you had found yourself a wife. I knew it in m' bones. The Holy Ghost woke me up and let me know my prayers had been answered."

Will covered the phone. He couldn't help but chuckle.

"What?" Terry asked him.

"Oh, nothing."

The Raiders started at their own twenty and drove down to the 49ers' twenty-seven-yard line. Napoleon Kaufman ran a draw up the middle on third and long for a Raiders touchdown. Will heard his dad screaming gleefully.

"It's tied up, woman!" his dad shouted. "It's tied up!"

His mother ignored his dad. She was more concerned about her son's happiness at that moment.

"Couldn't you be wrong this time?" Will asked.

"Have I ever been wrong before? Was I wrong when I told Jericho not to take you to the rail yard that day he got arrested? That decision set him on a course that changed his destiny. What would have happened if he had listened to me? Huh? I don't know but he wouldn't be livin' the kind of life he's livin' now. Would he? Was I wrong when I made you to take that scholarship to Harvard? You cried like a little baby. *I don't wanna go to Harvard. I don't wanna go to Harvard. It's too far from home.*' She sounded like a six-year-old having a tantrum. "Now look at you. You've got your own business. And what about Sterling? I told him to get outta that Air Force and practice law for real. He just wanted to stay in and travel around chasing them silly women. Shall I go on?"

"No, you don't have to. But are you sure about this? I mean, absolutely certain."

"Yes, I am. She's definitely the one. I've never been surer in my life."

"But you haven't even seen her." He was laughing under his breath.

"I don't need to see her. I'm sure she's a very nice girl. She's probably pretty, and can have lots of grandchildren."

"Nothing can change your mind?"

"Boy, the Holy Ghost ain't never wrong. You remember all them other women from the church you went out with?"

"Yeah."

"Well, as much as I wanted you to be with them, I never did get a confirmation from the Lord."

"So you sayin' God is endorsing this, then?"

"Yeah, boy. It's a match made in heaven, just like Isaac and Rebecca. And the Bible says, 'What God has put together, let no man put asunder.' So when can I meet her?"

"Uhhh, I don't know, Mom."

"Well, how about Thanksgiving? That would be a good time to meet her. The day of Thanksgiving to the Lord. That's only a week and a half away. I can wait that long."

"Are you coming out today though?"

"Yeah, we'll be out there right after the game. Okay?"

"Okay, Mom. I'll see you then."

"Okay, bye."

"Bye."

"So what was that all about?" Terry asked.

"My mother says you're the one, baby. She says the Holy Ghost told her so."

Terry laughed.

"Don't you believe in God?" he asked, looking at her.

"Yeah, but I don't believe God talks to people like that."

"Well, didn't God talk to Moses?"

"That was Moses."

"Well, let me put it to you this way. My mother is very religious. Her religious ways will eventually get you over the racial hump."

"How is that, Will?"

"My mother believes all that the Bible teaches. For example, the Bible in Genesis chapter two teaches that God made woman from man and brought her to him. My parents say it's God's job to do that for every man."

"What do you mean?"

"I mean, they believe what the Bible says about it not being good for a man to be alone. Just like God brought Eve to Adam, they believe God will bring a specific woman that was made for a specific man, into his life to complete him. That, according to my parents, was the reason for taking Adam's rib, making a woman for him with it, and bringing that woman to him. In other words, when God took the rib from Adam, it made him incomplete. Then when he gave him Eve, she brought completeness to his life, understand?"

"Hmm. That's an interesting theory, but I don't know if I believe that."

"It doesn't matter if you believe it, or not. They do. And that's your ticket to paradise. See, they think a man and woman can have the Garden of Eden experience if they wait on God. Anyway, it doesn't matter. She believes you're the woman so the only thing you have to worry about now is her changing her mind and saying she made a mistake, or something."

"Okay. So are you going to let me meet her today?"

"I don't know."

"Why not? I mean, this is ordained, isn't it?" she mocked.

"Because it could get ugly when I tell her and there's no telling what's going to come out of her mouth. I don't want you to hear something that might hurt you, you know?"

She laughed. "Yeah. Your mother might say some racist shit, even though she's religious, right?"

"Right."

"Oh, Lord. He agrees finally. I better write this down."

"Don't run the shit into the ground," he teased. "I've admitted it. What else do you want?"

"I want fifty years with you."

"Fifty years, huh?"

"Yeah...fifty."

Chapter 36:
Guess Who's Coming
to Dinner?

Terry left immediately after the game. They agreed it would be best if she wasn't there when Will's parents arrived, knowing full well it would be hard enough for his mother to deal with the situation as it was. However, she would come back and meet her later. She promised Will she would call before coming back. Will had no way of knowing if his mother would even meet her before the shock had a chance to wear off. The only good aspect of telling his mother, as far as he was concerned, was that his father had known for sometime and didn't have a problem with the relationship. Will hoped his father would prove to be an ally and a buffer between mother and son. He also hoped the 49ers win would help in easing some of the anticipated angst.

It was a quarter to five when Will heard his door chime. He was in the kitchen brewing New Orleans blend, his mother's favorite coffee. Terry had made lemonade and fresh hors d'oeuvres at half-time. His dad loved lemonade, no matter what the season.

Will took a deep breath and blew it out as he walked to the front door. He could see his parents through the white sheer curtains. His mom was wearing an authentic 49ers jersey with Jerry Rice's number eighty on it. Brenda was a big woman, with a big smile, and stood almost six feet tall. His dad was wearing a black Raiders jersey with Tim Brown's number eighty-one on it. Will opened the door.

"Hi, Mom! Hi, Dad!" Will said and hugged his parents.

"Hi, son!" his mother said with equal enthusiasm. "Did you see it? Did you see it?"

His dad curled his lips and rolled his eyes. "That's all she's been talking about all the way over here. Jerry this and Jerry that. Jerry, Jerry, Jerry."

"You just mad 'cause Jerry had a field day on y'all. They had six or seven guys on him and they still couldn't do nothin' with him."

"You see what I gotta put up with?"

Will laughed. "Come on in."

As they walked toward the kitchen, his mother asked, "Did you see that pass he caught at the fifty? He caught the ball six feet in the air, came down, and took off. They were tryin' to catch him. Jerry stopped on a dime and went the other way on them. He only had one man to beat. The man pulled up lame. He wasn't hurt! He wasn't hurt!" She laughed. "He was just embarrassed. He didn't want his kids gettin' teased in school tomorrow, that's all."

Will and his father looked at each other as if to say, "Is she ever going to stop talking about the game?"

They were about five feet or so away from the kitchen when his mother smelled the New Orleans blend; the chicory herb that gave the coffee its deeply rich blend and added tanginess to it.

"Umm," she said, taking a deep breath and holding it. "You made my favorite coffee, huh? Well, I'm still going to rub it in. Jer-ry! Jer-ry! Jer-ry!"

Will and his dad shook their heads as they walked into the kitchen. He wondered if he should spring it on her now, while she was still high from the victory. He decided he would.

"Terry made some lemonade for you, Dad."

"Did she? That sure was nice of her."

"It should be nice and cold now."

"So that's her name, huh?" Brenda asked.

"Yeah, that's her name. Do you want your favorite glass, Dad?"

"Yeah."

"You want your *Phantom of the Opera* cup, Mom?"

"Uh-huh."

Will opened the cabinet door and took out the *Phantom of the Opera* cup. He could hear the sound of chairs being pulled out in the near distance. Then he heard the air in the cushions deflate when they sat down. He opened the adjacent cabinet door and grabbed an old Oakland Raiders mug. It had number thirty-two, Jack Tatum's old number, on both sides of the glass.

"Just put the ice in it, son. Bring me the lemonade and I'll pour it myself."

Will and his mother watched his father meticulously pour his lemonade over the ice. It was like a ritual. They listened to the ice as it crackled when the beverage found its way into every nook and cranny. His father's mouth began to water in anticipation. He sat the pitcher down and picked up the glass. Like a wine connoisseur, he examined the color. Then he felt the glass for its coolness. He smelled the lemonade and just as he turned it up to drink it, he noticed his wife and son were staring at him.

"What are y'all looking at?"

Brenda laughed. "You, fool. It amazes me what lengths you go to drink a glass of lemonade. You've been doin' that little ritual for near 'bout fifty years now."

"Since I been doin' it so long, whatcha staring for?"

"You're just set in your ways, that's all. You're just set in your ways."

"You set in yours, too. That's why I love you, woman."

"You two amaze me." Will smiled. "You guys have been together that long and you're still in love. I only hope I can have that again."

"Speaking of being together, where's your friend?" Brenda asked.

"Who, Terry? She'll be here in a little while."

"I thought she would be here waiting for us. She must be on CP time."

When Brenda said that, his father choked on the lemonade. He started swallowing, then he began laughing when he heard the reference to colored people's time. His father was still coughing and trying to get some air into his windpipe.

Brenda slapped his back feverishly. "You all right, Benny?"

"Yeah," he said between coughs.

Brenda laughed, "I think you need to leave that lemonade alone, if you can't handle it."

Having regained his composure, Benny said, "I seriously doubt if she's on CP time."

Will laughed. "I doubt it, too." Then he laughed a little more.

"Oh?" Brenda said, with a questioningly look on her face. "Why is that?"

"Because she's white," Will blurted out.

Brenda laughed a little at first. Then she seemed to be contemplating the ridiculousness of the statement and laughed louder. She tried to talk, but every time she tried to say what she was thinking, she would start laughing all over again. The more she tried to stop, the funnier it became. As Will and his father listened, her laughter became contagious. They knew it wasn't a laughing matter, but they couldn't help themselves.

When their collective laughter began to wane, Brenda said, "So when is the white woman coming?" Then she laughed a little more.

"She should be callin' any minute now," Will said, looking at his watch.

"Who is it?" Brenda still didn't believe Terry was white. "Is it somebody I know?"

"No, it's nobody you know."

"I bet I do. What church does she go to? I know everybody in the church. Just tell me her mother's name, and I'll tell you the daughter's name." She looked confident.

"Her mother's name is Dyan, but you don't know her. She lives in New Haven, Connecticut."

"Don't nobody live in Connecticut but white folks," Brenda said, without thinking. It still hadn't hit her yet.

Will and his dad looked at her. They quietly consumed their beverages for a few seconds and watched the wheels turn in her mind. They could see she was realizing that this was not a joke after all. She looked at Will. He looked at her. He had a serious look on his face, which confirmed her suspicion. She turned to her husband and he had the same look as her son. She shook her head in disbelief.

"This ain't funny no more. Tell me the truth, Willy. You're scarin' me now."

"It is the truth, Mama. Why do you think I wanted to tell you to your face?"

Brenda's facial expression changed from pompous gaiety to that of fearful sobriety in microseconds. Now everything in her knew that he was telling the truth. It was a truth she hadn't prepared for. She could understand Sterling falling for a white woman. He was always running around with all kinds of women. *But not my Willy.* Brenda told him how white women always lusted after black men and how they would do anything to have one. Suddenly it occurred to her that Benny wasn't saying anything about this earth-shattering news.

She turned to him and said, "Benny, did you know about this?"

"Yeah, Brenda, I knew about it."

"Why didn't you tell me about this!?"

"Before you start rantin' and ravin', let me explain."

"Okay, explain why you would keep something like this from me after near 'bout fifty years? Explain how you could look me in the eye day after day and not say a word? How long have you known, huh?"

"Now, Mama, it ain't Daddy's fault."

"You shut your mouth, boy! This is between your daddy and me! Now hush up!"

"Mama, I'm thirty-six years old and—"

"And you ain't too old for me to go upside your head! Now shut-your-mouth!" Then she turned back to her husband and said, "Benny, don't you lie to me! How long have you known about this?"

"I've known about it since he came home from Toronto."

"THREE MONTHS! YOU KEPT THIS FROM ME FOR THREE MONTHS!"

"WOMAN, YOU GETTIN' BESIDE YOURSELF! DON'T BE HOLLERIN' AT ME LIKE I'M SOME CHILD YOU CARRIED FOR NINE MONTHS. I DON'T KNOW WHO YOU THINK YOU TALKIN' TO, BUT IT AIN'T ME. NOW IF HE DON'T WANT YOU KNOWING HIS BUSINESS, IT AIN'T FOR ME TO TELL YOU! AND DON'T BE JUMPIN' ON ME 'CAUSE YOU MAD AT HIM! IT'S HIS CHOICE NOW! NOT YOURS! NOW THAT'S ALL I GOT TO SAY ABOUT IT!"

"HOW Y'ALL EXPECT ME TO TAKE IT? WHAT? DID YOU EXPECT ME TO BE HAPPY ABOUT IT?"

"You were happy on the phone when I talked to you this afternoon," Will retorted in a caustic manner. "You were going on and on about how the Holy Ghost had told you this and told you that and how the Holy Ghost can't be wrong. You kept talking about this was the one and how she was going to have my children."

"BOY, DON'T YOU MOCK ME!" She bowed her head. "Besides, you tricked me."

"How did I trick you, Mama? Tell me. How did I trick you?"

"What is it? Sex? Is that what you want? You just gotta try it out before you die? Is that what this is about?"

"No, Mama. It isn't like that with her."

"Oh, she different from the rest of 'em, huh?"

"Yeah. She's a lot different from the rest. Black or white."

"So what you sayin'? She ain't freaky in bed? You know what they say 'bout them white girls. They'll do anything in bed; especially for a black man. You think she'd be with you if you didn't live in this house? Huh? You think she'd be with you if you didn't own your own business? Huh? You think she'd be with you if you didn't have deep pockets?"

"Mama, she's got money of her own."

"Oh, so she's rich and slummin', huh? How long do you think she's going to stick around when she tires of you? Huh? How long? She's just going to find another black buck to be freaky with. Y'all come a dime a dozen to her kind. Tell me this. How she look? Is she one of them mangy-looking white girls that y'all seem to go for or what?"

Will looked to his father for help.

His father looked back at him. "This is your show, son. I can't help you with this. Like I told you, you can't make folk except y'all. People gon' be people. That includes your mother. This is what you have to look forward to. You ready for it?"

Just as he finished, the phone rang. Will knew it was Terry. As he got up to answer the phone, he said, "Well, are you at least going to meet her?"

"Yeah, I'll meet her all right," Brenda blasted. "When I meet her, I'm going to tell her about herself. Where she at?"

"Hello."

"Well, at least you're still alive, and the house is still standin'." Terry laughed.

"Where are you?"

"In the driveway."

"Okay, I'll meet you at the front door," Will said, and hung up the phone.

"She finally showed up, huh? She got guts. I'll give her that much. But we're leaving."

"What? She's already here."

"I know. I heard you on the phone."

"Are you going to at least meet her before you go?"

"I said I would, didn't I?"

"Okay, I'll go get her."

Will left the kitchen and headed for the front door. Frantic, he opened it. "My mother will meet you, but they'll be leaving right after that. I'm sorry about this, but I told you she wouldn't go for it."

"Okay," she said nervously.

They walked into the kitchen hand in hand. Then Will said, "Mama, this is Dr. Terry Moretti. Terry, this is my mom."

"Pleased to meet you, Mrs. Wise." Terry extended her hand to greet his mother, but Brenda wouldn't shake hands with her.

"You let me tell you somethin', Ms. Thang," Brenda began loudly. "If you think I'm going to ever accept you and my son together, you outta yo' mind. I'll be waiting in the car, Benny." Then she stormed out.

"I'm sorry about this, Terry," Benny offered. "Give it time. But know this is a sample of what you're going to have to deal with. People simply don't like it and they like to ridicule people like y'all. Well, I gotta go. My wife is waitin' on me. Thanks for the lemonade. That was sweet of you. Y'all take it easy now." Then he walked out the room.

Terry turned to Will and said glibly, "I guess we can forget about Thanksgiving dinner, huh?"

†††

Will's parents rode all the way home in silence. Benny tried to talk to Brenda but she wouldn't respond. All she would do is grunt and groan. When they reached their home, Brenda got out of the car and slammed the car door. The car shook from the power of the door slamming. He sat in the car and watched his wife walk to the house in an angry hurry. She opened the front door and slammed it behind her. Then she picked up the phone and called her sister-in-law. The phone rang a couple of times before she picked up.

"Johnnie," Brenda groaned. "One of them white Barracudas done stole my Willy!"

Chapter 37:
The First Time

November 1997

Terry was sitting behind her desk thinking about her upcoming weekend in Boyes Hot Springs, California. As she listened to the O'Jays' "Stairway to Heaven" on the radio, she was becoming more and more aroused as she fantasized about Will. As soon as he called, she'd be out the door to pick him up and they would be on their way to the Sonoma Mission and Spa, where she booked them a suite for two nights and three days. They were supposed to leave at about twelve. She looked at her watch—11:07. Her phone beeped and her assistant said, "Dr. Moretti, you have a delivery."

"I'll be right out."

She opened her office door and saw a dozen long-stemmed roses in a black vase with her name inscribed in gold lettering. Taken completely by surprise, she almost shouted, but bottled her festive excitement.

"See who they're from," her assistant urged, excitedly.

Terry walked over to the flowers and smelled them. She took the card out of the envelope and read the message. *My heart and my soul longeth for thee. I shall withhold nothing from you. I am yours, now, forever, and always. Signed, you know who.* Terry's heart skipped a beat.

"What does it say? Who are they from?"

"A friend," she said, smiling from ear to ear.

Terry picked up the vase, went back into her office, and closed the door. She placed the roses on her desk and dialed Will's office at the clinic. Jeannine answered.

"Hi, Jeannine, is Will there?"

"No, he's been gone for about forty-five minutes. He's probably at home. I was about to leave myself."

"He sent me a dozen of the most beautiful roses."

"Yeah, I know. He told me he was going to."

"Did he tell you about our little excursion this weekend?"

"You know he did, girl. I hope y'all have a wonderful time."

"Oh, we will. Don't worry about that."

"I bet you will. You've been waiting three years," Jeannine said, laughing. "You probably won't last five minutes."

"Not even that long. I hope Will has a strong back, but if he doesn't, I do."

"You go, girl."

"I will. In fact, I plan on being that little Energizer bunny. You know the one that keeps going and going and going."

They laughed again.

"Don't let me hold you up, girl. I'll talk to you when you come back."

"Okay, bye."

"Bye."

Terry pushed a button on her phone that gave her a free line, and dialed Will's house. He had already picked up the phone. She could hear phone tones. He picked up the phone at the same moment she called. He kept pushing the button to get a dial tone.

"Will?"

"Terry?"

"Yes, darlin', it's me!"

"The phone didn't even ring. I was just about to call you and let you know I'm ready, if you are. Did you get the flowers?"

"Yes. They just got here. They're beautiful."

"They just got there? They were supposed to deliver them by nine."

"You worry about the most insignificant things," she said and laughed a little. "The only thing that matters is that you sent them to me."

"Did you like the card?"

"Yes. It was sweet. Thank you."

"Well, I meant every word of it."

"Did you?"

"Yes, I did."

"Well, I'm on my way to get you. Are you nervous?"

"A little. Are you?"

"Not really. A little, I suppose, but not much."

"Okay, I'll be waiting."

"I'm out the door now. See you in about six minutes, or so."

†††

Will was looking out the window when Terry pulled the red Mitsubishi into the circular driveway. The car had a high glossy shine and the chrome-plated alloy wheels sparkled. He picked up his bag, turned on the alarm, and walked out the house. Terry pulled a lever inside the car and the trunk opened. Will tossed his bags in and then he slid into the tan leather seats.

"Hi!" she bubbled, greeting him with a soft kiss on the mouth. He could feel himself beginning to stiffen already, but maintained his cool. "The seat adjustment button is on the side."

Will reached down on his right side and searched with his hand until he found it. Then he moved the seat all the way back and tilted back.

Terry waited for him to finish and she said, "Put your seat belt on."

"How fast are you gonna be driving?"

Terry laughed. "This baby has a top speed of 180 mph."

"You don't plan on going that fast, I know, right?"

Terry laughed again, put the stick in first, and peeled off out of the driveway. Will's head snapped back against the headrest. He grabbed the hand strap right above his door, and put his hand on the dashboard. Then he looked at her with a wild look in his eyes. She stopped at the corner and Will put on his seat belt. Moments later they were turning onto the expressway.

"Hey, Will, I've got a theme song for our weekend in the CD player. You wanna hear it?"

"Sure."

She pushed a button on the dash. Seconds later "Slippin' into Darkness" began. He looked at her and laughed, simultaneously shaking his head. He loved her sense of humor. Then she turned the music up and floored it. Will's head snapped back. He looked at her again. She was shifting gears like she was Jeff Gordon at the Indianapolis 500. She started passing cars, weaving in and out of traffic. Will looked at the speedometer—115 mph. He shook his head again.

Terry saw him looking at the speedometer and said, "Hey, this car is made to be driven like this."

"You think you can get us there in one piece?"

"Not a problem. We'll be there in less than forty minutes."

She shifted into fifth gear and the turbo kicked in as they picked up speed.

†††

They checked in at the Sonoma Mission Inn at 12:30. The suite was a blend of luxury and casual country elegance. Terry looked up and saw the white ceiling fan, and thought it might be better served in the bedroom where it would surely be hot. She wondered if there was one in there also. Will went over to the window and closed the plantation shutters. The room darkened a bit. Terry went into the bedroom and began unpacking. She was bending over her suitcase when Will came up behind her. She could feel his hard tool rubbing against her. She stood up and turned around. They kissed.

"I bought something special for you, Will."

"What?"

"You'll see. Why don't you plug in the CD player, but don't turn it on, okay? I'm going to go into the bathroom and change. I'll be right out." Terry kissed him again and squeezed his hardness a little. "I hope you have a strong back." Then she kissed him again, and went into the bathroom.

Will quickly unpacked his bag, undressed, and got in bed. Then he remembered he was supposed to plug in the CD player. He plugged it in, and wondered why she didn't want him to turn it on, but didn't dwell on it. He could hear water splashing in the bathroom. He picked up the remote and turned on the television. He was watching a rerun of *Deep Space Nine*. It was the episode when Dax and Worf decided to go on vacation together.

Terry came out of the bathroom about twenty minutes later, freshly perfumed, wearing a long-sleeved, black-lace cat suit that clung to every curve; her raven hair rested on her shoulders. She stood before him and he stared at her—his mouth open. Although he couldn't remember what it was, he remembered it was the same brand she had worn in his suite in Toronto, which seemed so long ago to him now. He looked at her from head to toe; occasionally stopping at her more sexual parts.

The sheer fabric of the suit made it possible to see her completely nude, yet she was completely covered. It was very erotic. The suit could be opened enough to expose her breasts, but he hoped there was an opening in the vagina area so he could have her while she was still wearing the suit. He took a deep anticipatory breath and let the air dissipate through his nostrils.

Terry watched him as he admired her body; seeing the unbridled lust in his eyes made her feel sexy and desirable. She had wanted him for so long. Now she would have the man of her dreams in the most intimate way. As her desire for him increased, she could feel herself beginning to lubricate. She remembered what had happened in Toronto, and how they might have been intimate then, but she was glad they had waited a while. She now understood that it was essential to wait because he needed to. She remembered the words on the card with the roses. *I shall withhold nothing from you. I am yours, now, forever, and always.*

Will picked up the remote and hit the power button. Then he got out of the bed, and stood before her in his black briefs. He could see that her mound area was completely covered with thick straight black hair. He walked over to her, and she put both of her hands on his well-muscled chest.

"I like the way you feel, Will." His stiff organ was protruding outward and pressing against her.

"I like the way you feel, too." He pulled her closer and kissed her gently on the lips. Then he picked her up and carried her to the bed.

"I want you to play the tape I brought."

"Okay."

He went over to the CD player, and pushed the play button on the tape player. "A Love of Your Own" by the Average White Band began playing.

"Is this the same tape you played in Toronto?"

"Umm, hmm. I wanted to finish what we started that night."

Will smiled. He went back over to the bed and got in with her. He kissed her again, and she kissed him back. He fondled her breasts, and she moaned softly. Then he slid his hand between her legs and into the opening of the cat suit, and felt her wetness. Her excitement was a natural aphrodisiac for him.

"I want you in me now," she beckoned softly.

He kissed her deeply, taking her warm tongue into his mouth, which made him even harder. Then he climbed on top of her and guided himself into her. She moaned again as he entered her, and said, "Oh, Will, I've wanted this for so long."

He looked down into her eyes and said, "I love you, Terry."

"I love you, too."

He stared at her for a minute, or so.

"What's the matter, Will?"

"Nothing. You're just so beautiful. We should have done this a long time ago."

"No darlin', we did the right thing."

He kissed her again and they slowly made love for the first time.

Chapter 38: Do We Have a Deal?

The Nighthawk landed at McCarran International at 11 PM and parked at terminal two. Jericho and the crew had spent the previous three months looking at apartment buildings that would be perfect houses of ill repute. Now they were in Vegas to check on the whorehouse Carlton Chadwick had won in the poker game in August. Prostitution was only legal outside the county line. The casino owners wanted the tourists to gamble their money away, not give it to ladies of the evening.

Cochise and Victor couldn't wait to get to the whorehouse, which was over an hour's ride south of Vegas. They were excited about owning a whorehouse, and talked about trying all the lovely ladies out since it would be free. But when they reached the ranch, they were very disappointed, having expected a big beautiful house with nothing but beautiful women running around in lingerie, if that. What they saw was a line of shabby-looking trailers lined up side by side, filled with women who were as far from beauty as the earth is from the moon. These women looked old and tired, like they had taken age injections or something.

Cochise and Victor were very disappointed and felt sorry for the girls.

Jericho called Carlton Chadwick on a satellite phone and told him he had been swindled.

Later, around 2:30 in the morning, on the way back to the Mandalay Bay Hotel, Cochise saw an exceptionally fine-looking "escort" sitting at a bus stop. She was a classy-looking woman with smooth chocolate skin, long sexy legs, firm perky breasts that begged to be admired, and a smile that could cause a traffic pileup. Cochise pulled the limousine over and retracted the window. "You working?"

"You buying?" she said, leaning in the window, showing him those perky nipples.

"How much, sweetheart?"

"More than a limo driver can afford, I'm afraid. Perhaps your boss can afford me."

"Perhaps. Get in. I'm sure he'd like to talk to you. We're looking for beautiful women like you."

Skeptical, the woman said, "I'm not into kinky shit. I don't do more than one man at a time and I don't do women. No gang-banging. Will he be okay with that?"

"Yes, his wife is back there also. I'm sure she won't allow anything. This is a business proposition, sweetheart. But, I'm going to need to sample the merchandise. You gotta pimp or are you with an agency in town?"

"Pimp."

Cochise picked up the phone. "Jerry, I got one you might wanna take a serious look at. The girl is fine as hell. Too fine to be on the streets. Got a pimp though." He hung up the phone. "Go ahead and get in. He wants to talk to you." She turned to leave. "Hey, what's your name, sweet thing?

"You can call me Plenty." She smiled.

"You definitely right about that. We'll talk later, I'm sure."

Plenty got into the limo and Cochise headed toward the Mandalay Bay. A minute passed and the phone rang. Cochise picked it up. "Yeah."

Pin said, "Head over to strip. We get her pimp. He drive a pink Caddy with pipes along the side."

Several minutes later, Cochise spotted the pink Caddy and stopped next to it. Victor Marshall got out of the car and tapped on the tinted window of the pimp's car. The window retracted. "Who wants Shaggy?" the pimp said and blew rings of smoke through the window. Victor reached inside the car and pulled the pimp through the open window and tossed him on the floor in the back of the limo. Cochise pulled off.

"The name's Victor Marshall, asshole."

Jericho said, "How much do you want for Plenty?"

Shaggy was so shaken by Victor manhandling him, he hadn't noticed that one of his girls was sitting on the seat facing the man who had just asked him about her. He whirled around and looked at her. Plenty was drinking from a champagne glass. He looked at the man who had asked him the question. "She's not for sale."

With that, Victor grabbed Shaggy by the collar and tossed him out of the moving limousine. Shaggy bounced off the pavement a couple of times. Cochise stopped the limo, backed up, and Victor got out of the car. He picked Shaggy up, who was scuffed up and bleeding from a variety of places, and tossed him into the back of the limo again. Cochise pulled off.

Before Shaggy could figure out what he wanted to say, Jericho politely said, "How much did you say you wanted for Plenty? I didn't quite hear you before."

Shaggy looked at Pin, who was laughing hysterically. "How about we trade? You take my whore and I'll take yours."

With that, Victor tossed Shaggy out of the limo again. Cochise stopped the limo, backed up, and Victor got out. He tossed Shaggy in the back of the limo a third time.

Jericho said, "Forgive me for being so rude. This beautiful lady is my wife. Her name is Pin. And since you had no idea who you were talking about when you called her a whore, I'm going to let you live, but I'm through bullshitting with you. Now…I'm willing to pay ten thousand for Plenty. Do we have a deal?" He pulled a thick wad of money out of his pocket and counted out ten thousand dollars. The wad was still thick.

"Plenty is worth ten times that, man."

Jericho took half of the money he offered and put it back with the wad. "She's worth much more, but I'm going to pay you five thousand for her, okay?"

"You said ten, man?"

"Do you want the five, or not?" Jericho asked, handing him the money. Shaggy took the money and counted it. It was all there. "Now get out."

"Stop the car."

Jericho picked up the phone and told Cochise, "Speed up every 60 seconds until Shaggy here jumps out of the car." He hung up. Shaggy got the message and jumped out of the limo, bouncing on the pavement as the limo sped away.

Chapter 39:
Family Secrets

Sonoma Mission
November 1997

It was a little after four in the afternoon and they had made mad passionate love several times. They were listening to New Birth's "Wildflower" for the second time when Terry said, "I love listening to this guy talk to the woman in this song. He sounds so sincere, you know what I mean?"

"Yeah."

While they basked in the glow of physical love, Will, who was pressing his body against Terry's, had his hand around her waist, lightly stroking her stomach and occasionally caressing her breasts. While he was stroking her, he heard her stomach growl; he felt the vibration, too.

"Sounds like somebody's hungry. You wanna order something to eat, babe?"

"Not right now. I want to talk to you and listen to the music a little longer, okay?"

"Okay," he said, and kissed the back of her head.

They were quiet for a moment.

"Will?"

"Yeah, baby," he said, nibbling on her right earlobe.

"Umm, I like that." She turned her head around and kissed him. Their lips made a smacking sound when they touched.

"Will?"

"Hmm," he said, nibbling on her neck. "You like that?"

"Yes, I do." She kissed him again. "Did you mean what you said on the card you sent with the roses?"

"Uh-huh." He felt himself stiffening, and wanted to make love again. He pulled her closer to him, and began biting her neck softly.

"I won't be mad if you didn't, but did you mean it when you said you loved me?"

"Yes."

"Are you sure?"

He stopped nibbling and turned her over, and looked her in the eyes. "I haven't been this sure in a long, long time. My feelings for you go way beyond simple attraction. I like you as a friend and much more." He stopped talking for a moment, and seemed to be contemplating what he'd just said.

Terry sensed he was thinking about something. "What's the matter?"

"Nothing. I was just thinking about something that my father always told me. I was thinking about it in Toronto as well."

"What did he say?"

"He talked about liking the person you're involved with. And I like everything about you."

"Everything?"

"Well, everything except your temper. But I'm willing to deal with it, if that's the worst of it. But you know..." He paused again.

"No, what?"

"It's strange how I can remember all that he said, ya know. It's like I'm becoming more like him every day. I used to get so tired of hearing him philosophizing about everything, but it all makes sense now."

Terry turned over, and laid her head on his chest. She could hear his heart beating. She rubbed her hands across his stomach, and inner thighs. "Will?"

"Huh?" He was still in deep thought.

"Were you teased as a child?"

"Yeah."

"Me, too." Her tone was more subdued. "Did they have a nickname for you that you absolutely couldn't stand?"

"Yeah." He laughed. "They used to call me B-B head."

"B-B head? Why did they call you that?"

"Because my hair used to be nappy as hell. I broke so many combs my mother said we oughta invest in Afro combs." He laughed a little more. "It's funny now, but that shit bothered me at the time, ya know?"

"Yes, I do."

"So what did they call you?"

"You promise not to laugh?"

"Nope. If it's funny, I'm going to laugh."

"Forget it then."

"You gon' be like that?"

"Yes."

"Does it bother you that much?"

"A little."

"Okay, I'll try not to laugh, but I can't promise not to, okay?"

"Okay," she said. "They used to call me Mr. Spock."

"The Doctor or the *Star Trek* character?"

"The *Star Trek* character."

"Okay, I'll bite. Why did they call you that?"

"Look at me, Will."

He raised himself up on his elbows, and looked at her—puzzled. "I don't see it."

"Look at my eyebrows," she said, in disbelief. "Do you see the natural arch?"

"Not really, no."

"You don't see it?"

"No."

Not believing her ears she frowned, but wasn't aware of it. "Maybe if I pull my hair back." Using both hands, she pulled her hair back. "Can you see it now?"

He looked at her eyebrows and the shape of her ears. Although her ears weren't pointed like Spock's, their size and shape did remind him of the famed television character. "Yes, I see it now."

"You do?"

"Yeah, but I don't see anything funny about it."

"Good, I'm glad you didn't laugh because I want to tell you how insecure I used to be."

"That's hard to believe."

"It's true. I was five-nine by the time I was twelve. I had my period, and my breasts were almost the size they are now. I was so different, ya know. Then I had to get these God-awful braces. To top that off, I was the smartest, and the youngest person in junior high school. I had always been the youngest in school because I was two grades ahead. Anyway, I used to wear these glasses that reminded the kids of Jerry Lewis. So they all called me the Nutty Professor. Some of them called me the Jolly Green Giant. Those kids were so ruthless sometimes. You know how quiet it is when you're taking a test?"

"Uh-huh," he said in a relaxed tone.

"I remember whipping through my biology test, and this boy I liked, but I didn't want him to know I liked him, wanted to look at my paper. He was making all kinds of gesticulations with his hands to get my attention. It made me feel good to have the upper hand. I pretended like I couldn't see him. The next thing I know, he's going, 'Ho Ho Ho, Green Giant.' Everybody turned around and looked at me. I could hear them snickering."

Will laughed a little and said, "Well, that is funny."

"I guess it is. But it certainly wasn't funny at the time."

"What made you tell me this now?"

"I'm not sure, really. I guess it came to me when you were talking about your dad, and things you remember about your childhood."

"Despite being teased, did you have a happy childhood?"

"For the most part, I did. If I had it to do all over again, I'd like to stay in my same grade, and be around children my own age. Was yours happy? Your childhood, I mean?"

"Yes, it was. We didn't have much, but we were happy."

"That's good."

"Yeah, in my neighborhood, you had to use your mind to have fun. You didn't have no Sega Genesis. Naw, you had to find a way to have fun. I remember playing tag with my friends. Sometimes we'd play volleyball and stuff. We played hopscotch and jumped rope. Then we'd play spades and Monopoly. By the way, whatever you do, don't play my mother in Monopoly. If you think the kids you grew up with were ruthless, my mother is the Simon Bar Sinister of Monopoly."

Terry laughed.

"Simon Bar Sinister," she reflected. "I haven't heard that name in so long. Who was your favorite Underdog character?"

"Underdog. Who else? But back to what I was saying. My mother loves to break people in Monopoly. You ain't gon' believe this—"

"Will, I love the way you can talk so different at times. One minute you sound like the Harvard graduate you are, and other times, like when we played cards with Cheryl and Cleve, you talk different. I noticed that you, Jeannine, and Jonathan talk differently when you're by yourselves than when you're with the entire staff. For example, did you know that when you get pissed you say git, instead of get?"

"Yeah, I know what you mean, but didn't you have a black roommate in college? Didn't she talk different also?"

"If she did, I never heard her."

"Well, let me hip you."

She looked at him, and said in as cool a voice as she could, "Well, hip me, darlin'." Then she laughed.

"Somehow it don't sound right when you try it. But stick with me, I'll get you through."

They laughed.

"So why do y'all do it? You know, talk different around each other."

"Have you ever noticed that Chinese Americans, and Japanese Americans, and Mexican Americans, and any other group that migrated here speak their language among themselves, but speak English to you?"

"Well, yeah. Whenever I get Chinese food, they'll be talking up a storm in Chinese, and then they tell you your bill in English."

Will laughed. "I heard Eddie Murphy say that on one of his early albums."

"Yeah. Me, too. That's when I first started noticing it, but what's your point?"

"My point is that every nationality in this country has their own language. Whether they speak it or not, they have one. Black people are the only ones who don't have a native tongue. So when I speak to a black person, I speak the only language that gives us some sort of identity. The problem is some of us don't know when it's appropriate, and when it isn't. Take Sterling, for example. That's why they fired him. He was lucky to get that big Bellamy case. If it wasn't for that case, he might be chasing ambulances right now."

"So it's an identity thing with you, huh?"

"Yes. Exactly."

"Oh, okay. Well, I like it."

"Good, I'm glad you do. Now can I finish tellin' you about my mother and Monopoly?"

"I'm sorry, darlin'. Please, continue."

"What was I saying?"

"You're not going to believe this—" she reminded him.

"Oh, yeah. You're not going to believe this but, playing Monopoly is how my mother got her real estate business going."

"Playing Monopoly? I wanna hear this."

"It's true. And the killin' part about it is, she didn't have any collateral when she went to the bank."

"What kind of bank doesn't require collateral? Did she have the money in the bank, or what?"

"No, she didn't. That's the strange thing about it. She wanted me to co-sign for her, but I told her no. I said, 'Just because you're the queen of Monopoly doesn't mean you can do it in the real world.'"

"What did she say?"

"She said, 'Fine. I don't need you. I can do it on my own. Jesus gon' help me out; even if you won't.'"

"I guess she was right, huh?"

"I guess."

"So what bank is this?"

"Why do you ask? You wanna see if you can get a loan?"

"Hell no. I wanna march my ass down there, and withdraw every penny of my hard-earned money, if they're making loans like this." She laughed. "No offense. I know it worked out for your mom, but Jesus! That's terrible banking!"

"I know, but I trust the bank and do nearly all my banking there. I financed my home and both my cars there. They were the ones who gave me my first business loan. I had nothing, except a doctorate from Harvard."

"And they gave you a loan?"

"Yeah. Well, not initially. I musta went to sixty banks before I went back to them."

"What's the name of the bank?"

"Chadwick International." He laughed a little. "I remember when Francis and I first—" He stopped in mid-sentence. "Did it bother you when I mentioned Francis just then? Be honest?"

"Honestly? No. Why would it? Just promise me you'll remember me long after I'm no longer around also. A girl likes to know she has a lasting effect on a man."

"So from time to time, if I should mention something that we did, or if something should remind me of her, it wouldn't bother you, right?"

"Right."

Will raised himself up, and kissed her. "You are so sweet, girl."

"You really think so?"

"Umm, hmm," he said, and kissed her again.

"Now…you will remember me when I'm no longer around, right?"

"Right. But you don't plan on going anywhere anytime soon, do you?"

"Naw. I plan to be around a long time."

"How long is a long time?"

"As long as you want me, darlin'."

"Good, 'cause I may never let you go." He kissed her again.

"Just so you know, I didn't change the subject this time, Will. You did."

"Oh yeah. You made me lose my train of thought."

"Sure, blame it on me. That's the first step to senility."

"Well, I gotta blame somebody." He laughed. "Anyway, Francis and I went in there and applied for a loan."

"Was this before or after you two got married?"

"After."

"Okay, did you lose your train of thought that time?" She teased.

"Don't run it into the ground." He grinned. "Anyway, we could tell by the way the man was trying to keep from laughing we weren't going to get the loan. We started to get up and leave, but we waited for the bad news."

"How did you get the loan then?"

"I really don't know, to be honest. One day, a loan officer from the bank called me, and asked if I still wanted the loan."

"The same guy that turned you down?"

"No, I asked about him when I got there, and they said he wasn't with the bank anymore. I was kinda glad, but I hope he didn't get fired, or anything."

"I doubt they fired him, but even if they did, I seriously doubt you had anything to do with it. If they fired him, he must have done something awfully terrible financially. Based on what you said, he did the right thing by turning you down."

"Yeah, you're probably right. Anyway, that's how I got the loan for my business."

"My mother has her own boutique in New Haven. She's had it for years. I don't know the particulars as to how she got it, or if she had to struggle, or anything. I just know she got it six years after we moved there. I think I was eighteen. It was during the summer of my sophomore year at Stanford. She was excited as hell to get it though."

"You were eighteen years old and a college sophomore, huh?"

"Yeah, wasn't everybody?" She laughed a little.

"I was twenty going into my junior year, but that was because I went to school year-round."

"Why did you do that?"

"I never wanted to go there in the first place. I only went because my mother wanted me to. I had scholarship offers from all the Ivy League schools. But she pushed me to go to Harvard. She said it was a 'prestige' thing. In retrospect, I'm glad I went."

"Well, didn't you like going to such a historical and prestigious school?"

"Not particularly. See, babe, what you have to understand is, I'm from the ghetto. Going to Harvard meant nothing to me at the time. Don't get me wrong. I don't want to sound ungrateful, but I was far too young to understand what it meant to go to Harvard. To me, all I was doing was going to some school that was almost three thousand miles away. I was leaving my family and friends. People I'd known all my life."

"People like Cleve?"

"Yeah. Cleve and I have been friends for years. We grew up together."

"So did you like anything about Harvard?"

"Yeah, I liked the school, but I did have some problems there."

"What problems?"

"You really wanna know?"

"I wouldn't ask if I didn't," she said, in a quiet attentive tone.

"To be honest, the shit started off bad."

"How did it start?"

"Well, ya know, when they award scholarships, they assign you a mentor and everything to help you get through school. I mean, after all, they would look bad awarding a student a full scholarship and then that student doesn't even make it through school. And being black didn't make it any easier. In fact, it made it more difficult."

"Why was it more difficult? It's not like they gave you anything. You won the scholarship on merit, didn't you?"

"Yep, but it's different if you win fair and square when you're black."

"How's it different?"

"It's different because white folk think somebody gave you something. No matter what you do, that's what they believe."

"What difference does it make what they believe? Ya just gotta go for it, ya know?"

"True. But the problem is people tend to treat you according to what they believe about you. It doesn't matter that what they believe may not be the truth. Truth is what people believe it to be. Am I making any sense to you?"

"Yeah." She wanted to say, "Yeah, people like your mother," but knew it wouldn't go over well. "So what happened at Harvard?"

"I told you about them assigning me a mentor, right?"

"Right."

"Well, his name was Professor Fairchild. I remember my first day on campus like it was yesterday. He was sitting behind his big desk staring at me, lookin' like John Houseman, with those bushy gray and black eyebrows that needed a haircut. You think your eyebrows make you look like an alien? You ain't got nothin' on this man."

Terry laughed, and hit him playfully.

"He had the nerve to sit there and tell me he didn't like niggas, but he thought everybody deserved an education. Then he said, if I told anybody, he'd just deny it. And he said he wasn't worried about it because he had tenure, and he couldn't be fired."

"What did you say?"

"I didn't say anything. He kept running his mouth. He told me I wasn't going to be an embarrassment to him, to Harvard, or to myself. He told me I would study harder than I'd ever studied in my life. And if I didn't have study skills, he'd see to it that I got them. What pissed me off was that he was right. I didn't know what the hell he was talking about. Study? I never had to. I was thinking what is this fool talking about?"

"But you graduated Magna Cum Laude, didn't you?"

"Yeah."

"How did you do that without studying?"

"I didn't say I didn't study at Harvard. But to be honest, I had no plans of studying when I left Fairchild's office. None whatsoever."

"Well, what changed your mind?"

"During orientation, I overheard some white boys taking bets as to how long I would last, and what kind of grades I'd get. And I don't mean no five-dollar bets either. I figured their parents were rich or something because these guys were betting in the thousands. Can you imagine that shit? Here we were in the library and they were discussing me. They referred to me as the Affirmative Action case. The shit pissed me off. My SAT scores were through the roof. But because I was black, it had to be Affirmative Action because there was no way a black kid from the ghetto was going to outperform whites without it.

"I think it was then that I started to hear my father's words. He had always said a black man had to be twice as good as a white man to even be considered half as good as him. Never did those words ring truer than right at that moment. I made up my mind right then and there that I was going to not only finish, but finish better than all of them. To be honest, that was the moment that defined my success. I had a choice to make, and I made it."

After saying this, he kind of chuckled and shook his head. He couldn't believe what he had just said.

Terry asked, "What's funny?"

"You know, Terry, my father's favorite subject was life choices. He always talked about how our decisions today, could forever affect our tomorrows. It's just so ironic, ya know?"

"Yeah, darlin', I do. Sounds like I owe those bigots a debt of gratitude then, huh?"

"What do you mean?"

"It's like what you told James in Toronto, and what you just said. You know, the part about how our decisions affect our future, or something like that, remember?"

"Yeah, I remember. And you're right. Those guys do have something to do with us being here right now. I didn't know it at the time, but now I know there is no way I would have made it through Harvard with the lackadaisical attitude I had. So in a way, they did me a favor. If my mother was here, she'd quote a scripture. She'd say, 'All things work together for good to them that know the Lord, Willy.'"

"But it was you who went for it, darlin'."

"Yes, I did."

"And I'm the beneficiary of their bet, in a way. We probably would never have met if you hadn't made it through Harvard. It's fate, Will. We were meant to be."

"I know. It's wild, isn't it? Decisions and whatnot."

"Will, it's not that I don't enjoy talking to you about Harvard and racism, but can I tell you something?"

"Yes, anything."

"I hope you don't get upset with me when I tell you this."

"What is it?" he asked.

"Let me just ask you this. How do you feel about gay people?"

"Fine. A lot of our clients are homosexuals. Why?"

"I think it's wrong."

"Is your brother a homosexual, Terry?"

Stunned that he guessed so easily, she lifted her head off his chest, and looked him in the eye. "How do you do that? I mean, how do you know things without knowing like that? I didn't say anything about my brother at all today. As a matter of fact, I rarely mention him. So how did you know?"

"I didn't know, really. It was the nature of the conversation that led me to ask the question. When two people feel close to each other the way we do, they tend to have an attitude of disclosure. Meaning, they want to reveal personal details, whether it be about themselves, or family secrets. It was logical, really."

"Well, he is, and it bothers the hell outta me."

"Why is that?"

"I think homosexuality is wrong."

"Why is that?"

"The Bible says it is, that's why."

"The Bible has been used to justify a lot of things. Some people try to use it to say you and I shouldn't be together because we black people have the curse of Ham on us or some stupid shit like that."

"Really? I never heard that before."

"Yeah, but back to your brother."

"I love Michael, but I don't agree with what he's doing."

"Is that his name?" He looked surprised. "My oldest brother's middle name is Michael, and I don't like his lifestyle either."

"Really? Is that why your father referred to Sterling as his other son in the restaurant that day?"

Will frowned. "You do have perceptive skills, huh?"

"I try, darlin'."

"I thought you missed that."

"Well, I didn't, and I'm also not missin' yo' ass tryin' to change the subject either. Did I say it right? It is yo', isn't it?"

"Yeah, that's right." He laughed. "But you have to get rid of that Southern drawl a little more, and you in there."

"Okay, so what's wrong with your brother's lifestyle?"

"It's complicated, babe. It could take a while to explain."

"Well, hip me," she said, as cool as she could. "Was that better?"

"It needs work, but I like the effort."

"Okay, now on to the story," Terry said and moved his arm so she could slide under it. His arm was around her neck and her face was close to his face. She whispered in his ear, "Now tell Doctor Moretti all about it."

"You are such a trip." He chuckled.

"I know. It's part of my charm," she said and nibbled on his ear.

"Am I supposed to concentrate while you're doing that?"

"No, you're supposed to tell me about your brother."

"Then stop that for a while."

"Okay, I'll stop for now, but you gon' be slipping' into darkness when you finish. How was that?"

"Work on it, babe, work on it," he said, acknowledging her effort. "You like boxing, right?"

"Yeah."

"You know who Roy Jones Jr. is then, right?"

"Of course."

"Well, my brother was better than Roy and all the rest of them."

"Really?"

"Hell yeah. I remember when I was about eight, or nine, my brother took me to the fights with him. Not boxing in a ring either. This was street fightin'."

"Why didn't he just become a boxer like Sugar Ray Leonard?"

"My father wouldn't let us box. He used to fight professionally. He said it was a brutal sport and a ruthless business."

"Yeah, it is. I wondered if he was a boxer. I intended to ask you about it the day I met him, but forgot."

"Anyway, they held their pugilistic bouts in the old rail yards. He took me up on top of one of the trains, and we watched the men fight. These guys were in their late twenties and thirties. It was brutal. They didn't have the same rules as boxing. You could use your feet, your knees, and your elbows. You could gouge an eye. The shit was out of control, ya know. Anyway, we were up there, and my brother would tell me who was going to lose, and why. He had a natural gift for it."

"What's his first name?"

"His name is Jericho. Anyway, we were sitting up there watching a couple of guys fight, and my brother would tell me the guy on the left was open for a hook. Or the guy on the right didn't have the distance for the kind of blow he was trying to deliver. It was exciting, for a little kid to be among the adults."

"I'll bet. So did Jericho have a fight that day?"

"Yeah, about four, or five, I think."

"Four or five?"

"Yes, maybe more. The way it works is that you can continue on fighting if you want to, if you win. You make more money that way. And the beauty of it was that my brother got the fights over quickly. A couple of blows and it was over, just like that."

Will had a boyish look in his eyes and expressed his immense pride in his brother's achievements. The corners of his mouth turned upward a little when he began describing the fight.

"My brother is short compared to me. He's only about five-eight, or -nine. The first guy was about his height, but he was about thirty. Hell, I don't know. They all looked old to me at the time. Anyway, the guy tried to hit him with the same left hook that knocked out a couple of guys before my brother's turn. But the guy didn't have the right distance and my brother ducked. And as he began rising, he hit the man with a lightning quick right hook of his own. The guy was out cold before he hit the ground. It was awesome."

"Is there a story about your brother's lifestyle in there anywhere?"

"What's the rush?"

"No rush. I'm having trouble seeing how any of this fits with his lifestyle, is all. Plus, I wanna climb you. I'm getting wet."

She slid her hand down his chest and over his stomach until she felt his pubic hair. Then she slid it further down until she felt his limp tool, which was soft from the earlier activity. Her touch felt good to him, and he began to rise again.

"I'm getting there."

"Yes, you are," she said, in a very sexy tone.

He laughed. "You know what I mean, girl."

"Yeah, but do you know what I want?"

"You want me to skip the fights then?"

"Yeah, he won them all. I got that. Then what happened?"

"Okay. To make a long story short, the police came. People were running everywhere. I was sitting on a train all alone. Then, next thing I know, a police officer grabbed him, but he broke loose and, *wham*, the police officer went down, and he wasn't movin'. Then they all jumped him and cuffed him. They took him to jail and they took me home to my mom and dad. I've never seen my dad so mad. The judge offered him Vietnam, or Berkeley. He went to Berkeley and for some reason, got into it with a professor, and knocked him out cold also. He went into the Marine Corps and became a highly decorated veteran. The next thing I know, he's a big-time drug dealer."

"Drug dealer? Why?"

"I don't know. All I know is that he and my dad argue whenever they're in the same room. He blames my dad for how his life turned out, I know that much. Other than that, I don't know what made him do it. They actually came to blows once, or twice. My dad won, but I don't know about today. My dad is old now."

"So you don't talk to him much, huh?"

"Hardly ever. I miss him. He always looked out for me when I was little. Kids in the neighborhood wouldn't mess with me once they knew I was his brother. It was cool, ya know."

"Yeah, I know. I was very protective of my sister, Ashleigh."

"So what my brother does for a living doesn't bother you?"

"No, why should it? Don't get me wrong, I'm not condoning it either. You're not involved with it, right?"

"No, I hate it, but he's my brother."

"Then we don't have a problem. Now, is that all you had to tell me about him?"

"Pretty much, why?"

"Because I'm getting ready to take you."

Chapter 40: Film at Eleven

Exhausted, Will and Terry had fallen asleep in each other's arms. Terry woke up and looked at Will. He looked so peaceful laying there next to her. She wondered what he was dreaming about, and hoped it was about her and their future life together. She wondered how far along they would be now if she had confronted him a long time ago like she wanted to. *Would we be married, and have at least one child with another on the way? What would their names be? Who would they look like? Me or Will? Would they look like both of us?*

Terry always thought that when black and white couples mixed, they had beautiful kids. She thought about all the advantages they would have, and how she wouldn't spoil them. She would give them what they needed, and not necessarily everything they wanted. They would have the best of both worlds. She decided to read those books in Will's den so she could teach them both sides of their heritage. She made up her mind to be the best wife any man would ever want.

You are so handsome, Terry thought when she looked at him. She reached under the covers with her left hand and began stroking him until she could feel him beginning to stiffen. Will awakened and looked at her—still half asleep. He was about to say something when Terry said, "Shhhhh-hhhhhhhh. Dr. Moretti knows best." She laughed in his ear and climbed on top of him.

†††

Satiated, she slid off him and was lying on her back looking up at the ceiling, still panting from the vigorous exertion. Will rolled over and looked at her, his elbow at a forty-five-degree angle—his head leaning against his clenched fist as he watched her chest move up and down rapidly. Small drops of perspiration appeared on her forehead. Her hazel eyes were scintillating. She looked at him and smiled between gasps for much needed oxygen.

He smiled back. "You gon' live?"

"Umm, Hmm, but if I were to die, now would be a good time." She stretched out her arms, and beckoned him to her bosom. He fell into her arms and they kissed. "I love you," she said, looking into his eyes.

"I know, and it feels wonderful. You ready to eat now?"

"Yeah, I'm starved."

"What do you want?"

"I don't know. Isn't that a menu over there near the television?"

"Yeah. Are you going to get it, Terry?"

"Why, so you can look at my ass?"

"Yep."

"How 'bout I turn over so you can get an eyeful and you get the menu?"

"Okay, but turn over first." She turned over onto her stomach and he looked at it. Then he slapped it hard enough to watch it shake.

"Ouch!" she yelped playfully.

"That didn't hurt you, girl."

He got up to get the menu. As he walked over to the television, she turned her head and looked at his ass. "You know, Will? Your ass is nice to look at, too."

"I knew that's all you really wanted, was to look at it."

"Yeah, I live for it."

He came back to the bed and she curled up next to him and they looked at the menu together.

"What looks good to you?" she asked.

"I like the club sandwich."

"Where's that?"

"Right under the hot roast beef and cheese."

"Oh, okay."

"I think I'm going to have the grilled chicken salad and a chardonnay. You want me to call it in?"

"Yeah, if you don't mind."

She picked up the phone and hit three for room service. Will picked up the remote control and channel-surfed while Terry called the order in. He stopped at TBS, and saw Clint Eastwood in one of the spaghetti westerns that made him famous. On TNT, Burt Lancaster was starring in *Twilight's Last Gleaming*. USA was showing *Patton*. Gymnastics were on ESPN. Showtime was showing *Deep Cover*. *Twister* was on HBO. While she was giving the order to the waiter, she tapped Will on the arm, and mouthed, "Let's watch that, okay?" Terry hung up the phone and pulled Will over to her. She guided his head to her bare chest and they watched the movie together. In the film, a cow flew past a truck in the middle of the road.

"Will, isn't it amazing what they can do with film nowadays?"

"Yeah, it is. They can do just about anything now; especially with computer-generated images. Hell, pretty soon, they won't need actors."

"That's amazing."

Her stomach growled again. This time it growled for almost twenty seconds. It stopped, and then started again.

Will gently rubbed her stomach. "How long will it take for the food to get here?"

"He said it would only take about twenty minutes. But you know what that means, right?"

"An hour."

They laughed and continued watching the movie for another thirty-five minutes and finally the waiter knocked on the door. "Room service."

"Just a minute!" Terry shouted to him.

She put on a lavish black cotton velour robe with a shawl collar, and walked to the door. She opened it, and the waiter said, "That'll be forty-seven dollars and sixty-one cents." The waiter couldn't have been more than eighteen years old. His eyes lit up when he saw Terry. He smiled the way young boys do when they have a crush on one their grade-school teachers.

"Do you want to charge it to the room, or pay cash?"

"I'll charge it to the room."

The waiter could see her breasts when she bent over a little to sign the check. As he gazed at them, a grin emerged. When she handed him the check, he offered an approving smile.

"Did you get a good look?" she asked.

Stunned, he said, "Huh?"

"That's rude." Then she pulled the table in the suite, and closed the door.

"What was that about, Terry?"

"Just a horny teenager looking at my tits. I think he came on himself, the way he was showing all thirty-twos."

Will laughed. "Can you blame the boy? I take it men have always had trouble looking you in the eye, huh?"

"Yeah, and it gets annoying after a while. The problem is men tend to associate a woman's breast size with her IQ. They think, thirty-eight D and the D stands for dumb-ho."

Will laughed. "Hide them bad boys and you won't have that trouble."

"I do, but there was nothing I could do just then, could I?"

"I guess not." He pulled her robe open and looked at her breasts. "They are nice to look at."

"I'm glad you approve."

Will squeezed her left breast. "I most certainly do."

She hit him playfully and they started eating their dinner. Helen Hunt and Bill Paxton were in the eye of the tornado, holding onto a strap in the movie.

"Could you see yourself doing something like that for a living, Will?"

"Nope. They crazy as hell doin' that shit. Could you?"

"Not without you, darlin'."

"That's sweet." He kissed her.

When the film credits began scrolling, Terry picked up the remote. "Let's see what's on the news." She pointed the remote at the television and hit the channel button until she saw Amy Ling giving a news brief.

"Coming up at the top of the hour, a man kills his ex-wife and children in a fit of rage. Film at eleven."

"Wow," Terry said. "I wonder what that's about."

Moments later the eleven o'clock news came on and Amy Ling began the broadcast. "At seven-thirty this evening the San Francisco police responded to a call from a man who claimed he had killed his wife and his children. According to Sergeant Bill Lacey, the police were called by a man who identified himself as Dr. James Friedrickson."

"Oh my God!" they said at the same time.

"He said he killed his wife, her lover, and his children. Friedrickson allegedly told Sergeant Lacey he didn't want to live and that he was going to kill himself. Sources inside the police department said the children were in their room playing with their dolls when their father burst into the room and shot both of them in the head one time each. It was a gruesomely bloody scene. Friedrickson apparently unloaded the gun in his wife and her lover while they were in the act. Then he went in the children's room and shot the children. He then reloaded the gun, returned to the bedroom where he found his wife, and her lover, and emptied the gun in their dead corpses."

"I can't believe it," Terry said, almost in a hypnotic trance.

They showed film of James being escorted into the police station with his hands cuffed; his head was bowed as they took him inside.

Visibly shaken by what he heard, Will picked up the phone and called Sterling. *This has to be a mistake. James wouldn't harm a flea, let alone kill Sharon and the children.* He put his hand over the transmitter. "Babe, pack our things, will you? James is going to need all the help he can get."

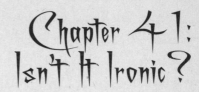

Chapter 41: Isn't It Ironic?

San Francisco
November 1997

Sterling and Will walked into the police station at 1:10 AM. They were given a booth and told to wait. Will was still stunned by what happened. One moment he was having the time of his life with Terry and the next minute he was witnessing the calamity of a trusted colleague. As Will pondered what he could have done to prevent this, he was reminded of the conversation he'd had with James in the safety deposit room at the Westin four months ago. He blamed himself for not spotting the stress James must have been under. He felt foolish for thinking that a simple promotion and a raise in salary would alleviate the mental anguish he must have felt.

I should have gotten him some help. Instead, I gave him even more responsibility, and pushed him to move on when what he really needed was a listening ear. Even the best professionals have breaking points. If Terry had of gone out with him, would that have made a difference?

He was full of questions, and Sterling could see it in his eyes. "Nothin' you could've done, bro." Then he put his hand on Will's shoulder to comfort him.

"I wonder," Will pondered aloud. "He told me about some things he was going through back in August and I pushed him when he wasn't ready."

"How were you to know?"

"Because I'm a professional. Can't you tell when a client or a witness is lying?"

Sterling nodded.

"Same thing. I was more concerned about my business than what he was going through."

"Okay, but we all go through things, Will. Some of us snap under the pressure. He made the decision. It didn't have anything to do with you. If it had, why didn't he kill her when you guys came back from Toronto?"

The door opened and James was brought into the room, wearing an orange prison suit, and clad in fetters. It was a ghastly sight of the macabre variety. He looked pale and disoriented.

"Remove the cuffs and chains," Sterling demanded. "My client poses no threat to anyone."

The officer uncuffed his hands, but left the shackles on his ankles. James sat down, but didn't say anything and he wouldn't look at Will.

"Let's see you get him off the way you got Samuelson off," the officer goaded, and left them alone.

Sterling waited for the officer to close the door. "James, this is important. What did you tell them?"

James didn't say anything for a moment or two. He just sat there with his head bowed in the shame that consumed him. Then he looked up at Will, clearly sorry for what he'd done. His eyes began to well with the tears he held back from the moment he committed the murders. Then he finally broke the silence. "I loved her. I loved her more than I loved myself. I took the humiliation, the verbal abuse, the public put-downs, and the insults in bed."

Sterling began taking notes feverishly, attempting to build a temporary insanity case.

"What happened, James?" Will asked, still floored by what happened. "I thought things were going well between you two."

"Start from the beginning," Sterling solicited. "Tell me the whole story."

"Things were never well, William. You wanna know what happened at the airport? I'll tell you. I went over to see what she wanted, remember?"

"I remember. Then you turned around and smiled at us."

"That's right. She said she wanted to be a family again. She said she wanted me back, and that she'd grown tired of Darren. She told me how much the kids missed and needed me. It was one of the happiest days of my life. I forgave her instantly. INSTANTLY! You remember how bitter I was, don't you?"

Will nodded.

"In the blink of an eye, I had forgotten everything she had ever done to me—the lying, the cheating, everything. We drove home and made love. I was so excited that I…that I…you know."

They both nodded, but Sterling said to himself, *that's the problem right there.*

"She had tried to get me to slow down," James began again. "But I couldn't control myself, ya know?"

They nodded again.

"I could tell she was disappointed, but she pretended not to be. So I told her about the promotion and the raise. It made her happy. Things were going well for a while, and then I noticed we started getting calls and people were hanging up again. I knew she was seeing Darren again, but I didn't care. I loved her anyway. Have you ever loved a woman with every fiber of your existence?" He didn't wait for an answer. He continued talking. Sterling was still writing at a quick pace. "I didn't like the idea of Sharon sleeping with another man, but I accepted it. She took care of home, and the children, so I just dealt with my ego. Men do it to women all the time, I told myself, and women deal with it. Why can't I?"

Sterling thought about Vanessa when he said that. He understood and could truly empathize. "So what happened tonight?"

The tears James had held back for so long worked their way down his cheeks. "What can ya do?" James asked, shaking his head. "What can ya do? I gave her everything. EVERYTHING! I even put up with her running around."

Then his facial expression changed. He stopped crying and rage filled his eyes. He started talking again, but it was different now. It was like an out-of-body experience. He was there again—in his home.

"I finished working early just so I could get home to be with Sharon and the kids. I walked in through the garage, and into the kitchen, and went upstairs to surprise everyone. I saw my kids' door was open, so I went in, and hugged them. I said, 'Where's Mommy?' And my six-year-old said, 'Mommy's in the bedroom with Darren.' When she said that, something snapped in me. I don't even remember leaving them. As I approached the bedroom, I could hear Sharon carrying on, making erotic sighs that had to have come from unimaginable pleasure—the kind of pleasure that made her forget her daughters were playing with their dolls in the very next room.

"Sharon's moans were so loud and so fierce that they didn't even hear me enter the room. I stood there, shocked at what I was seeing. Darren had her legs so high up on his shoulders that her toes were touching the wall. Still in shock, I just watched, unable to move as Darren thrust himself in and out of my wife over and over again. I don't know what bothered me more, the fact that she enjoyed sex more with him, or the fact that she was doing this with the kids in the next room. I walked out of the room, and got my gun.

"Then I walked back in and walked up to the bed. Sharon was about to orgasm when she saw me raise the gun, but she was so into the moment that she kept thrusting her body upward as Darren pumped her recklessly and hard. As she came, I shot Darren in the back of the head and I swear to you, I think she came even harder. She screamed, but it was not a scream of fear—it was ecstasy. I raised the gun and pointed at her while she was coming, and she got this look on her face, like she felt even more pleasure in the face of certain death. I squeezed the trigger and killed her also. When I realized what I'd done, I knew I had to kill myself, but I didn't want to make my kids orphans, so I killed them. I thought that maybe we could all be a family in the hereafter."

Will took a deep breath, and let it out slowly. He understood James's anger.

"Why didn't you kill yourself, James?" Sterling asked.

"Because I let Sergeant Lacey talk me out of it when I called the police. I wish I had though. Believe me. I wish I had. At least this nightmare would be over."

"What did you tell the police?"

"I told the whole story to Sergeant Lacey."

"Did he read you your rights?" Sterling asked, almost desperate for a way out.

"Yeah, he did. He read them to me twice. Once when he picked me up, and again when I gave him the confession on videotape."

Sterling thought, *You're through then. Ain't a damn thing I can do for you.* "Well, let me at least see the tape before we enter our plea."

"No need. I'll take my punishment. Hopefully they'll give me the death penalty. That's what I deserve."

"Are you sure about this?" Sterling asked.

"Yeah, I'm sure," James said and laughed halfheartedly. "Isn't it ironic, William? We had all those debates about the death penalty. I was always against it. And you were always for it. Now here I am praying for it, and you're trying to keep it from happening."

James stood up and tapped on the door glass. When the guard looked at him, he signaled him. The guard came in and cuffed him again. When the guard finished, he led him out the door. James stopped in mid-stride, turned back and looked at Will and said, "I'm sorry, William. I guess you couldn't count on me after all. I should have taken your advice, and gotten on with my life—sound advice. You told me right, but I didn't listen. You've been a good friend, and colleague."

Then James nodded to the guard and they left.

"Can you do anything for him, Sterling?"

"Nope. Ya boy's through. I can't do anything for him if he doesn't want to fight for his life. Hell, Johnnie Cochran couldn't get his ass out of this shit if he don't want to get out of it. Part of the defense is having a client who wants to fight for his life. And killin' them kids didn't help his case either. He might have had a chance if he hadn't killed the kids. Juries don't like that shit. I could have gotten him three to six, maybe less. Killin' those kids and the videotaped confession sealed his doom. But he's right about one thing. You told his ass right. He made the choice. So don't let this shit fuck with you."

"That's not all he's right about," Will said dryly. "He's right about the irony of the situation. The irony is he's lost the love of his life and I've found the love of mine. And while he was ending his life with Sharon, I was beginning mine with Terry."

✝✝✝

Will entered Terry's townhouse just before dawn. He and Sterling went to Denny's and had a light breakfast and talked for a while. When he walked into the bedroom, he heard Terry's purr-like snore. He looked down at her, and was grateful he had a chance to start a family with her. As he gazed at her, it became clear to him just how short life was. He had been alone for five years. It was like a death sentence, but he didn't realize it until now. He took off his clothes, and got in bed with Terry. He felt the warmth of her body when he touched her. She awakened.

"What time is it?" she asked, rubbing her eyes.

"A little after five."

"Why didn't you call me? I was waiting for you."

"I thought you'd be sleep, and I knew there was nothing you could do. I went out and got a bite to eat with Sterling."

"Next time, don't worry about waking me up," she admonished him. "Call me and let me know what's going on and where you are, okay?"

"Okay."

"So is it true? Did he do it?"

"Yes," he said, sadly.

"Why?"

Will looked at her. "Guess?"

When Will said that, she knew what had happened. "Well, why the children, Will? Why the children?" Her voice was full of sorrow.

"He said he didn't want to leave them as orphans after he killed himself."

"That is so sad. Children are innocent," she said, weeping. "Why did this have to happen?"

"I don't know, babe. I only know that this has taught me just how short life really is. And that a man's life is not to be wasted worrying about

338

petty people, and their petty ideology. I'm going to need you now more than I ever did before. Are you up to the challenge?"

"You mean at the office?"

"Yes, but I was referring to our relationship as well."

"Yes," she said, soberly. "You trust me that much? To run the offices, I mean?"

"Do you remember when we were in Toronto, and I told you why I hired you?"

"Uh-huh."

"I meant that. I have complete faith in you. This may sound insensitive, but you were the one I wanted to run things in the first place. Between the three of you, James was last on my list. I would have put Ivy there before him, but he deserved a chance, and I gave it to him. I guess it wasn't meant to be."

Chapter 42
Thanksgiving Dinner

San Francisco
November 1997

Benjamin Michael Wise tossed and turned in bed the entire night. He woke up suddenly and thought about his oldest son, who had chosen a life of organized crime. Benjamin had high hopes for Jericho, but was thoroughly disappointed by him. Jericho was the son who had embraced the brutal and often bloody art of pugilism for which he himself had become somewhat famous. Benjamin denied this same son the opportunity to enter the ring even though he displayed a considerable amount of natural talent for the sport.

Benjamin lived three completely different lives—lives that manifested themselves in the choices his three sons made. He was a rebellious hellion in his youth, fighting all the time and was brutal in and out of the ring. He fought magnificently and gained the number one ranking; earning him the right to fight Alvarez Sanchez for the Middleweight Championship of the World, an opportunity he'd wanted for three years. Sanchez had been the champion for years and avoided him. Unfortunately, Benjamin lost the fight on a stoppage in the waning seconds of the fifteenth and final round. He was winning big, but he had taken a lot of power shots. Finally, the referee stopped it and he lost the biggest fight of his life. He blamed the referee for years, and was never the same fighter again. He was relegated to relative obscurity after that.

During his years as a boxer, he had chased women and became well known as a ladies' man. Women were always throwing themselves at him and he was more than willing to oblige them. In his youth, he was hand-some and solidly built; some people called him a pretty boy. With his eyes open, he thought about all the women he'd slept with. Face after face came to mind—all meaningless trysts. He didn't know who they were or where they were now. He reflected on his part in the meaningless affairs and the women that seemed to flock after men of import and prominence.

But after the Sanchez fight, people started to change and the women stopped coming around. No one was chanting his name. No one cared, except Brenda. He thought of all the pain that he had caused his wife over the years and how she had stood by him in spite of himself. He loved her for it.

William was born years after his boxing career was over. By then, Benjamin was a changed man, no longer having the desire to run around, he became an excellent father and reared William to be like the man he was now. But it was too late for Jericho, who saw all the skirt-chasing, the late nights, the coming home drunk, and the arguing with Brenda. Jericho had seen it all, including the changes, but he was bent on doing things his own way, and it frustrated Benjamin. There wasn't a night he didn't think about his oldest son and what he might have done differently.

Brenda opened her eyes. She told her husband what might happen if he didn't change over forty years ago when they were visiting his sister in New Orleans. She thanked God she didn't have girls because, in spite of her trying to teach them to be chaste, the apple doesn't fall far from the tree. Benjamin's mother was a prostitute, which explained why he ran around so much. She watched her husband toss and turn for a while longer.

"How long you gon' let the past bother you, Benny?"

"You awake?"

"Naw. I'm talkin' in my sleep. Now how long you gon' let it bother you?"

"It's just hard to deal with. You know he blames me, don't you?"

"Yeah, I know. You know he uses it to push your buttons."

"I know."

"Then why do you let it bother you, Benny?"

"Because, I was wrong back then. I guess if I was the man I am now and he turned out the way he did, my conscience would be clear."

Brenda knew there was nothing she could say to make him feel better. She had tried unsuccessfully for years and decided to change the subject.

"You think she's going to show up?"

"Who?"

"Willy's filly. Who else?"

"More than likely. She's got gumption."

"Typical black male," she said scowling. "Black men seem to lose their minds when a white woman shows them the least bit of attention."

"Typical black female. Black women seem to lose their minds when one of them shows us the least bit of attention."

"Well, at least she's pretty. I'd like to think I had some influence on him."

"You did, Brenda. Why do you think he chose her? Simply because she's white? You really ought to talk to her. You know, woman to woman."

"You mean woman to barracuda, don't you?"

"If you're going to be rude like you were last week, you might as well tell him not to bring her. And if you think she ain't comin', you can forget about it. She's in it for the duration. A woman doesn't wait on a man for three years and when she finally gets him, gives him up easily."

"If that's true… If I have so much influence on him, she would be black." Brenda thought about talking to Terry for a moment or two. Then said, "Three years, huh? Okay, I'll talk to her woman to woman and see what she's bringing to the table besides her white skin."

"Woman, you're something else," Benny said, and shook his head.

Brenda got out of the bed and started preparing the feast. While she cooked, she began to consider the possibilities of Will getting too serious with Terry. She knew he was already, but believed it was just a phase black men had to go through at least once in their lives. She believed that if she saw them together as a couple, one way or the other, she'd know. She started humming one of her favorite spirituals. It was a song she had learned as a child in vacation Bible school. It was called "The Man from Galilee." As she hummed the tune, the song sounded so good in her mind that she began singing it out loud.

Put your hand in the hand of the man who stills the water
Put your hand in the hand of the man who calms the sea
Take a look at yourself and you will look at others differently
By putting your hand in the hand of the man from Galilee

††††

Terry and Will were lying in bed quietly; neither knew the other was awake. They buried Sharon and James's two daughters Wednesday and Terry spent the night with Will afterward. As a final favor to James, Will took care of the arrangements for the funeral. Even though Judge Jones gave him permission to attend the funeral, James refused. He thought it would be too traumatic for him. Will closed all the offices for the day and urged the staff to attend. It was a sad day for everyone. No one ever thought something like this would happen to their friend and colleague.

Will was considering the possibilities of dying without having a family. He always wanted children, but he was too busy building his business to be the kind of father he wanted to be. He and Francis put it off until it was too late. Now Francis was dead and Terry was in his life. *Was Terry as strong as she appeared? After all, what did she really know about racism? She had never experienced it. How could she really know how to handle it? What would she do when she experienced it the first time? How would she handle it?*

Terry's eyes were closed, but she was considering death also and how precious life could be snatched by the viselike jowls of the grim reaper. She thought about God, and the hereafter. It had been a long time since she'd been to church. She was raised Catholic, but had gotten away from it as soon as she was old enough to make her own decisions. But now, all the things she had been taught were coming back to her like a distant memory that had faded, but not vanished. She wondered if Sharon went to heaven or would she have to wait in purgatory for a predetermined time? She didn't know, but that's what she was taught. She opened her eyes and looked at Will; his eyes were open, too.

"Will?"

"Yeah, babe."

"Do you believe in God?"

"Yeah, I believe in God. Do you?"

"You think Sharon's in heaven? And yeah, to answer your question."

"Hard to say."

"Why is that?"

"Depends on what she believes, I guess."

"True, true. But ya know, whenever someone I know dies, I think about my own mortality. Do you?"

"Not really."

"Oh, okay." She sensed he didn't want to discuss it and changed the subject to something more conducive to his mood. "So how many people will be at your parents' house today?"

"Why? You nervous?"

"Yes. Very much so. Does that surprise you?"

Will rolled over so he could see her face. Terry was still on her back, looking at the ceiling. "Yeah. What would shake your confidence so? I mean, you're generally a tower of strength about this. Now, you don't seem so sure."

Terry rolled to her left and slid her body against his, feeling the warmth of his naked body against hers. She reached back for his arm and enveloped herself with it. She felt his erection rise the moment they touched.

"I love the way you feel against me, darlin'," she said. "Do you realize that?"

"No, but I do now."

"Are you going to get hard every time you touch me?"

"Why? You like it?"

"Umm, hmm. You want me to take the edge off for you?"

Without a word, he turned her over and climbed on top of her and entered her. He looked into her eyes.

"What are you afraid of?"

Her eyes welled and she pulled him close. Then she pulled his head down to the side of her neck and sobbed softly in his ear. Will just lay there inside her. He knew enough not to say anything. The harder she cried, the tighter her embrace became.

Between her sobs, she said, "Oh, Will. I love you so much. I don't think I could bear to lose you."

"You're not going to lose me, babe."

"I don't think your mother's ever going to accept me; just like she said."

"She will. It will take some getting used to, is all." He spoke in a pseudo Southern accent when he said, "is all."

Terry laughed. Then Will wiped the tears from her eyes.

"You really think so?"

"Yep. The key is when you go in there today, be yourself. Tell the truth about how you feel, no matter what. You may piss her off, but you'll win her respect. Her respect and her religion will get you over the racial hump. But if you try to assuage her, she'll see right through it and then you can forget about being accepted. The one thing my mother can't tolerate is a phoney person, understand?"

"Yeah, darlin'." She held his face in the palms of her hands and looked at him. "I love you, William Marcellus Wise, and don't you ever forget it." Then she kissed him passionately. Will's penis stiffened a little more. Terry could feel him move inside her. "I want to please you."

Then she pushed him over onto his back and climbed him.

✝✝✝

It was one-thirty when Will and Terry arrived at his parents' home. They were supposed to be there by one. Will was intentionally being late because he knew other members of his family would straggle in whenever they felt like it. But when they pulled up, he saw all of his relatives' cars already there. The one car he didn't want to see was the white Lexus Aunt Johnnie drove.

"Oh, shit."

"What?"

"Aunt Johnnie is here. As a matter of fact, all my relatives seem to be here."

"Don't you guys normally have family over for Thanksgiving?"

"Yeah, but not all of 'em. Well, almost all of 'em."

"So your mother decided to enlist some help, huh?"

"Yeah. You wanna go back to my place?"

"No. It's now, or never."

Terry and Will didn't know it, but many of his relatives were looking out the window and making their assessments of Terry. Will took her hand and led up the steps—laced fingers. When they got closer to the door, his relatives sat down quickly, attempting to be inconspicuous. Sterling opened the door.

"What happened?" Sterling laughed. "Did y'all get stuck together, or what? I'm tellin' y'all now, it's a trip up in here. These muthafuckas are killin' me. Drunkass cousin Sammy, who ain't never been on time for shit, got the nerve to be complainin' about you being late once. And Aunt Johnnie's in there havin' a field day about black men and white women. She keep that shit up, and I'm going to have to bust her little bubble. I'm tellin' you, the shit is off the hook, all right?"

"Thanks, bro."

"No problem. So how you doin', pretty lady?"

"Not too well at the moment. Nothing that a chilled chardonnay wouldn't cure."

"I know what you sayin', but you can handle this crowd."

"Ya think so?"

"Hell yeah. Just outthink 'em. When people pissed off, they don't think straight. You can kick a lot of ass when people pissed off. Why do you think lawyers try to get witnesses mad?"

"AIN'T NO SENSE IN HIDING HER ASS OUT IN THE HALL-WAY!" Aunt Johnnie shouted from the living room. "MIGHT AS WELL BRING Y'ALL LATE ASSES ON UP IN HERE!"

When Terry heard that, she took a deep breath and let it slowly dissipate naturally. Fear gripped her like never before—her heart pounded. She didn't know what to expect. This would be totally different from anything she had ever experienced.

"Hey, babe, I bet when you busted into my suite that night, you never expected this to happen, huh?"

Terry smiled nervously. She knew he was only trying to make her feel as comfortable as possible, but it wasn't working. Will placed Terry's hand in his and they took that all-important first step toward the living room where they had heard the thunderous voice of Aunt Johnnie. As they walked into the room, tension seemed to saturate the entire house. They reached the entryway of the living room and saw a mixture of faces.

To Terry's surprise, not all of the faces were hostile. Some were friendly. She could tell that there had been an argument prior to them coming into the house because the smiling faces were on one side of the room. On the other side, the facial expressions were that of total disgust. The natural thing for her to do was to gravitate toward the friendly side of the room, but her instincts and personal resolve told her to go directly into the storm. They told her to become an eagle and soar with the storm rather than giving into her desire for security and peace.

Will was about to introduce Terry to everyone when his four-year-old cousin walked up to her with his thumb in his mouth. Terry looked down at the child, and the child looked up at Terry. He took his thumb out of his mouth and said, "Hi. My name is Jordan. What's yours?" Then he put his thumb back into his mouth and resumed his sucking.

Terry stooped down and looked Jordan in the face. She smiled and said, "Hi, Jordan. My name is Terry."

"Terry? That's a boy's name and you a girl," Jordan said bashfully.

"Sweetie, Terry can be a boy's or a girl's name."

"Ohhhhhh." Jordan understood. "My daddy said you got a nice ass for a white girl."

"JORDAN!" His father yelled from across the room. He was standing with the friendly crowd. Jordan turned around and ran to the voice of his father. Will bent down and grabbed Terry's hand. They stood up together. Then Will said, "Everybody, this is Dr. Terry Moretti. This is the woman

I know y'all been discussin'. This is who I'm with now. I know some of y'all don't like it, but y'all don't have to like it. Since we're family, I know in time y'all will accept her just as y'all accept me."

"Who said we accept you?"

That was Karen, Jordan's mother and Will's favorite cousin. She walked over to them and stretched out her hand to Terry. "Pleased to meet you. You have to excuse my little boy. The more I try to teach him right, the more of his daddy seems to come outta him."

Terry took her hand and said, "Oh, it's okay. Don't worry about it."

"Come with me and I'll introduce you to everybody properly," Karen said. She looked at Will, who was about to accompany them, and rolled her eyes. He didn't want to leave her alone with the women in his family. Karen stopped him in his tracks and said, "Go away, Willy. I got this."

Will looked Karen in the eyes. He realized he was leaving Terry in good hands. "Are you going to be all right, babe?" Terry nodded nervously. He went into the kitchen to talk to his parents. His mother was standing at the stove over a large pot of candied yams. He walked up behind her and hugged her. "Hi, Mama."

"Hi," she said, reluctantly. It was more of a grunt than a greeting.

"You can't speak, boy," his father said. He was sitting at the kitchen table. Will turned around. "Hi, Dad. I didn't see you back there."

"Terry decided not to come after all, huh?"

"She's here." His mother grunted loud enough to be heard. "She's with Karen."

"Don't leave her alone too long; especially with my crazy sister in there. Ain't no tellin' what kinda trouble she's going to cause."

Will walked over to the table to sit down. The chair screeched when he slid it back on the tile floor. "Whose idea was it to have everybody over here?"

"Who do you think?" his father asked. They both looked at Brenda. "She didn't even tell me. People just started showing up with food already prepared. I asked her about it, and she said that if I could have secrets from her, she could have secrets from me. I was through with it."

Brenda could feel their stares burning a hole in her back. She didn't even bother to turn around when she said, "I don't know why y'all staring at me. I can have the whole family over if I want to." Will and his father shook their heads. "Benny," Brenda began again, "start carving the turkeys. It's time to eat now that Willy and Ms. Thang done finally showed up."

Benny got up and walked behind Brenda. He grabbed her left breast and squeezed. Then in her right ear, he whispered, "Ya better be glad I love you, girl." Brenda laughed. Then she swatted his hand. "I got somthin' for you upstairs later." Brenda laughed again.

Will had seen the scene a thousand times. It was like a classic film. He knew every line, every nuance. He loved seeing his parents together. It gave him reason to hope for that kind of love again. Then he wondered what was going on in the living room. It was too quiet in there. He knew he could count on Terry, Karen, and Sterling to give him the blow by blow, so he began chatting with his dad.

††††

The family understood why Brenda wanted them to come over for Thanksgiving, and they agreed something should be done to protect Will from the white woman. The men thought the matter would be best left to their wives, and had gone into the family room to watch the Detroit Lions play the Minnesota Vikings. From time to time, their cheers could be heard as Barry Sanders ran for thirty yards or a touchdown.

Since everyone brought prepared food, there wasn't a lot for the women to do, which was by design so they would have a chance to talk to Terry alone. Aunt Johnnie, Benjamin's sister, told all the women they would get down to the bottom of this new relationship Will had, and she would do the talking. After putting the children out, the women closed off the living room, and encircled her.

Terry knew she was in for a fight, and decided to listen to what they were and weren't saying to prepare for this battle. She hoped it wouldn't be too bloody, but if blood was what they wanted, she was going to open up an artery.

"What makes pale-faced bitches like you think you can just come up in here and take our black men?" Aunt Johnnie snapped. "What? You think you hot shit because you've got letters behind your goddamn name? Well, those letters don't mean a goddamn thing to me, Ms. Thang."

Karen said, "Now, Mama, ain't no need in gettin' upset with Terry. She's just—."

Terry cut her off. "Naw, Karen. Let your mother speak her mind. Then when she's done, I'll speak mine. Now, you were saying?"

Aunt Johnnie was taken aback by Terry's unexpected bravado, but undeterred. Terry, on the other hand, was gambling that if she dealt with Aunt Johnnie effectively, the others would be easier to handle. She recognized right away that, besides Will's mother, Aunt Johnnie was the leader of this mob. It was the classic bully syndrome.

"I just wanna know why you white bitches always comin' around a brotha when he's got money!" Aunt Johnnie yelled. "As soon as one of 'em get a little something, here come one of you bitches suckin' his dick, and spreadin' ya goddamn legs so wide a Mack truck can drive up in ya!"

"Are you through?" Terry said, impatiently.

"HELL NAW, BITCH!" Aunt Johnnie shouted. "I'M JUST GETTIN' STARTED!"

"MAMA!" Karen shouted. "You need to quit. You're embarrassing me and yourself."

"You think I give a damn! I speaks my mind, and let the chips fall where they may."

All the women in the room stared at Terry. Some felt sorry for her. She'd taken a vicious tongue-lashing and there was more to come. They all knew how Aunt Johnnie was. Many of them were former victims of her angry tirades. Although some of the family members didn't like her methods, many agreed with what she was saying. They were simply glad she was the one saying it, and not them.

Undaunted by Aunt Johnnie's hot outbursts, Terry said, "I understand how you feel, but—"

Aunt Johnnie looked at Terry—total disbelief defined her. She put her hands on her hips and said, "You understand how I feel? YOU under-stand how I feel? How the hell can you understand how I feel?"

Terry looked at Aunt Johnnie for a moment, or two. She seemed to be contemplating her answer. At that moment, it became clear to her how Will had felt all those years they tried prying information out of him. She could now feel what he must have felt, being alone among whites, who were more interested in justifying their own racial animus, rather than seeking common ground. The last Toronto trip particularly came to mind.

As Terry focused on the faces of the women that encircled her, it occurred to her that she didn't understand how Aunt Johnnie and the rest of the women were feeling. She knew she didn't have anything in common with them, other than Will. In fact, she didn't understand why black women felt the way they did about black men dating white women. How could she? After all, she only had two black women friends. Were it not for Jeannine, she would not have known there was a problem between black women and white women.

"You know what? You're right," Terry conceded. "I don't understand how you feel and why this is so upsetting to you, but I'm willing to learn. All I know so far, and I could be wrong, is that you seem to think that all white women are pale-faced bitches who, when it comes to dating a black man with money, suck their dicks and open their legs for them. Now as far as being pale-faced, as you can see, I have quite a bit of melanin in my skin. So the pale-faced comment doesn't apply. However, I can be a bitch from time to time so that doesn't bother me."

"Can't we all?" Karen asked, rhetorically.

The women laughed and the mood in the room was a little bit lighter than it was initially. But the venom was still visible.

"Now, to the comment about white women going down on a man, I take it black women don't go down. Is that right?" She was directing the question to all the women. Slowly at first, but one by one, they all turned their faces away from Terry, or diverted their eyes to something other than her. Terry smiled inwardly. She knew they all did it; even Aunt Johnnie. She had made some headway and she decided to milk it for all it was worth. "By your silence, I can only assume you've all engaged in it at one time or another. Perhaps some of you still do."

No one said anything. Terry smiled inwardly again. She had to keep a serious, yet inquisitive look on her face; otherwise, it would add fuel to a fire that was out of control. She knew she had to say her peace without sounding like a condescending white woman with letters behind her name. Aunt Johnnie had made this clear by her earlier comment.

"So I take it all of you were virgins when you got married."

The room was still silent. She wanted to say, "and I bet you all wore white on your wedding days, too." But she knew that was over the top so she left it alone.

"What the hell difference does it make what we do, or did before we got married?" Aunt Johnnie shouted. "That ain't none of yo' goddamn business."

"Precisely."

"Is that supposed to be some of that head-shrinking shit y'all do down at that clinic?"

Everyone got the point Terry was making except her. She wanted blood, and it blinded her to what Terry said with a single word. "Well, if it isn't my skin color, or my sexual habits that bother you, what is it?"

Brenda opened the door and said, "It's time to eat."

"We'll finish this later," Aunt Johnnie promised Terry.

"Looking forward to it," Terry replied.

The women went into the dining room where the men were already waiting. Terry looked for Will. She saw him near his dad and Sterling at the head of the table. She walked over to where he was standing.

"How did it go, babe?" Will whispered.

"I held my own."

The food was on a long, narrow, oak table on which sat three turkeys, honey-baked ham, mashed potatoes and gravy, greens, macaroni and cheese, fried chicken, potato salad, cole slaw, dressing, cranberry sauce, corn pudding, candied yams, and assorted pies and cakes. Brenda made lemonade for Benny. She had punch and soda for everyone else.

"Let's pray a prayer of thanksgiving to the Lord for his bountiful blessings," Brenda said. They all held hands and bowed their heads according to family tradition. Then Brenda began praying. "Thank you, oh God, for your many gracious blessings. You've given me everything a mother could want. You've given me a great family, a roof over my head, clothes on my back, and three wonderful sons. It's just too bad I ain't got no grandkids to speak of."

Sterling opened his eyes and looked at Will. They both laughed hard, but silently. Terry hit Will and Sterling playfully.

"But I thank you anyway, oh Lord of Heaven and Earth, and watcher of my soul, for you alone have made me glad. Hopefully, oh God, you'll let my youngest son know he needs to wait a little longer for some things and not to rush into marriage with the wrong woman."

Sterling laughed again. He looked at Will and Terry again and they were both laughing also. Then, they noticed that practically everyone was laughing silently. Their shoulders were hunching as they tried not to let the river of laughter break through the dam of silence.

"But most of all, oh God, watch over my oldest son, Jericho. See to it that no harm comes to him before he comes to know your son, Jesus Christ."

"AAAAAAA-MEN!" Jericho shouted. "Let's eat!"

Everybody turned to the direction of the voice. They saw Jericho and Pin standing there looking at them. Brenda ran to her favorite son and hugged him. Everyone left the table to great the prodigal son. Only Terry and Benjamin remained.

Terry looked at Benjamin. She could see the pain and disappointment in his eyes. In the near distance, they heard the family clamoring and falling all over themselves like Jericho was a celebrity. Benjamin hated the way they treated him; like he was a god, or something.

"Willy tell you what my oldest boy do for a livin'?"

Terry nodded. She wanted to say more, but kept her feelings to herself. The family came back into the dining room.

Jericho walked over to his father. "Hi, Daddy."

Benjamin returned the greeting without emotion. He didn't even look at him. Jericho accepted his father's stance, and respected him for it. They had argued about it enough and neither man would change, so they just quit talking about it. Jericho turned his attention to Terry. "You must be Desdemona."

Terry didn't acknowledge the Shakespearean reference. She simply stood up and extended her hand.

"You must be Jericho. Pleased to meet you. Hi, I'm Terry."

Jericho took her hand and looked deep into her eyes.

Terry got the feeling he was looking not into her eyes, but into her very soul. It was an eerie feeling to be probed with the naked eye. But she didn't look away. In his face she saw the uncanny resemblance to Benjamin. Except for the obvious age difference, they could be brothers instead of father and son.

"This is my wife, Pin," Jericho said politely.

Pin bowed. Terry bowed in like manner.

"Let's eat," Benjamin said. "Y'all kids get in line first and find a seat in the living room and kitchen, or wherever y'all wanna eat."

Chapter 43: Sins of the Father

Terry got the feeling she was being watched. She looked up and saw Pin and Jericho staring at her. They were very well-dressed in what looked like Armani suits, but they also looked angry and dangerous—both of them sporting painted-on scowls and sending threats with their eyes. *Was Pin in the drug business, too? Had either of them committed murder? Would they kill me over this silly race issue?*

"Brenda," Aunt Johnnie said, "did I tell you what happened at the grocery store?"

"Naw. What happened?"

"Girl, I'm standing in line and I hear these little black kids talking. They couldn't be more than nine or ten years old. And they were saying muthafucka this and muthafucka that. They acted like I wasn't even there. What's wrong with them?"

"Girl, I know what you mean. They don't respect their elders no more. They don't seem to care about nothin' these days."

Benjamin was staring at the son who resembled him in appearance only, furious with him still after so many years of arguing about his drug dealing. He tried logic and reason; philosophy and religion, but none of these could penetrate Jericho's unwavering commitment to the game he played so well.

"How do you expect them to respect anything or anybody when they haven't been taught to?" Benjamin asked. "They have very few role models where they live. And you can't expect athletes to be role models. That's the stupidest thing I've ever heard."

"Uncle Benny," Karen began, "maybe we can't expect them to be role models, but we can certainly expect them to act like they got some sense and a brain in their heads."

"Daddy, don't get too worked up," Will cautioned. "Your heart doesn't need the stress."

"On the other hand," Benjamin continued as though he didn't hear Will, "I can understand why people want athletes to be role models."

"Why is that?" Ronnie, Karen's husband asked.

"Because all the decent black men move out the neighborhood the first chance they get. And the ones that fail in life, and give up on themselves, blame everybody else for their life choices, and either end up in jail, or become drug dealers, or both."

Jericho knew that was a slap at him, but didn't say anything. He kept on eating as though he didn't hear it.

"So what are you sayin', Daddy?" Sterling asked. "You think we should all stay here in the ghetto, just so we can be role models?"

"Why not? The white man don't want you in his neighborhood. No offense, Terry."

"None taken."

"Why is that, Mary Dalton?" Jericho asked, referring to Richard Wright's classic novel, *Native Son*. "Is that an admission that you don't want niggas in yo' neighborhood? Or is that an admission that you only want the ones with money?"

Everybody stopped eating and looked at Terry, curious as to what she would say to that stinging accusation. Terry knew she was in dangerous territory and she had to choose her words carefully, yet not sound like they were contrived to pacify them at the moment. Brenda tried to contain the utter joy she felt, but a bright smile emerged and refused to go away. She was glad somebody finally said what she was feeling. And who better to say it than her favorite son.

"Neither actually."

"Oh, so you don't want niggas in yo' neighborhood, even if they got money, huh?"

"That's not what she said, Jerry," Will intervened.

"You sidin' with a white woman over your big brother, huh, Bigger Thomas?" That was another reference to *Native Son*.

"Listen, boy!" Benjamin shouted. "She's a guest in my house! Either treat her with respect, or get out!"

"Just like a house nigga to say some shit like that!" Aunt Johnnie yelled. "Here this white woman is taking another one of our good black men, and what does my brother do? He condones the shit and steps on his own flesh and blood to defend the white goddess. I'm so sick of you house niggas, I don't know what to do."

"You can get the hell out, too, Johnnie," Benjamin blared.

At that moment, Jordan came up to Terry and climbed in her lap and buried his head in her bosom. Terry embraced him as though he were her own.

"Would you look at that shit?" Johnnie pointed out. "That boy ain't but four years old, and look at him. What does he do? The first chance he gets, he climbs on the lap of a white woman. It must be in y'alls genes, or somethin'."

"It must be in y'all genes! It must be in y'all genes!" Jordan repeated while bouncing up and down on Terry's lap.

Terry put her forefinger to her lips. "Shhhhhhhhhhhh."

Jordan mimicked her. "Shhhhhhhhhhhh." Then he laughed.

No longer able to contain himself, Sterling said, "You gotta lot of nerve, Aunt Johnnie."

"What do you mean?"

"You know what I mean! Here you are sittin' in here doggin' black men when you've never married a black man in your life. You've had three husbands—all of 'em white. Ain't a dark face in the bunch. So you don't have nothin' to say about who Will sees."

"Yeah, and they all had money, too. You think I would marry one if they didn't? They were all typical white men who wanted some black poontang and I wasn't givin' it up without the money. If they want it that bad, they have to show me the money."

They all laughed, but Aunt Johnnie was quite serious.

"Ain't that what that fine Cuba Gooding Jr. said in that *Jerry Maguire* movie? I live by that shit! Look, if they want it that bad, why shouldn't they pay for it. I will not allow myself to be used and abused, then cast away with nothin'. Hell no. No man will ever have his way with me and not give me somethin' for what I gave him."

Now Terry understood why she was so angry with her. It wasn't only the color issue; it was a guilty conscience also. She wondered what else she would hear before dinner was over.

"This is so typical," Jericho chimed in again. "Here we are in our own neighborhood, in our own house, and the white man still got us pointing fingers at ourselves and putting each other down right in front of Scarlet O'Hara, who's trying to ruin my baby brother's life."

"How am I ruining his life?" Terry frowned. "I love him. Doesn't anybody understand that?"

"It's easy to love a rich black man, ain't it?" Jericho asked. "Would you love him if he didn't have a dime to his name?"

"Yes, I would."

"Get the hell outta here! You expect us to believe that? You wouldn't even know him if he wasn't rich."

"If I didn't know him, how could I love him?"

"Now we're gettin' somewhere. You don't love my brother any more than Aunt Johnnie loved those white men she married. What makes you any different?"

"I have my own money."

"Yeah, and it's the same money you got from your divorce settlement, isn't it?"

The room was quiet again. Jericho had just dropped a bomb that no one expected. They all looked at Terry, wondering what she was going to say. No one knew about the divorce settlement except for Will and Terry, or so they thought. They thought it would be best to keep it a secret, but now they knew they had made a mistake. Terry's mind raced. She knew she was in trouble. What could she say to appease their suspicions now? They already suspected she wanted him for his money. Now, they had real cause for concern.

"Is it true?" Benjamin asked.

"Yes," Terry said without hesitation.

Brenda could no longer contain herself. The joy within her found its way out; her scheme had brought about unexpected information and it looked bad for Terry. "Hallelujah! Thank you, Jesus!"

"I knew it! I knew it! I knew it!" Aunt Johnnie shouted in rapid succession. "She's a gold digger just like the rest of them barracudas!"

"Look, Othello!" Jericho said to Will, "You need to rethink this relationship of yours."

"I don't need to rethink anything," Will said sharply. "Do you know the details of the divorce settlement?"

"Yeah, Negro. I know," Jericho said smugly. "Desdemona got five hundred thousand dollars, a townhouse, and a brand-new, candy-apple red Mitsubishi 3000 GT. Anything else you wanna know, Negro? I got all the goods on her."

"How did you—" Terry began.

"How did I find out, Desdemona?" Jericho finished her question. "I know muthafuckas and they tell me all kind's a shit."

"Well, did they tell you she could have taken half?" Will asked. "This is California, you know. She only took ten percent of what she had coming to her, according to the law. And she didn't sign a prenuptial agreement."

"You mean she could have taken five million?" Karen questioned.

"Yep," Will answered. "I bet your mother would have taken the whole five million. What do you think, Karen?"

"Well, if you end up married to her, she won't mind signing a prenuptial agreement again, right?" Jericho asked. "Who knows, she might be kicking herself now when she looks back on what she gave up. But regardless, you need to protect yourself, just in case. You see what happened to the Juice. That might be you one day. Think about it, Bigger!"

"I will sign one, if it comes to that," Terry assured them.

"Terry and Cousin Will gettin' mar-read. Terry and Cousin Will gettin' mar-read," Jordan sang.

Terry shushed him again. Jordan mimicked her.

"Then it's all settled," Benjamin said.

"Unt Uh." Brenda shook her head. "Ain't nothin' settled. We a long ways from settlin' this."

"Why ain't it settled, Brenda?" Benjamin asked. "She agreed to a prenuptial. What else do you want?"

"I want her outta my Willy's life! That's what I want!"

"Now, Mama," Will pleaded.

"And don't 'Now, Mama' me, boy!"

"So I guess you would rather have a drug-dealing son than grandchildren then?" Benjamin asked.

"Now, Benny," Aunt Johnnie jumped back in. "You're wrong. I know this is your house, but you're wrong."

"How the hell am I wrong? He's the one selling drugs! Not me! Then he blames me for his own choices. I did all I could for the boy. He was just bound and determined to do things his own way."

"Just like you, Daddy. Just like you," Jericho told him.

"Just like you, Uncle Benny," Jordan repeated. "Just like you."

Terry put her hand over Jordan's mouth. He kept trying to talk. Then he started laughing.

"What do you mean, boy?" Benjamin shouted.

"You know what I mean, old man."

"Boy, I did all I knew how to do for you." His eyes filled with tears. "Tell me how I failed you? What did I do that was so wrong that you would hurt me like this?"

"Let's stop this, y'all," Karen pleaded. "We came over here to be with family for the holiday weekend. Let's act like we're family."

"Humph." Sterling grunted. "Tell ya mama. Her and daddy got white blood in their veins."

Johnnie said, "Don't be tellin' family business, boy!"

"Whateva! Y'all ain't been comin' over here for Thanksgivin'. What y'all come over here today for?"

"Because ya mama asked us to. That's why," Aunt Johnnie said.

"And you couldn't wait to bring your hypocritical ass over here, could you?" Sterling asked.

"You watch your mouth, boy!" Brenda shouted.

"Why don't you tell her to watch hers, Mama? Or Jerry, for that matter," Sterling asked. "She just cussin' up a storm over there and you ain't said a word to her."

"Don't you sass me, boy! You hush your mouth!"

Jericho stared at his father. His anger had reached its limit. He was tired of his father saying he'd done all he could do. He was tired of put-down after put-down; especially when he made it in spite of his father. "You wanna know how you failed me, old man? You failed me the day you quit in the Sanchez fight."

Benjamin looked at his son incredulously. He didn't know what he was talking about.

"Yeah. That's right. I've seen the fight a thousand times. You were winning that fight. You had the fight won. All you had to do was stay away, but you wanted to knock him out. You took too many shots you didn't have to take. And he broke your will to win, didn't he, Daddy?"

"NO!" Benjamin said, slamming his fist on the table. The silverware rattled. "I never quit! The referee took that fight from me! It ruined me as a fighter!"

"The referee took that fight from me!" Jordan repeated.

"Come here, Jordan!" Ronnie yelled from the other end of the table.

Jordan jumped off Terry's lap and ran into the living room with the other kids.

"When are you going to face the facts, old man? You're forever talkin' about life choices. What about your own choices in that fight with Sanchez? After Sanchez knocked you down in the fifteenth round, the referee asked you two times if you wanted to continue. And what did you say? You didn't say nothin'. You just looked over in your corner.

"What were you looking over there for? Everybody knows that even when a fighter is hurt, the first thing he does is put his gloves up and says he's okay, even when he's out on his feet. What did you do, Daddy? What did you do? I'll tell you what you did. You quit! That's what you did. Plain and simple! You had the Middleweight Championship of the World in your hands, and you quit in the last round. Now that was your life choice. Don't tell me about mine!"

Benjamin bowed his head and wept like a baby, finally facing a truth that he had run from for years. It was this same truth that kept him from letting Jericho in the ring. He didn't want him to take the kind of beating he had taken. Nevertheless, the naked truth, unencumbered by self-deception, penetrated the marrow of his bones and Benjamin could no longer escape its all-consuming grip.

"Jericho Michael Wise!" Brenda shouted. "Wasn't no cause for you doing that to your father."

"Yeah, it was. It was overdue, Mama. And that ain't all. I'm tired of this family looking down on me because of what I do, and did, to get out of the ghetto."

"Ain't nobody looking down on you, boy!" Brenda said. "Can't you see we love you?"

"Yeah, y'all do look down on me. Y'all just don't know ya do it. Except for Sterling and Aunt Johnnie, I have helped every last one of you Negroes get ahead! Every last one of you! Willy, how do you think you got that loan for ya business, huh? What about you, Mama? How do you think you got yours? Neither one of you had the kind of credit necessary to get the kind of loans you needed. How do you think you got 'em? Didn't you think something was fishy, Willy? You do have a doctorate from Harvard, don't you?

"How many banks do you know that'll give a black man a three hundred-fifty thousand-dollar unsecured loan? Didn't you think something was wrong there? What about lending you the money at three and a half percent interest? Didn't that seem strange to you? What about you, Mama? What about you, Sammie?" Sammie was nodded out. "Wake yo' drunkass up. I'm talking to you! What about the rest of you Negroes who have loans for houses and cars where you don't have to pay a lot of interest? What about your cab, Daddy? How do you think you got it? Like I said, I've helped all of you; except for Sterling and Aunt Johnnie."

Will frowned. "How do you figure you helped us get these loans?"

"Be careful what you divulge," Sterling cautioned. "I'm speaking as your attorney now, Jerry."

"All of you bank at Chadwick International, right?" Jericho asked.

"Yeah, so what?" Will asked, wondering where he was going with all of this.

"Well, Carlton Chadwick was my roommate at Berkeley. And that's all I have to say about it. Come on, Pin. Let's roll." As they walked past Benjamin, Jericho stopped and looked at his father. Benjamin's head was in his hands. He was still crying. "Let me tell you something, old man. The day you quit in that Sanchez fight, you played a pivotal role in how my life turned out. Not only did you end your career that night, but you closed the door on me ever having one. Think about it, old man. Would I have been street fightin' for money if I could have fought in a ring? WOULD I?

"And you say you did all you could do? You did all you could to make me the failure you became. That's what you tried to do. But it didn't work. Did it?" Jericho paused for a moment to calculate the damage he'd done. Then he continued the verbal assault. "I was better than you could have ever dreamed of being. I was better than all of them that came after you, too. Now you live with that! All I ever heard you do is spout off about your little wisdom and your little philosophy. What has wisdom and philosophy gotten you? Nothing! That's what it's gotten you! I have gone my own way! You're right about that, but I made it, Daddy! BIG TIME! And what did I do? I helped you and Mama, and the rest of you Negroes. And for that, y'all wanna disown me. Then y'all wonder why I don't come around."

With his final words to his father, Jericho ended the war between them with one blow. It was a knockout. There was nothing Benjamin could say.

He just cried in his hands. They all knew Jericho was wrong, but who was going to say something to him? They knew he was a killer. And even if he wouldn't kill them, they didn't stand a chance in a fistfight. So they just watched as Jericho and Pin swaggered out of the room. When they heard the door slam shut, they looked at each other and questioned the validity of what they'd just heard.

Brenda comforted her husband. She had known the truth, too. She knew it would kill Benjamin if he ever realized what she had always known. Now that he knew the truth, maybe he could sleep better at night, she thought as she rocked him in her arms.

Chapter 44: Woman to Woman

Brenda came back downstairs after having been up there for two hours or so talking to Benny. When she entered the dining room, no one was there. The table had been cleared and wiped clean. She could hear the television in the family room. She wondered if everyone was in there, or if they had all gone home, thankful they cleaned up before they left. She had hoped she wouldn't have to do it herself. She walked down the hallway and looked into the family room. She saw Sterling and Will watching the game.

"Where is everybody?"

"They left about a half-hour ago, Mama," Sterling told her. "How's Daddy doin'?"

"He's sleepin' right now. He'll be all right."

"That's good," Will said. "I'm glad he's all right."

"Where's your friend at, Willy? Did she leave?"

"She's in the kitchen washin' dishes."

"And you two lazy niggas didn't bother to help her either, did you?" Will and Sterling looked at each other and rolled their eyes. "You two would have to embarrass me the first time she comes over here, wouldn't you; like you have no manners at all. Why would you have a guest cleaning up while you two sit around watching the football game?"

"Now I know you ain't takin' up for the white woman, are you, Mama?" Sterling laughed.

"It's not about takin' up for her. It's about manners, fool. Now what is she thinking of me? She's thinkin' I done raised two lazy niggas. That's what she's thinkin'."

"Well, you better run in there and help her then. That way, you can show her you got manners, even if we don't. In the meantime, we'll be watchin' this game."

Then the two brothers slapped high-fives and laughed. Brenda turned around and walked out of the family room and headed for the kitchen, wondering what she was going to say to Terry. She watched them during dinner and she was more than a little concerned about her relationship with Will. She knew Will loved her. But still, she didn't like the idea of Will being with a white woman.

Right before she walked into the kitchen, Brenda stealthily looked in on her to see what Terry was doing. She smelled coffee brewing. Terry's back was to her. She was at the sink washing dishes. It was very awkward for Brenda to see some white woman in her kitchen washing her dishes like she belonged there. Brenda wondered if she kept a clean home, or if she was putting on a front for her.

Terry could see Brenda looking at her through the reflection in the window. She pretended not to know she was there watching her. Terry wondered what was going through Brenda's mind as she watched her. *Should I be in here, in her kitchen? What is she thinking? Does she think I'm trying to butter her up by cleaning up after everyone? Maybe I should be in the family room with Will and Sterling. I'd rather be watching the game anyway. But if I did that, what would she think of me? She would probably think that I'm a lazy white woman, who wants her son's money. Yeah, I did the right thing by coming in here. At least she can't say I'm lazy.*

"Thanks for cleaning up, Terry."

"Oh, it's no problem."

"I'm sorry my lazy sons didn't help you."

"That's okay. Karen helped me before she and Ronnie left."

"I bet Jordan didn't want to leave, did he?"

"As a matter of fact, he didn't. He cried before they left, and fell asleep."

"I bet you're proud of yourself, aren't you?"

"What's that supposed to mean, Mrs. Wise?"

"You know what it means. You seem to have a way with men. Or is it just black men?"

"If you're asking me if men are attracted to me, I'd have to say yes, they are. But it doesn't make me proud."

"I'm talking specifically about my Willy, my Sterling, my Benny, and now my little Jordan. Or do you just like black men period? Is Willy your first black man? How many of them have you had? How many of them have money?"

Terry washed the last dish and put it in the rack. She pulled the plug and the water swirled into the pipe. Then she picked up a towel and dried her hands. "May I ask you a question, Mrs. Wise?"

"Yeah. Right after you answer mine."

"Fair enough. Will is the first black man I've ever dated, and he happens to have money. There's nothing I can do about that, other than what I said, Mrs. Wise. I will sign a prenuptial if we get married."

"So that's not your plan? You're not planning to marry him?"

"Mrs. Wise, that's an unfair question."

"Unfair? How is that unfair?"

"Well, it's similar to the one Jericho asked me earlier. No matter what I say, it won't be right. If I say, I'm not planning to marry him, you'll say, well why are you wasting his time? Or you'll say something vulgar like I am using him for sex, or whatever it was you said at his place. Something about a black buck, I believe you said. But if I say I do plan to marry him, then you'll say it's because he has money."

Brenda laughed. "You're smart. I'll give you that."

"May I ask my question now, please?"

"Ask away."

Brenda poured herself a cup of coffee. Then she pulled out a chair from the kitchen table and sat down.

"May I be frank?"

"Please do be. I can't stand phony people."

"What have I done that makes me so undesirable for Will?"

"What have you done personally? Nothing."

"Then it's because I'm white?"

"Yeah, but it's even beyond that. It's the very fact that you represent all the white women before you that wanted a black man and got him hung because you didn't have the strength to tell the truth. The truth being, you were the instigator, the initiator, and in many cases, his false accuser, which in a very real sense makes you, the white woman, his executioner."

Terry looked at her and frowned. She was stunned by her provocative commentary.

"What? Are you surprised I can think even though I don't have a PhD from Stanford? I'll have you know, we think in this house. We always have, and we always will. So don't let my speech patterns fool you."

"I'm sorry I gave you that impression. I didn't mean to sound snobbish."

"Whether you intended it or not, that's what your body language said."

"Well, I'm sorry. I didn't mean to offend you. You just spoke so well that I was a little stunned, is all."

"In other words, you didn't think I would be able to converse on your level, right?"

"I meant, I didn't expect you to say what you did. To be completely honest, I didn't think you had a good reason for not liking me."

"Really? So you think my reasons are good reasons then?"

"Yes, I do. But not good enough."

"Why not?"

"Because you've lumped me in with all the bad white women that have, and would do such a thing."

"So then you acknowledge the past?"

"Yes, but I don't dwell on it. In this case, you're doing to me what you don't want done to you. For example, you don't want me to think you're lazy simply because you're black, right?" Brenda looked at her. "You want to be judged as an individual, right? Well, I don't want you to judge me by the few white women that did what you said to black men. Judge me by my own deeds, not the deeds of others."

"The few? You make it sound like it was only a handful, or something. What about the Scottsboro Boys down there in Alabama? And what about Susan Smith in South Carolina?"

"Mrs. Wise, I can't argue with you on those cases. I can only tell you I'm not like those women."

"Are you even familiar with the Scottsboro case?"

"Yes, I am. But not as much as you are, I'm sure."

"What do you know about the case?"

"I know nine or ten black boys were accused of raping two white women. The jury found them guilty and the judge disagreed with them and ordered a new trial. I also know that one woman who was supposedly raped, changed her testimony in the second trial."

"Is that supposed to make it all right that she accused them in the first place?"

"No, it just means some of us are willing to do the right thing. What about the judge in that case? He disagreed with the jury and ordered a new trial. And he was never elected again. Doesn't that say something for the white race?"

"Yeah, it says something. But like you said earlier, not enough."

"Well, I think it says you could be wrong about me." Then she thought for a moment. "What about the Underground Railroad?"

"What about it?"

"Well, since you're bringing up the faults of white people in the past, it's only right that I bring up their virtues as well. You do acknowledge that it was primarily white people running the Underground Railroad, don't you?"

"So what? I suppose you're going to tell me it was a white man that freed the slaves, too."

"No, but it's true."

Brenda laughed a little. "The good deeds of the few don't erase the evil deeds of the many."

"True," Terry said. "True. However, do we allow the good deeds of the few to be forever lost in the evil deeds of the many?"

"Good point but let me ask you this. If the good deeds of the many black people are lost in the evil deeds of a few black people, and the many are judged by the few, am I not justified in judging the few good white people with the many evil white people?"

"No, Mrs. Wise. It's unfair to the few."

"That's just it. The many in our case have been treated unfairly. Why should I be any different from prejudiced whites?"

"Because it's right, Mrs. Wise. Because it's right."

"That's so typical. White people always want us to turn the other cheek. Then when we do, they slap us again. We just keep turning the other cheek, and we keep gettin' slapped. Well, I'm tired of being slapped around by white people."

"Okay, what will it take for you to accept me?"

"Black skin."

"That's the only qualification?"

"In this case, yeah."

"Okay. Tell me something. What can a black woman do for Will that I couldn't do for him?"

"Pour yourself a cup of coffee and have a seat."

Terry poured some coffee into a cup and sat down. She assumed she was making headway; Brenda had at least offered her a chair—that was a start. She was wondering if her question would perplex her the way it had perplexed Will. She was counting on it. The only question that remained was, would it be the viable vehicle to acceptance? The women looked at each other as they sipped their coffee.

"What can a black woman do for him that you can't do for him? First of all, she can identify with him, Terry. That's something you will never ever be able to do."

Terry frowned. "What do you mean, identify with him?"

"See, that's what I mean. You have no idea what I'm talkin' about, do you?"

"No, I'm sorry to say I don't."

"Okay, let's say you two get married. Willy comes home and he's seein' red and he's madder than a bull being repeatedly stabbed by a bullfighter in Mexico. You say, what's wrong, baby, honey, sweetie, or whatever pet names you have for each other. And Willy says, nothin'. You say, sweetie, I know something's wrong, otherwise you wouldn't be so upset. Now tell me what it is. He says, he was at the store buying whatever and he wanted to use his credit card. He pulls out his MasterCard, and the woman waiting on him asks for five pieces of identification besides his driver's license. What is your first response?"

"My first response is, you bitch, get the manager out here!"

"Okay, but what if he told you he thought she did it because he was black. What would you think?"

"What do you mean, what would I think?"

"I mean, would you think he was right, or wrong?"

"I would think the lady was being ridiculous, but not because he's black."

"See, and that's the difference between you and a black woman. A black woman would immediately know where he's comin' from, even if it wasn't racism in that case, because she's been through it all her life, just—like—him. He wouldn't hesitate to tell his black wife what happened. But with you, he'd learn to not be as open about what he thinks because white people have the tendency to think black people are paranoid when they sense they're being treated unfairly."

"Well, I admit, I do think some black people are paranoid. I also think some black people make excuses for why they don't get ahead in life. And I think in some of these cases, I'm right. Now do you fault me for that, Mrs. Wise?"

"It's hard to fault people when they tell the truth. But you have to keep in mind that Willy is a catch for black women."

"He's a catch for most, if not all women. But I'm having a hard time understanding why black women are so hostile about the interracial thing in general. I don't get upset when I see white men with black women."

"That's because all you understand is what you know about yourself and your white world. Step out of your sphere of understanding for a second or two. Why would you get upset about it? Is there a shortage of good and decent white men?"

"No."

"There are plenty of well-to-do white men out there, right?"

"Yes, that's true."

"Black well-to-do men are hard to find. If this were true of white men, you might have a problem with it, just like the Massa's wife had a problem with him running specifically after black women. What you have to understand is that there isn't enough men, period. And in the black community, the problem is even worse. Let's turn the situation around. What if most of the men you had to choose from were not the marrying kind, or so you believe? Then you were left with the choice of staying at home alone, or going outside the white race? What if your female ancestors had been repeatedly raped by black men and it was legal to do so? What if you had educated yourself, but white men were so beaten down physically and mentally by black men that many have very little self-esteem, or they're just plain good for nothin'?

"Now, you find a white Willy out there. And you see many white Willys marrying black women once they've made it. How would that make you feel? Now you're stuck with dating the black man who is well-established and thinks well of himself, or dating a good-for-nothing white man who has nothing on the ball, but he wants to lay you anyway. But these black men don't have the same mental baggage the white men have.

"They are clean-cut and well-educated doctors and lawyers—men of renown. And it's considered a privilege to marry one. And let's say you're encouraged to do so, knowing these men had raped your mothers, and broken your fathers. In fact, they broke the strong ones and let the weak ones live to propagate more weak men. Now, because a lot of white men have lost their way, and many don't know who they are, they can't be considered serious prospects for husbands. But the black man is, because he doesn't bring along the same baggage, understand?"

"Yes, I understand now, but I still think that in my case, I am the woman for Will."

"There's another reason, too, Terry. Do you realize that it's still dangerous for a black man to date, or marry a white woman? It isn't just white men either. It's the white woman, too. A black man has to be just as concerned about her as he is about him. See, Terry, a white woman wields a lot of power because she controls the white man. If she says a black man did anything to her, and I mean anything, he'll use all of the power available to him to make that black man an example. Case in point: Susan Smith. That's too much power for any woman to have over a man. You would have to be one unique individual to convince me that my Willy is safe with you. And I don't think there's that much convincing in the world."

"So you're worried I would cause him some harm?"

"Frankly, Terry, I am very worried. Even if you don't mean him any harm, there are a lot of white men out there who do mean him some harm. They would want to hurt him simply because you're pretty. If you were some old alley cat-lookin' white woman, he'd be a little safer, but even they have the power to hurt a black man. Let me give you an example of what I'm talkin' about."

"The Scottsboro Boys is good enough, Mrs. Wise."

"That was in the early thirties. You need something more up-to-date. Take the O.J. Simpson trial. Just for the sake of argument, let's assume he did it, okay?"

"I believe he did do it, but okay."

"White people were mad because they think he got off. Again, let's assume he did. See, Terry, what pisses me off is I don't see the same furor when murders are committed on a regular basis. And I don't care what anyone says, had Nicole and Ron been black, white America would not be so enraged still. To prove this point to you, did you notice that people only thought the jury came back too soon after they reached a verdict of not guilty?

"To me, in order for these naysayers to be taken seriously, they should have said to Judge Ito, 'Look, this is a volatile situation. You should make them deliberate much longer. That way, no matter what their decision, it will be more acceptable to all of America.' But no one said that until after they came back with a not guilty verdict. In my opinion, they thought it was going to be guilty. Generally speaking, when a jury comes back that quick, Sterling says it's usually a guilty verdict.

"White people ain't stupid. I think most of y'all thought this was great at first. White people thought a quick guilty verdict by a predominately black jury would be great because no racism could be laid at the feet of white America for the injustices we've suffered. I bet if it had been guilty, you wouldn't hear white America saying they should have thought about it longer. To prove my point, sooner, or later, another black football player will be accused of killing a woman, but this time she'll be black. And I guarantee you white folk will barely notice. If a guilty verdict is reached quickly, you won't hear white people saying they should have thought about it longer."

"I absolutely agree with you on that. When they came back with the verdict so quickly, I thought for sure it was guilty. And you're right, I didn't even think about how quickly they came to a decision because he was obviously guilty. But when they said he wasn't guilty, I did just what you said. And I'm sure a lot of other white people did the same. But back to the subject. Does the fact that I've been honest with you today mean anything to you? Will says you know people without having known them very long. He says it's a gift, or something. He says you could have been a psychologist."

Brenda laughed. "Willy said that about me?"

"Yes. He knows things without knowing them, too. It amazes me sometimes. Like last weekend. We were in Sonoma and I was telling him I had a problem with homosexuality. And that's all I said, right? The first thing out of his mouth was, 'Is your brother a homosexual?' And he was right."

"I'm against homosexuality, too. It's not a personal dislike. The Bible says it's wrong. Why are you against it?"

"I'm not sure. I just think it's unnatural."

"You go to church?"

"I haven't been in a long time."

"Why don't you come to church Sunday? I promise you'll have a good time in the Lord."

Terry laughed within herself. *So I can go to church and worship your God, but I'm not good enough for your son. That doesn't make any sense.* "Okay. I'll be there this Sunday."

"Good, I'll be looking for you all; it's been a while since Willy's been to church. You make sure he comes with you, okay?"

"Okay."

"Do you realize Willy hasn't been to the community center since he came back from Toronto?"

"Well, you know he recently opened a new clinic and we've been seeing each other."

"I think it's more than that, Terry. Willy loves going down there and helping people learn to read and write. He gives lectures and everything. They need him. You ever heard Willy give a speech?"

Terry laughed. "Only when he's mad at me about something or someone else in the office."

Brenda laughed. "No, I mean at a high school, or a college?"

"No, I haven't."

"Well, he's very active in the community. He hasn't told you this, but I know he's thinking he'll have to give all of that up for you."

"Why would he have to?"

"Willy's not like most men. He's not going to hide you forever. Like he told his daddy about it the day he got back in town. That's how he is. He doesn't make decisions without having thought them through. We taught him that. We taught him to look down the road and look at all that could happen on any given decision. I don't know what his decision is, but I'm sure Willy's considering it."

"I'm considering what?" Will asked, as he walked into the kitchen.

"That ain't none of yo' business, boy. That's between Terry and me."

"Boy, you sho' do speak good English when you want to, Mama." Will laughed.

"Hush yo' mouth, boy," Brenda said playfully. "I can speak English as good as you."

"I know, Mama. I know." Then he looked at Terry. "Jerry called and he wants to know if we'll go out with him and Pin tonight?"

"Where we goin', darlin'?"

"The Perfect Indulgence Club."

"Sure. Tell him Desdemona will be dressed and ready for the ball."

"I already did. I knew you would want to go."

"How did you know that?"

"I knew you would want the chance to win Jericho over, that's how."

"See what I mean, Mrs. Wise. It's like he can read my mind, or something."

"I can. And don't you forget it."

"I won't, darlin'."

"Well, we better be going then."

"Okay, Will." She looked at Brenda. "Mrs. Wise, I really enjoyed our talk. I hope we can do it again sometime."

"I'm sure we will. Benny says you've been waitin' three years, and you're in it for the duration. So I figure I'll be seeing a lot of you, whether I want to or not."

"That's true."

Will hugged his mother and she hugged him back. She kissed him and hugged him again. "You be careful, now."

It was her way of saying you're a man now and you're old enough to make your own decisions. She hadn't accepted Terry, but it was the first step. Will knew that whatever happened between them, it was a huge triumph for Terry. He could tell by the way she hugged him. He sensed the hostility leaving. She was closer to accepting her, and it made him feel good.

"Mama," Sterling said, "Jerry wants to talk to you."

"Okay, let me see y'all to the door." They walked out of the kitchen and into the hallway. When they reached the door, Brenda said, "Willy, bring Terry to church Sunday."

"Okay."

"Did you hear what I said? I said bring her. That means don't drop her off. That means you come in the church also."

Will laughed. "Okay."

"And that goes double for you, Sterling. And don't be goin' into the nursery botherin' the women in there either."

Sterling laughed. "Okay, but what if they botherin' me?"

"Boy, get on outta here. You somethin' else."

Sterling laughed. Then he hugged his mother and they left. Brenda closed the door and watched them walk to their cars. Then she went to the phone and said, "Hi, Jerry."

Jericho said. "Mama, I'm sorry. Is Daddy all right?"

Chapter 45: Perfect Indulgence

Will looked in the mirror as he brushed his teeth. A red terrycloth towel was wrapped around his waist. He was thinking about James and wondered how he was faring in prison, still questioning why he hadn't noticed that James was on the edge, still wondering if Sharon and the two girls would be alive if he had taken the time to counsel James properly.

Terry was putting on the finishing touches of her makeup in the other mirror. Her hair was up and held together tightly with four bobby pins in a bun shape. She looked at Will who seemed to be brushing his teeth on autopilot and in deep thought. She looked at the reflection of his bare chest and the thickness of his biceps in the mirror, and noticed how his chest muscles moved as he brushed his teeth. She laughed to herself because they made love twice that day and here she was thinking about it again.

"You gon' scrape the enamel off, if you keep that up."

"Huh? I didn't hear you, babe. What?"

Terry smiled. "You gon' scrape the enamel off, if you keep that up."

"You gon'? What kind of English is that?"

"It is pretty bad, ain't it? Must be the riff-raff I been hangin' out with lately. What do you think?"

Will spit the residual toothpaste he had in his mouth into the sink. Then he rinsed with water and spit again. "Yeah, it's bad, but I like it."

"You do, huh? Why?"

"I don't know. Maybe it's the way you say it with that Southern accent you been tryin' to hide since I met you."

"You don't think I sound like an old country hick with this accent?"

"Yeah, you sound just like some ol' bumpkin."

Terry hit him playfully.

Will stood behind her and kissed her neck.

"Umm," she said and closed her eyes. "So what were you thinkin' so hard about?"

They looked at each other in the mirror.

"When?"

"When you were brushing your teeth, silly."

"Oh, I was just thinking about James. I was wondering how he was doing in prison. The funeral was yesterday and I was just wondering how he was doing on Thanksgiving without his family for the first time, ya know?"

"Yeah, I know. It must be rough on him right now."

Will stopped kissing her neck and looked at her in the mirror again. Terry wished she hadn't asked what he was thinking. She wanted him again, but now she knew he was in the mood to talk about James' situation.

"You think he's all right?"

"James?" he asked in disbelief. "The man has probably never even been in a fistfight. Now he's in Folsom doing time with hardened criminals. What do you think is happening?"

"He's probably having a hard time." Terry thought about what she said and laughed.

Will looked at her sternly. He didn't think it was a laughing matter.

When she saw that he was serious, she stopped laughing. "I'm sorry, darlin'. It's not funny. Forgive me?"

"Yeah, you know I do." He resumed kissing her neck.

"Umm, I like that."

Terry turned around and kissed his lips. As the kiss became more passionate, she put her arms around him, pulling him closer until she felt his hardness pressing against her. She pulled the towel away from his loins and caressed his love joint.

He responded to her caresses by gripping her tight derriere as he felt himself being pulled into the moment. "Do you think we have time, babe?"

"Umm-hmm, but don't mess up my hair, okay?"

†††

Sterling, Le'sett, Jericho, and Pin were talking near their vehicles when Will and Terry pulled into the parking lot of the Perfect Indulgence Club. Victor and Cochise were leaning against the limousine, watching the beautiful women that went into the club unescorted. Terry looked at Pin who was standing close to Jericho, and wondered if she was as devoted to Will as Pin was to Jericho. Then it occurred to her that no one questioned the fact that Pin was Asian. She had noticed Pin's Southeast Asia good looks earlier at dinner, but she didn't think anything of it until now.

Will pulled into a parking space about six cars away from Jericho's limo and turned off the ignition. He was about to get out of the car when Terry said, "Will, why didn't you tell me Jericho's wife was Asian?"

Will frowned. "What difference does it make?"

"It makes a lot of difference. Did Pin have to go through the screening process also, or what?"

"What do you mean, screening process?"

She curled her lips. "You can be so evasive sometimes. Was Pin accosted by Aunt Johnnie and the rest of the women in your family the way I was? Or is this just a white thing?"

"Look, Terry," he said in a firm voice. "When Jerry came home from Vietnam, he brought her with him. It wasn't like they had a choice in the matter. It was already done."

"Oh, so then, if we had gotten married, I'd be accepted just like Pin, right?"

Will looked at her and took a deep breath. He was growing tired of the questions. "You sho' like to sweat a brotha."

"Oh, so I'm sweating you when I ask you a logical question?"

"You're making a mountain out of a molehill."

"Really? I don't think so. You know, your mother was telling me I could never identify with you because I'm white. She was talking about how I would respond if you came home one day upset about the way you'd been treated by some white nobody. She said I'd probably think you were paranoid if you told me you thought it was racism."

"Yeah, and?"

"What if I told you, you were making a mountain out of a molehill in that situation?"

"Point taken. Now…can we go inside?"

"I know you don't like being cross-examined, but don't patronize me, Will. I'm serious. Don't you think there's something wrong with your mother accepting Pin, and not accepting me?"

"I'm not tryin' to patronize you, babe. But you know, I'm getting a little tired of these questions."

"Okay, fine. Just answer this last question. Isn't there something wrong with her accepting Pin, and not me?"

"Yes. We've covered this," he said, obviously irritated.

"Well, I just don't think it's fair, is all."

"Welcome to the club. We've been sayin' that for four hundred years. Now let's go."

They got out of the car and walked over to where the others were standing. Terry wondered if things would ever get better between her and Will's mother. They seemed to be getting somewhere earlier, but she wondered what his mother would say if she asked her the same questions about Pin and Jericho.

"You startin' to make being late a habit," Sterling told Will.

"We had something to take care of before we got here." Will winked.

"I'll bet you did." Sterling laughed. "Hello, Terry. This is Le'sett Santiago."

The women shook hands and greeted each other with pleasant smiles.

"Santiago? Santiago?" Terry repeated. "Where do I know that name?" Then it hit her. "Weren't you the District Attorney in the Samuelson case?"

"Yes, as a matter of fact, I was."

"Well, if it's any consolation, I think you won. No offense, Sterling."

"Thank you," Le'sett said.

"Humph." Sterling grunted. "Do you think she won because she put on a better case, or because you think Samuelson's guilty?"

"Both," Terry said.

"Thanks again," Le'sett said. "We women have to stick together."

"Yeah, we do," Terry said, looking at Will. "Some of them like to ask hard questions, but they don't like to answer them."

Will pinched Terry's ass hard, but no one noticed. She wanted to cry out, but held it in.

Sterling thought she was talking about him, and said, "Well, I'm glad you weren't on the jury."

"Can we go in the club now, if y'all through talkin' shop?" Jericho asked.

"Yeah. I'm outnumbered anyway. Let's go have some fun."

As they walked toward the club, Terry and Will had their arms around each other, pinching each other's ass all the way to the entrance; each attempting to pinch the other harder than they were being pinched.

The group walked into the lobby of the club and heard moderately loud music being played. There were a couple of bouncers wearing white and green togas; one black, the other white, standing near the club entrance. Both looked like bodybuilders, sporting thick rippling muscles. The black bouncer had a bandanna tied around his head that had Hercules written on it. The white bouncer was wearing one that had Samson on it. His hair was shoulder-length and curly. He looked like soul singer Michael Bolton. Several women stared at him, admiring his body.

Jericho stared at Sampson and he stared at Jericho. Then Jericho whispered to Pin, Victor and Cochise, "They got that shit backwards, don't they? Samson was the brotha, and Hercules was the myth." They laughed.

Sterling saw what was happening between the two men and whispered, "Jerry, don't start no shit up in here. We can't afford an incident in our professions."

"I'm not going to start anything. But you know me. I'm not going to run from it either."

"Look, man, Le'sett doesn't know anything about you. She's an Assistant

District Attorney. If some shit happens, she could be in real trouble. So just chill out, okay?"

"Okay."

Samson walked over to Jericho. At five-eleven he looked down at him. "Can I help you with something, pal?"

Jericho looked him in the eye. "I seriously doubt it."

"Well, what the hell are you laughing about?"

Victor was about to approach Samson, but Jericho put his arm out and stopped him.

Terry and Will were wondering what happened to provoke the response they were witnessing. But Will wanted to see some action.

"What's going on?" Terry whispered to Will.

"I don't know."

Terry detected a little childlike glee in his voice, reminiscent of when he told her about Jericho in Sonoma.

"Is it against the club rules to laugh?" Jericho asked.

"You just be careful, pal," Samson said, and flexed his chest muscles.

Jericho laughed. "Okay, pal. I'll be real careful."

Samson watched them as they walked away. He called the other bouncers over. As he talked to the bouncers, he pointed at Jericho.

Inside the club were white massive columns positioned around the circular room, which resembled a Roman Coliseum. Between each column, there hung a statue of a Greek or Roman god.

Sterling saw a vacant table near the Aphrodite statue and led them there through the mammoth crowd. Victor and Cochise were on duty and took a table near them. A group of black men and women were drinking and talking among themselves at the table next to theirs. As soon as they sat down, Terry heard one of the women at the table say, "Look at that shit." Terry ignored the comment, even though she sensed the woman was referring to her.

While they waited for the drinks they ordered, Terry could hear the women making more comments about her. Now they were loud enough for Will to hear. The men at the table laughed at what their women were saying about Terry.

"Do you wanna move, babe?"

Terry shook her head, but he could tell she was getting upset. "You sure?" Terry nodded.

"Hey, Jerry," Will said. "I've been meaning to tell you that Cleve wants you to back a business venture of his."

"What scheme is he tryin' now?" Sterling asked.

"He wants you to back him financially, Jerry."

"I figured that much, baby brotha," Jericho said. "What's he looking to do?"

"He wants you to buy Scott Tyler's three McDonald's," Will said.

"Three, huh? At least he thinks big. Why does he think I'll help him?"

"Because you helped Alicia with her salons."

"Cheryl still kickin' his ass?" Jericho asked.

"Like clockwork." Sterling laughed. "Every Friday night. When Cleve gets home from the post office, he knows he's going take an ass whuppin'!"

When Sterling said that, Terry remembered when she had first met Cleve at the airport and how bad he looked.

"Ain't that some shit," Sterling continued. "You work in a place where you can get ya ass shot off. Then ya go home knowin' you gotta take an ass whuppin'."

"Is that true?" Terry whispered to Will. He nodded. "So that's why he had that patch over his eye at the airport?" He nodded again.

"Alicia got skills," Jericho said. "What's he bringin' to the table?"

"Alicia Harris?" Le'sett questioned.

"Yeah," Will confirmed. "Do you know her?"

"Not personally, no," Le'sett told him. "I do go to her salon though."

"So do I," Terry admitted. "But I had no idea she was black."

"What difference does her color make?" Jericho asked. "Do you get what you pay for when you go in?"

The waitress came back with their drinks. Jericho paid the check.

Terry took a small sip of her chardonnay. Then she looked at Jericho. She couldn't believe he had the nerve to ask her what difference color made. She knew she had to handle this situation delicately. "Yes, I get what I pay for. All the stylists are white at the salon I go to. And I've never seen any black people there, so I assumed the owner was white. As far as color is concerned, it doesn't bother me any more than it bothers you."

Will and Sterling looked at each other. They wanted to laugh, but didn't.

Sensing the onset of an argument, Le'sett said, "So, Pin, Sterling says you're a wonderful dancer. Is that right?"

Pin nodded. "Dance, I like. Yes."

"Jerry, you don't mind if I dance with her, do you?" Sterling said.

"That's up to her."

"You wanna dance, Pin?"

Pin nodded. They went to the dance floor and danced to the SOS Band's "Take Your Time (Do It Right)."

"Do you dance also, Will?" Le'sett asked.

"Not really. I like to slow dance. That's about it. Sterling's the dancer in the family."

"What about you, Terry?" Le'sett asked.

"Huh?" Terry kind of grunted. "I'm sorry, I didn't hear you. What?"

She couldn't help but listen to what the black women at the table next to theirs were saying about her. The women were getting bolder and louder. Jericho could hear what they were saying, but pretended not to.

"Do you dance?" Le'sett repeated.

"A little."

"I'll be right back, y'all," Will announced. "I gotta go to the little boys' room."

"Yeah, me too," Le'sett said.

"Take care of my girl until I get back, Jerry."

Left alone, Terry and Jericho stared at each other, but she didn't sense any hostility from him. She saw being alone with him as opportunity to question him about what he'd said earlier at dinner and what he'd said only moments ago. She was just about to open her mouth when he said, "I understand you know something about the fight game. Is that right?"

"I like boxing, if that's what you mean. I don't know anything about street fighting though."

Jericho's eyes lit up. "Will told you about me, huh?"

"Yeah, he did."

"I'll tell you what, you tell me who you like in boxing, and I'll school you on street fightin'."

Terry continued sipping her chardonnay. She could still hear the vicious insults being hurled at her, but found a way to concentrate more on what Jericho was saying rather than what the women behind her were saying. "Are you talking about contemporary fighters, or fighters of the past?"

"Do you know the fight game well enough to talk factually about boxing's greatest fighters?"

"No. I don't know many from the past."

"You probably know Ali, Frazier, Louis, and Robinson, huh?"

"What about Jake Lamotta?"

"Saw the movie, huh?"

Terry laughed. "Yeah, I did."

"Okay. Well, who do you like today besides Oscar De La Hoya?"

"What makes you think I like him?"

"'Cause all the women like Oscar."

"He's handsome," she said, feeling a little more relaxed. "But he can also fight. Quick powerful jab. Nice short hook, too."

"True, but he wouldn't last long in a street fight though."

"Why is that?"

"No rules."

"Hmm, I see. What do you think of Roy Jones Jr.?"

"He's good. Probably the only one of all the guys fighting since the eighties that would have given me trouble in the ring. But on the street, it wouldn't even be close. Hell, I would beat all they asses on the street. You name 'em, I'd beat 'em. That goes for Hagler, Leonard, Hearns, and Duran. See, the key to winnin' a fight is to get yours off first. I don't mean throwing one punch, then assessing the damage. Naw, I mean throwing a variety of punches to a man's center."

"What do you mean by that? A man's center, I mean."

"I mean attack the center of him. For example, the eyes, the nose, the throat, the chest, and the groin are a man's center. Attack those areas swiftly and he'll be at your mercy in seconds. Take Samson, for example. Somebody gon' end up kickin' his ass because he thinks people are intimidated by him. One day, he's going to run into somebody who's not afraid of his muscles. And he's going to be in a lot of trouble. I'll bet you he ain't been seriously challenged in a long time. He's overconfident.

"Let me give you some advice. If you're ever in a bind and you know your life's on the line, attack the attacker with everything. Let your adrenaline take over. What I mean by that is, use it to fight, not to flee. Hit first, and hit hard. Let the element of surprise be your ally. Believe me, it's the last thing the attacker will expect. The hard thing is to control the fear. If you're not careful, you could kill someone if you're outta control."

"Okay, I will, but I seriously doubt I'll ever need to do that."

"If you never have to, good. But be prepared just in case. You never know."

"Okay." Terry was surprised by his change in attitude. Will was right, she thought. Fighting was his passion. She wondered if what he told his father was true. Would he be a drug dealer if he'd had the chance to box?

Jericho said, "By the way, Sterling told me what you said."

"What was that?"

"Sterling said that when you guys left the house you had said something about Desdemona being ready for the ball."

"Yeah, I said that. Does it bother you that I said it?"

"No, just wondered why you chose that name out of the three that I called you."

"Well, it was the only one that—"

Terry stopped in mid-sentence. One of the women at the next table shouted, "IT'S JUST A GODDAMN SHAME! THREE BLACK MEN GON' COME UP IN HERE WITH WOMEN, AND NOT ONE OF 'EM BLACK! A HONKY, A WETBACK, AND A CHINK!"

Terry turned around and shouted, "NOW JUST A MINUTE!"

"You want some of this, bitch?" the woman retorted.

Jericho stood and went over to the table. He looked at the man nearest to the woman and said, "Is that yo' woman?" The man nodded. Jericho backhanded him in the mouth. The man fell backwards out of his chair.

Victor and Cochise stood up and watched the crowd. The people in the club gasped. Jericho looked down at the man and said, "I want a heartfelt apology. My wife is Asian. I don't like the idea of somebody calling her a chink. The last man that called her that, ended up dead."

The man was terrified. Blood trickled from the corner of his mouth. "I didn't say it! I didn't say it!" he said. His breathing was erratic.

"I know you ain't' gon' take that shit," the woman said to her boyfriend.

The man looked at his girlfriend angrily.

"It's bitches like her that get brothas like you killed," Jericho told him. "Apologize, and we can forget this happened."

"Jerry!" Victor called out. "Here comes Samson. You want me to stop him?"

"Naw. Let his ass on through." Jericho looked at the man on the floor again. "Well, I don't hear you apologizin'."

Just then, Samson grabbed Jericho around the collar, but Jericho lifted his left arm up in an inside sweeping motion and wrapped it around Samson's right arm, locking it so he couldn't move it. Then Jericho hit him in the groin. Samson grunted and doubled over. Jericho grabbed his hair and pulled his head back and chopped him in the throat. While Samson was holding his throat and gasping for air, Jericho grabbed his hair again and slammed his face into the table. The music stopped. Pin pulled out her pistol and ran over to where Jericho was standing. Jericho turned back to the man on the floor.

"Now...apologize," Jericho demanded in an eerie calm voice.

"I'm sorry, man," he said hurriedly.

Still dazed from the blows, Samson shouted, "I'm gonna kill you, man!"

He grabbed Jericho around the waist from the back. Jericho snapped his head backward, bloodying Samson in the nose. Then he quickly pinched the nerve between Samson's forefinger and thumb, and squeezed hard. Samson yelped in pain and released him. Jericho held on to his hand and grabbed his arm. He spun around quickly so that he ended up behind him. He had Samson's right arm locked again. Jericho was behind him pulling his hair back—veins bulging in his neck. Samson felt his arm going numb from the pressure on the nerve in his elbow. Jericho bounced his head off the table again. Then he looked at the man on the floor and said, "So you think yo' woman is funny, huh? Well, laugh."

The man chuckled a little. Jericho bounced Samson's head off the table again. "I SAID LAUGH, MUTHAFUCKA, NOT CHUCKLE!" Each time the man laughed, Jericho bounced Samson's head off the table. His face was bloodied by the constant pounding.

"LOOK OUT BEHIND YOU, JERRY!" Cochise shouted.

The black guy who wore the Hercules bandanna was running toward Jericho at full speed. Pin tripped him and he fell face forward to the floor. Jericho let Samson go and he slumped to the floor. Then Jericho drew his weapon and pointed it at Hercules who was lying at his feet. Hercules was about to get up.

"Relax, brotha," Jericho said, with the same calmness. Hercules lay back down when he felt the muzzle of the gun at his temple.

Pin came over and kicked Hercules in the face. Then she bent down and placed her gun between his eyes and she whispered in his ear, "Move again, you die."

Jericho spotted Will and said, "Y'all get on outta here before the cops get here."

"Come on," Will said and snatched Terry by the arm.

Chapter 46: Retribution

As they sped away from the club, Terry looked at Will. He was seething. They rode in the Jeep for about fifteen minutes and hadn't said a word. She looked out the window for a moment, and then looked at him again. He looked as if he was about to explode. She decided to lighten the atmosphere.

"I guess we won't be going back to the Perfect Indulgence Club, huh?"

Will whipped his head in her direction and shot her the meanest look she had ever seen. "I bet you think that shit is funny. Well, it ain't!"

She laughed. "Well, it's a little funny."

"That's yo' problem! You don't know when shit is serious! Yo' ass always gotta make a joke outta everything! Don't you get tired of it! I do! I get sick and tired of it!"

"Will, why are you pissed at me? I wasn't the one who slapped one man around, beat another one senseless, and held a gun to yet another man's head! Yet you have the nerve to be mad at me?"

"You damn right, I'm mad at you."

"Why? What did I do?"

"Didn't I ask you if you wanted to move?! Didn't I?!"

"What does that have to do with anything, Will?"

"You know damn well what that has to do with it!"

"So it's my fault your brother slapped people around? Is that it?"

"Yeah, it's your fault!"

"I want you to explain that to me." Her voice rose a few octaves. "Assuming it was my fault, which it wasn't. How the hell would you know what happened when your ass was in the john?"

"'Cause I know yo' ass! That's how!"

"Prove it!"

"Prove what!"

"Prove you know what happened." Her voice sounded calm and confident now. "This ought to be good, too."

Will thought for a moment and said, "Well, I can't prove it. But—"

Terry laughed a little, which angered Will even more.

"See that's what I'm talkin' 'bout. You think everything is funny! The shit ain't funny!"

Terry thought, *Boy, your grammar really gets bad when you're mad*, but she didn't say anything. *Why antagonize the situation?*

"Here's what I think happened!" He was still shouting. "See, I think somebody at that table said one thing too many and yo' ass turned around and said somethin'! And that's how the shit started! I asked yo' ass if you wanted to move and what did you say? 'No', that's what you said! I said, are you sure? And you nodded your head, yes. Right, or wrong?"

"You're right, Will," she said, still calm. "But do you have to keep shouting at me?"

"Why didn't you just move? The shit wouldn't have happened if you would have just moved."

"Maybe it wouldn't have tonight. It may have happened some other time though."

"Maybe, but my brother wouldn't be there at some other time," he said, having composed himself. "What if he had killed somebody, Terry? What if the bouncer has some sort of permanent brain damage?"

"Will, I admit I didn't think about all of that, but that doesn't make it my fault completely either. Yes, I could have moved. But Jericho could have dealt with the situation better, too."

"That's just it. That's how he deals with things."

"Can I be honest with you, Will? A part of me is glad he did what he did. I don't think it was right, but sometimes people need to know they can't just walk all over people. Those people at that table were using all kinds of racial slurs against me. The thing that set him off was what they said about Pin."

"What did they say?"

"They called her a chink; they called me a honky, and Le'sett a wetback. That's when he went off. If it had just stopped with the bouncer, I wouldn't be too worried about it. But when they drew their guns, it got out of hand. Besides, if you were honest with yourself, you would have to admit you wanted something like that to happen. And don't say you didn't. I saw that look in your eyes when the bouncer and Jericho had the confrontation in the lobby. You hoped you'd see some action then. You may not have wanted it to go as far as it did, but you wanted something to happen. Frankly, I'm glad he loved his wife enough to put a stop to what they were saying about her and me. I just wish it hadn't gotten out of control."

He stopped the Jeep in front of Terry's townhouse and turned the ignition off. "So you condone what he did?"

"No, but I understand. And you're evading the issue."

"What issue?"

"Did you, or did you not want something to happen with Jericho and the bouncer?"

"The question is irrelevant. What I wanted had no bearing on what he did, and what you didn't do. Both of you made decisions that brought the situation to a head. That's the point. So even if I did want something to happen, he didn't do it for me. You said it yourself. He did it for Pin and you."

"I don't know if he did it for me, but he certainly did it for Pin. And I respect that."

"Fine, I'll talk to you tomorrow."

"You're not coming in?"

"No."

"You still mad?"

"Yeah! Why wouldn't I be? If someone had gotten killed in there, ain't no tellin' what the repercussions would be."

"You're overreacting."

"Maybe I am. But you're not reacting enough."

"Why don't you come on in, have a glass of wine, and relax. I'll give you a full body massage, and we can get in the Jacuzzi for a while. How does that sound?"

"Not tonight."

"Well, fine. Be that way."

Terry got out of the Jeep. Will retracted the window and said, "Do you have your keys?"

Without turning around, she pulled them out of her purse and dangled them.

"Goodnight!" he shouted and pulled off.

†††

Terry walked into the dark house and switched on the lights. She decided to take a long hot bubble bath. She went into the kitchen and poured herself a glass of white wine and then went into the bathroom. She took a sip and sat the glass on the edge of the tub. She turned on both the hot and cold water and adjusted the temperature until it was just right. Then she sprinkled some bubble bath in the sunken tub. As the tub filled, she thought about her argument with Will. *Maybe I should have moved. Maybe they should have kept their mouths shut.* "Live and let live."

She thought she was being silly because she missed Will and wanted to be with him, in his arms; to have him hold her and feel the warmth of his body against her skin. She thought about their one night in Sonoma and how wonderful it was. If only they could be there, together, right now.

The tub finally reached the level she was accustomed to. She disrobed and looked at herself in the three-way mirror. Then she remembered her pinching game with Will earlier. She positioned herself to see her back-side, and saw between twelve and fifteen pinch marks. She shook her head and eased into the tub. When the hot water touched the marks, it caused her a fair amount of pain. She thought about Will and said, "I hope yours hurts, too." She eased her body all the way in the tub and the bubbles came up to her neck. She took a sip of wine, closed her eyes, and moments later, fell asleep.

In a dream she was having, she told her parents about her relationship with Will. An argument ensued and someone called her parents' house. The ringing in the dream jerked her out of sleep and she opened her eyes. She thought the phone in her house was really ringing. Hoping it was Will, she stood up, grabbed a towel, and wrapped it around herself. Her wet feet splashed hastily across the ceramic floor. She opened the bathroom door and realized the phone wasn't ringing at all. It was only a dream. Disappointed, she dried herself off and got in bed in the raw.

†††

Terry slept for about half an hour when, suddenly, she felt someone put their hand over her mouth. She struggled and tried to scream. But the hand muffled the sound. Wanting to see, but afraid to open her eyes, she squeezed them tighter than before. She grabbed and pulled at the hand, but it was much too powerful. She felt the body of the hand sit down on the bed next to her. Then she heard the click of the lamp and saw the familiar brightness everyone knows intimately. Her mind raced. She wondered if she was about to be raped and murdered right there in her own house—in her own bed. She grew angry with Will for not coming in. If he was there, this wouldn't be happening to her, she told herself.

After struggling for a while, it occurred to her that the body sitting next to her and the hand wasn't being aggressive. It was only covering her mouth. She realized it was only Will playing a game and stopped struggling. Instead of opening her eyes, she decided to play along. This was obviously one of his sexual fantasies. She read somewhere that a lot of men like to pretend to be burglars and take advantage of their wives, or girlfriends. She felt the hand being pulled away. She remembered she was nude, and smiled. She opened her legs as wide as she could get them and with her eyes still closed, she threw back the cover, exposing her nakedness. "Take me, big boy."

She felt the covers being pulled back on her. She became uncomfortable, but not afraid. She wondered what Will was doing. Keeping one eye closed tightly, she opened the other and looked to see. Jericho was looking down at her. She gasped and grabbed the cover, pulling it tightly up to her neck. She looked around the room and saw Pin standing right beside Jericho. She had what looked like a Japanese sword strapped on her back. Victor was at the foot of the bed showing his pearly whites. And Cochise was standing on the right side of the bed looking down at her.

"That's some kinda body you got there, Ms. Lady." Victor smiled.

"WHAT THE HELL ARE YOU DOING IN MY HOUSE?"

"See, Desdemona." Jericho stared at her. "You never know when you're going to be attacked."

"What are you doing here?" Terry asked again, but more calm.

"I'm here to finish that little conversation we started. Get dressed," Jericho said in a commanding tone. Then he turned to Pin and said, "Stay with her. Bring her into the living room when she's decent."

The men left the women alone and went into the living room. The two women stared at each other for a few seconds. Terry knew she would be all right, but she also knew this was a serious situation. She was still uncomfortable with what was going on and wanted to call Will and have him come over, just in case things got out of control.

"May I call Will?"

Pin shook her head.

"What's this all about?"

Pin picked up Terry's black robe and handed it to her. Then she tilted her head in the direction of the living room. They had already seen her naked and she didn't want to feel uncovered. She took the robe, and put it on. Then she went to her drawer and pulled out a pair of jeans and a sweatshirt that read: Stanford Athletic Department. After sliding into her jeans and putting on the sweatshirt, the two women walked into the living room and saw Victor and Cochise watching ESPN's *Sportscenter.* Jericho was standing near the front door reading a poem on the wall.

Retribution
I would have done that which is unseemly
I was loyal to you and you betrayed me
I told you things,
intimate things,
things so personal…
I trusted you
And you humiliated me in front of all of them
you treated me like dung.

I would have done that which is unseemly
ruined my reputation!
ruined my marriage!
abandoned my faith!
For what!? For who!?
To embrace Lucifer?
That essential part, known only to a few,
that which he hasn't seen in a year,
I laid at your feet!
I would have embraced the onyx stone
And rendered it smooth
leaving you as motionless us a warm cadaver

I would have done that which is unseemly!
But you have poisoned the dream
Your treachery has turned it into a nightmare
blood turned cold
No refuge, no peace
A maniacal guest in the east wing of St. Joseph's now
Model patient: FREEDOM!

For this, you shall pay with your life
Not by death
Humiliation is yours,
Until the debt is paid.

Jericho heard the women come into the room. Still looking at the poem, he said, "This yours?"

"Yes. Do you understand it?"

"Do people normally have trouble understanding your work?"

Terry wondered if avoiding questions ran in the family. If it did, she knew she would have a hard time getting an answer out of him. She assumed he would be difficult to pin down, so she decided to play the same game. If he answered her questions, she would answer his.

"How did you get past the alarm system?"

"Don't worry about it? Do people normally have trouble understanding your work?" he repeated, still looking at the poem.

"Did you have to beat the bouncer like that?"

Jericho turned around and looked at her. Their eyes met. He was about to repeat the question a third time when it occurred to him that she'd heard him the first time. "What kind of game you playin', woman?"

"Same one you playin', man," she said, flippantly.

Pin started walking toward her.

Terry no longer saw the innocent, childlike demure quality that was characteristic of her. She could tell Pin was approaching her to do some harm. The look in Pin's eyes frightened her. Her heart was pounding. She tried not to show her fear, but fear was about to consume her. In those brief seconds that passed, Terry remembered what Will said on the way home from the club about taking things seriously. She knew this was one of those times.

"Relax, Pin," Jericho said. Pin bowed to her husband, and backed off. "Now, what kind of game are you playin'?"

Feeling her heart rate decrease, she could breathe normally again. She looked at Jericho and said, "I just don't think it's fair for you to ask me questions only. I think I should be allowed to ask you as many questions as you ask me. This is my home, and y'all broke in here, which means you're uninvited guests. You scare me half to death in my own bed and to top that off, you ask questions of me, yet you won't answer mine. So unless we come to some sort of agreement, it's going to be a long night."

"I guess she told you, Jay." Cochise laughed.

"Sho' did," Victor joined in. The two men slapped high-fives.

"Ya got spunk, Desdemona," Jericho told Terry. "I'll give you that, but don't push your luck." He paused for a few seconds to let what he said sink in. Terry nodded her head. "Now, how you wanna do this?"

Terry remembered what Will said when he was in a similar situation in Toronto. She decided to use the same technique. "Let's have a quid pro quo-type deal."

Jericho laughed. "Quid pro quo, huh? Okay. Deal."

"Good. Let's go into the den. I think we'll be more comfortable in there."

"Lead the way."

Terry turned around and walked in the direction of the den. Then she stopped and turned around. "Can I get anyone coffee or something to drink?"

Victor shook his head no.

"Naw, we fine," Cochise said.

As they left the living room, they could hear that ESPN's *Superbouts* was about to come on. "Hold on, let me see who they're showin'," Jericho said. He turned around and listened to Al Bernstein talk about the "Thrilla in Manila" as Muhammad Ali had coined it.

Terry could tell he wanted to watch it and said, "You want me to tape it for you?"

"Naw, I've seen it about fifty times already. I have it on tape."

"Really? And you still get excited about it?"

"I wouldn't say I get excited, but I do enjoy watching those two gladiators battle each other."

"Okay."

They continued down the hall and entered the den. Terry sat behind her desk in a leather swivel chair. Pin and Jericho sat on the couch.

"Now, where were we?" Terry asked.

Jericho could tell she was used to being in charge by her demeanor. That piece of information gave him a little insight as to who she was. He'd had her background checked out, but as far as he was concerned, there wasn't anything like doing a face to face. That way he could see how a person reacted to questions. He could see when a person was attempting to hide something and when they were lying.

In Vietnamese, Pin said, "She likes to be in charge."

"I know," Jericho said in English.

Terry frowned, wondering what Pin said.

"You like being in charge, don't you?" Jericho said. "That's what she said, just in case you were wondering."

"Yes, I do. And yes, I was wondering."

"I bet you try to control Will, too, don't you?"

"I try, but he won't let me. It's part of the allure, you might say."

"That's good. A woman loses respect for a man when she can control him. She tends to walk all over him. But anyway, what inspired the poem?"

"Did you understand it?"

"Yeah, but listen, I don't have a lot of time. I came here for two reasons only. One, to finish what we started at the club. And two, to talk to you about my baby brother, understand?"

"Fine, but before you go, I want you to tell me what you think the poem means, deal?"

"You mean stanza by stanza or what?"

"Any way you want, but explain the story itself; not one or two lines."

"Okay. Now, why did you choose Desdemona over the other names?"

"I read the play and the books, just like you did. And of the three, she was the only one who meant no harm to the man she loved."

"You chose your words carefully. I'm here to hear that Stanford acumen."

"What do you mean?"

"I mean, you said the man she loved as though it doesn't make a difference that the man she loved was a black general."

"True, but I don't know if it makes a difference that he was black, just as it apparently didn't make a difference to her. The point is Mary Dalton was a liberal-minded white woman who was ignorant to what position she was putting Bigger in the night of her death. Scarlet O'Hara was a scheming white woman who'd do anything to get a rich man. Desdemona was the only true woman of the three I completely identified with."

"You're very good. You tend to use race when it suits you and when it doesn't suit your purpose, you leave it out."

"What do you mean?"

"You know what I mean. When you talk about Mary Dalton and Scarlet O'Hara, you make sure you mention skin color. When you talk about Desdemona, you leave color out. Just like you left color out when you indirectly spoke of Othello."

Terry laughed. "You caught that, huh?"

"Yeah. I don't miss much."

"Why did you do that to the bouncer? You didn't have to do it. I heard Victor ask you if you wanted him to stop him. And you said no. So why did you do it?"

"Because he needed it. You saw him flexin' his muscles in the lobby. He had the nerve to be questionin' me on why I'm laughin'. Like I said, he was used to intimidating people. He needed to see he couldn't push people around just because he was bigger than everybody else."

"So it had nothing to do with him being white?"

"No, not at all."

"So you're not racist then?"

"No, I'm not. But I admit, I don't like how black people have been treated in this country by the white man."

Skeptical, she said, "So your problem with me has nothing to do with me being white?"

"Yeah, it does, but not as much as you think. If you think it's just because you're white, you're wrong. Did you know Francis?"

"Yes, I did."

"Frankly, I don't know a lot of good women. They don't make 'em like they used to. I've known about four in my life. My mother, my wife, Francis, and Vanessa."

"Vanessa?"

"Sterling's old girlfriend from some years back. I just don't trust 'em. They're always up to no good."

"The same argument could be made about men."

"True, but Will's not in love with a man. Therefore, that argument is moot. My baby brother means the world to me. He reminds me of what I could have been if I had stayed in school. One of the proudest moments in my life was when he walked across that stage and got his doctorate. It was like I was getting mine, too, ya know? I'm proud of him and his accomplishments.

"I want him to be happy. And I'll be damned if I'm going to let anybody, I mean anybody, take advantage of his kindness. Will ain't like me. If he brought you to meet my mother, it's pretty serious. So basically, I came here to tell you that if you can't be true to him, and do right by him, you need to leave him now. 'Cause if you're in it for his money, I will make your life a living hell and then bring it to an abrupt end."

Terry stared at him. From the look in his eyes, she could tell that the threat was real. Besides, she had witnessed, to a certain extent, the level of brutality he was willing to inflict on an adversary. She admired how he felt about his brother. The gravity of the situation notwithstanding, she felt no fear because she loved Will.

Terry said, "You don't have to worry about that."

"Good. Now, I've said my peace. If there's nothing else, I'll leave your home."

"May I ask you a personal question?"

Jericho could sense her question before she even asked because people, after talking to him, invariably asked the same question. He nodded.

"You're an intelligent man, Jericho. I'm sure you could do something else if you wanted. Why do you sell drugs?"

"Same reason yo' daddy sells them. Profit."

Terry frowned. "What do you mean? My father doesn't sell drugs."

"Sure, he does. Isn't he the Chief Executive Officer of Seagreens Liquor and Coolers?

"Yes, but that's different."

"How's it different? Oh, I get it. One's legal and the other isn't, right?" Terry didn't say anything. "Both are drugs. And given the fact that liquor used to be illegal, and the fact that the long-term effects of either can kill you, what's the difference?"

Terry sat in her chair watching his every move, every facial expression; the personal analysis was well on its way.

"I know what you're thinkin'," Jericho continued. "What about all the black people on drugs, right?"

Terry gave no indication of her thoughts. She only listened.

"Well, I say what about all the white people on drugs now? You have no idea what's happenin' across this country, do you? See, doctor, the drug problem is way beyond the black community now. I saw the trend back in the late sixties when I was at Berkeley. White people were gettin' into LSD and other hallucinogens way back then. I saw the opportunity and I took it. And now my investment has paid considerable dividends."

"So it doesn't bother you that drugs are devastating families?"

"Does it bother you that liquor is devastating families? Hell naw, it don't. While yo' ass was livin' in the lap of luxury in New Haven, ya daddy was peddlin' drugs under the guise of legitimacy, and the aegis of the United States Government in the form of taxes; all of which spawned economic growth. In fact, that very growth has created an ever-growin' and vital community of psychologists and social workers whose livelihood depends on the so-called source of what ails society itself. Now we have to have family counseling for alcoholics. What about what it does to the gene pool? It's no different than drugs. No different at all.

"People are just more willing to accept the legality of it. What's really interesting is how you have doctors out there peddling prescription drugs and gettin' kickbacks under the table from pharmaceutical companies who make billions of dollars a year. You never even hear about that shit. How do you think so many celebrities and athletes get hooked on painkillers and shit? And I won't even bother going into steroid usage. That's big business, too. But they point at me, because it makes white America comfortable.

"The irony of all of this is my business has opened a door for Will's latest business venture. If it wasn't for people like ya daddy and me, and the doctors that prescribe drugs for their so-called patients, Betty Ford wouldn't be in business. So when you talk about why I sell drugs, understand that it was drugs that paid for your Stanford education. Hell, my biggest competitors are people like ya daddy who have the means to get into the homes of the very families you talk about and advertise their drugs to children."

"Oh, come on now. They hardly advertise to children."

"Really, doctor? Then you're more naive than I imagined. You don't think that part of the business is to get a new generation of drinkers? You think they don't do research? If you believe that, you need to spend some much needed time on your own couch. Not only are they guilty of advertising to children, they have access to college campuses around the country. These guys sponsor frat parties and shit, providin' free barrels of beer to their unwitting scholastic achievers, many of which are doctors, lawyers, and engineers of every kind. Not to mention pilots. Or do you think drinkin' problems are reserved for the poor and indigent?"

"Of course not. There's no need to insult my intelligence, Jericho."

"Is that what I'm doing? Insulting your intelligence? I thought I was making an intellectual argument against the sale of legitimate drugs."

"That's just it. Although I contend that your premise is seriously flawed, and that's putting it mildly, it's clear you have good morals and strong reasoning skills."

"Yeah, well, too bad I didn't use them the day I knocked out the professor."

"May I ask you one more question?"

"What?"

"You promise not to get mad at me and knock me out?"

Jericho laughed. "Promise."

"Do you really think it's your father's fault for what you've done with your life?"

"Yes and no. Sure, I made the decisions, but we can't discount what influenced my decisions. Do you know why I was named Jericho Michael Wise?"

Terry shook her head.

"Are you familiar with the Bible?"

"A little."

"You are familiar with Joshua and Jericho, I trust?"

She nodded.

"Well, I was named after that city—that battle. I was also named after Michael, the Archangel—the warrior of God."

Terry looked confused.

"Don't you get it? I'm a born warrior. Born to kick ass and take names. I've got fightin' in my veins. Do you know what I studied at Berkeley? Philosophy. That's what I studied. I really liked reading it. Then I got into the philosophy of battle. I had a natural affinity for it. I read about Hannibal, Alexander, the Moors, et cetera. That's how I got through Vietnam virtually unscathed. The point I'm makin' is fightin' is a part of who I am. Hell, my father even nurtured my natural inclinations for the sport until he lost his nerve."

"You seem like a strong-willed person. Why didn't you rebel and do what you wanted to do? Why didn't you box anyway and deal with the consequences?"

"Out of respect to my father; I didn't go against his wishes at first."

"At first?"

"Yeah. I kept hoping he'd change his mind, but he never did. Then I started sneakin' to the gym. I'd spar with the best in there. I'd beat them so badly that their trainers would stop it and wouldn't let me spar with 'em anymore. Eventually, one of them saw I was a natural and he was going to sign me up. He told me he thought I could go all the way, ya know?" His mind seemed to wander back to that time as he talked.

"Well, what happened?"

"I had a chance to make some serious money at the rail yards. It was going to be my last street fight. Hell, I was even considerin' leaving the Chiefs if it worked out for me. Anyway, there was some out-of-town talent coming in to take on all challengers. I saved up about two hundred dollars worth of my winnings. I was going to use it to get my boxing equipment. But I figured I would need more than that. So I bet on myself to win. I would have won about five grand if I made it to the last man.

But the cops came and broke that shit up and threw my ass in jail. Judge told me to either go to college or go to Vietnam. And the rest is history."

Terry smiled. "Hmm, I see."

"You see what? You ain't gon' tell me none of that psycho babble bullshit about me hatin' my father, are you?"

Terry laughed. "No."

"Okay then. We're through, if you have no more questions."

"No. No more questions."

They left the den and went into the living room. Victor and Cochise were still watching ESPN when they walked into the room. "Let's roll, y'all," Jericho said. "My business is complete here."

They were walking toward the door when it occurred to Terry that Jericho hadn't given his interpretation of the poem. "One last thing," Terry said.

But before she could ask the question, Jericho began, "It's about a tripped-out white woman, probably a close friend, or relative of yours, maybe even a patient, who fell in love with a brotha who didn't want to have anything to do with her. When she realized there wasn't gonna be no romance, homegirl went the hell off. She went off because she wasn't fuckin' her husband like she shoulda been doin' in hopes of being with said brotha. Somehow or another, the brotha made it clear he wasn't interested, and she flipped. Ended up in a psycho ward for a while and got out seeking retribution."

"That's very good. Most people don't even come close to interpreting the poem. You should like this. It's about the reincarnation of Desdemona. I wrote it while I was in college."

"Hmm. Interesting. Listen, I like you, Terry."

She smiled. "Thanks."

"But know this, you fuck over my brother, and yo' life is over. That, I promise you. And understand this, it will not be quick. You write about retribution; I carry the shit out. We understand each other?"

Terry nodded. This time she took what he said seriously.

"All right, y'all. Let's roll."

Chapter 47: Lock and Load!

Thanksgiving Friday
Not long after leaving Terry's place

As the dawn of a new day approached, Jericho stared out the window of an all-night diner. At a nearby booth, Victor and Cochise ate their breakfast, and chatted. Throughout the diner, the sound of forks coming into contact with plates could be heard. There was a young couple in a booth on the other side of the diner staring mindlessly into each other's eyes, listening to Foreigner's "I Want to Know What Love Is."

Jericho sipped his coffee and watched them for a moment, then looked out the window again. As he watched the sun rise, he contemplated the discussion he had with Terry. She asked some tough questions.

He wondered what would have happened if he had listened to his mother, and not gone to the rail yards that day so many years ago. He knew he could have boxed professionally, but he wondered if he could have been the doctor or lawyer his father hoped he'd be. He toyed with the idea of him and Sterling putting a practice together and wondered what that would have been like. Then he laughed within himself when he thought about Sterling and all of his women. For some reason, Vanessa came to mind. He wondered if Sterling would ever get her back.

He remembered walking into his parents' house on Thanksgiving and hearing his mother praying that God would protect him until he came to know Christ as his personal savior. She'd always talked to him about Jesus whenever they spoke. In fact, when he called her to apologize for his behavior, it wasn't thirty seconds before she brought Jesus into the conversation. She talked so much about God that he knew what she was going to say before she said it. He would take the phone away from his ear so he wouldn't have to hear it. Then she'd talk to him about settling down. And as usual, she got around to talking about having grandchildren. But children just didn't fit in the kind of life he led. Now, he was almost fifty and children were almost out of the question. Nevertheless, he wondered what kind of father he'd be.

I wonder if Pin still wants to have children. She asked me about it several times. She's not too old. Maybe we can do it. Maybe we can walk away from this life. We've got the hotel and plenty of cash. Why not? Why not walk away from it all and live a normal life at the hotel? Why not raise children? Mama would be so happy.

He was smiling, but didn't know it.

Pin smiled, too. "What you think about that give you pleasure without me?"

Her words awakened him from the hypnotic daze. He looked at her. "How you feel about gettin' outta this life?"

In Vietnamese, she told him, "I'm ready if you are. I would die for you. You know that, right?"

"Yeah, I know," he said, in her native tongue. Then he took her hand in his. "And I love you for it. But I want you to know that I don't want to live without you either. I'm less than a man without you. You make me feel like I can accomplish anything." He paused for a moment. "Look at that young couple over there."

Pin turned around. She smiled. "Just say the word, and we're out for good."

"You still want to have my children?"

"You know I do."

"Let's do it then. Let's leave all of this behind and start again."

They stared at each other for a moment. Then a squad car pulled into an opening next to the limo. One of the officers got out of the car and walked into the diner. He didn't seem to notice them. The officer chatted with the owner like they were old friends.

Victor looked at Jericho and said in a hushed tone, "What do you wanna do?"

"They don't know nothin'. He came to get his doughnuts. Just relax."

Pin watched the other officer who was still in the squad car. She could see him talking on the radio. He got out of the car, walked around it, and looked at the limo's license plate. When he saw the other officer come out of the diner, he got back into the car. Then they pulled off.

"What do you think?" Victor asked.

"I don't think they know anything," Jericho told him. He looked at his watch. It was approaching six o'clock. "But just to be safe, when we leave here, we better go straight to the airport, and get outta dodge."

Jericho and Pin talked about their future together for another hour, or so. They told Victor and Cochise of their plans to leave the business. Victor resisted the idea at first, but eventually succumbed to Jericho's will, having learned over the years that it was pointless, and a huge waste of time to try and change his mind once it was made up. Rather than break the gang up, they all decided to leave together. Their crew was like a finely tuned body. Jericho was the brain of the operation, Pin was the heart, and Victor was the muscle. If Jericho thought it was time to quit, it was time to quit.

It was almost nine o'clock when they left the restaurant. Cochise looked at the fuel gauge and saw they had less than a quarter of a tank left. He picked up the phone and said, "Jerry, we need some gas. I'm gonna pull into this gas station at the corner, okay?"

"Yeah, go 'head. I need to call Chadwick before we leave anyway."

Cochise pulled up next to the full-service pump. A shapely young female came out of the store section of the service station, wearing a tight pair of blue jeans and a yellow University of California T-shirt. She came to the window.

"We're offering a free car wash for every fill-up. Would you like to fill your tank today, sir?"

"Why not?"

He watched her ass sway from side to side as she walked back to the pump. Occasionally, she looked at the dark glass, wondering who could be in there, hoping it was probably a big movie star, or somebody really important. She put the nozzle in the gas tank opening and locked the handle so it would continue pumping without her assistance, and went back to the front where Cochise was. As she approached him, she saw him looking at her in the driver's side mirror.

She put her breasts in his face. "So, who's back there?"

"Nobody you know."

"It's a big star, isn't it?"

Cochise decided to have a little fun with her. "You might say that."

"Really? Who is it? I'm from Omaha. I'm dying to meet a celebrity."

"You wouldn't know him if I told you his name."

The pump clicked off. She pulled the nozzle from the tank, and returned it to the pump. Cochise paid her, and she handed him the coupon for a free car wash.

As his window ascended, the young woman said, "You're not going to tell me who it is, are you?"

Cochise retracted the window and motioned for her to come closer. She bent down again. "You promise not to tell anyone?" She nodded. "It's the President."

Her mouth fell open. Then she realized he was only kidding.

"Hey, I told you it wasn't anybody you know. But you wouldn't be satisfied with that because you're starstruck. Now where's the car wash?"

"It's right down the street, at the corner," she said, grudgingly. Then she walked back into the service station. A minute later, he pulled into the car wash. The phone rang.

"What the hell are you going in here for?" Jericho shouted.

"Hey, it's free. You know I can't pass up free shit."

"I guess another five or ten minutes won't make much difference. But when we leave here, go straight to the airport."

"Cool."

Cochise pulled into the tunnel-like car wash. It was the kind that cleaned inside and out. They got out of the car and walked toward the front of the carwash to give the cashier the coupon when Jericho spotted two men who worked there arguing over a bet on the Raider-49er game. Apparently, one guy welshed on the bet. And the other was making an attempt to collect.

Jericho smiled. "Let's watch this."

"Where my goddamn money at?" one guy said to the other.

"I don't owe you no money!"

As soon as he finished the sentence, the second guy caught a right in the face. The employees stopped working and watched while the two men fought their way out the side door. Jericho followed them outside. But when he walked out the side door, he saw what looked at first glance like ten or eleven shotgun-toting police officers converging on the car-wash. Jericho quickly drew his weapon. He grabbed the man who threw the first punch, and put the gun to his head. He could tell the other man was thinking of running. He pointed the gun at him. "INSIDE, NOW!"

When the police saw Jericho take the hostages, they pointed their weapons at him. One of the officers called the station and informed them of the situation. More cops were on the way.

Victor and Cochise pulled their guns out and controlled a couple who had just pulled in and the employees who were stationed at the entrance of the car wash.

"Cochise," Victor said. "Run up there and get the cashier and the rest of the employees before they run outta here."

He ran through the narrow hallway and out the glass door where the men dried the cars. A car pulled out onto the street. The occupants had no idea how lucky they were.

"CLOSE THE DOORS!" Cochise shouted. Hurriedly, they obeyed. "NOW...UP AGAINST THE WALL AND SIT YA ASSES DOWN!"

The man who was thinking of running was still weighing his options. Jericho cocked his gun and motioned for him to go inside. The man reluctantly did as instructed. Jericho backed inside the car wash with the hostage, and closed the door.

†††

Terry was lying in bed thinking about Will. She hadn't slept well because of all the excitement of the previous night. She wondered if he was still mad at her. *He should have called by now.* She picked up the phone to call him and then decided against it. *If he's still mad, he might hang up the phone.* She decided to go over to his place. And if he was still mad at her, he'd just have to be mad. *At least we'll be together.*

Terry hit the automatic garage-door opener and drove inside a half-hour later. She saw both cars were parked, so she knew he was there. She turned off the alarm system and went inside. The house was quiet. She went into the kitchen and opened the refrigerator and decided to make him a nice breakfast and serve it to him in bed. *He needs some pampering. Let me see what he wants for breakfast.*

She walked down the hallway to the rear of the house, where the master suite was and listened at the door for the sound of the television. *Maybe he's up and watching ESPN, or something.* Hearing nothing, she slowly turned the doorknob. If he was asleep, she didn't want to wake him. She stuck her head in and looked at him. It was a little chilly in the room, but he was still asleep, buried under the burgundy and gray comforter. Quietly, she walked over to him to see if he was asleep or just lying there. If he was still asleep, she would get in bed with him. If not, she would make him breakfast.

She looked down at him. He looked so peaceful. She went around to the other side of the bed, kicked off her shoes, took off her Stanford sweater, and she slid out of her jeans. She was wearing a red bra and matching panties. She eased in and immediately felt Will's body heat. She slid over to him and looked at the back of his head. Then she put her arm around him.

"A person can get killed sneakin' into peoples' houses."

Surprised he was awake, she said, "Did I wake you?"

"No. I was just lyin' here thinkin'."

"Before you say anything more, I'm sorry I didn't move last night. I know I should have, but I didn't. And you're right, if I had moved, none of that stuff would've happened. Do you forgive me?"

"Yes. I'm sorry I put all the blame on you. Jerry should have handled the situation better. And those people were wrong, too."

She hugged him. "You want some breakfast, Will?"

"You cookin'?"

"Umm-hmm."

She slid her hand between his legs and felt his hardness. She nibbled on his ear and said, "Let's do it first."

✝✝✝

"How many?" Victor asked.

"I'd say about ten," Jericho told him. "But you know more on the way."

"What you wanna do?"

"We call Smitty. That's what we do. We're ready for this contingency. They're the ones unprepared. They have no idea who we are or what we're capable of. All they know is that we have handguns. They probably got an all-points bulletin from the club last night, or some shit like that."

"HEY!" Cochise yelled. "What are we going to do?"

"Pin," Jericho commanded. "Relieve Cochise and have him come down here so I can brief him."

Pin ran through the same hallway and seconds later Cochise came down to the entrance. There was a nervous sweat building up on his forehead. Jericho could tell he was scared. He had never been in battle before.

"Look, man," Jericho began. "I know looking at all them cops is scary right now. But you gotta stay focused. We gon' get outta this shit, okay? They're outgunned. Most cops never even fire a shot. They're more scared than you, believe me. This is why we bring all this shit. Just for times like this."

"Yeah," Victor agreed. "Too bad Charlie never understood that shit. His ass would be alive today if he did."

"What's the plan, Jerry?" Cochise asked nervously.

"We call Smitty, and have him do according to plan," Jericho reminded

413

him. "But we gotta move quickly. We've got a hostage situation now. And that means reinforcements will be here soon. We gotta move before SWAT gets here because if they have a chance to set up, we're through. Ain't none of us leavin' alive once they get into position. We're going to attack them before they know what hit 'em.

"I'll have Smitty come up behind them with about fifteen or twenty street soldiers, and lay down some suppression fire. When they take cover, we'll launch a few concussion grenades, and roll the fuck outta here. Then a few blocks from here, I'll have Smitty set up another ten men or so to cover our escape route. It'll be over quicker than the Gulf War."

"Got it." Cochise's confidence returned. He believed Jericho would get them out in one piece.

"I'll call Smitty while y'all prepare for battle."

While Victor and Cochise put on bulletproof vests and checked the weapons, Jericho called Smitty. "Smitty, this is Jericho, we have a Tango Echo. I repeat we have a tactical emergency situation. I'm at the corner of Howard Street and Fourth. I'm surrounded by the police. I need ten street soldiers here in less than fifteen minutes. Ya got that?"

"Yeah I got it, but you can save ya breath," Smitty said calmly. "You on yo' own. Ain't nobody here to help you."

"WHAT? Didn't I tell you when I got here to put the usual fifty street soldiers on alert?"

"Yeah, but you never need them. So they're all makin' deliveries, or with their women. I don't know where all of 'em are. It would take at least an hour to get that many together."

Pin brought the other hostages down just in time to hear the gist of what was happening.

"You mean they ain't comin'?" Cochise said with renewed fear. "Oh, shit. We gon' die."

Pin sat the hostages down and then put on her vest and strapped her sword to her back. She glared at Cochise. She had the same look in her eyes as the night she beat Charlie mercilessly. Cochise got the point immediately and closed his mouth. They could hear the sirens.

"You stupid muthafucka!" Jericho shouted, and pushed the end button.

"What the hell happened?" Victor wondered.

"We're on our own," Jericho told them. "Smitty said ain't nobody there to cover our flank. The sonofabitch is lyin'. I could hear it in his voice."

"I kill him!" Pin shouted. "He not see another sunrise!"

"Here's the new plan," Jericho said. "We still launch the grenades. But we use the rocket launcher to clear a path. We hit the cars. The cops will scatter. We lay down our own suppression fire. Then we roll the fuck on outta here."

"What about them?" Cochise said, referring to the hostages.

"We don't need 'em. They stay here. NOW, LOCK AND LOAD!"

They got out the rocket launcher and some concussion grenades. They all had automatic weapons now, ready to begin the assault. Jericho looked outside. There were more cops now.

"Y'all ready?" Jericho asked.

"Ready," they said.

"Cochise, you stay here with the hostages until we clear a path," Victor said. "Fire at the cops occasionally to keep them from advancing on our position."

Cochise nodded.

They went up to the front and opened the garage door. Jericho and Pin fired at the cops behind their cars. Shell casings dropped on the cement as the shots rang out. They sounded like miniature bells when they hit the ground. The cops took cover behind their squad cars. Innocent by-standers ran in all directions. Victor launched a rocket at the cars and they exploded on impact. Then he launched another. Jericho and Pin were still firing at will. Victor launched the concussion grenades. Explosions could be heard ten blocks away. They could hear the high-pitched sound of more sirens. Jericho looked up and saw a police helicopter. They could hear Cochise discharging his weapon now.

"Advance, Pin!" Jericho shouted.

Pin changed clips, and moved forward, still discharging her weapon.

"Victor, relieve Cochise! Have him bring the car out! We're leaving! Put the rocket launcher in the back seat!"

Victor ran back to the entrance and told Cochise to get the car. He took his weapon and began firing. As he fired, he could hear the female hostages screaming. Pin and Jericho were still shooting at the other end of the building.

"They're going to kill us all!" one of the hostages shouted.

Victor changed clips and continued the assault. Then he closed the door and ran down to the other end of the building. They got into the back of the limo and Cochise floored it. Victor stood up through the sunroof, and continued firing at the police. Most of the cars were riddled with bullets, but about four or five cars were completely untouched.

"They comin'?" Jericho asked.

"Yeah, they're right on our ass," Victor told him.

"I get out here," Pin told Jericho. "Make sure they no follow."

The limo stopped. Pin got out. They looked at each other as though they would never see each other again.

"I die for you," she said, with staunch resolve. "But before I die, I kill Smitty."

Jericho and Pin embraced.

"Jerry!" Victor shouted. "They're almost here! We gotta go, man!"

Pin strapped her sword on again and grabbed her bag of ammunition. She looked at Jericho one last time. Jericho looked at her as the limo sped away. He saw her take cover behind some cars.

"Victor," Jericho called out. "Is the helicopter still with us?"

Victor looked up. "Yeah, but now there's a news team up there also. They're probably filmin' all this shit."

"Take out the police helicopter."

Cochise stopped the limo. They could hear Pin firing at the police now. Tires screeched. The sound of bullets penetrating glass and metal could be heard. Then they heard more screeching, and loud collisions. Victor aimed the rocket launcher at the police helicopter. The pilot tried to turn around, but it was too late. Victor fired. Seconds later, the helicopter exploded and crashed. Victor then turned on the news team, but when he saw them turn and leave, he let them go.

†††

After spending the day together in bed, Will and Terry decided to invite Cleve and Cheryl over to play cards. They played for hours and Cleve, as usual, was telling post office stories. They were listening to music and watching college football games on the giant-screen television. The television volume was turned down. Cheryl was a big fan of Penn State. She used to have a crush on Tony Dorsett, and followed them ever since. Penn State was playing the Miami Hurricanes. The game was just about over and it looked as though the Hurricanes were going to win. It was almost 11 PM.

Cleve picked up the remote control and changed the channel to the news. "Let's see if they have any more news about that shootout this mornin'."

"Was there another shootout in Chinatown?" Terry asked.

"Y'all didn't see it?" Cleve couldn't believe his ears.

"Naw," Will said. "What happened?"

"I can't believe y'all didn't see it. It was on at twelve and six," Cleve told them. "Y'all was probably fuckin'."

Will and Terry looked at each other and smiled. Cheryl and Cleve laughed.

"Was it good to you, babe?" Will asked.

"Real good, darlin'. Did you enjoy it?"

"Sho' did. Had to be better than anything we missed on the news. What do you think, babe?"

"Two out of two doctors agree."

"Y'all a trip." Cleve laughed.

The eleven o'clock news came on and Amy Ling was standing in the back of a warehouse. The camera focused on an exploded fuse box. Amy was talking now, but they couldn't hear what she was saying. Will picked up the remote and muted the stereo. Then he hit the volume button on the television.

"The police found the bodies of thirteen members of the notorious Chiefs street gang. Apparently, the assailants blew up this fuse box to my left and went on a killing rampage. Some of the bodies were decapitated.

Antowain Smith, better known as 'Smitty,' was one of the members found at the macabre scene. His head has yet to be found. The police also found dismembered hands holding guns with their forefingers still squeezing the trigger. Inspector Franklin, of the San Francisco Police Department, said she's never seen anything like it. Right now, she's espousing one of two theories until forensics has a chance to go over the crime scene. Since the Japanese Mafia are known to use swords as a means of killing their enemies, she says it could be the act of a rival Japanese gang. She also says it could be the act of one perpetrator. She bases this theory on the positions of the bodies. She thinks some of the men shot each other in the confusion. If that was the case, it could have been the work of one man wearing night-vision goggles. Right now, they don't know anything for sure. This is Amy Ling reporting for WTSF News."

The news report sent a chill down Terry's spine. Instantly, she knew the assailant was Pin.

Chapter 48: Happy Birthday!

San Francisco
February 1998

S everal months passed since that strange and volatile Thanksgiving weekend. Christmas had come and gone, so had New Years' Day. The weather was unseasonably warm. Generally, around this time of year, San Francisco was a brisk fifty-nine degrees. But this year, it was a warm seventy-six degrees. Will woke up and looked at the clock, which was more of a habit than an innate desire to know what time it was. He knew what time it would be. But this day was a little different than any of the other days. It was his birthday.

He got out of bed and went into the bathroom to look at himself in the mirror for changes in his face, but he looked like he always did. Being thirty-seven didn't feel any different from thirty-six, or eighteen for that matter. Still, he looked at himself and thought about having Terry as his wife, wondering if she would change if he married her. He loved her the way she was and hoped she wouldn't change, but he'd seen it happen a dozen times. Most of the time during a counseling session, the husband would complain about his wife changing after they had gotten married.

Larry and Louise McVicker came to mind. They were the typical couple whose relationship fell apart. The couple had a great relationship before the marriage—that was the one thing they agreed on. He remembered counseling them separately. Louise complained that Larry was a pig who not only expected her to do all the chores in the house, but wouldn't even pick up behind himself, and was unwilling to change. He wouldn't even change the way he dressed. She tried to make him over, but he would always revert to wearing the same old blue overalls and yellow work boots.

Larry, on the other hand, complained that Louise had changed so much that he didn't even recognize her. Before they got married, Louise would willingly pick up behind him. She'd come to his apartment and clean it for him. He didn't understand why she changed. Why all of a sudden did she expect him to clean up when he never had before? And what was wrong with the way he dressed? "I was dressing this way when I met her," he said. "I'm a contractor. My company isn't big enough for me to quit working and wear suits and hold meetings." He thought the relationship would continue as it had prior to the marriage. To Larry, marrying Louise was a mere formality, nothing more. Louise wanted to change and grow together. She wanted to become one with him, but not if he was unwilling to change.

Will counseled numerous couples and discovered that problems in relationships stemmed from unrealistic expectations and incompatibility. Most of the couples hadn't really known each other well enough to get married. They saw the negative aspects of their partner's personality, yet chose to ignore it. But after the marriage, for some reason, they could no longer ignore the idiosyncrasies of their partners.

He wondered what surprises Terry had for him. The phone rang.

"Hello, Mama."

"Happy birthday, son. I guess you knew it was me, huh?"

"Well, when you do it every year around the same time, yeah."

"So what are you two doing on your birthday?"

"We goin' to see *The Phantom of the Opera* at the Curran."

"Y'all can go there anytime. They show it eight times a week, don't they?"

"Yeah, but this is a special engagement."

"Special? Special how? Ain't it the same play?"

Will laughed. "Mama, you kill me sometimes."

"I just think y'all oughta do somethin' special on your birthday."

"We are. The original Canadian cast is going to be there for a special AIDS Benefit. It cost five hundred dollars just to sit in the balcony."

"Five hundred dollars! Why would you pay five hundred dollars to see some ol' play that you've seen ten times? I don't understand how young folk can throw away good money like that. I remember when I was growin' up. We was lucky to have five hundred dollars in one year. And y'all gon' spend that in one night?"

"That's five hundred a ticket, Mama."

"WHAT! Y'all sho' is crazy. Y'all gon' spend a thousand dollars in one night?"

"That's just to get in. We're being driven to the theater in a limousine. Then there's the cost of Terry's dress. She's going to Alicia's to get her hair and nails done. She gotta have shoes and everything. You know how y'all women folk are. Ya can't wear the same dress twice."

"How much is all that going to cost?"

"I don't know for sure. Terry's payin'."

"Oh Lord. She's gon' expect Christmas in July when her birthday come."

"Done come and gone."

"What'd you give her?"

"Something special."

"You not gon' tell me?"

"No."

"Well, if she's doing all this for you, you musta went all out for her."

"Maybe I did, maybe I didn't."

"You love her that much, son?"

"Yep."

"Y'all gon' get married?"

"Maybe. I'm having lunch with her today at Fisherman's Wharf. I'll discuss it with her. Do you still think she's the right one?"

"Don't you sass me, boy."

"Okay, Mama." He chuckled. "I gotta go. I gotta work at both clinics today."

"Why you gotta do that?"

"Because I still have clients I'm counseling."

"You're going to wear yourself out doin' that."

"I don't do it every day. Just once or twice a week."

"Oh, okay. Well, don't work too hard on ya birthday now."

"Okay, I won't. Take it easy."

"You, too. Bye."

"Bye."

†††

The black stretch Lincoln limousine pulled into Will's driveway at 6:30. Terry called him from the phone in the limo.

"You ready, darlin'?"

"You supposed to be here by now."

"Keep your shorts on; I'm in the driveway waitin' on yo' late ass."

"I'm not late. It's 6:30."

"Well, what are you waiting for? Let's roll, as Jericho would say."

"I'm on my way," he said, and hung up the phone.

Seconds later, Will came out of the house wearing the black collarless Fumagalli tuxedo he owned, which was offset by a Harrison lavender vest. The driver opened the door for him. He took one look at Terry and his mouth fell open.

She was wearing a sleeveless formal gown that glittered like it was made of diamonds. Her hair was pulled back and tight. She wore a tiara that glittered as much as the dress. She looked at Will and smiled. His reaction made all the work she put into her appearance please her.

Before long, they were on the Golden Gate Bridge. The traffic was unusually light that night. They rode past the Presido and on through MacAuthur's Tunnel. Soon they were turning left on to Geary Boulevard.

"So when are we getting married?" Terry asked.

Will laughed. "You sho' like to sweat a brotha when you wanna know somethin'."

"I like sweatin' you. Now, is this somethin' you plan on doin', or what?"

"We'll see."

"I'm not trying to rush you, but what are you worried about?"

"I just want it to be the way it is now, ya know? I wanna be sure that what we have is not a figment of my imagination and that we don't end up in the twilight zone, wondering what happened, and why. Understand?"

She nodded.

"Like this morning. I was thinking about some of the couples I've counseled. They all thought it would work before they married. You know what I mean?"

"Yes, but we're different."

"That's what I believe, too, but doesn't every couple think they're different from every other failed couple?"

"You gotta point. I thought Roger and I were different, too. Now I'm with you, and only God knows who he's with tonight."

"So you understand, then?"

"Umm-hmm." She kissed him. "I absolutely love you."

"I love you, too."

When the limo stopped in front of the Curran Theatre, Terry couldn't resist the urge to rub Will's crotch. She felt him hardening again. As much as Will wanted to hear Colm Wilkinson, who was playing the Phantom, he couldn't wait until the opera was over. The driver opened the door and they got out.

They entered the theater and heard the orchestra warming up. The lobby was full of elegantly dressed women wearing lavish necklaces and luxurious stoles. This was a night for the rich and famous.

"Tickets," the usher said.

Their seats were first-row center in the balcony. But there were two small children sitting behind Terry. She thought it was strange that children were there, but she didn't dwell on it. Soon, the lights were turned off and the opera began with the auction scene. The little boy sitting behind Terry started swinging his leg and accidentally kicked the back of Terry's seat while the chandelier was being raised. Moments later, she felt the boy put his shoe on the back of her seat. Then he started pushing. She pushed back and the boy seemed to think it was a game.

Will was into the opera and totally oblivious to Terry and the boy's infantile power struggle over control of her seat. The more she tried to ignore him, the more he pushed her seat. She paid over a thousand dollars for those tickets and she wanted to enjoy the show. She also wanted to turn around and tell his mother what was going on, but she thought that if she continued to ignore him, he'd get bored with the game he was playing with her.

Twenty minutes into the opera and the boy was still kicking the back of Terry's seat and she was seriously pissed now. Then his mother decided she would sing along with the Phantom and Christine. Terry found this equally irritating. She turned around and stared at the woman. The woman looked at her and continued singing. Will looked at Terry and whispered, "What's wrong?"

"This rotten little kid keeps kicking the back of my seat."

She said it loud enough for the mother to hear. But she either didn't hear her, or she ignored her. Will saw how frustrated Terry was, but what could he do? Terry decided to tough it out until the intermission, and then she'd give the woman a piece of her mind. As each minute passed, the constant kicking fueled her indignation. She didn't want to ruin Will's birthday, but she was going to tell the woman how she felt. *This is ridiculous!* Then the woman started the singalong again. The mother's failed attempt at singing was more fuel for the flame. Exasperated, Terry took a deep breath and blew it out loudly. Mercifully, the intermission finally came.

"Excuse me, Miss," Terry began. "But could you refrain from singing during the opera! And could you control your brat! He's been kicking the back of my seat all night!" Terry thought she was saying it nice, but her face expressed the frustration and anger that had built up over the past hour. A few of the people near them turned around and looked at her.

"I'm sorry," the woman said. "I'll take care of it."

Terry looked at Will. She could tell he was a little embarrassed at the way she handled the situation. "I'm sorry, Will, but that's ridiculous. I don't blame the boy as much as I blame her. The boy is bored, but he should still have manners. When we have children, we won't bring them to places like this, unless they're well-behaved. And if they're not, we'll beat their little asses 'til they are."

Will laughed.

"I'm serious, Will. I can't stand badass kids."

Will laughed harder. Soon Terry was laughing, too. "You feel better now," he said.

"Now that I've said my piece, yes!"

Chapter 49:
Passion

The pace was quick and direct after they exited the limousine and made their way to the entrance of Terry's townhouse, caught up by emotion and desire. They stumbled through the door—their sexual urges dominating their minds, helpless to their ravenous craving. He started with a kiss on her wide inviting mouth. As her tongue found its way into his mouth, he sucked it, tasting her cinnamon breath as this kiss was far more passionate than the first.

Terry suddenly felt the familiar twitch in her private parts, and welcomed it. She began to swell and felt like a busted geyser down there. Her body responded involuntarily to his powerful embrace. Dazed by what her body was feeling, she would have done anything to please him at that moment. And when he turned her around so her back was against his chest, she hoped he would bend her over and enter her recklessly.

Out of the corner of her eye, Terry could see the red light on the answering machine flashing, but she was into the moment. The sensation of having her neck kissed, her ears nibbled, and her breasts squeezed through her clothes drove her wild. She sighed. "Oh, Will, you make me so hot." She tried to turn around to face him, but he firmly held her there so she turned her head instead and offered him her lips and tongue once more.

Sliding his right hand down her right thigh, he pulled up her dress. She wasn't wearing panties, which turned him on even more. The blood flow to his love joint increased and throbbed against her back. With her left hand, she reached around and gently massaged him through his pants while he massaged her swelled secret place. He felt her wetness against his fingers and stroked her there slowly in small circular motions. She felt the twitch again.

Her knees weakened as the passion, the sensation, and the anticipation of the forthcoming eruption drew her in. Her knees started to bend by themselves, but she stood firm. Again her knees bent due to the rhythm of his touch. But again, she stood firm. The back and forth motion continued, until she surrendered herself to the clitoral massage, the breast massage, and the neck kissing. As the pleasure heightened between her legs, she felt herself release all that the massage had built.

Weakened by the sudden and violent explosion, he practically dragged her to the bedroom. Unzipping her, the formal gown dropped to the floor. She turned around and faced him, feeling more desirable as he leered at her awesome body. The desire to have him inside was overwhelming. She began undressing him feverishly, almost ripping off his Fumagalli and pushed him on the bed.

Climbing on top of him, she kissed him hard on the lips, nibbling on his ears and licking his neck while her hands roamed all over his chest and abdomen. When she began to ache with the anticipation of him being inside her, she straddled him, sliding onto his hardness. She found a steady rhythm and kept it for a while, moaning uncontrollably as each stroke plunged ever deeper, sending wave after wave through her entire body.

He withdrew himself and laid her on her back, kissing her again and massaged both of her exquisite breasts. He took her left nipple into his mouth and made miniature circles with his tongue. Then he did the same to the right breast. He went back and forth to each nipple slowly at first, then rapidly, giving her the sensation of having both breasts sucked at the same time. Desire having reached its limit, he lifted her legs onto his shoulders and entered her with reckless abandon and she received him anxiously. He pumped her hard, entering her over and over again. The heat of their bodies in close proximity, and the physical exertion of their lovemaking caused Will to sweat. As he moved, he looked into her eyes, and she into his.

"You're sweating, darlin'," she told him—gasping.

"I know."

Then a single drop of sweat fell off his forehead and into her eye. The salt in the sweat stung her eye momentarily. She wiped his forehead with the palm of her hand and wrapped her arms around him, pulling him closer. He felt her breasts on his chest.

Terry was sweating, too. She felt the thickness of his back, grabbed his ass, and squeezed in rhythm with each thrust. She arched her back more, which allowed him to go even deeper than he already was. They moaned in each other's ears.

"It's so good," she said softly. "I'm going to cum."

"Right now?"

"Yes. Don't stop…Don't stop."

She gripped his back and held on tight, sighing in high-pitched tones and seemed to be gagging in between the sighs. The intensity of the orgasm caused her to babble incoherently for a moment. She bit into his shoulder, needing to taste him, but she didn't break the skin. Slowly, she released the firm grip of his back and relaxed a little.

Will was still pumping her with the same voracious vigor. He was on the verge of release also as the sensations he felt mounted, taking him ever closer to orgasmic bliss. Then suddenly he felt a surge and his body jerked in response, but he was still hard.

Ashleigh, Terry's sister, walked into the townhouse and tossed her bag on the floor. She saw the red light flashing and realized that Terry may not have gotten the message she left. She could hear movement coming from Terry's room, and decided to tell her sister she was in town. As Ashleigh approached the bedroom, she realized the sounds she heard were of a sexual nature and decided to go to bed and talk to Terry in the morning. But as she walked past the bedroom door, she was captivated by the howling bedsprings, and the loudness of her sister's sighs. "Don't make me cum again! Don't make me cum again! Oh God! Oh God!" she heard her sister scream.

Ashleigh laughed at first because she couldn't believe how loud her sister was when she made love. However, after several moments of intense listening, the sounds began to excite her a little. Realizing what was happening to her, she went into the bedroom adjacent to theirs, and got in bed, but could still hear their intense lovemaking. The sensual sighs and slamming of the headboard became unbearable. When she heard Terry screaming like a woman in a horror film, she got up and went into the den across the hall.

"That's ridiculous," Ashleigh said.

She started reading one of Terry's psychological journals and fell asleep. About an hour later, a car alarm awakened her. She hoped the sexual interlude was over and went back into the spare bedroom, crawled into bed, and listened for a moment. Hearing only quiet, she drifted off to sleep.

✝✝✝

Having quelled their sexual desire, Will talked to Terry while he rubbed his hands all over her back, buttocks, thighs, and calves giving her a soothing sensation all over. After talking softly to her for several minutes, Terry was breathing deeply and had fallen asleep. Pleased she was satisfied, he removed his hand and smiled to himself.

Terry opened her eyes and looked at him. "Was I asleep?" Will nodded. "Come here," she said, taking him into her arms. He laid his head on her bosom. "I love you."

Will woke up at 10:30 and looked at Terry, who was still asleep. He wished he could go back to sleep, but he seldom could. Instead, he decided to serve Terry breakfast in bed and thank her for the wonderful birthday present. He went into the kitchen in the nude and started preparing the food. While the bacon fried, he whistled and took the Aunt Jemima pancake mix from the cupboard. He heard Terry get up. Moments later, he heard the toilet flush and decided to tell her he would be serving her breakfast in bed in about fifteen minutes. He heard the bathroom door open and he wanted to catch Terry before she came out.

Hurriedly, he walked into the hallway; Ashleigh was about to go into the spare bedroom. She heard him and thought it was her sister. They saw each other at the same time. He gasped and tried to cover himself. He was amazed she didn't scream, but could tell she was shocked. Ashleigh's eyes dropped to his thick tool and then back up into his face. She smiled and said in a hushed tone, "Hi, you must be Terry's friend. I'm Ashleigh."

Embarrassed and still trying to cover himself, with a half-smile, he said, "I'm Will." Then he ducked into the master bedroom. He could hear Ashleigh laughing in the hallway.

"Terry! Terry!"

She awakened. "What time is it?"

"Hey, get up," he told her in hushed tones as he put on his shirt and slid into his trousers. "Ashleigh's here, the breakfast is about to burn and she saw me naked. That is not how I wanted to meet her."

"That's what you get for walking around naked."

Will looked at her sternly. He didn't think it was funny. "Look, get up and talk to her or something."

"Hey, it was your idea to keep this a secret, not mine. You could have met her a long time ago, if you wanted. But nooooo, let's keep this between you and me, you said."

Angry that she didn't take the situation seriously, he left the room without a word. Terry got out of bed and put on a black cotton velour robe and followed him. She knew he was embarrassed, but didn't think it was that big of a deal. "Will, you're making too big a deal of this," she said, entering the kitchen.

"Oh, so if we were at my place and you were naked when my mother walked in, I guess you'd just take it in stride."

"You're comparing apples to oranges. Of course if your mother came over, let herself in, and met me for the first time, and I was naked, yes, I would be upset. But it's just Ashleigh. She's nobody."

"Hi, all," Ashleigh said. "It's always good to know you're well thought of, sis." She laughed. "But she's right, Will, is it?"

"Yes, it is," he said, still a little embarrassed.

"Now if Dad were here, that would be a different story, right, Terr?" She laughed again.

"Ha, Ha," Terry mocked.

Will served them breakfast and asked if they wanted coffee. "No," Terry said. "I'll have some orange juice this morning."

"I'll have a cup," Ashleigh said. "So, wild night, huh, guys?"

They knew what she meant, but said nothing.

Terry said, "So what time did you get here, Ashleigh?"

"Let's just say I would have given my left tit for some earplugs." She said it with such a straight face that if you didn't know her, you'd think she was angry, but she liked to lighten things up with references to her anatomy.

"Don't mind her," Terry told Will.

"Speaking of tits," Ashleigh began again as though Terry hadn't said a word. "You remember old man Brody?"

"Yeah. What about him?"

"I had to pull his wisdom teeth, Friday. You know what babies men can be. He was scared of the needle so I gave him the gas. And do you know that old buzzard grabbed my tits and held on for dear life? It was easier to get his wisdom teeth out than it was to pry his hands off my tits. My assistant literally peed on herself, she was laughing so hard."

They all laughed and continued eating. It was quiet for a moment and then Will said, "Well, I'm sure you guys have a lot to talk about. I'm gonna take a shower and get outta here."

Ashleigh smiled. "Don't leave on my account."

"Well, I do have some things I need to take care of," he lied. He knew she didn't come all the way from New Haven to talk about her tits and old man Brody. He excused himself and went into the bathroom. He turned on the shower and then went back into the bedroom and took off his clothes. The door wasn't completely closed and he could hear them talking.

"What the hell was going on in there last night?" Ashleigh mused aloud.

Terry rolled her eyes. "What do you think was going on?"

"Was he going down on you or what?" As if she knew the answer, Ashleigh continued, "He had to be as loud as you were. Either that or you were fakin' it for his ego."

"Hey, he can probably hear you, you know?"

"How? He's in the shower. Can't you hear it?"

"Does that mean he's in it? For all you know, he could be at the door listening."

"Well, even if he is, I still want to know. Was he, or wasn't he?"

"No, he was not."

"So you were fakin' it then."

"No, I wasn't. I'm crazy about him. He's the most wonderful man I've ever met."

"I guess it doesn't hurt that he's your boss, huh?"

"What's that supposed to mean?"

"It means he has money."

"Are you saying that I only want his money?"

"Hey, the way you sounded last night, you must want something more than what he was giving you. Why else would you fake it unless you're trying to get something?"

"I really do love him, Ashleigh. And I didn't fake anything last night. It took us some time to get to the point of what you heard last night. The first time we did it, I was a little disappointed. I liked it with him, but I was disappointed. You know how you hear this and you hear that. If you're not careful, without even knowing it, what you've heard becomes a part of you. I was a victim of the stereotype. I expected him to be this great lover and he wasn't. He wasn't lousy or anything, just not great, okay? It was a sobering lesson, you know? But I really liked him. As we became closer, the sex got better and better. And what you heard last night was the result of a lotta practice."

Will smiled and got into the shower. He wondered if she ever faked with him, but never asked.

"Well," Ashleigh began again, "he's cute. Does he have any brothers?"

It was clear now why she had flown all the way from New Haven in the middle of the night. Terry wanted to ask a thousand questions at that moment, but the psychologist in her knew to be silent and listen. There was stillness in the kitchen—an emotional quiet that both sisters were familiar with. It was the same quiet that Terry experienced with Roger, her ex-husband. And now her baby sister would taste the bitterness of marital betrayal. Ashleigh now knew the shock and disappointment that millions, perhaps billions, of other women had known throughout the annals of time. It was gut-wrenching. And then the tears came.

Chapter 50: What Are You Going to Do Now?

Terry hugged her sister and listened, feeling the anguish of her emotional affliction as she wept. She wanted to kill Jeffery for what he had done to her. *Men could be so cruel sometimes.* As she held Ashleigh, during those precious moments, she thought about Will, and was glad he was a one-woman man. She knew he was human, but she believed he wouldn't do to her what Roger had done, no matter how tempting the offer. *But what if he did? What if he had an affair? Would I leave him because he did? How would I handle it if it happened again?*

Ashleigh said, "I'm sorry to come all this way to dump on you, but I needed to get away, you know?"

"I know."

"The trouble is, I still love him, Terr. God help me, I still love him." Then she cried again.

"What are you going to do now, Ashleigh?"

Between sobs, Ashleigh said, "I don't know. Do you think I should leave him?"

Ashleigh collected herself. This was the first time she cried since she found out Jeffery had been having an affair yesterday afternoon. She was only stunned when she saw him kissing his girlfriend as they entered The Colony Hotel in downtown New Haven.

"I can't tell you what to do, sis. That's a decision you're going to have to make on your own."

"You left Roger when it happened to you."

"That's different."

"Different how? They both fooled around. I think I should walk away."

"Well, that's up to you. Just remember you have two small children who need their father. Roger and I didn't have any children to consider. So that's what makes our situation unique. Besides that, we were having big problems anyway. We just weren't meant to be together. His philandering was my out."

"You love this Will guy, right? What if he did it? Would you leave him?"

"I sincerely doubt he would."

"Of course he would. What man do you know that could turn down a piece of ass; especially if he could get away with it? They're all dogs."

"No, not all of 'em."

"So he's different, huh?"

"Yes, he is."

"Okay, let's assume he did it and you found out about it, would you leave him?"

"I don't know, sis. It depends."

"On what?"

"On why he did it. What our relationship was like... If we had kids... A lot of things. It's not that simple."

"You must really love this Will guy, because I know you. And it wouldn't matter about all that stuff. The Terry I know wouldn't hesitate to leave any man who did that." She paused for a second. "I guess you weren't faking last night after all, huh?"

The two women laughed.

After a moment or two, Terry said, "Look, I have to be honest. The fact of the matter is, he's human, so it could happen. But so am I, okay? Sometimes shit like this happens. And although it hurts me that Jeffery hurt you, I realize people make mistakes. I just hope I'm never in that position again, is all. I hope he never does, because it would be hard to forget it. But I love him enough to try and work through it, if he wanted me to stay with him. But again, I don't believe he would do it."

They heard the door of the bedroom open. Will was coming down the hall. The two women stopped talking. Ashleigh dried her eyes. He walked into the kitchen wearing the black Fumagalli he'd worn the night before.

"Were your ears burning, Will?" Ashleigh asked.

He dropped two slices of bread into the toaster. "Yep. So what did you tell her about me, Terry?"

"Nothing about you. I only talked about how much I love you and what I'd do in certain situations, is all."

"Uh-huh. What situations would that be?"

"You don't need to know everything a woman says about the man she loves. You might take advantage of me."

The toast popped up and he put some butter and strawberry jelly on it. Then he put some bacon and eggs on it and put it in the microwave.

"You just want me to take advantage of you, is all," he said, mocking her.

"Sure do. When are you going to take advantage of me again?"

Will looked at Ashleigh. She was looking at them, mesmerized by their open conversation. In the time that she had been around them, she thought they were good together and hoped it would work out for them. Will looked at Terry again and smiled. The microwave beeped and he took the sandwich out. "I'll be back later. I need to change clothes."

"You don't have any in the closet, huh?" Ashleigh asked.

"No, I don't. I need to use your car for a while, okay, babe?"

"Okay. But don't waste any of that in my car, and try not to strip the gears. And whatever you do, don't have an accident in my car. If you do, don't even bother coming back."

"Deal. But I hope you realize you'll be losing two things you love." Will drank his apple juice. Then he kissed Terry. "Catch you later, babe. Nice to meet you, Ashleigh." Then he went out the door.

"He's nice," Ashleigh said.

"Yeah, I think so, too."

"When's the last time you talked to Michael?"

"I don't know, why?"

"Because he has full-blown AIDS and he's still too proud to tell you. I had promised I wouldn't tell you when he first contracted the virus. But I didn't promise not to tell you about this. He has pneumonia and he's going to die soon."

†††

Will was enjoying the Mitsubishi so much that he decided to take his time getting home. He turned left off Fulton Street, onto Arguello Boulevard and drove past the Conservatory of Flowers. Then he turned right onto John F. Kennedy Drive. He was shifting gears like a maniac, and having a lot of fun. He slowed down when he saw he was approaching Eighth Avenue and turned left and drove past the Asian Art Museum. Then he floored it. The Japanese Tea Garden was a blur as he zoomed past. The tires screeched as he turned right onto Martin Luther King Drive. He followed King Drive until he got to Ninth Avenue where he turned right and drove back to Kennedy Drive, then onto Park Presidio Boulevard. Once he got on Park Presidio Boulevard, he opened it up to see how fast it could go. In no time, he was in the MacArthur Tunnel.

Before long, he was on the Golden Gate Bridge and off again. He stopped at a light as he entered Sausalito. He had set his sandwich on a napkin in the passenger seat and almost forgot he had it. He figured it was cold now, but he picked it up and took a bite. The light changed but he wasn't aware of it.

A driver blew the horn and he pulled off again, taking another bite of the sandwich. Some jelly dripped onto his shirt. He looked down for a second. "Damn," he said. He wiped the jelly off the shirt with his napkin. Then he looked up again and saw he was about to run into the back of a car. He put on brakes but it was too late. Bam! It was a brand-new black Lexus 400 trimmed in gold. Although he hadn't hit the car hard, he hit it hard enough to do damage to both cars.

Seconds later, a black woman got out of the car and slammed the door. She was yelling at him, but he couldn't understand what she was saying. He got out of the car and her words became abundantly clear.

436

"What the fuck's wrong with you?" she shouted. "Didn't you see that the light was red?"

Will looked at the woman closer—she looked familiar.

She looked at him and thought he looked familiar, too.

"Jade Wilson?"

"Willy?" Her expression changed. "It's been a long time," she said. "I remember when you used to have that crush on me, too."

"Yeah, but that was a long time ago, Jade. You're still looking good though."

"So what did you do with your life, Willy?"

"I'm a psychologist now."

"Wise Counseling Services?"

"Yeah, that's me."

"Wow! I heard your commercial on the radio station that just hired me."

"Which one is that? I advertise on several."

"WJAM, the beat of the Bay. My show is syndicated now. I was in Atlanta for seven years and they called and said they wanted to bring my show to the coast. They bought me a house here in Sausalito and everything."

"That's great, Jade. Well here, this is my card. My insurance will cover everything."

"You married?"

"Widower. You?"

"For five years. He was a bum. I had to get rid of the fool. Got a couple of great kids though. Girlfriend?"

"Yeah, this is her car and she gon' be mad as hell. She told me not to have an accident just before I left."

"That's why ya had one. So is it serious between you?"

"Yeah."

"Well, listen, if it doesn't work out, give me a call, okay. I gotta be goin'. I'm running late as it is. And this is my first day."

"Okay, but I doubt that I'll be callin'."

"Ya never know. It might be fate. Well, I gotta run. I'll be talking to you, I'm sure."

"Okay, Jade. It was nice seeing you and sorry about hitting your new car."

"That's okay since it was you, Willy. Try and catch the show. It comes on at twelve noon. I'm going to be late, thanks to you. So that's the least you can do." Then she got in her car, and left.

Will walked back to the Mitsubishi and got in. He picked up the phone and called Terry.

"Hello."

"Hey, babe, you're not going to believe this, but guess what?"

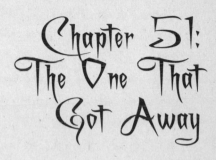

Chapter 51: The One That Got Away

"Are you okay, Will?"

"Yeah, I'm fine. It was a fender-bender. I'm sorry, baby. I'll have it fixed. There's only minor damage."

"Well, what happened?"

"I was feedin' my face and some jelly dripped onto my shirt. I looked down for a second and boom, an accident."

"You are so lucky that I love you. Because if I didn't, I'd get my .9mm out and it would be open season on any black doctors who graduated from Harvard, own two businesses, live in Sausalito, happen to be wearing a black Fumagalli, and crashed their girlfriend's beloved candy-apple red Mitsubishi 3000 GT."

"You know that's one of the reasons I love you, girl."

"And why is that, darlin'?"

"Your sense of humor and your ability to take so many things in stride."

"You didn't think so when we left the Perfect Indulgence Club that night, did you? You thought I needed to take things more seriously then, huh? Then when you wreck my car, suddenly you're glad I take things in stride. But on a serious note, I need to take some time off from work. We have a family crisis back in New Haven. I need you to get back here by three so you can take us to the airport."

"Oh, wow. What happened? Is Michael okay?"

"How do you do that?"

"Do what?"

"You know, Will. How did you know it was Michael?"

"Simple deduction. If it were your mom, or dad, you would have simply said so. Ashleigh's already here, so no need to go back to New Haven for her. That leaves Michael. But the real clue was when you said family crisis."

"Why would that be a clue?"

"The words 'family crisis' denotes unwanted responsibility and obligation. So how long has he had the virus? He does have AIDS, right?"

"Do you analyze everything that quickly? Or do you just go on visceral instincts on things like this?"

"Both actually. Listen, I'm home now. I'm going to change as quickly as I can. I should be there in plenty of time. What time does your flight leave?

"Four-thirty."

"Okay."

†††

Will was in his black BMW and had almost reached Terry's townhouse when he decided to see if he could find Jade's radio show. He had forgotten the dial numbers, so he hit the search button, which automatically locked in FM stations for about five seconds. After going through about seven stations, he heard the WJAM jingle. They were going to commercial.

He stopped in front of the townhouse and parked. Terry and Ashleigh were coming out of the house. He opened the trunk and put their luggage in.

"Minor damage, huh, Will? I suppose that's why you drove the BMW."

"Yeah, the damage is minor. It'll be fixed by the time you get back. I'll take care of everything. It'll look like new."

"It better."

"Do you guys interact like this all the time?" Ashleigh asked.

Terry said, "After good sex and traffic accidents, yes."

Will shook his head and finished putting their bags in the trunk. They got into the car. WJAM was coming out of the commercial break when they pulled off.

"This is Jade Wilson on 99.9 WJAM, JAM-FM, the beat of the Bay. As y'all know I was late this afternoon, my first day back in the Bay Area. That sho' is sad, ain't it? Ya get a new gig in your hometown and ya gettin' paid large; then ya have nerve enough to show up late the first day. At the top of the hour, I told y'all that I was going to explain why I was late this afternoon.

"And those of you who are familiar with the show when I was in Atlanta know that I always have a call-in segment where I give y'all a chance to say what's on your mind within the confines of the show, all right? For all you new listeners out there, since I'm the host, I have to tell my personal story first, then I take your calls, all right? Now, today's topic is the one that got away, all right? That's what we in the biz call a segue. In fact, I got the idea this morning when some fool ran into the back of my brand-new Lexus."

Terry looked at Will. "Are you the fool, darlin'?"

Will smiled. "Shut up."

"So not only did you tear up my car, but you tore up hers, too, huh?"

"See, girl, that's yo' problem. You don't know how to leave shit alone."

Ashleigh said, "You two are crazy. But that's good though."

"That's right," Jade began again. "That's why I was late. I'm sittin' at a traffic light, waitin' for the light to change, and this fool runs right into me. So I'm seein' red, right? I mean, I'm fired up. I get out the car, forget all that my mama taught me about being a lady, and was cussin' up a storm. I mean, my head was goin' from side to side and everything. I didn't care how I looked either. I mean, I didn't worry about my hair, my nails, or my outfit. The sistas out there know what I'm talkin' about. All I could think about was how this idiot had hit my new ride and how I was gon' let him have it, all right? I can't say everything 'cause this is live radio, but y'all know what I'm talkin' about.

"So anyway, this brotha gets outta this red sports car. And yes, he was fine, ladies, but I didn't give a damn. Fine or not, you don't hit a sista's new car, okay? Now here's the segue for today's topic. Anyway, y'all, I'm lightin' into that place where the sun don't shine, right? And he says,

'Jade Wilson?' And I say, 'Willy?' Turns out to be a guy who had liked me from elementary school to high school. I wouldn't give the brotha the time of day either, right? And guess what? That's right, you guessed it. Not only is he fine now, but the brotha's paid.

"It's San Francisco's own William Wise of Wise Counseling Services. When I think about that fool I married when I could've had Willy, I think damn! So ladies, everywhere, especially you young sistas, be nice to the ones you don't like as much as others. That'll be the one that got away. We gon' take a short break here, and do a little business. But when we come back, I'll be takin' your calls. I wanna hear your stories about the one that got away, or your comments about my story. And to put you in the mood, here's the Average White Band singing 'School Boy Crush.'"

"Sounds like somebody's got some serious com-pe-titiooooooon," Ashleigh sang.

Will looked at her through the rear view. "No. There's no competition."

Although Terry was glad Will made his feelings clear to Ashleigh, she couldn't help wondering if he had any residual interest in Jade. She knew not to ask him about it, but curiosity got the better of her.

"So when were you going to tell me you ran into someone you had a crush on?"

Will looked at her. He didn't want the conversation to go any further. "There's nothing to tell. End of story." He heard the show coming back on after the break and turned the radio off.

Terry cut her eyes at him and said, "I was listening to that, Will."

He could tell she was anxious to hear what was going to be said, and knew it could only lead to trouble. "Fine. You wanna hear the show, listen to it. But I'm not answering any more questions about what happened. It was a fender-bender. So what! I knew her way back when. So what!"

Terry didn't even bother to acknowledge what he said. She simply reached over and turned the radio back on. Then she looked at him and rolled her eyes.

"I don't know why you rollin' yo' eyes at me. I told you what happened."

Jade was talking to a caller.

"So was this guy married, or what?" the caller asked.

"No, but he has a girlfriend. It was her car."

"Well you know what they say, girl. All's fair in love and war," the caller went on, and laughed. "If I was you, I'd go after him before Ms. Thang gets him."

Jade laughed. "For all my Caucasian listeners, Ms. Thang is slang for white woman."

"Why you wanna listen to this?" Will asked.

Terry looked at him. "Because it's interesting."

Ashleigh laughed. "You're damn right, it's interesting. It sounds like it's about to get real interesting."

"I take it you have a problem with black men dating white women?" Jade asked the caller.

"You know how it works, girl," the caller said. "If the brotha's that successful, you can bet he got one. And if he don't, one has already painted a bulls-eye on his back. She's already made up her mind that she gon' get 'em, no matter what it takes. I mean, whatever, too. You know what I'm sayin', Jade? I can't say it on the radio, girl."

Jade laughed. "Yeah, I know."

"So, Will, black women refer to white women as Ms. Thing, huh?" Ashleigh asked. "Or are we only known by that term when we have a black man?"

Will looked at his watch. He thought if he sped up, he could at least get them to the airport faster. It was bad enough they were discussing him on the radio, but now they were talking about him and the white woman he was dating. He switched lanes and floored it.

Terry laughed. "You in a hurry, darlin'?"

"Not at all," Will told her, and drove even faster.

"Oh, I forgot to tell you, sis. Will doesn't like to answer tough questions."

Will looked at her and rolled his eyes. Then he looked at his watch again.

"We have a male caller from the Florida Keys on the line who wants to dispute the previous caller," Jade said. "Go ahead, caller."

"You bitches kill me," the caller said. "The segment is supposed to be about the one who got away, and now y'all talkin' 'bout the brotha like you know he got a white woman. I mean, damn, ya just said how successful the brotha was. I get so sick and tired of sistas always puttin' a brotha down when he doin' the best he can. And to top that off, ya wasn't even interested in the brotha 'til ya found out he was paid. Soon as ya find out the brotha got a few nickels, now ya talkin' about the one who got away. I'll even take it a step further. Ya sittin' up in there talkin' 'bout what Ms. Thang is willin' tuh do, but what about y'all? Ya know the brotha's in a relationship, and then she gon' say some mess like, all's fair in love and war. If that's the case, I guess it's okay for men to be dogs, right?"

"Let me ask you a question, caller," Jade said.

"Sure, but don't cut me off if you don't like my answer, okay?"

"Okay, I won't cut you off. Now here's the question. Is your wife, or current girlfriend, white?"

"I knew that would be your question. And yes, she's white. So what?!"

"It's just typical, caller. That's the only reason you called in, I'll bet."

"Let me ask you a question, Jade? Have you ever dated a white man, or wanted to date one?"

"No."

"So you've never seen a white man you found attractive then?"

"I didn't say that."

"That's my point, Jade. Sistas see white men they find attractive, but won't date 'em because of the color issue. But what gets me is, they tend tuh wanna put a brotha down for doing what deep down they wanna do. And if that ain't the case, they tend to harbor the same racist attitudes that whites have, yet don't want whites to exhibit prejudicial behavior toward them. You know what I think? I think that black men and white women have the freedom that white men and black women had years ago. And both the white man and the black woman are pissed about it. That's what I think."

"Okay, caller, is that all you have to say? I mean, I don't want people out there in radio land to say that Jade Wilson, the soul sista extraordinaire, wouldn't give equal time to a brotha who obviously doesn't know who he is."

"Talk about typical. When ya argue from a logical point of view, y'all get pissed. But it's cool. Thanks for lettin' me speak my mind." Then he hung up the phone.

"You're welcome, caller. And just to show you that I don't have any hard feelings, I hope you and yo' white girlfriend are very happy. We'll be right back with more calls. The phones are lit up, y'all. We gon' stay with this one for a while."

"Soooooooo," Ashleigh began, "How did you two get together? I mean, who was the aggressor in this relationship?"

"What difference does it make?" Terry asked.

"I see. So you went after Will like the lady said, huh?"

Will looked at Ashleigh through the rear view again. When they made eye contact, he nodded his head slightly.

Ashleigh laughed. "Terr, are you going to answer the question?"

"So what if I did go after him? Is that so wrong? What's wrong with going after what you want? Yeah, I'm aggressive. So what? You gotta be to get anything worth havin' in this world."

"Bothered you, huh, sis? Are you guys prepared for what's going to happen in the future? It sounds to me like a lot of people still don't like the idea of a black man screwing a white woman. I don't mean to be crass, but isn't that what it's all about? Plain ol' fucking?"

"So what if they don't," Terry snapped. "I don't give a damn who likes it and who doesn't like it. We're together and that's the end of it."

The show's jingle began again. Shortly after the jingle ended, Stevie Wonder sang the chorus of "Jungle Fever." Then they heard Jade saying, "We have a female caller from Dallas on the line. You're on the air with Jade Wilson."

"Yeah, is this Jade?"

"This is Jade. Go ahead with your comment, caller."

"I think that last guy is what you call a bitter brotha. He seems to be so mad. And where does he get off calling us bitches?"

"What's your point of contention with him, caller?"

"Well, I just think he's wrong."

"What specifically do you think he's wrong about?"

"He was talkin' about logic and reason, right? Is it logical that black women are mad because they want to date white men, and can't? I don't see no logic in that statement. None at all."

Will pulled into San Francisco International Airport, got into the departure lane, and drove past the south terminal boarding area.

"You're looking for United, right?" Will asked.

"Yeah."

"That's in the northern terminal, right?

"Right," Terry said quickly. She was still trying to hear the radio show.

"Okay. Do you mind answering his questions, then?" Jade said.

"What are they?"

"Have you ever wanted to date a white man?"

"Yeah, who hasn't? But I think it was more of a jungle fever type thing. You know, curiosity. I know you've at least thought about it, right, Jade?"

"I think you just legitimized the brotha's question, caller."

"What do you mean?"

"I think that's what he was tryin' to say, but he was too pissed and too inarticulate to say that everyone has at least thought about it. So can I ask you why you never explored the idea?"

"You tell me why you never have first, Jade. I know you've had offers from white men, haven't you?"

"What black woman hasn't? We got a lot of callers with requests. So when we come back, we're going to get back to the music."

"What a cop-out," Ashleigh said.

Will pulled up to the United Airlines terminal and stopped the BMW. Then he turned around and said, "Ashleigh, have you ever thought about dating a black man?"

"I did more than think about it, let me tell you. But he was the aggressor, Terr, not me."

They got out of the BMW. Will took their luggage out of the trunk.

"So when were you going to tell me about it?" Terry asked.

"You got a lot of nerve. I had to find out about Will on my own."

"That was his idea, not mine."

"I gotta go, babe," Will told Terry. "I can't park here."

"I know. I wish you could see me off though." Then she kissed him. "I'll call you when we get to Philadelphia, okay?"

"Okay. How long will it take to get to Philly?"

"The lady told me five hours and ten minutes to Philadelphia, provided we leave on time. And besides that, they've had a lot of flight delays due to weather problems back east. When we get to Philadelphia, we have an hour and fifty-five minute layover. Hopefully, we'll leave there on time."

"You could be flying all night then. When you add in the time differential, you guys will be lucky to get there by three-thirty or four in the mornin'."

"I know. But we gotta take this flight. Otherwise it'll be even longer. Ashleigh believes he's going to die soon and I need to tell him a few things."

"Okay, babe. I understand."

"I believe you do, darlin'."

They kissed again. It was a deeper kiss this time.

"Nice to meet you, Will," Ashleigh said. "Too bad I didn't get the chance to know you better."

"Maybe next time."

"Yeah, maybe next time."

"Bye. I love you," Terry said.

"I love you, too. Bye."

As they walked toward the terminal, Will heard Terry say, "So who was this black guy? And when did this happen?"

"It was this guy I met in college."

Will shook his head and got in the car. When he pulled off, he could hear Jade and her audience still talking about the same subject.

"Ya know, I think the earlier caller had a point," Jade said. "We were supposed to be talkin' about the one that got away, and I haven't heard one caller tell me about their experience. Maybe Van from the Motor City has a story about the one that got away. You're on the air with Jade Wilson."

"Yeah, Jade?"

"Go ahead, this is Jade."

"CAN WE PLEASE HEAR SOME MUSIC?!"

Will laughed and turned onto Highway 101. "It's about time!"

Chapter 52: When are you going to tell Dad?

Terry and Ashleigh hurriedly pulled their luggage down the concourse, looking for gate eighty-three. They heard their flight being told to board the 757 to Philadelphia. Ashleigh promised to tell Terry all about her college romance as soon as they took off. They finally got to gate eighty-three and saw passengers boarding.

As they stood in line waiting to enter the plane, Terry thought about Jade, and the women on the radio show. *What if Will still finds Jade attractive? If so, does he find Jade more attractive than me? Is Ashleigh right? Can Will turn down a proposition?* Her mind began to wander on its own, conjuring up all sorts of mental images about Will's secret desires to be with Jade. *After all, Jade is black and I'm white. It would be better for him in the long run anyway. And what if black women are right about aggressive white women? Maybe there is something to this interracial thing where white women are concerned. But, I've never gone after a black man before Will. They always asked me out. But why did I turn them down, yet I went after Will? Was it because he has money? Roger had money, too, and he's white. Hell, I have money. I've always had money. I grew up with money. I never wanted for anything. In fact, if Will and I broke up today, I'd still have money and an inheritance from my parents. Naw, it's not the money.*

Is it jungle fever then? Did I really want to try it all the time that I was turning black men down? I don't know. I should have listened to Will. I should have just let him turn the damn radio off, and I wouldn't be questioning my motives. Will is a great guy for any woman to have. That's why I went after him. Not because he's black and rich like they think. But would I date him if he didn't have the money? The other black guys I turned down didn't have any. At least, I don't think they did. No. I didn't even think about money then. I was with Roger.

"Terry, Terry," Ashleigh repeated.

Terry finally looked at her. "Huh? I'm sorry. What did you say?"

"I've been talking to you for five minutes and you haven't heard a word I've said, have you?"

"I'm sorry, sis. What were you saying?"

"It's that radio show, isn't it? What they said really bothers you, doesn't it?"

"Yes, and it bothers me that it bothers me, ya know?"

They entered the plane and stored their carry on bags in the hatch above their heads in the first-class section. Then they sat down and continued talking.

"Well, what bothers you more? The fact that they said it or that there may be some truth to it?"

"I think it bothers me because I think there is some truth to it, ya know? The fact of the matter is if Will weren't in the position he's in, I wouldn't even know him. If I met him on the street, sure, I'd think he's a fine brotha, and keep right on steppin'."

Ashleigh frowned.

"What's the matter?" Terry said, seeing the look on Ashleigh's face.

"Are you aware of what you just said, Terr? You sounded just like a black person for a second there."

"I did? What did I say?"

"Let's just say you're having trouble with your suffixes. I used to do it, too. I was always afraid I'd slip up when I came home from college on vacations."

A tall, well-dressed black woman boarded the plane. Her seat was directly in front of them. She placed her carry on bags in the hatch and was about to sit down when a female flight attendant walked up to her, and asked if she could see her ticket. The attendant asked her nicely, but the black woman didn't like the idea of the attendant asking for her ticket. She was attempting to suppress her rage, but Terry could tell she was really angry.

"Excuse me," Terry interrupted, looking at the name on her vest, "Lucy, but you didn't ask me or my sister for our tickets. Why are you asking this woman for hers?"

Then one of the other passengers said, "You didn't ask for mine either."

One by one, all the passengers in the first-class section said the same thing.

Embarrassed, Lucy said, "I was going to ask to see everyone's ticket. I haven't gotten around to the rest of you yet."

"OH, BULLSHIT!" Terry said loudly. The passengers stared at Lucy. "We've been here for ten minutes now, and you saw us sitting here," Terry scolded. "This woman hasn't even taken her seat and you're asking her for a ticket before anyone else? BULLSHIT!"

The captain came out of the cockpit. "What seems to be the trouble?" he asked, speaking to the black woman.

"Captain, may I ask why I need to show your flight attendant my ticket when she hasn't asked anyone else in the first-class section to see theirs?"

"I'm sorry for the inconvenience, ma'am," the captain said. "Lucy, I need to speak with you in the cockpit." The two of them turned around and entered the cockpit.

"I see you're as bold as ever." Ashleigh laughed.

"More of us need to be. That's why it goes on so much."

"Well, I'm not as bold as you, Terr," Ashleigh said, feeling guilty.

"It's that kind of attitude that allowed the Holocaust to happen, not to mention slavery. If we don't stand up, it will continue to go on unchecked."

Seconds later, a humbled Lucy returned and apologized to the woman, but she wasn't receptive. The black woman turned around and said, "Thank you for speaking up and I agree with you one hundred percent. We wouldn't have to complain so much if there were more people like you who see injustice, and refuse to look the other way. This happens to me all the time, but this is the first time someone said something about it. Thank you."

"You're welcome." Terry understood what she meant by someone saying something, too. She meant someone white saying something about it. "Hi, I'm Dr. Terry Moretti and this is my sister Ashleigh."

"I'm Dr. Tara Ali. Please to meet you."

"Are you a surgeon, or family practitioner?"

"I'm a gynecologist."

"You practice in San Francisco?"

"No, I was here to give a seminar. I practice in Philadelphia. And you?"

"I'm a psychologist, and my sister's a dentist. I practice in San Francisco and she practices in New Haven, Connecticut."

As the 757 started taxiing out to the runway, they heard a flight attendant ask everyone to put on their seat belts. Dr. Ali thanked Terry again. Then she turned around and slid into her seat. Terry wanted to ask her a myriad of questions, but didn't want to bother her. She looked at Ashleigh and asked, "So are you going to tell me about this guy you met in college, or what?"

"There's really not a lot to tell, Terr. When are you going to tell Dad about you and Will?"

"I'll tell him before I leave New Haven."

"How do you think he'll take it?"

"He'll probably be pissed, but so what?"

The plane taxied down the runway, picked up speed, and before long, they were in the air.

"The guy's name was Brian Manning. He was studying economics at Boston College when I was there. He was so arrogant."

"You like arrogant men, don't you? Or have you changed your opinion of them?"

"No, I haven't changed. I still like an arrogant man. I don't know what it is, but it's a real turn-on. The fact that it was taboo sex made it even better. Every time we got together, I kept wondering what Dad would do if he found out."

"Did you love this guy, or what?"

"I told myself that at first, but it was sex, plain and simple."

"So he was good, huh?"

"Very good. But not anywhere near as good as Will is. I thought there was an opera going on in your bedroom last night."

They could hear Dr. Ali laughing after that comment.

"I'm serious, Terr. You were loud as hell last night. I went into the guest-room and I couldn't stay in there. And it went on and on and on. It was funny at first, but then it got ridiculous. That's why I asked you about it this morning. I just knew you were faking or something."

"Well, if you had loved Brian, maybe you would have experienced that kind of pleasure also. There's more to lovemaking than just going for it. So what happened to Brian?"

"I got pregnant and aborted the baby. He didn't want to see me anymore after that."

"Why did you have an abortion?"

Ashleigh looked at Terry incredulously. "Are you kidding? Do you really think I would have that man's baby, knowing how Daddy feels about it? You must be out of your mind."

"If Dad felt differently, would you have had the baby then?"

"I doubt it. Besides, I couldn't have a baby. I hadn't completed my bachelor's degree yet. Dad would have stopped paying for college or something crazy like that. You know how he is."

"You ever wonder why he feels that way, sis?"

"Yeah, but I'm not going to ask him about it."

"Well, I am, but not before talking to Mom first. I bet she knows something. It just doesn't make sense to be involved in civil rights with that kind of attitude."

"I know. It's puzzling, isn't it?"

"Well, he's going to tell me something when I tell him about Will."

"I'm sure he'll tell you, Terr. You're still his little peaches and cream."

"You still jealous about that, sis?"

"Not as much as I used to be, but yeah. You're my sister and I love you. When I left last night, I knew I could come out to the coast without notice. You've always been there for me."

"And I always will be, sis."

The two women hugged.

"Now, let me get some rest. I didn't get any sleep last night because some opera singer kept singing high notes in my ear all night long."

Terry laughed a little and said, "Okay, sis, you get some rest."

†††

"So anyway, Dr. Ali," Terry said. She was sitting next to her now. "What do you think? Do you think the woman on the radio could be right about me?"

Dr. Ali looked Terry in the eye and said, "About you specifically? No. A lot of white women, yes. Definitely." Terry looked at her as though she wanted more of an explanation. "Look, Dr. Moretti," she continued, "I don't know what you want me to say. I told you what I think. But if that isn't good enough for you, I don't know what more I can say, and still be honest with you."

"Well, tell me this. And I realize you don't know me, but, would you have a problem with me dating the guy I was telling you about?"

"With you? No. But with a lot of white women, yes."

Terry looked at her again, hoping for a more complete answer.

Dr. Ali took a deep breath and let it out the way people do when they're irritated. Then she said, "What do you want from me, Dr. Moretti?"

"I just want you to explain, if you don't mind too much, why you feel this way about white women in general, and not me."

"Because you're different from most I've encountered. In fact you're different from most people, period. Your sister said it right. You're bold as hell. And trust me, if you love Will the way you say, you're going to need to be that way, especially with what's her name again?"

"Aunt Johnnie. What do you mean by, I'm different from most people, period?"

"Take the flight attendant, for example. Like I said, it happens to me all the time. White people never say a word. They just look at me as though they want to see if I belong in the first-class section with them. Then they sit around and discuss me. They say things like I wonder what she does for a living. I'm not saying it's wrong to wonder what I do that I can afford a first-class ticket, but what I find deplorable is them knowing why I'm being singled out, and not saying a word about it. I look at them and I see their guilt because they obviously thought I didn't belong in this section. If you hadn't said something, I might have gone off. And that would have made matters worse."

"Why is that?"

"Because, if I go off, and it doesn't matter how many times I behave in a dignified manner, it gives black people a bad name with people who are in a position to hire and fire black people. I think a lot of people who sit in the first-class section either own businesses, or know people who do, which means they have influence. I know white people discuss black people because we discuss white people. The difference is, most of us are not in a position to hire and fire people because of quote unquote 'perception.' You got loud with the flight attendant and that will do nothing in the way of denigrating your image to other whites. In fact, about the only thing you could do to lose some sort of status, real, or imagined, is become a whore, or marry someone black who doesn't have any money. Black people, on the other hand, have to bear the sins of other black people all the time. We're seen as a collective, not as individuals."

"But, Dr. Ali, white women are seen as a collective when they date black men."

"That's true, Dr. Moretti. However, that's where it ends."

"What do you mean by that?"

"I mean that you're talking about an isolated situation. I'm talking about an American institution. Therefore, I don't see much of a comparison. When you have to bear the weight of white people, the way I have to bear the weight of black people, then we can talk. But until then, it is sheer folly to try and make a comparison between the two peoples."

"You married?"

"Divorced. And he was black."

Terry laughed.

"That was your next question, wasn't it?"

"Yep."

"Now you want to know if I'd date, or marry a white man, right?"

"Yep."

"Depends on the white man. If he's in a financial situation comparable to mine; if he understands that I'm an independent woman; if he makes a sincere attempt to understand my blackness; and if he's as good in bed as your Will is, I'd give it some serious consideration." The two women laughed. Between their laughter, Dr. Ali said, "I'm willing to give any man a chance if he can turn my bedroom into an operatic theater!"

Chapter 53: Infidelity?

A Philadelphia snowstorm caused a five-hour delay. The flight to New Haven finally took off at 6:20 AM and they arrived at the hospital at about 8:30. Ashleigh couldn't stand to see Michael so weak and helpless and went to the relatives' waiting room. After reading an article in *Vogue* magazine, she called their mother to let her know Terry was in town visiting Michael at the hospital.

Terry was in the intensive care unit, standing over her comatose brother. She looked down at the unrecognizable shell of a man that used to be so alive and full of life. She remembered the games they played when they were children and how mad she used to get when Michael gloated after beating her at her favorite games. A smile surfaced, but only for a moment. All of that was behind them now.

She looked at him through the plastic, closed her eyes, and tried to remember the man he used to be. She remembered the day he told her about his homosexuality, and how painful it was when he confirmed what she'd suspected for years. He was her brother, but their relationship would never be what it was. *Why did you have to tell me? Why couldn't you stay in the closet?* Her eyes filled with tears and found their way down her cheeks.

"Why couldn't I be more accepting of you, Mikey?" she said. "I've always been so strong-willed. I was foolish enough to believe that if I wouldn't talk to you, or acknowledge you, you'd leave that life."

She remembered how he looked the day she rejected him, the disbelief, the disappointment in his eyes. He told her she was the one person in the family he thought would understand and accept him the way he was, but she was his staunchest opposition. When she thought of the years that had gone by without so much as a word between them, she felt the sting of what her willful stubbornness had cost her. As the tears slid down her cheeks, she lifted the plastic and touched his frail arm.

"Mikey, I know it's too late, but I'm sorry I wasn't there for you. I'm sorry I rejected you when you needed me most. I'm sorry for all the years that passed without one single phone call."

Terry paused for a second and thought about what she was saying to her brother, who for all she knew, couldn't hear a word she was saying, and realized that what she had done to her brother, was now being done to her by Will's mother. It had become so clear at that moment. Just as she was convinced that homosexuality was wrong, and had rejected her brother, Will's mother felt the same way and rejected her. The realization finally broke what pride she had left, and the grief she felt within gushed out of her like a sudden unpredictable storm.

†††

As they drove to their parents' house in a white Rodeo, Terry looked out the window at the snow-covered landscape and listened to Ashleigh talk to Jeffery, her wayward husband, on the cell phone.

"You gotta lot of nerve asking me where I've been when you've been spending your time downtown at the Colony Hotel!" Ashleigh practically screamed.

"When are you coming home?" Jeffery asked. "This isn't something I think we should be discussing on a cell phone."

"Don't worry about when I'm coming home. I only called to make sure the kids are okay. Did you make breakfast for them?"

"Yes. We had breakfast together. Did you tell your parents?"

"You mean, did I tell Daddy? Why? You afraid he's going to come over there and kick your ass?"

"Can't we at least discuss this face to face?" Jeffery asked, avoiding the question.

"I don't think we have anything to discuss, Jeffery. Pack your things! I'm coming home and when I do, I want you to leave!" She hit the end button.

Ashleigh pulled into the driveway and parked the Rodeo. The garage door was open and they saw their mother putting the snow blower away. Terry got her bags out of the truck and hugged her mother.

"Where's Dad?" Terry asked her mother. "He should be doing this."

"He got stuck in Manhattan." Her mother's Southern drawl was thick. Dyan was five-eight and still shapely for a woman approaching sixty. She was wearing a pair of Levis, duck boots, and a New England Patriots down coat. Her curly brown hair could be seen at the outer edges of her Patriots ski cap. "He should be home this evening though."

Good. That'll give me a chance to tell you about the man I'm going to marry.

"You gettin' out?" Dyan asked Ashleigh.

"No, Mom. I have some things at the house I need to get rid of. Today's a good day to do it."

Terry laughed a little.

"Okay, don't work too hard. Bye."

"Thanks for picking me up, sis." Terry winked.

Ashleigh smiled at Terry and backed out of the driveway.

Mother and daughter entered the warm Tudor dwelling and took her bags up to her room. Her mother always kept her room the same way she left it, which was full of trophies she'd won in volleyball, and track and field.

"So what did you want to talk to me about, dear?"

"Well, Mom," she said nervously, "I actually need to tell you something and then talk to you about it. When Dad comes home, I'm going to talk to him, too."

Concerned, her mother asked, "What is it?"

"I've found someone, Mom. It's someone I'm deeply in love with."

Relieved, her mom said, "Is that all? The way you sounded on the answering machine had me worried it was going to be more terrible news. I thought you had something dreadful to tell me. So who is this guy? That's good news. God knows we could use some good news around here, with Mikey being so sick and all. Can you believe that sister of yours knew all this time and didn't say a word until last week when the boy was on his death bed? I swear I couldn't stand any more bad news right now. If I hear another bad thing right now, I'll go out of my mind. Who did you say this guy is? It's about time. I've always said you were too picky."

Terry laughed. "Are you going to let me tell you about this person? Or are you going to keep on rambling?"

"I don't ramble. I like to talk, is all."

"Well, to have a conversation, you have to let me talk a little, Mom."

"Okay, but get to it. You know how I hate suspense."

Terry sat on her bed. Then she patted it. "Sit down, Mom."

Her mother sat down. She could see the seriousness of what she was about to be told in her daughter's eyes. She wondered what it could be. "This is good news, isn't it?"

"It's great news, Mom."

"Then what's wrong? Why are you so hesitant to tell me about this man you've met? It is a man, isn't it?"

Terry laughed a little. "Of course, it's a man."

"Thank God. One gay child is more than enough for any parent. Who would have ever guessed Mikey would have turned out gay?"

Terry looked at her mother and rolled her eyes.

Her mother realized she was rambling again. "I'm sorry. I won't interrupt again. Go on, I'm listening."

"Since you won't let me ease into it, I might as well come on out with it. The man I love is black, Mom."

Terry paused for a moment or two to let it sink in. Her mother sat there expressionless for a few seconds. Then she slowly began shaking her head. Her head tilted. Tears fell.

"Mom, I'm sorry you feel this way, but my mind is made up. I'm really shocked that you would be so upset about it. I expected you to support me in this."

"No, no, honey," her mother said between sobs. "Don't you ever think that. My tears are both tears of joy and tears of shame. I guess deep down I knew this day was going to come."

Confused, Terry asked. "What are you talking about, Mom?"

"I guess I'd better tell you now before your dad gets home. Lord knows this is going to kill him. But it's time to get it out."

"What? Get what out, Mom? What have you done that could be so terrible?"

"Promise me you won't hate me, honey. Promise me."

"Mom, there's nothing you could do that would make me hate you. I learned a lot from how I handled Mikey's gay lifestyle. And I won't allow myself to be so full of pride that I can't accept you. Believe me, Mom, there's nothing you did in the past that I can hate you for, okay?"

With her head still tilted in humility, she said, "Okay." Then she took a deep breath. "It happened over thirty-four years ago, honey."

Terry fought the urge to ask a thousand questions. But she knew her mother would tell it all. It was her nature to do so. She held her mother's hand. "Go on."

"This happened during our Civil Rights days. As you know, we were highly involved back then."

Terry knew what she was about to hear would provide her the information as to why her father had changed since those days.

"Anyway, we worked hard every day organizing marches and sit-ins. Your father didn't want me to march because when you marched in those days, or participated in a sit-in, you were taking your life into your hands. So I worked in the office. If I wasn't organizing, I was teaching Negroes— that's what we called black people back then—to read and write so they could vote when the law forbidding them to was overturned. In that office, I met Joseph."

Instinctively, Terry knew Joseph was black. And with that knowledge she knew the rest, but allowed her mother to get it all out. She needed to after all these years. Terry looked into her mother's eyes as she spoke and could tell her mother was reliving the whole incident in her mind.

Her mother was no longer in her bedroom. She was in the South, thirty-four years ago.

"I remember it like it happened yesterday. I was filing some papers in my office when he came in. He was so tall and so dark. His skin was as smooth as silk and he had the prettiest smile you ever did see." She was smiling now, but didn't realize it. "I remember his first words to me. He said, 'Excuse me, Miss, but are you Dyan Moretti?' I about fell off my feet. He had the deepest, sexiest voice I ever heard. We were both instantly attracted to each other, and we knew it. Right then, right at that moment, I knew this was a man I didn't need to be around.

"But instead of staying away from him, I found myself drawn to him. He was well-educated and he'd traveled the world. He'd tell me about his trips to India, Senegal, China, et cetera. He told me how different things were for black people in Paris. He told me it wasn't anything for blacks and whites to mix there. I knew we were on dangerous ground but I couldn't stop thinking about him. After a while, I lost my will to resist my desire to be with him in that way. Then we started seeing each other. As dangerous as it was, we couldn't help ourselves. We tried to stop, but deep down, we really didn't want to.

"After a while, your dad figured out what was going on. He confronted me and I told him the truth. I thought he'd leave me, but your father told me he loved me and he wanted me to stay with him. He threatened to tell my parents if I left. I wanted to leave your father for him, honey, but the truth is I was too scared to leave. I wanted Joseph more than anything on earth, but I knew I couldn't deal with my parents knowing what I'd done. My father and I were close and I didn't want him thinking he'd raised a whore. Your father knew that and used it to keep me with him. But it wasn't just that. I was also afraid of the times we were living in, too.

"In those days, people were being killed all the time. I felt bad about what I'd done and I promised him I wouldn't see Joseph again. I quit working in that office and I hadn't seen Joseph in a year, or so. Somehow, he got our phone number and called me, and we started meeting again. It was just as intense as it was before we quit seeing each other. A few months later, Joseph was killed in a plane crash. He was on his way back to Biloxi from a trip to New York. I was devastated. It turns out I was a couple months pregnant at the time he died. And—"

"Is Joseph my father, Mom?"

"No, honey, he isn't. But there was some doubt for a while. I named you after him just the same. I wanted to remember him when I saw you because you could have been his child."

"Does Dad know I'm named after Joseph?"

"Douglas doesn't know. He thinks you're named after his grandfather."

"What was his full name? Joseph, I mean."

"Joseph Terrance Shaw. Now…do you hate me?"

"No, Mom. I could never hate you. And I'm glad you told me. You must have really loved this guy."

"I still do, honey. After all these years, I still do."

The two women embraced and held each other.

Dyan said, "So, who is this guy?"

"His name is William Marcellus Wise."

"The man you work for?"

"Uh-huh?"

"Well, honey, if you love him, I'm all for it."

"So I can count on your support when I tell Dad?"

"If it comes to that, yes."

"What do you mean?"

"That's why I told you about Joseph, honey. You've fallen in love with a black man. How do you think your father's going to feel? You know it's going to bring up the past. That's the first thing that's going to pop into his head."

"Infidelity? Is that what this is all about? Let me ask you something, Mom. Has Dad ever seen another woman that you know of?"

"Yes, but I put up with it because of what I'd done myself. What could I say? If I did it, he could also."

"If that's the case, then he's had his revenge. No need to bring up the past unless we bring it all up. I'm sure he won't want to do that, Mom."

"Probably not, but you never know with men. You know how they have their double standards in these matters. He probably thinks it's natural for a man to lust after a woman, but it's unladylike for a woman to lust after a man. That way he can justify what he does."

Terry yawned. "Okay, Mom, I'm sleepy now. I've been up all night. I'm gonna take a nap. What are you making for dinner?"

"Just some of your favorites."

"Steak smothered in gravy and onions?"

"Umm-hmm."

"Mashed potatoes, yams, green beans, and apple pie, too?"

"Umm-hmm."

"What about the potato rolls? Are you going to make some?"

"Yep, just for you, honey. You get some sleep now, okay?"

"Okay, Mom. It's good to be home." Dyan left the room.

Terry undressed and got in bed. She closed her eyes and pondered her mother's story. Although she would never admit it, a part of her was a little disappointed Joseph wasn't her father. If he were, Will's mother wouldn't have a reason to reject her. Terry's eyes suddenly popped open when she realized that all the women in her immediate family had been involved with black men at one time or another. *Was the woman on the radio right about me?*

"I wonder…" she said out loud.

A few minutes later, she was sound asleep.

Chapter 54: That was a fairy tale, wasn't it?

Terry was sound asleep when her father looked in on her. The room was dark, but he could see her from the light in the hallway. Her mouth was open and he could hear her faint snore. He remembered looking in on her every night when she was a child. Looking at her now brought back happy memories for him. It was hard to believe she was over thirty now. It seemed like such a short time ago when he rushed Dyan to the hospital at three in the morning. He wished they let fathers guide their children out of wives back then. He wanted to be the first face she saw. He wanted to be the first to touch her so she would know her daddy loved and wanted her. He smiled and closed the door gently.

Terry woke up suddenly when the door closed. She heard footsteps going away from her room and realized her father had looked in on her. It was dark outside and in the room. She reached over to the nightstand and turned the light on. The bright light stung her eyes at first. She picked up her watch. 3:30. *I couldn't have slept that long.* Then she realized she forgot to set the time ahead. She picked up the phone and called Will at the clinic.

"Wise Choice Substance Abuse Center. Jeannine speaking. May I help you?"

"Hi, Jeannine, this is Terry. How you doin'?"

"Girl, I know your voice. How was your flight?"

"It was fine until I got to Philadelphia." She yawned. "I was only supposed to be there for an hour or so, but a storm hit and we ended up being stuck there for five hours."

"You sound like you just woke up. The jet lag kickin' yo' ass, huh?"

"You know it is." She yawned again. "I woke up a couple of minutes ago and looked at my watch. It was still on Pacific Time. I thought it was 3:30 in the morning for a second, or two."

"Woke up thinkin' about 'em, huh? Girl, you got it bad."

"I suppose you never woke up with Jonathan on your mind, huh?"

"What can I say? He knows how to work me, which reminds me of what happened earlier today."

"What happened?"

"Poison quit today."

"Ivy? Are you serious? Why?"

"Girl, it was a big mess up in here today. Well, not at this office, at the Counseling Center. You know how Dr. Wise still has clients there that he sees from time to time?"

"Uh-huh."

"Well, we were over there this morning because he had an appointment with the rump wranglers and—"

"The who?"

"You know, Nick and Nathan." Jeannine laughed. "That's what I call them. Dr. Wise doesn't like it, but he lets me get away with it."

Terry assumed Will didn't tell her why she had come home, so she let the comment slide. "So what happened with Ivy?"

"Ivy had the nerve to try to get with Jonathan."

"What? You have to be kiddin'."

"No joke. The trouble started when he told her he wasn't interested. Then she had the nerve to get indignant. She started shoutin' some shit about him leadin' her on. They were in the break room and I heard her screamin'. I was wondering who she was screamin' at like that. Then, I see Jonathan walkin' past my desk real fast. Then here she comes following him like a puppy. To make a long story short, I had to put her ass in her place. You know I never liked her anyway. There we were goin' at it and Dr. Wise comes out his office. He was mad as hell. You know how he tries to be cool about everything, but I could tell he was fired up. Then Ivy said either I go, or she goes. He tried to get her to calm down, but she wouldn't have it. Then Ivy said, 'Fine, I quit.' And she walked out of the office."

"So who's covering for her?"

"Dr. Wise and some of the associates."

"Wow. So there's only two PhDs left?"

"Four. You, Dr. Beverly, Dr. Wise, and you might as well count Jonathan. He's almost done with his dissertation."

"He must be pullin' his hair out with all of us gone so quickly. Just six months ago, we were all in Toronto together. And now look what happened. James is in jail, Ivy quit, and I'm in New Haven."

"Oh, yeah," Jeannine said. "I heard Jade's show yesterday. Ain't that some shit?"

"You got that right."

"And she's been callin' here leavin' messages for Dr. Wise to call her, too."

Terry resisted the urge to ask if he returned her calls. "So is he there right now?"

"Yeah. Hold on, I'll put you through."

"Okay, thanks for bringing me up to speed on what's been going on."

"No problem, girl. Hold on a second."

A couple of minutes passed and Will said, "Hi, babe. How's Michael?"

She could tell he didn't want her to know things weren't going very well since she left, so she played along. "Not well, darlin'. I don't think he's going to live much longer."

"You did talk to him though, right? I mean, you did make your peace, right?"

"Yeah, I'm all right with it now. I'll tell you about it when I get home, okay?"

"Okay. Sounds like you just woke up."

"I did. You were the first thing on my mind, so I called."

"Thanks, babe. I was thinking about you, too."

"Well, I told my mother about us. Now I'm going to talk to my dad."

"How did she react?"

"Very well. I'll tell you all about it."

"Okay, good. Listen, I'm real busy right now. I'm gonna have to go. Let me know how it goes, okay?"

"Okay. I love you."

"I love you, too. Bye."

✝✝✝

Terry got out of bed and put on a red Stanford jogging suit. Then she left her room and entered the bathroom across the hall. She smelled the food her mother promised her. She especially liked the smell of butter on the potato rolls. She washed her face and brushed her teeth. Then she went back into her room and pulled her hair back tightly and put a red Scrunchie on. The doorbell rang. Then she heard her mother talking to Ashleigh.

"Where's Jeff and the kids?" Dyan asked.

"They're with Jeff. He took them to the movies so I could spend some time with Terr."

Terry smiled. Then she went downstairs to dinner.

"Hi, Terr," Ashleigh said. "I was just telling Mom Jeff was taking the kids to a movie tonight."

She had a grin on her face, which confirmed what Terry had thought all along. The kids were with Jeff, but not because of some movie. Ashleigh had come over for the anticipated fireworks. She wanted to see her father's face when Terry told her secret.

"How did you sleep, honey?" her mother asked.

"Great. I made a long distance call to San Francisco, Mom. Send me the bill and I'll pay for it."

"Any particular reason you're calling San Francisco, Terr?" Ashleigh grinned.

"Mom already knows, Ashleigh. I already told her."

"Told her what?" her father asked. Douglas was six-four with broad shoulders and resembled ESPN'S Mark Malone, thick moustache included.

Dyan and Ashleigh looked at Terry, wondering if she'd tell him now.

Terry smiled. "Hi, Daddy." She wrapped her arm around his in an escort fashion and began walking toward the dining room. "How was New York?"

Ashleigh laughed a little, but her father didn't hear her.

"New York was fine, Peaches. How are things in San Francisco these days?"

"I got a promotion a few months back."

They entered the dining room and took their normal seats. Terry sat next to her father. Her mother sat opposite her husband and Ashleigh sat opposite Terry.

"Where's your family, honey?" Douglas asked Ashleigh.

"Douglas," Dyan interrupted, "how about we bless the food? Then y'all can talk all y'all want."

"I'm sorry," he said.

They bowed their heads and Dyan thanked God for providing. They all said amen and filled their plates. Douglas briefly looked at Ashleigh and furrowed his brow as if he expected her to answer his question. Then he reached for the potato rolls.

"Jeff and the kids went to a movie, Daddy."

Ashleigh looked at Terry. Terry smiled and winked. Ashleigh couldn't help but smile.

Douglas picked up a forkful of his steak and put it into his mouth. "Are you guys having trouble?"

"No, Daddy. Why would you think that?"

"Because I've never seen you without the kids. Why are you being so defensive?"

"I'm not being defensive, Daddy. We were all supposed to be going out tonight. Terry came in town and you know we hardly see her as it is, with her living way out in San Francisco. I didn't want the kids to be disappointed. You know how kids are when you promise them something. You can't just pull the rug out from under them like that, Dad. You taught me that much."

Terry had to bite her tongue to keep from laughing uncontrollably. She was absolutely amazed at how well Ashleigh could lie and look so sincere while doing so. Ashleigh looked at Terry and winked as if to say your turn to manipulate Dad.

To get the conversation away from her and Jeff, Ashleigh said, "Terr, didn't you have something to tell Daddy?"

Douglas was looking down at his food. Then, with his fork, he put some more steak and mashed potatoes in his mouth. "Yeah, that's right," he said as he sopped up some gravy with his potato roll. "It almost slipped my mind."

Ashleigh smiled at Terry and mouthed, "You might as well get on with it."

Terry rolled her eyes.

"Well," he said impatiently. "What is it, Peaches?"

Terry stopped eating and wiped her mouth with her napkin. She looked at her mother and she nodded. She was nervous, but knowing she had her mother's support made it a little better. She understood how her mother must have felt thirty years ago. Reluctantly, she said, "I'm in love, Daddy."

"Is that all?" he said and resumed eating. "I thought you had some bad news or something. That's good. I hoped you and Roger would get back together, but I guess that's over for sure now. Why were you afraid to tell me?" He thought for a second. "Oh, you were afraid I wouldn't pay for another big wedding, right? You were right, too." Then he laughed, but nobody was laughing with him. "I'm only kidding with you, Peaches. I'll pay for it again. You just make sure this is the last one. Weddings are expensive these days." Then he laughed. Again, nobody was laughing with him. "What's wrong with you guys? That was funny." As he was eating and enjoying his food, he noticed that none of them were eating. They were staring at him. It occurred to him that there was more to tell. He put his fork down. With a frown on his face, he said, "Are you pregnant, or what?"

"No, Daddy. I'm not."

"What is it then?" He stared at her.

"You remember that time we went to the video store together?"

"We've been to the video store a thousand times together. Which time am I supposed to remember?"

"The one when you told me about Jennifer Silverman."

"Jennifer Silverman? I don't remember telling you anything about her."
Terry frowned. "I can't believe you don't remember telling me about her."

"Okay, I'll bite. What am I supposed to have told you about her?"

"You didn't tell me she ran away with a black man. You didn't tell me about the eighteen-inch erect penis they put in Mr. Silverman's locker either, huh?"

Ashleigh said. "Eighteen inches, huh? I guess they made their point."

"You watch your mouth, young lady," Dyan said.

Still confused, Douglas said, "What does that have to do—" Now he understood what she was trying to tell him. "I know you're not going to tell me this guy is black, are you, Peaches?"

"Do you remember me asking you, after you talked about that interracial couple leaving the store, what if I was involved with a black man? That's when you told me about the Silvermans. That was a fairy tale, wasn't it? There was no eighteen-inch penis in the locker, was there?"

Ashleigh laughed. "What is this? The *Get Smart* show? Are you supposed to be Agent 86 or something?"

"Ashleigh!" Dyan said sternly. "This is serious."

"But, Mom, think about it," Ashleigh continued. "Doesn't that sound like something Maxwell Smart would say? The old eighteen-inch black penis in the locker trick." She laughed again. They had sullen looks on their faces, which made it funnier to her. "Don't you guys get it?"

"We get it, Ashleigh," Dyan said sternly. "It just isn't funny right now."

"It's funny to me. Can't you just picture him saying that?"

"I thought you told me you would never do that to me, Peaches?" Douglas shifted the attention back to Terry.

"I never told you that, Dad, and you know it. You told me why you didn't want me to. But that wasn't the truth. It wasn't that Jennifer ran away with a black man. It wasn't even that fictitious story you told me. What bothers you about me being with a man who happens to be black?"

Douglas looked at Dyan. He wondered if she told her about Joseph.

Sensing what he was thinking, Dyan intervened, "I told her all about Joseph, Douglas."

"Told her all about what?" Ashleigh said, no longer laughing.

"This isn't about Mom, Daddy," Terry told him. "It's about me and the man I love."

"Told her all about what?" Ashleigh said again. "Who is Joseph?"

They ignored Ashleigh and kept talking.

"I can't believe you told her, Dyan. Why would you tell her about that?"

"It needed to be told, Douglas. It's been a secret long enough. Like the Bible says, 'The truth shall set you free.'"

"I suppose you're sleeping with him, too. Just like your mother."

"Joseph is black?" Ashleigh said without thinking. "And you slept with him, Mom?" It just came out of her mouth spontaneously. She didn't even know she was going to say it.

"Yes, she did," Douglas said. "And she did it while we were married. Now that Peaches and your mother have slept with black men, I suppose you're going to sleep with one, too."

"I suppose you've lived your life above reproach, huh, Douglas?" Dyan asked. "You've never violated your vows, have you?"

"DON'T YOU DARE TRY AND TURN THIS AROUND!" he screamed loudly. "ANYTHING I'VE DONE WAS DONE BY YOU, LONG BEFORE I DID IT! AND DON'T YOU FORGET IT!"

"HOW CAN I FORGET IT, DOUGLAS, WHEN YOU KEEP REMINDING ME OF WHAT HAPPENED THIRTY YEARS AGO?! WHAT BOTHERS YOU MORE, DOUGLAS!? THE FACT THAT I COULD LOVE ANOTHER MAN? OR THE FACT THAT THE MAN HAPPENED TO BE BLACK!?"

Before he could answer, Terry interrupted, "I'd be interested in knowing if any of these women you've been seeing are black."

"I'm not going to even dignify that, Terry."

"Why not, Daddy? Does the truth make you that uncomfortable? I'd be willing to bet that if you let it bother you for over thirty years, you probably had to find out what the attraction was yourself, didn't you, Daddy?"

"After all I've done for you? I can't believe you would talk to me like this." Then he looked at her jogging suit. "Thirty-two thousand dollars a year for a Stanford education. For what? To be psychoanalyzed by my own daughter?"

"I'm only being who you raised me to be," Terry said, ignoring the tuition comment. "A strong, aggressive woman, who can make decisions on her own. It was you who said I should question everything and everyone to find the truth. Why should I exclude you? You've proven to be just as fallible as anyone in this room. Should I not question you, Daddy?"

Douglas looked at Ashleigh and again said, "I guess you're going to get involved with a black man, too."

"No, Daddy," Ashleigh said desperately. "I would never do that. I could never hurt you that way."

Terry looked at her and frowned. Ashleigh's eyes pleaded for her not to say anything. She couldn't believe Ashleigh had the nerve to deny her involvement with Brian Manning; especially since she just told her yesterday. Terry thought about exposing Ashleigh, but decided not to. If she didn't want him knowing her business, it wasn't for her to tell him.

The phone rang.

"I'll get it," Ashleigh said, wanting to get away from the scrutiny. "It's probably Jeff anyway." Then she got up and left the room.

"Daddy, my mind is made up. Now either you trust my judgment, or you don't. That's up to you."

"You're willing to give up your inheritance for him?"

"DOUGLAS!" Dyan shouted. "ENOUGH! YOU'RE ACTING LIKE A CHILD! IT WAS THIRTY YEARS AGO! IT'S TIME TO EITHER PUT IT BEHIND US, OR WE NEED TO GO OUR SEPARATE WAYS! YOU'RE NOT GOING TO HOLD THIS OVER MY HEAD ANY LONGER! I'VE PUT UP WITH IT LONG ENOUGH! I'VE PAID MY DEBT! AND I'LL NOT PAY ANOTHER DAY!"

"AND DADDY," Terry shouted, "YOU HAVE TO KNOW YOU CAN'T CONTROL ME WITH MONEY! BESIDES, I HAVE MORE THAN ENOUGH ALREADY! NOW, YOU DON'T HAVE TO LIKE THE IDEA OF ME BEING WITH A BLACK MAN, BUT I'LL STILL BE YOUR DAUGHTER NO MATTER WHAT! IT'S UP TO YOU! YOU CAN EITHER GAIN A SON-IN-LAW, OR LOSE A DAUGHTER. THAT'S UP TO YOU, DADDY!"

Ashleigh walked back into the dining room and said, "Michael just died."

Chapter 55:
The Beat Down

San Francisco
May 1998

Will and Terry were working sixteen-hour days, six days a week at the counseling center. In addition to their heavy workload, they went through resumes and conducted interviews, painstakingly looking for qualified people, who had a good blend of professionalism and the personality to mesh with the current staff. Fortunately, the substance abuse clinic was practically running itself. All things considered, it wasn't that bad without Ivy and James. Jonathan would be graduating in less than a month and things would be even better. They hired a black couple from Washington, D.C., both former professors at Howard University, who specialized in family therapy and child psychology.

During this hurried time in their lives, Will and Terry practically lived at each other's homes. One night it would be his place, the next night hers. But it was hard for them to spend quality time together. When they got home, they were too exhausted to enjoy each other the way they had before. They were discussing marriage more and more now; especially since Terry's parents were in therapy and Douglas was becoming more accepting of the relationship. It was getting to the point where it just didn't make sense to maintain two homes anymore.

Will was on his way home from a long day of catching up on paperwork at the clinic. He promised Terry he would come by her place as soon as he got his paperwork caught up. It was about 11:40 PM when he walked out of the office. He tossed his briefcase on the back seat. As he closed the passenger door, it occurred to him that he forgot to call Terry before he left. He opened the driver's door and got in. When he cleared the garage, he picked up his cell and called her.

"Hello."

"Hey, babe, I'm on my way. I just have to stop at the store on the way," he said, while checking his mirrors for oncoming traffic.

"Are you real tired?" she asked as though she had something on her mind.

"Not real tired. Why?"

"We haven't been out in a while and I was wondering if you'd like to see a movie tonight."

"What movie?"

"The Michael Douglas film," she said. It felt funny saying her brother's and father's name like that, but she didn't dwell on it. "I think it's called *A Perfect Murder*."

"Yeah, we can go."

Now that he finally had some time, he was about to start touring because thanks to Oprah Winfrey's book club, his book, *Don't Settle For Second Best*, hit The New York Times nonfiction bestseller's list.

"Okay, but you won't have time to go to the store. You'll have to stop on the way back. I'll be looking for you."

"All right. I'll be there in about twenty minutes."

When he arrived at Terry's townhouse, he blew the horn and she came out. She was looking out the window, watching for the hunter-green Cherokee from the foyer.

Will watched her walk from the stairs to the passenger door. She was wearing an ivory beret, slacks, shoes, and an ivory swing jacket with a pleated tuxedo collar. When she got into the Jeep, she put her purse in the back seat. As she stretched to place the purse on the back seat, he saw the gold chain he had given her for her birthday. At the end of the chain was a pearl pendant with a gold lobster clasp closure with matching earrings. Will loved the way she would put so much time into looking good for him. He looked at her for a few moments and smiled. He was thinking about parking the Jeep and going up to her place for the evening.

"What?" she said naively.

Will furrowed his eyebrows a few times and tilted his head toward her place as if to say, "Do you want to go in?"

She laughed and kissed him. "There'll be time for that later."

They arrived at the theater at 12:23 AM, just prior to the start of the film. He stopped at the entrance. Terry reached in the back seat to get her purse.

"I'll get the tickets," she said, and got out of the car.

Will parked the car and stepped out into the cool night. It always amazed him how San Francisco could get so cold in May, but when he was at Harvard, in May, it could get extremely hot. When he got inside the theater, he saw Terry getting the tickets.

"Two for *A Perfect Murder*," she said.

Will walked over and said, "What time does it start?"

"12:30, darlin'."

The clerk handed her the tickets and said, "Two screens down on the left."

"Do you want to get anything from the snack bar?" Will asked.

"No thanks. If I get hungry, I'll eat something later."

She wrapped her arm around his and laid her head on his shoulder as they walked into the theater. There were only about twelve people in the theater, including them. Will was going to sit closer to the front in the center, but Terry gently grabbed his hand and led him to a seat in the back. They took their seats and watched the last preview before the film started.

Thirty minutes into the movie, Terry laid her head on Will's shoulder again. Then she rubbed his right inner thigh. Will's leg twitched from the stimulation. He wanted to enjoy the movie, but her touch was far more enjoyable.

Five minutes later, Terry moved her hand further up his thigh and caressed his crotch, which caused Will to throb. He looked at Terry and she looked at him and said, "What?" Will looked around the theater to see if anyone was looking. No one was, so he didn't say anything about it. A couple of minutes later, she was fumbling around trying to find the zipper, and when she found it, unzipped him slowly.

She unbuttoned his pants, reached inside his underwear, and stroked him. He looked at her, and again she said, "What?" He looked around the theater again to see if anyone was looking. Again, no one was. She continued to stroke him. Then without warning, she took him into her mouth. As the pleasure increased, it became more and more difficult to pay attention to the movie.

Finally, he stopped her and said, "Let's go."

He zipped his pants, grabbed her by the hand, and walked briskly toward the exit. Terry didn't object to leaving early because that was all a part of her plan. She wanted to bring him to the theater and fellate him, believing that it would be exciting for both of them. If he had not led the way, she would have.

When they reached the exit, Will said, "Hey, I gotta go to the restroom."

He gave her the keys and reminded her to lock the doors. The Jeep was just outside the exit door, so he was able to watch her until she was safe.

Just as Will turned to go to the restroom, a San Francisco Police cruiser went by.

The two officers were watching Terry get into the Jeep, too, but for different reasons. One of the officers said, "Goddamn, would ya look at that?"

The other officer excitedly said, "That's what they call a rich man's woman."

They turned the cruiser around and went back for a second look and about that time, Will had come out of the theater. As he walked to the Jeep, one officer said, "I know she's not with that nigger."

When Will got into the Jeep, the same officer said, "Goddammit. Why the fuck is she with him? She's too fuckin' beautiful to be with some coon."

Will said, "I need to go over to that grocery store across the street."

He started the Jeep, and headed toward the grocery store. The police cruiser followed them at a distance, but Will and Terry were oblivious to it. Will parked in the space nearest to the door and got out of the Jeep. One of the police officers followed him to the pharmacy section, where Will looked, but he didn't see any condoms.

He went over to a cashier who didn't have anyone in her line. "Excuse me, Miss. Can you tell me where the prophylactics are?"

Frowning, the cashier said, "What?"

By this time, the line was starting to fill. Will thought she didn't hear him, so he repeated the question.

The cashier said, "Just a second."

She picked up the phone, punched two numbers and said, "Stan, what aisle are the condoms in?"

A teenager came over and said, "Who wanted to know about the rubbers?"

Everybody was staring at Will. He felt about two inches tall. Nevertheless, he maintained his cool. "I am."

"Come with me," the young man said.

Will followed.

"What kind do you want?" he asked. "I recommend Durex, because they're more sensitive than most of the others."

Will smiled. "Thanks for the suggestion."

"You're welcome."

Will followed the young man to the pharmacy area. "Just ask the pharmacist for the kind you want," the young man said and he left.

The police officer heard the announcement and went back to the cruiser. "The nigger's in there buyin' rubbers."

His partner said, "That's one pretty piece of ass he won't be gettin' tonight. Let's pull their asses over."

"You sure you want to do it, with that shit in the back seat?"

"Why not? It's just a nigger and a woman."

"Why don't we just get their license number and catch them another time? I don't feel right about this one."

"They won't give us a problem. Trust me."

Will got into the car, still a little embarrassed.

"What happened?" Terry asked.

As he backed out of the parking space, he told her what happened. She tried not to laugh, but she couldn't help it. Her laughter finally erupted. The more she tried to stop laughing, the harder she laughed. Between breaths and laughter, she kept saying, "I'm sorry. I'm sorry." Then she'd stop laughing for a second or two and laughed again, saying, "I'm sorry. I'm sorry."

Will listened to her laugh hysterically for a about minute, then he laughed also. He glanced in his rear view. "Oh shit!" His voice was a mixture of fear and dread.

"What's the matter?" Terry asked, still trying to contain her laughter. She looked at Will and saw the concern on his face. Will was still looking in the mirror. She stopped laughing and turned around to see what he was looking at. She saw the police cruiser and said, "It's only the police. Relax."

"Relax! Are you kiddin'?!" he shouted.

"Will, calm down. You don't have to bite my head off."

Will looked at her and said, "Those are the same police officers I saw in the parking lot when we left the theater. One of 'em was in the store."

"Don't you think you're being a little paranoid? It's their job to patrol parking lots. And I don't know but, maybe, just maybe, they needed something from the grocery store."

"Maybe you're right," he lied. As far as he was concerned, they were being followed. He knew it was pointless to continue telling her how he really felt. She was white and probably never experienced unprovoked harassment.

"So, where we goin'?" Terry asked in a sexy tone. "Your place or mine?"

"Huh? Oh, uh, where do you want to go," he said, trying to hide his concern.

"What are you thinking about?"

"What do you mean?"

"I don't know. You seem distant."

Will was trying to figure out what the police were going to do next. They had been following them for ten minutes. *I know that's enough time to run my plates.*

"Well?"

"Well what?" he said, and picked up the phone.

"What are you thinking about?"

"I'm thinking about calling Sterling and telling him a police cruiser has been following me for over ten minutes now," he said sternly.

Terry turned around to see for herself. Just as her head turned, bright red and blue lights flashed.

"Hello," Sterling said, groggily.

"Sterling, it's me, Will," he said frantically.

"What's the matter, man?" Sterling said, realizing this wasn't a social call.

"'Hey, man, a couple of cops have been following me for the last ten minutes, or so. They're signaling me to pull over and I've got Terry with me."

"Oh shit! You think they know she's in the car?"

"Yeah, man. They were at the theater and the store I went to. They had to see her."

"Where are you?"

"I'm on 101 headin' home."

"How's the traffic? Are there any other cars?"

"No. We're all alone out here."

"Pull over, be courteous, and don't do anything to provoke 'em. I'm on my way."

"Hurry up, man! It just don't feel right, ya know?"

"I'm there, bro. It'll take about twenty minutes. I'm bringin' my camcorder."

"Okay, bye."

"Bye," Sterling said.

Will pulled over and looked at Terry. "Be courteous, no matter what. Can you do that, babe?"

"Yes," she said, taking the matter much more seriously.

He saw both officers get out of the cruiser. One was coming on his side of the Jeep, and one on Terry's side. "When they say, 'License and registration,' slowly reach into the glove compartment and hand the vehicle registration to me. Okay?" he said, trying to be confident.

"Why don't I just get it now?"

"Because it could be interpreted as a hostile action. We want them to be cool. So we have to be cool. Understand?"

She nodded her head.

While he was still looking at Terry, he heard the rapid tapping of a flashlight on his window. Tap, tap, tap, tap, tap. Will took a deep breath, and then turned to the officer. He forced himself to smile and retracted his window. The window's motor hummed as it slid down. He could see the officer's name was Leslie.

"License and registration."

Terry reached into the glove compartment, grabbed the registration, and handed it to Will. He took the registration from her and gave it to Officer Leslie. Then he slowly reached into his jacket and pulled out his wallet. He opened it up and showed him the license.

"Sir, please remove the license from the wallet."

Will complied.

"Thank you, sir."

First he flashed the light on the license, then in Will's face and then on Terry.

"I need your identification, too, ma'am."

When Terry reached in the backseat to get her purse, Officer Leslie drew his .9mm and yelled, "FREEZE, BITCH!"

Terry stopped what she was doing, turned around, and looked at the officer on her side of the Jeep. "What's goin' on!? What did we do!?" she said, rattled by what was happening.

"OUTTA THE FUCKIN' CAR! NOW!" Leslie shouted.

Will got out of the Jeep. He raised his hands and shouted, "I'M NOT RESISTING! I'M NOT RESISTING!"

"You too, bitch," the other officer said, striking the palm of his hand with his nightstick. As Terry got out of the Jeep, she could see that his name was Sykes.

"Turn around, nigger, and assume the position," Leslie said.

When Will turned around, Leslie put his nine back in its holster, and pulled out his nightstick. Gripping the nightstick with both hands, Leslie hit Will in the back of his right leg. Will screamed as he fell against the hood of the Jeep in excruciating pain.

Leslie shouted, "Boy, you must think you can fuck a white woman whenever you feel like it! Ain't that right?"

Will didn't answer him. Leslie hit him again. Will screamed and fell back onto the hood again.

"Answer me when I'm talkin' to you, boy."

Officer Sykes dragged Terry to the cruiser. He put the nightstick on the hood and ripped her blouse.

Will heard Terry screaming, "Don't touch me!" in the distance. He was still lying on the hood and felt the heat of the engine; his leg was throbbing from the blows he received. He turned his head around to see what was happening to her. He looked through the glass of the Jeep and saw her ripped blouse.

"That's right, look," Leslie told him. "When he's done, I'm next. And you, you get to watch it all before you go to the emergency room—if you live."

"You fuckin' that nigger?" Officer Sykes shouted.

"None of your fuckin' business!" Terry shouted back.

He slapped Terry with the back of his hand and she fell against the cruiser. Then she screamed maniacally and charged the officer ferociously. Her sudden offensive stunned Sykes momentarily, just as Jericho said it would, and gave her the opportunity to kick him in the balls. He didn't expect her to put up any fight. He thought the most she'd do was scream. This wasn't the first time he and Leslie had done this. Women gave them little, if any, trouble. When he doubled over, she kicked him again.

Officer Leslie heard his partner grunt and when he turned to see what was happening, Will found the strength to punch him flush in the nose, breaking it. He put his weight behind the punch the way his father had taught him. Leslie's blood poured down his face to his neck, and finally to his shirt. Leslie dropped the nightstick immediately as he crumbled to the ground.

Will picked up the nightstick and beat him with it. He could hear Terry in the distance shouting, "I'll kill you! I'll kill you!" When Officer Sykes doubled over, Terry grabbed his nightstick and pummeled him. Will stopped beating Leslie and turned him over on his stomach and handcuffed his hands behind his back. Then he pulled his Baretta from its holster and limped over to help Terry, who had already subdued Sykes, beating him mercilessly with his own nightstick.

She hit him in the head, in the arms and legs, and anything that he moved. She was swinging like a crazed maniac. The officer was screaming, "No more! No more!" over and over, trying to cover any exposed area. Terry was out of control. She kept swinging and screaming, "I'll kill you! I'll kill you!" By the time Will got over there, the officer had passed out; blood oozed out the back of his head. From the way his body was contorted, he could tell his right arm was broken in several places.

Will grabbed Terry and held her, saying, "It's okay. It's okay."

When she felt Will's embrace, her senses returned to her. "Is he dead?" she kept asking.

"I don't know. You okay?" he whispered.

"I am now."

Will was about to let Terry go and cuff the other officer, when he saw Sterling's black Jaguar pull up. He got out of the car and looked at the pummeled officers. Then he said, "Y'all some bad muthafuckas. Here I come to save y'all's asses, and y'all done whupped they asses." Then he laughed and said, "I'll get the camcorder."

Chapter 56: Damage Control

S terling called Amy Ling before he left his house and asked her to bring a camera crew to the scene. He wanted to broadcast the incident on the six o'clock news in the morning. That way, the district attorney would be scrambling to do damage control. As he got the camcorder out of the car, he thought it would be a good idea to call the local chapter of the NAACP to the scene, too. He knew Reverend Persons would eat this up. Persons loved to expose this sort of thing. Finally, Sterling called an ambulance. He tried to make it sound as though their injuries weren't bad, hoping they would take their time.

Sterling came back with the camcorder and told Will he had made a number of calls to the right people and to let him handle the situation. Will agreed and took Terry to the Jeep. He was still limping.

Terry was still shaken by the events, but much more composed now. She wondered what Will's mother was going to say, now that her fears had come true. The thought of having to face Brenda bothered her more than anything. She remembered her words. *"Frankly, Terry, I'm very worried."*

"How could this happen, Will?"

Will didn't answer.

"Why did this have to happen, right when your mother was starting to accept me?" She seemed to be thinking out loud.

Again, Will didn't say anything.

"Will, please say something. You don't think it was my fault, do you?"

"No, it wasn't your fault, babe. They're the ones with the problem, not you. Try and remember that, okay?"

"What are we going to tell your mother?"

"The truth. What else?"

As Sterling filmed the scene, he happened to look in the back seat of the squad car. There were two large black garbage bags sitting on the back seat. He thought it was peculiar so he opened the door, grabbed a bag, and looked inside. He saw brick-sized packages of aluminum foil. He opened the other bag, which was full of money in small denominations. *The cops robbed a drug dealer*, Sterling thought. Otherwise, where are the perpetrators? Why would ordinary police officers be entrusted with this kind of evidence? Wouldn't the Drug Enforcement Agency or someone else have handled this? He knew evidence could disappear in a police station so he began filming again.

Moments later, Amy Ling and the camera crew arrived. Sterling filled her in on all the details of the assault. Her crew filmed the scene as she wrote her script. She wanted to interview Will and Terry, but they declined. Reverend Persons, the police, and the ambulance all arrived at about the same time. After being informed of the situation, Reverend Persons talked to Will and Terry. Amy asked him if she could interview him on camera. He agreed.

Chapter 57: Mercy

Brenda Wise was in the kitchen making breakfast like she had done for almost fifty years, humming her favorite spiritual as she stirred grits into the boiling water. Benjamin loved eating breakfast with her and they always ate together before they went to work. Their meals together were the one constant in their marriage during his time as a boxer, and ladies' man. At breakfast they shared their thoughts and feelings. Brenda often spoke of how she would either buy or sell one of her houses. But lately, she fussed about not having any grandchildren.

Benjamin walked into the kitchen. "Hello, you vivacious beauty from the motherland." He was standing right behind her now. He placed both hands on her breasts and squeezed. Brenda laughed. "I love you, girl."

"I love you, too, Benny."

Benjamin inhaled deeply, smelling the butter in the grits, the homemade biscuits, the French toast, and the bacon all at once. "You sho' do make a mean breakfast, woman."

"Let me go and set the table before you get yourself all worked up. You know how you hate to be late to your spot at the airport."

"Maybe just a quickie then."

"Maybe. Let's see how you feel after you eat, okay?"

"Okay."

Benjamin opened the cabinet and took out the plates, the bowls, and the cups. Then he opened the drawer and took the silverware out and set everything on the kitchen table while Brenda poured the eggs she'd beaten into the skillet.

"You want a cup of coffee, Brenda?"

"Umm-hmm. Everything will be ready in another minute or two."

"Okay. You goin' to Oakland today?"

"I had planned on it. But since you feelin' frisky, I might just cancel."

"You want to?"

"Yeah, if you do."

"Okay, good," he said. "Let's eat first though. Then we can get to it."

"You sure you can handle what I'm going to put on you, Benny?"

"No, but I'm sure as hell gon' try."

They both laughed.

Brenda brought the skillet over to the table and put the eggs on their plates. Steam rose as Benjamin poured the grits into the bowls. Brenda watched him salivate prior to digging in. He was very meticulous about his food, and had to be situated just right before he could begin eating. Benjamin was about to put some eggs into his mouth when he heard Brenda clear her throat to get his attention. It was time to give thanks to the Lord. They bowed their heads and said grace. The phone rang.

"Hello," Brenda said.

"Are you watchin' the news?" Aunt Johnnie asked.

"Naw. We're eating."

"Well, Reverend Persons is on. And I saw Sterling getting into his car and pull off. I thought I saw Willy's Jeep, too. But I'm not sure."

"What?" Brenda said with concern in her voice and switched on the nine-inch portable television that sat on the counter.

"What's goin' on, Brenda?" Benjamin asked.

Brenda fanned him in such a way that he knew to be quiet and watch the television.

"What are they talkin' about?" Brenda asked Johnnie.

"I don't know; it just started. Somethin' about an incident with the police."

"And you saw Sterling and Willy's car?"

"Umm-hmm. What you bet Ms. Thang is in this somewhere?"

The two women quieted themselves and began watching the telecast. Reverend Persons was speaking.

"That's right, Amy," Persons said. "I received a call from Attorney Wise at about two o'clock, or so. He told me his brother might be in trouble with the police and that I should get down here as soon as possible. All I can say is that I'm glad he thought enough to call the media to the scene. Otherwise, we probably wouldn't know what happened here."

"Well, let's be fair, Reverend," Amy said. "We still don't know exactly what happened."

"No, Amy, I don't know what happened. However, when two police officers, who are not a part of the Drug Enforcement Agency's Task Force, are found with what looks to me like several kilos of cocaine and large quantities of money in small bills, it doesn't take a genius to figure out what's going on."

"Reverend Persons, are you saying the San Francisco Police Department is corrupt?"

"No. Not at all. However, I'm saying these two officers are. I'm further saying that if you and your camera crew hadn't been here, somehow or another, the victims of this abominable crime would probably be charged with resisting arrest, and assaulting police officers. Let's set the record straight right now, Amy. A man and a woman were assaulted by criminals posing as police officers. Were it not for their personal resolve and initiative, only the Lord knows what would have happened."

"Why do you suppose the police chose to pull them over, knowing they had drugs and money in the back seat of the squad car?"

"Isn't it obvious? She's white, and he's black. This kind of thing shows you that we haven't even approached Dr. King's dream. What's frightening is that this happened in San Francisco."

Amy frowned. "What do you mean by that?"

"I mean, we live in a city that prides itself in making the unnatural natural. In other words, it's natural for two women, or two men to be together. But it still isn't natural for a white woman to be with a black man. The evidence is right before you in living color, along with the drugs and the drug money. It'll be interesting to see if this incident will be enough to wake up a comatose America—an America that sleeps while its citizens are attacked by men who are sworn to protect and serve them. Any time a prominent black doctor can't date a white doctor without being assaulted by the police, of all people, in a city like this, it shows you where we are in terms of race relations."

"Thank you, Reverend Persons," Amy said, turning back to the camera. "While you may disagree with Reverend Persons' religious ideology, one thing's for sure. Two people say they were attacked tonight by peace officers. We can only speculate as to their reasons for doing so. But the question that comes to my mind is this. What were they doing with the drugs? And where did they get the money? This is Amy Ling for WTSF News."

"Did you hear that shit?" Aunt Johnnie asked Brenda. "If this doesn't wake Willy's ass up, nothing will."

The phone beeped in Brenda's ear.

"Hold on for a second, Johnnie," Brenda said. "Hello."

"Mama, Will and Terry had some trouble early this morning," Sterling said. "You and Daddy should come down to General Hospital."

"Yeah, we just saw it on the news. We'll be right there." She switched back to Johnnie. "Let me talk to you later," Brenda said, in a subdued tone and hung up the phone. "Let's go, Benny."

✝✝✝

Brenda was furious when they walked into the hospital. She knew this would happen. As far as she was concerned, this was all Terry's fault and she would let her know how she felt. This time she wouldn't be as nice about it. This time she would give it to her with both barrels.

They stopped at the receptionist station. "What room is William Wise in?" Brenda asked.

The receptionist hit a few buttons on her computer keyboard. "He's in the ER. His injuries were not that serious. He'll be released shortly."

As they approached the emergency room, they saw what looked like a battalion of angry police officers standing around like they were waiting

490

for something or someone. Brenda hoped it wasn't her Willy. Her anger was swallowed by concern.

Will was lying on the bed while a nurse wrapped his leg. Terry was sitting on the bed beside him, holding his hand. There was a bruise on the right side of Terry's face. Sterling was talking to police detectives. No one noticed when Brenda and Benjamin entered the room.

Then Terry slowly turned her head toward them as though she sensed Brenda's presence. When she saw Brenda standing there with a look on her face that could only be described as outrage, she bowed her head.

When Brenda saw Terry's eyes, she saw a different woman. At that pivotal moment, Brenda realized that Terry now understood what she was trying to tell her. Instead of making matters worse, Brenda asked her if she was okay.

A couple of police officers walked in and whispered something to the detectives Sterling was talking to. Then one of them came over and said, "Terry Moretti, you're under arrest for the murder of Peter Sykes. You have the right to remain silent..."

†††

Having survived the humiliation of the cavity search, Terry lay on her cot in the city jail, desperately trying to go to sleep, hoping the nightmare would be over when she awoke. But she couldn't sleep. The events of the previous night kept resurfacing in her mind. She kept seeing herself beating Sykes, even though he'd begged her to stop. She vomited several times. The thought of killing another human being was totally unacceptable. She tried telling herself it was self-defense, but deep down she didn't believe it was.

Then she remembered what Jericho had told her the night they went to the Perfect Indulgence Club. *You could kill someone if you lose control.* Like flashes of light, everything that happened since the Toronto trip came to mind in uncontrolled images. One second she'd be talking to Will in his suite. The next, she'd be having an argument with Ivy.

She tried to stop the images, but couldn't. Her mind just kept going from one event to the next. She wondered what Sykes' wife and children must be going through right now. Powerless and frustrated that she couldn't go back and stop the beating, she cried and fell asleep.

"Moretti!" the guard yelled. "Your attorney's here."

Terry opened one eye to see if it was all a dream. When she saw the bars and the uniformed guard, she knew it had really happened. She had no idea how long she'd been asleep or how long she'd been in jail, but she was glad to be leaving the cell, if only for a little while.

"How long have I been in here?" Terry asked the guard.

"Three hours."

"Three hours? Is that all?"

"That's all."

It felt more like three days.

The guard brought Terry out of the holding area of the jail. She was wearing an orange jumpsuit, much like the one James had worn. She was so glad to see Will and Sterling that she practically ran to them. Will hugged her, holding her tight.

"You all right?" Will asked.

"Now that you're here, I am."

Sterling thought about Vanessa. His mind went back to the last day he saw her, the day she left him forever. When he looked at Will and Terry, it made him want that kind of relationship again. He tried to put it behind him, but couldn't. Sometimes when he walked through the mall, he would smell her perfume, and look around for her, but it would always be someone else. As long as she was alive, Sterling knew he'd never marry.

Sterling cleared his throat. "Excuse me, you two, but we've got some decisions to make."

They reluctantly released each other and sat down at the table.

Sterling sat down in a chair across from them. "After reviewing the tape that Amy recorded last night, the District Attorney's office decided to drop the charges. It turns out that these police officers are a part of some whacked-out racist priesthood or some shit like that. They've got swastikas tattooed on their arms. That goddamned Leslie has 'I hate niggers' tattooed on his chest. I talked to Le'sett an hour ago and you're free to go."

"Well, what are we waiting for? Let's get out of here," Terry said.

Sterling looked at Will. "Are you sure you want to pursue this?"

"You damn right, I am."

"Pursue what?" Terry asked.

"Will wants to sue the police department for what happened last night, Terry. And he's well within his rights to do so. But if we do this, we need to be absolutely sure. Le'sett has assured me that if we bring a lawsuit, you will be recharged with murder and they intend to prosecute you to the fullest extent of the law."

"It was self-defense, Sterling," Terry said.

"I know that, but the state will attempt to prove you went well beyond defending yourself. They'll call Will to the stand as a witness against you. They've already got Leslie's sworn affidavit stating that he heard Sykes begging you to stop the beating. He says you continued hitting him without mercy. Do you understand what I'm saying here?"

Terry was quiet.

"But you can win the case, right?" Will asked.

"Yes, I can, and they know it. But the catch is you're going to get a lot of bad publicity at the clinics. And who knows, Jerry will probably come into this. Hell, they may try and make it sound like you were doing a pick-up for him."

"THAT'S LUDICROUS!" Will shouted.

"Calm down, Will," Sterling urged. "Let's think about this."

"WHAT IS THERE TO THINK ABOUT?" Will shouted.

"Will, I know you're pissed, but you're going to have to calm down so cooler heads can prevail. They know its bullshit, but the last thing they want is bad publicity for the city. Their strategy is to give your business bad publicity, too. All they have to do is go on camera and say you were suspected of drug dealing and it could cost you your business. You know how people are. They won't even consider your innocence.

"The media will play the shit up big just to sell some newspapers, just like they did the Richard Jewell case in Atlanta during the Olympics. Can't you see the headlines? DRUG COUNSELOR SELLS DRUGS TO PATIENTS. They'll dig up everything in your life and put it on public display. And you know they'll drag James into it, too, just to spice it up more. All of this will be bad for business. They could track Ivy down and, knowing her, she might say sexual harassment was going on at the clinic. The clients at the rehabilitation clinic will start to wonder. Many of them will leave and spread the stories further. What if they look into how you got your loans to begin with, Will? What if some clerk at the bank gives the media your financial documents? You see where I'm going with this? If it were me prosecuting this case, you'd get off, Terry, but it would cost you your business, Will."

"I say we cut our losses and get the hell outta here," Terry said.

"Hell no." Will frowned. "We go to court. How the fuck are they going to pull me over and beat me like some kind of animal, and expect me to let it go? And for what? Because my girlfriend's white? FUCK THAT! I say we fight this shit. I say we sue all them muthafuckas. And if the papers want to try that shit, I say we sue their asses, too. I'm sick of this shit, Sterling. If I want to see her, then goddammit, I'll see her. You tell them we'll sec their asses in court."

"I can't take this anymore, Will!" Terry said, almost yelling.

"What? What are you saying?"

"I'm saying it isn't worth it, Will. It isn't worth having our lives intruded upon. It's bad enough I'm made to feel guilty because I'm white. Now, I have to have my life inspected by sheepish sycophants who will stop at nothing to find out any and everything about me. What if they go back to New Haven and bother my family, Will? My parents don't need that. And are you really willing to take the chance of losing a business you worked so hard to build? Is your pride worth that? IS IT?"

"Listen to her, Will," Sterling said. "I know how you feel, bro. If you were some nobody, it would be a lot easier. But since you have a business, and you're an outstanding citizen, that makes it big news. Do you understand what I'm saying here?"

"What's the alternative?" Will said, still frustrated.

"The alternative is, we sign the papers not to sue and they'll see to it that Leslie goes to jail for a long, long time," Sterling said. "After all, the entire police department didn't do this. Let's allow justice to prevail here. I know it hurts, but there'll be another day."

Will look at Terry. "You sure about this, babe?"

Terry nodded. "I just want this to be over."

Reluctantly, Will said, "Where are the papers?"

Chapter 58:
Trapped?

San Francisco
August 1998

Two months later Officer Leslie cut a deal with the District Attorney's office. He turned states' evidence and signed an agreement to testify against the people he was doing business with. In return, he was sentenced to two years jail time with the possibility of parole after serving nine months.

Terry stood at the window of Will's bedroom, wearing cotton pajamas underneath her robe. The room was chilly. She was looking out at the gathering fog under the Golden Gate Bridge, thinking about Will's family reunion and how she really didn't want to go. She would much rather go to Toronto with the new staff, but she knew Will expected her to go to the reunion with him.

Terry became distant and intolerant of people. She lost the desire to go out in public with Will because she always felt as if people were staring at them. To her, it seemed as though every place they went, they were the center of attention. She was paranoid and it bothered her tremendously; especially since she accused Will of it a number of times. She remembered how he'd get mad at her for even bringing it up. Now she understood. When Will asked why she didn't want to go out, she would say she wasn't ready yet.

She still loved him, but it just wasn't the same. She wished she could put the images out of her mind and go on, but she couldn't. *Is this how it's going to be? Am I going to be paranoid from now on?* When she learned of

Officer Leslie's sentence, she wondered if their relationship was worth Will being beaten, her being molested and possibly raped, and a man's life.

Her temper was getting more and more out of control. She found herself snapping at everyone, except Will. He was her only refuge, her place of peace and security. But he was also the cause of much of the scrutiny she felt intruding into their lives. She didn't blame him, but she couldn't help thinking that if he wasn't black, or if she wasn't white, they wouldn't have this problem, and Officer Sykes would be alive.

Will wasn't making things any better for the couple. Since the incident, he wanted to go out more and more. He didn't like the idea of people telling him who he could date and who he couldn't. He was talking about marriage more and more and Terry found herself constantly changing the subject. She laughed a little when she thought about this, and remembered telling him he shouldn't let people control him. Now she was developing the same attitude he once had.

"What's the matter, babe?" Will asked.

"Nothing."

"Why are you staring off into space then?"

"I was just thinking about the family reunion today."

"You're still thinking about Sykes, huh?"

"Yeah," she said. She had grown used to him knowing her thoughts before she expressed them.

He could tell she still had some residual regret, but as far as Will was concerned, Sykes got what he deserved. "I don't mean to be insensitive, but that probably wasn't their first time pulling someone over. I bet they did it all the time, and had gotten away with it until we stopped them. Isn't that what they assume about first-time criminals? Don't they assume they've committed the crime before since this is the first time they got caught?"

"But, Will, it's different for me. I've never had to deal with this sort of thing before. I've been so naive. All this time you've been trying to tell me what it's like, and I just couldn't understand it. As a matter of fact, I didn't believe it was happening to us until he slapped me and I fell up against the squad car."

"Well, you can feel sorry for him if you want to. But I don't. I'm not the least bit sorry for him. It's too bad for his family, but who made him pull us over? Who made him fondle you? Who made him pimp slap you like some whore? Do you know what Leslie said while you were being attacked? He told me to watch because he was going to be next. And I'm supposed to feel sorry for these guys? I could care less. If their families are homeless, that's just too damn bad.

"They're lucky I didn't sue everybody involved in this shit. And I'll tell you something else. I'll bet other officers knew what they were doing to people, too. I'll bet they did and not one of 'em lifted a finger to help any of the victims. I want you to think about something, Terry. What if you hadn't fought back? What if you hadn't distracted Leslie long enough for me to surprise him? He told me I was to watch what happened to you before I went to the hospital. And what about all the drugs? What about all that money? These were bad cops, and bad men, period. I say fuck 'em, because one, or both of us could be in our graves once they had their fun. You think about that while you're feeling sorry for 'em."

"Will, I know, but it still bothers me that people would do something like this."

"Welcome to the real world."

†††

Will and Terry arrived at his parents' house at two o'clock. They were carrying the watermelons they picked up at the grocery store. Benjamin was working the grill and Jericho was helping him. Pin was right next to her husband, as usual. Sterling was behind the microphone, playing CDs. Brenda was involved in a game of Monopoly with Aunt Johnnie, Cleve, and Cheryl. From the looks of things, Brenda was winning. There were children everywhere, playing everything from jacks to volleyball.

Will and Terry approached the table where his mother was. Both of them had angry looks on their faces, and everyone noticed.

"Where you want these?" Will asked his mother.

Cleve asked, "Well, if it ain't Batman and Batgirl. Or do you prefer Catwoman?"

"I think I prefer you shut up!" Terry snapped.

Cleve laughed. "Okay, killer."

"Put 'em on one of the tables," Brenda told Will.

"Cleve, we have some more in the Jeep," Will said. "Help me out?"

"Okay, bro. Why don't you take my place, Terry?"

"Okay," she said. She didn't want to, but she didn't want to be too dis-agreeable. "Which one are you?"

"I'm the boot. You should appreciate the irony of that since you like to kick ass."

Will and Cleve went to get the rest of the watermelons, and the women continued the game. They looked at Terry, wondering what was wrong. *What were she and Will arguing about?* They continued playing the game in silence for a while. Then Jordan came over to the table and looked at Terry. He wanted to climb in her lap, but even he saw she was fuming about something.

"Cousin Terry," Jordan began. "What's the matter? Why you so mad?"

Everybody looked at her as if to say, "Yeah, what's the matter?"

Terry looked into his brown eyes and melted. The rage she felt seemed to drain out of her like air out of a balloon. She smiled at him and he smiled at her.

"Can I sit on yo' lap?" Jordan asked.

"Sure," she said, and picked him up.

Will and Cleve came back with the watermelons. "Did she tell y'all what happened at the grocery store?" Cleve grinned.

They all said, "No," and looked at Terry as if to say, "What happened at the grocery store?" But no one asked. Will and Cleve went to get the last two watermelons.

"Cousin Terry," Jordan said. "What happened at the grocery store?"

Everybody looked at Terry again. She could tell they all wanted to know, even Aunt Johnnie.

"There was a bad woman at the store, honey," Terry told him.

"What you mean, a bad woman?"

"I mean there was a racist woman there."

Now the women understood, but they still wanted to know what happened.

"What do racist mean?"

"Well, honey, it's complicated. It basically means to dislike someone because of their color." She put her arm against his arm so he could see the contrasting colors. "See, your skin is darker than mine. Some people don't like people because of their color, and for no other reason. The woman in the grocery store was like that, and it angered me, okay?"

"Ohhhhhh," Jordan said like the light had suddenly come on. "Grandmama Johnnie and Aunt Brenda is a racist, too, then."

Terry wanted to say, "Yeah, that's right," but didn't. She just looked at them and they got the point. Cheryl was laughing under her breath.

"Jordan, go play with the other kids," Aunt Johnnie told him.

Jordan jumped off Terry's knee and ran over to the other kids. Will and Cleve came back with the last of the watermelons.

"Did she tell y'all what happened yet?" Cleve asked.

"Here, Cleve, you can have your spot back." Terry frowned, and left the table.

†††

Karen came out of the house with the homemade barbecue sauce that Benjamin made. Terry watched her take the sauce over to the grill. As Karen walked back to the table, Terry met her about halfway and said, "Can I talk to you?"

"Yeah, what's up?"

"Is there someplace we can talk?"

"Yeah, let's go in the house."

Terry heard Cleve enthusiastically telling the women about the grocery store incident as she walked past the Monopoly table. Will, who was now talking to his dad and Jericho, obviously told him all about it. The women went into the dining room and sat down at the table.

"So what's up?" Karen repeated.

Terry was quiet for a minute or so, and then she started crying. Karen hugged her and waited for the words to come. "I think I'm losing my mind. Everywhere we go people seem to be staring at us, watching our every move, like we're celebrities or something. Then when I look at them, they turn away as though they weren't staring. I think I'm paranoid." Karen resisted the urge to jump in there and explain what was going on. "Like today, Will and I were asked to pick up the watermelons, right?"

Karen nodded.

"I was looking over the watermelons, and Will was looking at some grapes or something. Two white women were looking over watermelons, too. One says to the other, 'I think they got that backwards. He should be looking over the watermelons, and she should be looking over the grapes.' Then they laughed. And, Karen, I can't even begin to describe the rage I felt. I mean, I felt a surge of fiery energy like I've never felt before. Without even thinking about it, I walked over to her and slapped her face."

Karen wanted to laugh, but held it in.

"Then she said she didn't mean it the way it sounded, and that made me even angrier. So I slapped her again for lying about it."

Karen was smiling now, but Terry didn't notice because her head was tilted toward the floor.

"Then what happened?" Karen asked, still fighting her laughter.

"She said, 'I'm sorry,' and wanted to shake my hand."

Laughing now, Karen said, "Did you shake her hand?"

"Hell no. I felt like slapping her again, but she walked away."

Karen couldn't resist the urge to say, "I guess she got tired of being slapped." Then she laughed hysterically.

"You think this is funny, Karen?" She was looking at her now.

"Hell yeah. The bitch got what she deserved."

"Don't you think I was being irrational?"

"Yeah, but sometimes, being irrational is the best course of action that brings real satisfaction. She knew she was wrong before she opened her mouth. What possible reason could she have for sayin' some shit like that?

No reason. No reason at all. She thought she could make her friend laugh at your expense without any repercussions. That's what she gets, as far as I'm concerned. I bet she won't do that shit again. Frankly, I think we ought to just start a slappin' line for people like that. We can start with my mother. But I doubt you'll have any more trouble outta her."

"Why is that?"

"Ever since she found out you beat that cop to death she hasn't had much to say about you and Will. She probably thinks you'll kick her ass, too."

"Oh, so that's why she was so subdued at the table, huh?"

"Yep. Look, Terry, I know what you're goin' through. Do you want me to explain it to you?"

"Would you, please?" Terry asked, almost beseeching her.

"Well, first, ya gotta understand that people are more than likely watching you and Will. They can't help it. It's still taboo. I don't care what people say, when they see it, their eyes are drawn to it. And that's on both sides of the fence. Second, you're developing what we black people call the sixth sense."

Terry frowned. "What?"

"The sixth sense for us is when we know, without proof, that white people are doing something racist—some of the time they aren't even aware of it. But you see it in their eyes, in their facial expressions, in their body language, and something inside you lets you know what's happening."

"Oh, I remember Will telling me something about that some time ago. But it sounds like paranoia to me, Karen."

"It generally does to white people. If you talk to the average white person, male, or female, who's dated or married someone black, I bet they'll agree with what I'm saying. Right now, you're in the beginning stages of it. It may take a while for you to fully understand and sense it the way we do. Black people have had to deal with it all our lives, and over a period of years, it becomes second nature to us. You stay with Will long enough, and you'll see what I'm talking about."

"But, Karen, I don't want to develop a paranoid sixth sense. I don't want to live my life wondering who's saying what about me. I don't want to sense those sorts of things about people. I just want to live my life the way I've always lived it."

"You mean carefree?"

"Pretty much, yes."

"Well, those days are over, Terry. You no longer have that option. Look, Will has to deal with people thinking he's with you because you're white. You think he likes that? I know it pisses him off, but he puts up with it because he loves you. Now, what are you willing to put up with for him? Are you willing to put up with racist people who think they aren't racist? Because if you aren't, you should leave Will alone. He's committed to you. Are you committed to him?"

"Yes, but I never thought this sort of thing could happen to me, Karen."

"Time to grow up. This is how things are. If you're going to do this with Will, you better know it could cost you your life at some point. Isn't that obvious? I know it sounds ridiculous to say these days, but this sort of thing still happens, as quiet as it's kept. Is Will worth all of this? That's the question you have to answer, Terry."

"Honestly, Karen, I don't know. I love him. I mean, I really love him, but this is a little too much for me. Do you understand what I'm saying? A man is dead because of our relationship." She paused for a moment of reflection. "I remember talking to Will's mom in the kitchen back on Thanksgiving. She told me how concerned she was about Will's safety because of me. I thought she was being paranoid, but now it seems so prophetic."

"Yeah, Aunt Brenda's like that. Didn't she also say that you were the one for Will before she knew you were white?"

"Yes, but—"

"Then go with that. This is obvious, but life isn't always a bed of roses. You can't run and hide from trouble, Terry."

"Yeah, you're right, but I haven't felt unsure of myself since junior high school. Right now, I feel like the same person I was back then, ya know? I mean, I had no confidence for a long time. And now that's been taken from me."

"You'll get it back. It'll just take some time. You've been through a lot this last year. Ya gotta work through this thing, okay?"

"Okay."

"You feel better now?"

"Yes, but it's still hard to deal with killing a man, even though he may have killed me, ya know?"

"Yeah, I guess it is. You gon' be all right?"

"Yeah, in time."

"You ready to go back to the party?"

"Yeah. Let's go. And thanks for listening."

"You're welcome."

The two women left the dining room and went back outside with the rest of the family. Jeannine and Jonathan had arrived. Jeannine was showing everyone her engagement ring. Cleve, Cheryl, and Will were playing three-man spades. Terry and Karen were coming through the doorway when Cleve spotted them.

"Hey, killer!" Cleve shouted. "Why don't you and ya boy, Will, team up again for some spades so me and Cheryl can beat that ass again!"

As soon as he finished the sentence, Brenda, who was standing right behind Cleve, slapped him upside the head and said, "Boy, what did I tell you about your mouth?!"

Chapter 59: That's All You Can Talk About These Days

Sterling, as usual, was the life of the party. Ever since he got the Warren family to take the five million dollars that Adrienne Bellamy offered, he had been on a roll. He had plenty of cases and signed several pro prospects. He was still behind the microphone talking to the family members and playing requests. From time to time, he would play a blast from the past and go out and dance with someone. Occasionally, he'd dance with the women his cousins brought with them. Sometimes he would dance with two at a time. Now, he wanted to dance with Terry. He played Maze's "Southern Girl" and then grabbed the mike. "This is for you, Terry."

Terry didn't want to dance, but he kept on talking to her on the mike, and the family kept telling her to dance. Eventually, she agreed. Sterling started the song over and they danced together. Having been a stiff board all day, she finally let herself go and relaxed. While she was dancing, it occurred to her that she had lost her sense of humor, and had become solemn. She had lost a vital part of her personality and wanted it back.

The song ended and everybody applauded. She was about to go back to the table when Jericho came up to her unexpectedly. He hadn't said anything to her all day.

"Can I talk to you for a moment, Terry?" Jericho whispered in her ear.

"Sure." She wondered what he wanted to talk to her about this time.

They walked over to a nearby tree. Jericho sat down. Then he looked up at her. "Have a seat." It was more of a command than an invitation. Nevertheless, she sat down next to him. "So…how you doin'?"

"I'm doin' okay. Thanks for askin'."

"Naw, I mean, how you really doin'?"

"I've been better," she said, festively, trying to lighten the seriousness of the question. "Everybody seems to be taking this whole thing in stride."

"That's because we're used to it. You, this is your first time, but it won't be your last. You understand what I'm sayin'?"

Terry nodded.

"That's fucked up the way they let Leslie off with two years because he turned states' evidence, ain't it?"

"Real fucked up!" She frowned as the anger began to stir within.

"You know y'all was lucky as hell that night, don't you? If you hadn't done what I told you in that kind of situation, both of you would probably be dead now."

"Yeah, I know."

"I could take care of him for you. All you have to do is say the word. It's creepy muthafuckas like Leslie that'll try and blame y'all for what he and his partner did, ya know?"

"You think he might come after us?"

"Not right away, but when the smoke clears, and he realizes he doesn't have a job, a pension, a family, or a partner, he could start trippin'. On the other hand, if his wife sticks around, he might be okay. I say we close the chapter on the whole thing now while he's in prison. I know some people on the inside who would consider it an honor to kill his ass. It ain't like he don't deserve the shit. And damn, if I got caught, I'd be looking at some serious time. They would've put my ass up under the jail. He's got several kilos of uncut cocaine in a squad car, of all places, a million-two of drug money, and he walks. Ain't that some shit?"

"Ain't life grand?" she mumbled, shaking her head slowly, deliberately.

Pin came over and sat down next to Jericho. She looked at Terry and smiled. Terry smiled back.

"It's yo' call, Terry. What do you wanna do?"

"I can't believe you're asking me if I want you to kill someone."

"I don't have to kill him. I can just make sure he understands not to bother either of you again, okay?"

"No, don't touch him," she demanded. "This is difficult enough. The last thing I need to worry about is you sending him a message."

"Okay, but if you change your mind, let me know."

"Okay, but I don't think…"

Jericho furrowed his brow and Terry stopped in mid-sentence, remembering what he told her in the Perfect Indulgence Club. They both understood what was happening between them.

Terry said, "I'll let you know if I change my mind."

†††

Will drove the BMW into the garage and parked between the Mitsubishi and the Jeep he seldom drove. Terry was quiet all the way home. It made him apprehensive. He wasn't used to her being so quiet— so deflated. She always had a zest for life. Now she was a mere shell of the Terry he fell in love with. He wanted her back. He missed her pithy comments; especially when they were debating an issue. Now, no matter what he said, it was okay with her.

They got out of the BMW and entered the house. Will knew something was terribly wrong between them and it was much deeper than wanting to stay in and not be bothered by onlookers, who stared at them mindlessly. One way, or another, he decided to find out tonight. When they entered the kitchen, he opened the refrigerator and took out the Minute Maid orange juice, and poured some in a glass.

"Terry, did you see Jeannine's engagement ring?"

"Umm-hmm."

"You know they're getting married in June."

"Yeah, Jeannine told me."

"You know, I was thinkin'—"

"Will, please, not tonight, okay?"

He frowned. "You don't even know what I'm going to say."

"Yes, I do, Will. That's all you can talk about these days."

"What have I been talkin' about these days, Terry? Huh? What have I been talking about?"

"Getting married, Will. That seems to occupy your mind more than anything else. Knowing you, you were probably thinking about a double wedding, or something."

Will smiled, but tried not to.

"So you were thinking about a double wedding?"

"Yeah. What's wrong with that?"

"Will, I'm tired. Let's just go to bed, okay?"

"NO! Let's not. Now what's the problem? This is what you've wanted for years. Now you don't want to get married? Is that it?"

"Will, you know I love you, but now isn't the time, okay?"

"No, it's not okay! Now look, I know it's only been two months since the incident, but I love you and I want to do this. Do you?"

"I don't know, Will. I just don't know anymore."

Will frowned. It hurt him far more than he let her see. His stomach was flip-flopping. "What do you mean, you don't know?"

"I just don't know, Will."

"What's the problem? Is it the incident? Talk to me, Terry!"

"Yes, it's the incident," she said, almost shouting. "But it's more than that, Will. It's everything that's happened to me in the last year. Ever since we got together, it's been one thing or another. First we're hiding how we feel and everything is great between us. The moment we start telling people and going out in public, all hell breaks loose."

"I thought you said you'd thought about all of that stuff. Isn't that what you told me in Toronto? You said you weren't going to let anybody control you. Isn't that what you said?"

"Dammit, Will!" she shouted. "You don't have to rub it in! I know what the hell I said! You don't need to remind me! I feel bad enough!"

"The hell I don't. The next thing ya know, you'll be tellin' me you need to get away or some shit like that."

Terry turned away from him. She hated when he did that.

Realizing he was right, he said, "So you leavin' me, huh? I don't believe this. After all that talk, you're just as weak as I was. Now I find out it was all a sham."

Terry turned around quickly. She had a puzzled look on her face, unable to believe what she heard. "Is that what you think, Will?"

"Yeah, that's exactly what I think!"

"I suppose you think I want your money, too, then, huh?"

"Do you?"

"After all the shit I put up with since we got together, how can you possibly ask me that? I have been through a lot to be with you, Will. How much more do I have to put up with? Do I have to die before you know how much you mean to me?" She paused and stared at him for a second. "Do you even realize that this wasn't the first time my life was threatened since I've been with you? Do you?"

Will frowned. He had no idea what she was talking about. "What do you mean? Who threatened you?"

"Your brother. That's who." She waited until she was sure he knew who she was talking about. "That's right, it was Jericho. He broke into my house that night after we left the club on Thanksgiving. He told me I better not fuck you over, or he'd kill me. He also told me that it wouldn't be quick. Now, if I didn't love you as much as I say, wouldn't that be a good time to leave yo' ass? I saw what he did to the bouncer in a matter of seconds. Frankly, I think it was a demonstration for me, now that I think about it."

Will was smiling from ear to ear. "Ya know, you're picking up the language better." The comment momentarily broke the intensity of the argument.

"What?"

"You said, 'Yo ass' instead of your ass."

"I did?"

"Yep. Do you remember when you had me memorize this?" He looked deep into her eyes. 'All I know is I've wanted this moment for a long time. And now that it's finally here, I don't want to lose it. Marriage is a long way off, but I'm not opposed to it. But since we're being totally honest, let me tell you how I feel, and what I want from you, my man of choice. I want your heart in the palm of my hand. I want all that you are. I want you to give it to me unreservedly and without regret or remorse. I want you to lose yourself in my love, and not have a second thought about it. I want you to free yourself of all the burdens that afflict you and embrace my love and be forever freed from doubt.' Do you remember saying those words to me, Terry?"

"You know I do, Will." She wanted him now. "Thank you for remembering them."

"If I could only explain how I felt when I heard you speak to me from your heart that way. It really moved me."

"Really, I couldn't tell," she said, calmly. "You're always so nonchalant."

"Yes, it awakened love in me and set it afire. And like a pressure cooker, it brought forth the intensity of it and broke the fetters of a love long since departed. I have placed my heart in the palm of your hands, Terry. I have given you all that I am, unreservedly, without regret, and without remorse. I have freed myself of every affliction so that I could embrace your love. And I am forever free from doubt."

They stared at each other for a second or two. Then it was seriously on. They groped and fondled each other as they ripped and pulled at each other's clothing. Moments later, he was inside her. It was something about the words that turned them both on. They made love there, on the kitchen floor. Then they went into the bedroom and made love for hours in every way imaginable. Moments after the end of their vigorous love-making, Will fell asleep.

††††

The rays of the sun filled the room as Will slept. He felt the heat on his face. With his eyes still closed, he rolled over and reached out for Terry, but she wasn't there. He searched the bed with his hands, but still couldn't find her. He opened his eyes to look for her, and saw she wasn't in bed. He listened for her in the adjacent bathroom, but he heard no semblance of activity. He got up and went to the door and listened closely. Hearing nothing, he knocked on the door. "Terry?" He didn't hear a response so he opened the door. She wasn't in the bathroom. *She must be in the kitchen.*

He put on his robe and walked out of the bedroom, stopping at every room on the way to the kitchen, but she wasn't in any of them. He searched the whole house for her. Deep within he knew that not only was she not in the house, she was gone for good. He couldn't believe it. They had just made love so intensely, that he thought she was going to stay. He thought they had an understanding. *She wouldn't leave without saying goodbye. She wouldn't leave like a thief in the night. Is that why she was so passionate last night? Is it because she knew it would be the last time?* His heart raced as the truth began to sink in. She had left him.

In the distance, he could hear his answering machine beeping at regular intervals. He hoped there was a message that would explain all of this. *Yeah, that's it. She probably went out to get something to eat for us.* Relieved, but still anxious, he went into the living room and pushed the message button on the machine.

"Will, I'm sorry I had to do this, but you know I can never resist you. I tried to tell you last night that I needed some time away to sort things out."

He knew what he was about to hear would be nothing but bad news. He sat down on the couch and continued listening.

"But I've thought about it and I know I should go. Will, I know you're hurt, but believe me, hurting you was the furthest thing from my mind. If someone would have told me a year ago I'd leave you once I had you, I would have laughed in their face. But after all that I've gone through, I know this will be best for both of us in the long run. I didn't tell you this last night, but Jericho actually offered to kill Leslie. And don't tell him I told you either. I thought it was morbid, but sweet in a weird sorta way, ya know? Especially coming from him.

"But back to you and me. Please let me go, Will. And please don't call me. You know I can refuse you nothing. If you call me now, I'll be right back in your arms. But, don't, Will. Don't call me. I've never been more miserable than I am at this moment. This is something I need to do. I hope you understand. I really do. I'm going to play you a song, okay?" Then she laughed a little and said, "You know, I remember playing the Dramatics for you that day in Toronto. Do you remember me asking you to pay attention to the words? It's ironic because we got together after that. And now, I'm going to play you another song. I'm going to ask you to listen to the words again, because I really mean them. Listen closely, darlin'," she said in between her sobs. "I love you, William Marcellus Wise."

He recognized the tune immediately. It was Whitney Houston's "I Will Always Love You." Instantly, his eyes filled with tears. As he listened to the words, the tears rolled down his cheeks and when the song ended, he picked up the phone to call her and then hung it up.

Chapter 60: Moving On?

San Francisco
October 1998

T erry lay under the covers of her bed in deep thought. The conversation with Father Powell came to mind. She walked into Saint Mary's Cathedral and entered the confessional. Father Powell asked her when she last confessed her sins. She told him she hadn't attended church regularly since she was about twelve years old Her parents quit going to mass when they moved to New Haven.

She lost interest in the church, but now, the death of Sykes, by her hand, forced her to think about the hereafter. She told the priest she parked down the street from Sykes' home to see how his family was coping without him. She went on to tell him how it hurt to see the little boy playing catch with his mother instead of his father. Then she told him about her situation with Will and his family and just about everything else that had gone wrong the past year.

Father Powell told her that killing someone in self-defense was not a sin. He also told her that any problems she and Will were experiencing weren't too great to overcome with the help of the Lord. He recited specific verses in the Bible to support what he was saying, and Terry listened. His words comforted her. When she left, she felt as if a great burden was lifted from her narrow shoulders. Now all she needed to do was decide if she was willing to put up with ignorant people. She wondered if Will still wanted her, or if he was glad to be out of the situation. The alarm went off again. This time, instead of hitting the snooze button, she turned it off.

While in the process of deciding what to wear to the office, she looked at her reflection in the oval mirror in her bedroom. As she gazed at herself, she was transported backward in time, to the night she and Will were pulled over by Leslie and Sykes, and wondered for the thousandth time if she could have done something differently. If she had, they would be together now. She had hoped her sexual aggression that night, in the theater, would be exciting for them. They had been so busy trying to make up for the absences of James and Ivy that they didn't have time to really be together the way they wanted to. Everything seemed to be happening all at once. *If I hadn't turned him on in that theater, we wouldn't even be in this shit. The cops wouldn't have pulled us over. They wouldn't even know who we are. That was probably fate, too.*

She could see herself with Will at the hotel in Sonoma now. She smiled, but didn't realize it. Then she thought about watching the news and hearing Amy Ling describe how James had killed his wife and children. Still staring blankly at her reflection, she could now see herself with Will at his parents' house. Jordan brought the smile back, but it disappeared when she thought about the conversations she had that day; especially with Will's mother. Then the night of the theater, on Will's birthday, and the erotic pleasure they gave each other came to mind.

Michael's death and the talk show she, Will, and Ashleigh listened to on the way to the airport came to mind. She wondered if Jade was still calling Will. She heard that WJAM offered Will the opportunity to be a regular guest on the show to answer calls. She believed it was only Jade's attempt to worm her way into his life. *Maybe she's what Will needs*, she thought. Suddenly, her stomach felt queasy. She felt the uncontrollable need to throw up and ran into the bathroom and leaned over the toilet, vomiting. Instantly, she knew she was pregnant.

†††

Will was sitting in the Compass Rose restaurant at the Westin St. Francis Hotel, waiting for Sterling. They were supposed to meet for lunch at Nick's Lighthouse before he left for Toledo, Ohio, to do a booksigning he promised the Dare to Imagine Book Club. Will and Sterling were going to discuss the broadcasting contract WJAM offered him to answer questions from the audience on Jade's show. But Chase Davenport had flown in from Manhattan and Sterling spent the night with her in the hotel.

Will was about fifteen minutes early. He saw a couple sitting across the room staring into each other's eyes. The couple reminded him of Terry. It had been a month and a half since she walked out of his life. He picked up the phone a thousand times to call her, but always hung up before dialing her number. He wanted to give her the time she wanted, but he also knew she could be right. Maybe they were better off without each other. But still, he couldn't help thinking about her and the intimate moments they shared. He thought about the last time they were together and how special that night was, and the cruel morning that followed. He wondered if she missed him as much as he missed her.

"Are you ready to order, sir?" the waitress asked.

He came back to the present and looked at her. The waitress was an attractive woman with long sexy legs, five feet three inches tall with perfect teeth. She smiled when he looked into her brown eyes and could tell he found her attractive. Will looked at her name tag. "I'm waiting on my brother to show up, Melanie. He should be here any moment."

"He's here," Sterling said, placing his briefcase in one of the four chairs at the table. "And you're early."

"Why don't I give you gentlemen a few minutes," she said, and turned to leave.

Sterling looked at her shapely legs and said, "I'll need more than a few minutes with you, girl."

Although she heard what Sterling said, she didn't bother to respond. Sexual innuendoes were part and parcel of being a waitress. It was something she learned to deal with, but she did find him attractive.

"So what's up, baby brotha?" Sterling asked.

"Not much. You got the contract?"

"Yeah, I got it." He opened the briefcase and pulled out a contract that was the size of a small manuscript.

"What the hell is that?"

Sterling laughed. "It's for your protection as well as theirs, Will. Jade's show is on in over four hundred markets. For what they're paying you, they wanted to try and close all the loopholes."

"So all I have to do is call in twice a day in the four hours the show is on while I'm doing the book tour, and come in the studio once, or twice a week when I'm in town, right?"

"Right, but Will, this could be bigger than that. If this works out, you could end up with your own show. Think about that shit for a minute. Jade talked about you on the air, right? Next thing ya know, people wanted her to ask you for advice. Now they want you to do the show. That's how this shit happens, bro. I predict that they're eventually going to want you to co-host the show. And from there, ya never know."

"Well, right now I'm not interested in all of that."

"What's the matter, Will? You have everything. The world is yours, man." Will was quiet for a moment, or two. Sterling could tell he had something on his mind. "You and Terry okay?"

"Naw, man. She left me a couple of months ago."

Shocked, Sterling said, "What? You kiddin' me?"

"Naw, man. I'm dead serious."

"What did you do?"

"Why are you assuming I did something?'

Melanie came back to take their order. She had expected more sexual remarks from Sterling, but she could tell the two men were thoroughly engrossed in whatever they were talking about. They stopped talking, and ordered. Then she quietly left them.

"If you didn't run her off, what happened?"

"It was a number of things and the death of Sykes specifically. She said she couldn't deal with it all. She needed time away from me. I hoped she would've call by now, but she hasn't."

"Well, why haven't you called her?"

"Because she told me not to. If she comes back, it has to be her decision. I don't want her coming back because I can't let her go. If she came back because I asked her to, that would be hangin' over my head forever. She'd end up resenting me and leaving again. I don't need that."

"Is it pride, Will?"

"No, it's reason, period."

"Look, man, don't make the same stupid ass mistake I made. Did I ever tell you what really happened with me and Vanessa?"

"No, I assumed you just got tired of her like you do with all the rest."

"Naw, man. I knew that's what everybody would think. So I let y'all think it. But what really happened was one day Vanessa had a Mary Kay show right here in this hotel. And one of her friends, who was always hittin' on me, came by."

Melanie brought out their lunches, and said, "Can I get you anything else?"

"Not right now," Will said, without looking at her.

Sterling looked at her legs again as she walked over to another table. "Anyway, she came by as soon as Vanessa left. She was wearing this spandex bicycle suit that was fittin' her perfectly. And to make a long story short—"

"Vanessa came back, right?"

"Umm-hmm. And she brought two of her friends. So I'm standing there, naked as a jaybird, with cum drippin' on the carpet. And Vanessa's standin' there in shock. The shit was fucked up."

"So that's why she left, huh?"

"Yeah, but I know I could have gotten her back had I gone after her. But like a fool, I let my pride get in the way and now she's gone forever. I wish like hell I had gone after her."

"How do you know she would have come back if you had?"

"I just know, man, all right. That's why you need to at least call Terry and see if that's what she really wants you to do. One call ain't going hurt nothin'. If she really doesn't want you back, you'll know. If she does, you'll know that, too. I'm just sayin', man, I fucked up. I lost the woman of my dreams. I hate to see you do the same thing."

"So you think I should call her, huh?"

"Hell yeah, man. How long she been gone? What, two months? That's long enough to know one way or the other. She don't need no more time. She probably needs yo' dick up in her. That's what she needs."

The two men laughed.

"So you goin' to Toledo first, then you're doin' *Oprah*, right?"

"Right."

"Okay, well look, Chase is waiting for me. All you have to do is sign on the dotted line, and you're all set."

†††

Will looked at his watch as he walked toward gate forty-five. He still had a few minutes before the plane was ready to board. He stopped at a payphone and called Terry's office. When he heard the phone ring, he thought about hanging up, but didn't.

"Wise Counseling Services Sausalito. Sally speaking. How my I direct your call?"

"Hi, Sally. This is Dr. Wise. Is Dr. Moretti available?"

"I'm sorry, sir, she called in this morning. Can I give her a message?"

"Uh, no. It's not important. I'll talk to her when I come home."

"Oh yeah, that's right. You're going to be on *Oprah*. I almost forgot."

He heard his flight being told to board the plane.

"Yes, I'm going to be on. I just don't know when they'll air it. Well, Sally, I've gotta board the plane now. I'll talk to you later, bye."

"Okay, have a nice time in Chicago. Bye."

Chapter 61:
That's My Only Mission

San Francisco
October 1998

Terry anxiously walked into the townhouse. Will left one song on her answering machine every day that week. Monday, he left Smokey Robinson and the Miracles' "The Tracks of My Tears." Tuesday, Barry White's "I've Got So Much to Give." Wednesday, the Commodores' "Three Times a Lady." Thursday, the Spinners' "How Could I Let You Get Away." And now it was Friday, and she wondered what he would play for her today.

To Terry, each song seemed to express his feelings for her. She kept listening to the songs over and over, opening her heart a little more each time she heard them. The songs brightened her days and changed her attitude. She could smile again. Will never left a message. He just played the music.

She practically ran over to the answering machine to see if there was a message. The light was flashing. She pushed the button and the messages began playing. The first one was from her doctor reminding her of today's appointment. She forgot to erase it. She pushed the skip button, but none of the messages were from Will. Disappointed, she went into the bedroom to change clothes. She kicked off her shoes, sat on the bed, and massaged her feet. Then she took off her suit and hung it in the closet.

Looking in the mirror, she placed both of her hands on her belly, and felt the new life inside her. It was too early to determine the sex, but the ultrasound confirmed that she was definitely carrying twins. A couple of weeks ago, she considered aborting the babies. But now, those thoughts were far, far away. She wondered how Will would respond to the news. She knew Brenda was going to be happy. *This is going to change everything.* Sterling called and told her Will was coming home today. She would have called him, but she wanted to hear her song of the day first.

She raced to the living room when she heard the phone ring. Prince's version of "Betcha by Golly Wow" began right after she heard her personal greeting. She sat down and listened to the words—a smile emerged. When the song ended, she waited to see if he would leave a message this time. He did.

"Terry, this is Will. I've got something important to tell you. I want you to meet me tonight at the Coconut Grove Supper Club on Van Ness Avenue. I know this is late notice, but it's really important to me that you meet me there."

"I'll be there, darlin'."

"Oh, you're there, huh?"

"Yes, I am. After all the songs you played this week, you didn't think I'd miss Friday's song, did you?"

"I guess not."

"Will?"

"Yeah?"

"Do you hear it?"

Will strained to hear whatever it was she was hearing, but couldn't. "Hear what?"

"The pitter patter of little feet."

The pitter patter of little feet? "You pregnant?"

"Twice, darlin'."

"Twins?" He shouted. "Oh my God!!"

"Umm-hmm. I guess yo' daddy was wrong."

"What was he wrong about?"

"Apparently, your gun is fully loaded. 'Cause I got two of 'em in me. Just found out an hour ago."

"Wow, that's great! That's great! Mama will really be happy! How many months are you?"

"About two."

"You mean it happened the night you left me?"

"Apparently. It's fate, babe. Do you believe me now?"

"Yeah, I think you're right. It's fate."

"You know, I think that was our best session yet. I've thought about it practically every day since that night. Have you?"

"Yeah. Just about every day."

"I take it you want them, huh?"

"So you seriously thought about aborting my children, huh?"

"Will, how in the hell do you do that?"

"It's a gift, baby. I know you could never take my children from me. Besides, Mama would lose her religion and kill yo' ass, and you know it."

Terry laughed. "I know."

"Do me a favor, babe?"

"Anything, darlin'."

"Wear that dress you wore on my birthday. This will be a night to remember."

"Okay."

"The way I feel right now, you wouldn't be wearin' it long if I was there."

"Are you hard?"

"Yep."

"I guess you expect me to give it up tonight, huh?"

"Either give it up, or I'll just have to take it. It's been a while."

"Promises, promises."

"All right, babe. Until tonight then."

"Until tonight, darlin'."

†††

Terry walked into the opulent surroundings of the Coconut Grove Supper Club, wearing the dress that revealed her curvaceous body like she promised. The lights were dim, adding to the romantic atmosphere. She spotted Will and walked over to his table. Practically every eye in the restaurant was on her, but all Terry could see was the man she adored.

Will stood when she reached the table, looking quite dashing in a white sports coat and shirt, a black bowtie, and black slacks. They both stared nervously into each other's eyes for a couple of seconds before sitting.

Will said, "I knew you wouldn't be late, so I took the liberty of ordering for us."

"Oh? And what did you order, sir?"

"It's a surprise. Trust me. You'll love it."

"Hmm," she uttered with a teasing grin. "Well, whatever it is, I hope it's good. I'm starving."

"I know. You're eating for two, right?"

"Three, darlin'," she said, smiling. "Three."

"I'm so glad you're back, baby. It's been so long since I saw that infectious smile of yours. You know how your smile lights up an entire room. Every man in here wants to know who you are. And every woman is jealous. You know that, don't you?"

"Oh, really? I hadn't noticed any other man. So what did you want to talk about?"

"You and me, babe. You and me."

"Will, you know I'm forever yours. We don't need to talk about it. We just need to be together, is all."

"You know I missed hearing you say that."

"What? Is all?"

"Uh-huh. It's your trademark, girl."

"I missed you calling me babe, and girl, and just talking to me in general."

"Well, I want to rectify that. But before we do, let's eat. I hope you're very hungry."

He raised his hand and the chef came over. He was wearing the traditional white garb the Pillsbury Doughboy made famous, and carrying a large tray with a single plate covered by a silver lid. He placed the tray in front of Terry.

"Be careful, ma'am. This is hot," the chef said. "As a matter of fact, you better let me take the lid off for you." He lifted the lid.

Terry frowned when she saw a steak with mashed potatoes, creamed corn, and hot potato rolls. She looked at Will and wondered what was going on. She expected a diamond ring, not her favorite meal. *Why would you have me get all dressed up if you're not going to pop the question? I could have come here in a jogging suit for this. Jesus!* She forced a smile to hide her enormous disappointment.

"Enjoy, mom-to-be," Will said.

"Well…I am eating for three and I am starved," she said, still forcing herself to smile.

"What's wrong, babe?" Will asked. "Are you feeling okay?"

"Sure. Why?"

"I don't know…you seem a little disappointed. Isn't this your favorite meal?"

"Well, now you know," she said with a ho-hum tone.

Will looked at the chef and nodded. He reached into his pocket and pulled out a ring case and put it on the table. Terry gasped. Tears welled in her hazel eyes.

"Well… open it," Will told her.

Terry's hands shook when she reached for the ring case. She opened it and saw a ten-karat diamond ring, which glittered in spite of the scantily lit room. Terry gasped. She was taken completely by surprise. Will picked up the ring and got down on both knees—customers applauded. Two tears slid down Terry's cheeks. Will took her left hand and eased the ring onto her finger. "Grow old with me, Terry. Be my wife and make my life complete."

Terry was so overwhelmed with emotion that all she could do was nod her head. She grabbed and held on to him with all her might. The customers applauded again. Finally, she was able to say, "Yes, Will. I'll marry you."

Will stood and took her hand. "Come on, I have my brother's plane waiting to take us to Vegas."

"You mean you want to get married right now?"

"Yes, right now. Everything's planned. We'll fly to Vegas, get married, and honeymoon in the penthouse of the Mandalay Bay Hotel."

"Isn't this kind of sudden? Is this because I'm pregnant?"

"Terry, my life has been empty since you left. As you know, a lot of good things have happened to me while you were gone. The book is going through the roof. I just did *Oprah*. And I'm going to be doing a national radio show that could turn into something down the road. The only thing missing is you, baby. I don't want to be apart from you ever again. I wanna do this tonight. But if you're unsure, it would be best not to."

"I'm sure. I just don't want you to do this because I'm pregnant."

"I want to grow old with you—that's my only mission."

He kissed her and led her out of the restaurant amidst more applause. A black stretch Lincoln limousine was waiting for them when they got outside.

"What about our cars?" Terry asked.

"We'll get them later."

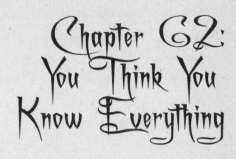
Chapter 62:
You Think You
Know Everything

Las Vegas
October 1998

Mr. and Mrs. Wise had just made love for the fourth time, and their breathing was starting to return to normal. Although she knew her mother would be disappointed she wasn't able to attend the wedding, she couldn't wait to tell her. She hoped her father would be happy for her, but if he wasn't, it was too late now. The deed was done.

"You hungry, babe?" Will asked.

"I'm starved. Some kind of husband you are. You whisk me away to Las Vegas, screw my brains out, and you don't even bother to feed me."

"There's food in the refrigerator. At least there's supposed to be."

"I suppose you want me to get up and cook for you now, huh?"

"That would be nice." He grinned. "I guess I better get my club out of the closet and start things off right, huh?" She hit him playfully. "I saw a fruit basket in the living room when we came in. You want me to get it for you?"

"Yeah, so I can see yo' ass," she said, playfully. "It's been a while." Will went into the living room to get the fruit. "And you better not have let Jade see it either," she shouted as he disappeared.

He came back a moment or two later with the basket in tow. Terry was lying on her side, her arm at a forty-five-degree angle, supporting her head. Will sat down beside her and peeled an orange for her.

"What makes you think Jade wants to see it?"

"Puh-lease, men are so stupid sometimes. You're the one that got away, remember? She probably got you that job at the station to better her chances."

"Is working with her from time to time going to bother you?

"You gon' let her see yo' ass?" she asked, smiling.

"Not if you don't want me to."

"Then no, it won't bother me."

"Okay, good."

Having finished peeling the orange, he handed it to her. "You want me to make you something to eat while you call your mother?"

She decided not to acknowledge that he knew what she was thinking, wondering how he would respond if he was wrong for a change. She popped a slice of orange into her mouth and said, "Ya know, that's a good idea. I think I'll call her." Will rolled his eyes. "What?" she said, trying not to smile. Will just kept looking at her. He knew sooner or later she would start laughing. Seconds later, the dam broke. She laughed hard and rolled over onto her back. Her laugh brought a smile to his face.

"I can see right now, this marriage is gon' be a real trip," she said, still laughing. "You think you know everything."

"Do I know everything? Or do you think I know everything?"

"You know everything, darlin'. And I love you for it." She kissed him. "Now, go cook my food before I have to get my club outta the closet."

A half-hour later, Terry came into the kitchen and sat down at the table, wearing a white monogrammed Mandalay Bay Hotel complimentary robe. She showered and combed her hair. Breakfast smelled great and she couldn't wait to dig in.

Will smelled the perfume she sprayed on and wanted to take her there, on the table, but bridled his passion; there would be time for that later. In fact, it was his plan to have her as soon as they finished eating. "So how did it go?"

"Great. She was kinda disappointed she couldn't be there, but glad. Are you going to call your mom?"

"She already knows. Told her all about it about a month and a half ago when I planned all of this."

"Really?" Her eyebrows furrowed. "How did she take it?"

"Pretty well, actually. I didn't ask for her permission, Terry. I told her what I was going to do, and she said okay. She wasn't thrilled, or anything; she just said okay, and that was that."

Will sat a plate, piled high with bacon, eggs, hash browns, buttered toast, and a bowl of grits, on the table.

"So you planned all of this stuff a month and a half ago, huh?" she asked, and began eating. "Umm. This is so good."

"Yeah. I called your office just before I boarded the plane to Toledo, but Sally said you called in. That's when I started planning. I called my brother and he was happy to let me use his jet. As a matter of fact, he got us this penthouse for free. He knows the guy who owns the place."

"Really?" she said, between mouthfuls. "That was very gracious of him."

"Yeah, it was. You want some coffee?"

She shook her head. "Will, how would you feel about having a real wedding? I'm not saying right now. Maybe a year from now when I can get into my dress."

"She was real disappointed, huh?" Terry nodded. "That's fine with me. I'm going to be busy touring for a few more months, or so, anyway. Plus, I've got the businesses and the radio spots."

"So you don't mind?"

"No, I figured you'd want one complete with a honeymoon package someplace far away. I even thought of what we could do."

"And what's that, darlin'?"

"Well, first, I thought we'd fly to Pennsylvania, and—"

"The Poconos Mountains," she said excitedly, interrupting him.

"Yeah, then I thought we'd take a cruise someplace. Then after that, maybe fly to Rome, Paris, and Madrid. Maybe even Sydney. How does that sound?"

She looked at him admiringly, and said, "I love you so much."

"I love you, too." He kissed her. "I suppose you want a big wedding, right?"

"The biggest!"

"Can your dad afford the biggest?"

"Not the biggest, but a big one."

"You're not going to believe this, but Jerry said he'd pay for it if we wanted him to. He offered his plane and everything. It's going to be great."

"Did he, really?" She reflected for a moment. "I guess he really does like me after all."

"He offered to kill for you, didn't he? I think that says it all."

"Wow, so you really planned all of this, huh?"

"Yep, but we need to start making arrangements right away. We have to hire some more people pronto. That way, when we're gone, we won't have to worry about the business. Oh, and that reminds me. We're going to need a babysitter. My mother doesn't even know you're pregnant. I'll call her right now."

He picked up the phone and dialed. His mother answered. "Hello."

"Are you up already?"

"Yeah, you know I have to fix yo' daddy's breakfast every mornin'. You know how cranky he gets when his belly ain't full. So did you get married?"

"Yep. Sure did."

Terry went over to Will. She took off her robe and he looked at her naked body. She could see he was hard again. She opened his robe and massaged him.

"Mom, I've got great news. Terry's pregnant."

Brenda screamed and praised the Lord, thanking Jesus for answering her prayers. He could hear his dad say, "What? What happened?"

Facing him, Terry slid down his erect pole and began a slow steady grind. She kissed his neck, and whispered, "What did she say?"

"She's praising God right now."

"Congratulations, son," Benjamin beamed. "So you got some sap left, huh?"

"Yep. Enough sap for twins."

He heard his father cover up the phone and say to Brenda, "She havin' twins."

Terry was grinding faster now, and Will was trying not to get too involved in their lovemaking. Terry knew he was holding back, which turned her on even more. Will could hear his mother praising God. Then he heard her say, "Let me talk to Terry, Willy."

"Okay." He looked at Terry. "Here, she wants to talk to you."

Terry stopped grinding and composed herself. "Hello, Mrs. Wise."

"Hello to you, Mrs. Wise," Brenda said.

As Will pumped her, orgasmic blushes flooded Terry's face as the sensation overwhelmed her. Seeing how much she was enjoying it, he moved faster. He didn't know what his mother was saying, but whatever she was saying, must have all been questions because Terry kept saying yes, and okay. Occasionally, Terry bit her bottom lip. He could tell she was on the verge of orgasm, so he moved even faster.

"Here, honey. She wants to talk to you now."

Will took the phone and said, "Hello."

Terry placed both hands on the back of Will's chair and furiously slammed her body against his. The chair squealed and threatened to clasp. Will said, "Okay, Mom. I gotta go, bye."

Brenda laughed. "What now?" Benjamin asked.

"They were doing it the whole time we was talkin'."

Chapter 63:
With This Ring

Westin St. Francis Hotel
San Francisco, California
The Wise Wedding
August 20, 1999

It was her wedding day! Terry was standing in front of the full-length mirror in her suite at the Westin St. Francis Hotel, admiring her new figure. She took the advice of her gynecologist and exercised during the pregnancy while meticulously counting calories. She'd lost the extra weight quickly, and was feeling quite sexy in her wedding lingerie.

She laughed when she remembered how uncomfortable it was, walking down the aisle with her father, wearing sexy panties and a wire cup bra the first time she got married. The wire bra was cutting into her flesh and her panties were riding up her ass and there was nothing she could do about it with every eye in the church on her. With each step she took, her panties seemed to shrink. This time she was a little bit wiser. She went for comfort over sexy. Who was going to see her panties through the dress anyway?

Ashleigh bought Terry a pair of frantics, which were scented panties designed to be extremely comfortable because they had a full cut over the buttocks, which prevented those uncomfortable ride-ups. Each pair had a small, heart-shaped fragrance sachet stitched in just below her belly button. They weren't all that great to look at, but she was comfortable and that's all that mattered.

Although this would be her second marriage, she wanted to wear a white formal gown. Her mother emailed her the web address of Priscilla of Boston, with an attached link, which took her directly to a diamond white gown with a sweetheart neckline and a cathedral train. Her mother thought the sweetheart neckline would look good on her because she was what dressmakers called a fuller-chested woman. And having given birth, her breasts were constantly filling with milk, making the sweetheart neckline the more appropriate choice.

The wedding was going to be performed at the hotel and the entire wedding party was staying there. Jericho flew Ashleigh and her parents in from New Haven on his private jet. He was also paying for their hotel bill, the caterer they had flown in from New York, the use of the banquet room, and any other last-minute, unexpected expenses. Terry remembered how annoying Jericho found her dad to be and smiled.

During the entire rehearsal dinner, her father kept trying to find out what Jericho did for a living because he could afford his own plane. When no one would tell him, he decided to ask Jericho himself. Jericho told him he owned the Renegade Hotel and Casino in the Caymans, but her father wasn't satisfied with that answer. He kept asking more and more questions. Jericho finally looked at him with those steel eyes of his and said, "Mr. Moretti, you ask a lot of questions of people you hardly know. Do you think that's wise?" Douglas eventually got the point and left him alone.

As she waited for Alicia Harris, her hairstylist, to arrive Terry wondered if Ashleigh ended up staying in Sterling's room last night. They appeared to be instantly attracted to each other upon meeting at rehearsal. She watched them from time to time during the dinner portion of the evening's festivities. Sterling was the Best Man and Ashleigh was the Maid of Honor, which meant Sterling would be her escort that evening, and tonight at the reception. *Since Jeffery's still in New Haven with the children, who knows what's transpired between them*, she thought. The last time she saw Ashleigh was when she came out of the lobby restroom after the rehearsal dinner was over.

The wedding party left the banquet hall and went up to their rooms. Ashleigh and Sterling were standing near the water fountain talking. It looked like they were well on their way to doing more than that. Ashleigh told Terry that Jeffrey's construction project was behind schedule and he couldn't leave until it was finished. Since she was the Maid of Honor, she had too many responsibilities to bring her children along. So she left them with Jeffrey's parents for the weekend. Terry knew Ashleigh was still bothered by Jeffrey's indiscretion last year, and that was probably the real reason he and the children didn't come to San Francisco.

Terry meticulously planned the wedding with her mother, sparing no expense, knowing their resources were practically unlimited. She would have the very best of everything on her day. Their pictures were in the society section of the *San Francisco Chronicle* along with short biographies of the couple. The event was billed as one of the biggest weddings of the year, having everything imaginable, including the best food, the best wine, the best musicians, the best caterer, the best florist, and the best hotel in the city.

Terry wanted a unique meal, preferring a feast rather than the traditional baked chicken for the thousand or so people coming to the wedding. The menu included filet mignon in a succulent merlot sauce, lobster, shrimp, and crab. The guests could also have chicken breasts stuffed with goat cheese, sun-dried tomatoes and spinach, drenched in a tomato-basil sauce; grilled salmon and smoked bacon hash served with oven-roasted root vegetables in a port-wine demi-glace. Strict vegetarians could choose assorted grilled vegetables nestled on a potato pancake, served with French green lentils and warm balsamic vinaigrette.

Dyan hired Howard Rose, of New York, to cater the wedding. He would be expensive, but worth it. He only did about ten weddings a year. Securing his services was difficult, but if you could get him, you knew your reception would be done with class. Howard had been in San Francisco for a week preparing for the wedding reception. He had flown in his own servers, waiters, and bartenders. He rented plates, silverware, serving pieces, fifteen fountains, and several different sized wine glasses. Even though Douglas was paying for the liquor with a company discount, Howard went to Napa Valley and picked out the wines they would serve the wedding party.

Terry was impressed with his professionalism and particularly impressed with his timetable for the reception. Depending on the length of the reception, he would serve anywhere between six and twelve different hors d'oeuvres. He would begin serving hors d'oeuvres while the wedding party took pictures and rode around for a while in the limousines. He understood that the one thing guests hated was to wait for the wedding party, which generally took a long time depending on the photographer.

As a final touch, Howard made three different multitiered wedding cakes. He prepared a white, multitiered bridal cake, which was to be served to the guests at the reception. He also prepared a chocolate, multitiered groom's cake which was traditionally sliced and given to the guests when they left the reception. The third cake was made of chocolate and vanilla swirl.

Terry looked at her watch. 9 AM. The wedding was going to start at four. She called Ashleigh's room, but she didn't answer. She assumed Ashleigh was with Sterling, but didn't feel right calling his room so she called Will's room instead.

"Hello," he said, groggily.

"Sorry to wake you, darlin', but is Ashleigh with Sterling?"

"Yep, and it sounds like they been at it all night long. Who can sleep? Here, listen to this." He put the phone against the wall for a few seconds. Ashleigh moaned in rhythm with the violently slamming of the head-board against the adjacent wall. Then Will put the phone back to his ear. "There, you hear that?"

"Not really."

"Take my word for it." He laughed. "They're goin' at it somethin' fierce. How 'bout you come over here for a few so we can make some noise of our own."

"Will, you know I'm waiting on Alicia to do my hair."

She heard a knock at the door. "There she is now. I gotta go. Tell Ashleigh she better not be late. Bye." Then she hung up the phone.

Will banged on the wall. Silence suddenly filled the room. Then he heard the headboard slamming against the wall again. Will banged on the wall again. Again, it got quiet. This time he heard Sterling yell, "WHAT!"

"Hey, man. Terry's looking for her."

"OKAY!" Sterling yelled back.

Will laughed when he heard the slamming again.

†††

At five minutes to four, Will and his groomsmen, Sterling, Jericho, Cleve, Jonathan, Ronnie, and Bernie, were standing outside the wedding hall, dressed in black tails, checking each other over one last time before they went in, removing lint and cutting off loose strings. A moment or two later, the minister came out and said, "They're ready."

Will and Sterling stayed behind while the other men went to their appointed stations. Suddenly he wished he hadn't agreed to such an elaborate event. He took comfort in knowing they would have a very short ceremony and a long-deserved honeymoon.

"You nervous, bro?" Sterling asked Will.

"Yeah, man." Small perspiration circles were forming on Will's forehead. Sterling pulled out his handkerchief and wiped the sweat away. "You think Terry's nervous, too?"

"Probably." Sterling laughed. "Ya should've knocked it out this morning. Then you'd be more relaxed like me."

"You're not going to see Ashleigh again, are you?"

"I don't know. One can never tell about these things. Now come on, you've stalled long enough."

"You got the ring, Sterling?"

"Yeah."

"Let me see it."

Sterling shook his head and pulled the ring out of his trouser pocket. "See, I got it. Now let's go."

Sterling opened the door and Will walked into the hall and saw his mother and father sitting in the front row. Aunt Johnnie was sitting right behind them, along with the rest of his family and friends. On the other side of the aisle, he saw Terry's mother sitting by herself. She was smiling at him. Behind her was Terry's extended family and friends. He saw a distinguished-looking black woman sitting behind Dyan and wondered if she was Terry's college roommate.

When they reached the portable altar, Sterling whispered in Will's ear, "Who's the babe sitting over there with the white folk?"

"That would be the first thing you'd notice," Will whispered.

Ronnie was escorting Karen, his wife, down the aisle now. He had a frown on his face, like they had just got into it about something.

"Well, you know me," Sterling said. "I might have to shoot some game to her at the reception. The girl got it goin' on, big time. Who is she?"

"I don't know, but I can only guess that it's Debbie, Terry's roommate from Stanford."

"Oh yeah? The woman is fine with a mind. Yeah, I gotta shoot some game. What does she do for a livin'?"

"She's a doctor."

"Another headshrinker? Forget it. She'll probably be analyzin' my every move while I'm tryin' tuh get my swerve on."

Will laughed. "Naw man, she's a medical doctor."

"Oh, so she's paid, huh?"

Jericho and Pin, who was three months' pregnant, were coming down the aisle now. They could see Cleve and Cheryl were next, Jonathan and Jeannine, and then Bernie Beverly and Jade Wilson.

"Probably," Will answered. "Hey, ain't that Vanessa in the back?"

"Where?" Sterling said excitedly.

"She just walked in. She's over there near the usher by the entrance."

"Yeah, that's her. Wow, she came. She won't talk to me, but she came to your wedding."

"What can I say? I'm not the dog in the family. You own those rights exclusively."

Ashleigh was coming down the aisle now. She was five-seven, very pretty, with dark hair, brown bedroom eyes, and a killer body.

Sterling whispered, "Just in case you wonderin', the girl can screw. She almost broke my dick off this mornin'."

Will laughed. "I knew there was a reason I picked you to be my best man. Who can be nervous with you around?"

The preacher looked at them sternly and cleared his throat.

"Be cool, man," Will said.

"Don't worry about him. He just needs a piece. That's how a brotha look when his dick is hard. He needs to douse that bad boy. He'll be all right then."

Will laughed again.

Jordan was coming down the aisle carrying Will's ring. Terry and her father were standing at the entrance, watching Jordan. The organist played the bridal march—all the guests stood.

Will smiled as his bride and her father marched down the aisle. Thanks to Sterling, he was completely relaxed. As they approached the altar, he saw her face through the veil. She was smiling. Will looked at Terry's mother and saw tears roll down her rose-colored cheeks.

When they reached the altar, the minister said, "Who gives this woman to be wed to this man?"

"Her mother and I do," Douglas said and sat down next to his wife.

Will walked over to Terry, took her hand, and whispered in her ear, "Did the franties work?" Terry hit him playfully.

"Dearly beloved, we are gathered together in the sight of God to join this man with this woman…"

Chapter 64: The Reception

Seven Lincoln limousines stopped in front of the Westin St. Francis Hotel. Will and his wife were in the only stretch limo of the seven. The chauffeurs drove them to Pier 39, where their photographer took an incredible amount of pictures. They couldn't wait to see them. Now they were about to make their grand entrance into the reception hall in order of importance.

Thunderous applause and cheers rang out when they entered the reception hall. Sister Sledge's "We are Family" served as background music while a video of Terry and Will exchanging vows was being shown on the giant-screen television. Purple and white candles and champagne were on every table.

They made it easy for parents who had children to attend the reception by renting additional halls for their children; one for teenagers, another for preteens, and a nursery for infants. Although they hired a nanny, both sets of grandparents promised to look in on the twins from time to time so Terry and Will could enjoy their wedding day.

After dinner, Sterling walked through the hall, looking for Vanessa but she wasn't there. She left right after the wedding. Unable to find Vanessa, the insatiable lothario looked for Terry's college roommate, Debbie. She was sitting at a table, a few feet away from the disk jockey's set-up. She smiled invitingly at him. Just as he approached her table, an usher told him it was time to do the toast. He heard someone on the mike say, "Can we have the best man come up and make the toast?" Sterling mouthed, "Can I talk to you later?" Debbie nodded.

The usher handed him a glass of champagne. Sterling grabbed the mike and said, "My brother's first wife died about seven years ago. And since her death, he hasn't really been happy. His business life has been a great success, but personally, there's been a huge void. Then Terry came into his life and turned his house into a home. When they decided to become a couple, my mother, who's been trying to get all of us married off so she can have grandchildren, woke up in the middle of the night and called my brother at his hotel in Toronto. She knew in her heart that God had answered her prayers.

"My mother is seldom wrong on these things. If anyone doubts that, just go into the nursery and look at the twins Terry had three months ago." The audience laughed. He raised his glass and said, "To my baby brother, and his beautiful bride, may your life together be filled with happiness and good cheer. May your lives be long and healthy, and may God bless your home with plenty of children so my mother can quit bothering God about me every night!" They laughed and drank their champagne. "Now, I'd like to dedicate a song for their first dance." He nodded to the disk jockey. LTD's "Concentrate on You" began.

Will took Terry's hand and led her to the dance floor. Will whispered in her ear, "Are you happy, babe?"

"Very. Are you?"

"Very happy. I'm glad all the madness is behind us."

"So am I."

"I bought you a wedding present I know you gon' love."

Terry pulled back from his embrace and said, "What did you get me, Will?"

"It's a surprise, girl."

"You not gon' tell me?"

"Nope, but I'll take you to see it right after this dance, okay?"

"Okay." She smiled. "I love you so much."

"I love you, too. You think I can get a little when I give you your present?"

"Maybe," she said, playfully. "Depends on the gift. If it's a really good gift, ain't no tellin' what you might get."

"You makin' me hard, girl."

"Really, I can't feel you with all this stuff on. What do we tell the guests when we leave?"

"We'll tell them we're going to check on the children and we'll be right back."

"You think it'll work."

"Umm-hmm."

A few minutes later, the song ended. Now everyone was up dancing. As they were leaving the dance-floor, Douglas came up to Terry and said, "Don't I get to dance with you, Peaches?"

"Yeah, Dad. But can it wait until I see my wedding gift? Will wants to show it to me now."

"Okay, but don't keep your old man waiting too long, okay?"

"Okay, Dad, I won't."

Will looked at his watch as he and Terry slipped out the door, hoping the delivery people would be on time. As they walked through the lobby, people stared admiringly at them, offering enthusiastic congratulations. They smiled and thanked them. Just before they reached the exit, Will stopped walking, faced Terry, and said, "Okay, I want you to close your eyes before we go outside and keep them closed, okay?"

"Okay." She grinned.

Skeptical, Will said, "I guess I have to trust you."

"You can trust me, darlin'. I won't open my eyes. Promise."

When they were within range of the motion detector, the automatic doors opened and they went outside. Terry heard the movement of traffic, horns blowing, footsteps moving in all directions. Her desire to open her eyes was overwhelming, but she kept them closed. Will led her a few more feet to the left. She felt awkward walking with her eyes closed.

"Okay, we're here."

"Can I open my eyes now?"

"Yeah, open them."

She opened her eyes and gasped when she saw the brand-new black Mercedes Benz convertible. It was wrapped in a red ribbon and bow.

"Is this mine?" she said, spontaneously.

"Yep."

"Thank you, honey. You're the best husband in the whole world." Then she frowned. "What about the twins? Don't you think a two-door coupe will be too small for them?"

"The twins can ride in the Jeep. Or we can get a station wagon. It's up to you."

"Can we go for a ride?" she said, excitedly.

"No, babe. That would be rude. We've already been gone too long as it is. I just couldn't wait any longer to surprise you. Besides, you wouldn't be able to get in there with that dress on anyway."

"I wanna do it, Will," she whispered in his ear.

Will smiled. "Me, too."

"Let's go back inside, cut the cake, throw the garter, and go upstairs for some nookey," she said.

Will laughed. "Okay, but cut the ribbon off first so the valet can park it for you."

After cutting the ribbon, they went back inside the hotel. As they approached the reception hall, Terry thought about the children and decided to visit the nursery.

"Will, let's check on the twins before we go inside."

"You go ahead. I'll go and make an appearance so they won't worry about us, okay?"

"Okay, I won't be long, darlin'."

†††

Thirty minutes passed and Terry was still visiting the twins. Will was so busy mingling with the guests, he hadn't missed her. One of the ushers came over to him and said, "Sir, it's time for the bride and groom to cut the cake. But we can't find her."

"She's in the nursery. I'll have her sister go get her."

He walked over to the wedding party's table and said, "Hey, Ashleigh, you mind getting your sister out of the nursery. It's time to cut the cake."

"Is she in there again? She was in there twice today." Ashleigh joked. "She can't seem to leave them for a second. I'll get her."

Ten minutes passed and Ashleigh hadn't come back yet. Will wondered what was going on. He was about to go check on them when Ashleigh came running into the hall. She was screaming something, but the music was so loud he couldn't hear what she was saying. Will practically ran over to her. She looked like she'd seen a ghost. After Ashleigh told him what was going on in the nursery, Will ran out of the hall.

Jericho, being ever vigilant, watched the way Will hurried out of the hall.

"I'll be right back," Jericho whispered in Pin's ear.

"I go with you," Pin said.

"No, not this time. It may be nothing. But if it's what I think, I don't want to take any chances with the baby."

✝✝✝

"Eight...Seven...Six..."

Seeing no other way out, Will picked up the gun, squeezed the trigger and heard the clicking of an empty gun. He looked at Leslie and saw the rush he was getting from the threat of killing Terry. He seemed to relish the idea of knowing that Will knew there was nothing he could do about it.

"See, you're just as powerless to keep me from killing her as you were the night she saved your ass."

Jericho snatched the door open and stepped into the room with his gun drawn. Seeing the gun, Leslie hid behind Terry, using her as a shield. "I don't know who you are, but are you a good enough shot to shoot me without hitting her?"

"Better," Jericho said.

"What makes you think I'm not prepared to die in the process of killing her?"

"Prepared or not, only way you leavin' this room is in a body bag. Cowards like you need killin'. You're one of them fools who thinks he's a hunter because he shot a duck, or a deer. Shootin' ducks and deer is for weak men like you. A real man would only hunt and kill an animal that could hunt and kill him."

Jericho could see he was getting to the man holding a gun to Terry's head, so he kept talking, hoping he would give him a little more head space to work with.

"Look at you, hidin' behind a defenseless woman in a nursery. You probably been a loser all ya life. It's weak pathetic men like you that join the police force to get a little power. It just proves how puny, how trivial, how inconsequential you really are. That's the real reason why your wife left you, ain't it? Deep down, you know I'm telling the truth, don't you? Weak man like you probably can't even get it up. What did your fellow officers say when they found out that a woman beat yo' punkass partner to death with his own nightstick? Is that the real reason she's gotta die? Because she humiliated you and him? It musta been some kinda funeral, huh? All of San Francisco's finest dressed in their pretty blue uniforms, givin' an honor burial for a despicable fool who lost his life, not on the field of battle, but on a darkened highway in the wee hours of the morning, by a woman with more gumption than him. The shit is funny to me." Then he laughed in his face.

As Leslie watched Jericho's body shake with laughter, the rage within exploded. Without so much as a change in expression, Leslie pulled the trigger. Terry was dead before she hit the floor. She seemed to be floating as she fell. Then Leslie pointed the gun at Will and fired.

"Nooooo!" Will screamed in horror, as he ran to Terry. Everything seemed to be happening in slow motion.

Jericho squeezed the trigger, but Will had stepped into his line of sight, and took the bullet in the shoulder. As he was going down, he felt the bullet Leslie fired pierce the collarbone of the same shoulder.

Jericho adjusted his aim and unloaded his weapon into Leslie before he had a chance to shoot Will again. His body jerked in different directions each time a bullet hit him. He fell to the floor and convulsed, gurgling blood. Then he convulsed again and died. Will crawled to Terry and rocked her lifeless body.

As he wept, he kept repeating, "Terry, you gotta wake up, baby. It's time to go on our honeymoon."

Epilogue

San Francisco
June 2001

Radio personality Jade Wilson married Dr. Bernie Beverly. After a few drinks and a friendly chat near the water cooler at a Wise Choice Counseling Center party, Jade, who found Bernie extremely attractive, went to his home that night and never left. Even though her husband is white, she still hates the idea of black men dating and marrying white women. When she was asked about this on her syndicated radio show, she said, "Well, if black men didn't treat black women so badly, they wouldn't have to turn to white men for comfort." Then she refused to discuss the subject on her show again, saying, "The subject is too trivial to discuss and there are far more important issues than who I fell in love with and married."

As for Jericho, getting out of the drug business was far more difficult than he imagined. The drug economy was much like the world economy in that each consortium was dependent on the other to keep the peace. If Jericho removed himself from the mix, a war would ensue for ownership of his territory. And a bloody war on the streets of the United States was bad for business.

Jericho's partners, who were already irate about the Hawthorne murder, told him he would have to find someone else to take over his territory. They also told him he was responsible for the actions of that person, even though he was no longer in the business. To get out, he had several options. One option was to kill all of his partners, which would cause unprecedented chaos in the drug underworld. Another option was to work for the United States Government so that everything would collapse. But that would open the door for the New York Mafia to gain a foothold again. A third option was to stay in the business for the duration. Jericho decided to stay in the business until he decided what he would do.

Adrienne Bellamy kept her word to Sterling. His agency, Wise Choice Sports, was booming; so was his law practice. He finally gave Le'sett Santiago what she wanted—partnership. The deal between Officer Leslie and the District Attorney's office left a bad taste in Le'sett's mouth. She was now running Sterling's law practice, hiring new talent, and taking the business to a whole new level. Much to Le'sett's chagrin, Sterling never slept with her again after they became business partners.

Thanks to Adrienne Bellamy, Sterling was living a privileged life, making more money than he ever dreamed of, doing everything first class. He even bought a nine million-dollar home in Mill Valley. The lavish two-story French Normandy home offered five bedrooms, five and a half baths, a library, a den, five fireplaces, an in-ground swimming pool, a pool house, a sprinkler system, a three-car garage, and a view of San Francisco. Yes, Sterling was living high and loving it. He was on his way to Denver with Tiffany, his personal assistant, to renegotiate a contract for Dante King, a done deal, he thought.

Almost two years had passed since Terry was murdered in front of Will. From time to time, he relived the tragic event spontaneously. No one was more hurt about her death than Will's mother—not even Terry's parents. It took her death to make Brenda recognize her own shortcomings in the matter of race. He buried Terry next to Francis, leaving space for himself to be placed between both of his wives whenever his time came. Three months after burying Terry, Will left his twin sons, Terrance and Michael, with his parents and took an extended vacation, visiting the Pyramids of Egypt and the Nile River; the Coliseum in Rome, the Sistine Chapel, the Pantheon, and many other locales in Europe.

As the irony of fate prevailed, he met Dr. Tara Ali, the woman Terry met on the plane to New Haven two years earlier, who happened to be taking an extended vacation, too. Terry had made enough of an impression on her that Dr. Ali remembered her and their conversation on the plane. On the balcony of his suite at the Negresco Hotel in Nice, they enjoyed the stunning view of the Riviera coastline as she listened to Will pour out his soul over coffee. When their vacation was over, they parted, but promised to keep in touch, which they did.

During the next six months, they made numerous phone calls to each other, talking non-stop for hours, becoming more attached with each conversation. Soon after, they made plans to vacation together in the Presidential Suite of the Intercontinental Castellana Hotel in Madrid, which is where they first made love, over a year after Terry was buried. After that magical time in Madrid, Dr. Ali closed her practice in Philadelphia and moved to San Francisco, where she opened an office in Sausalito.

William Marcellus Wise wondered if God had played some cruel trick on him, giving him a loving wife to replace the one taken from him. If it was a cruel trick, could it have been any colder than seeing a second wife taken away right before his very eyes? Was Terry's fate sealed the moment he decided to go to Toronto? Was the last two years all a part of some twist of fate? What if he hadn't gone to Toronto? Would Terry be alive?

Although Will had met another beautiful woman and moved on with his life, his sons were a daily reminder of the woman he still loved. Terrance and Michael were the only redemptive aspect of a love long gone, but never forgotten.

Author's Note

When I look back on how this novel began, and how I became an author, I shake my head because all of this was so unintentional. An unforeseeable set of circumstances, words were spoken behind closed doors, all made this novel happen. I was going to school to learn psychology, not to become an author, which is why Freudian psychoanalytic theory is depicted in this book in the persons of Jericho [the superego], Sterling [the id], and William [the ego].

Fate's Redemption was formerly titled *Life Choices*, which actually came from a seven-page, double-spaced short story for a literature class I took at the Community College I attended. The short story was titled "The Conversation," which you have already read in this novel. That short was never supposed to see the light of day. I was simply getting back at the teacher for comments he made. Although I do not remember what he said, I don't think the man knew the impact of his words. I do not think he meant any harm, but, words are so very powerful, taking the individual to the highest highs and the lowest lows.

Well, "The Conversation" struck a nerve and the next thing I knew, my creative writing teacher, Leonard Kress, the man I dedicated this novel to, wanted to read it. I refused, as "The Conversation" was not meant for him, but for his colleague. It had done what it was intended to do as evidenced by Kress' earnest desire to read the short. After relentless prodding, I acquiesced, wondering how he would feel about the short. To my surprise, he told me he thought the story had potential and wanted me to continue writing it in his class. This seriously blew me away. Again—words—a powerful medium.

Then Kress added, "I think you should build the story around Will and Barbara." Barbara was Terry's name at the time. I frowned. "You want this to be an interracial love story?" I questioned. "Yes. That's the story, Keith." We went back and forth about this as I had no intention of writing a story about a rich black man falling in love with a white woman. None whatsoever. But after much prodding, I said fine. What difference did it make? Who was ever going to read it? Kress and the other four students in the class would be the only people looking at it. This, I could live with because even then, I knew this story would push a lot of buttons.

When I wrote "The Conversation," it was powerful, truthful, and very revealing on both sides, I thought. And I wanted to keep the same edge—keep the same truths coming forth. That was the only thing that could keep me remotely interested in a story of this kind. I asked myself, what would happen in real life if this were to occur? I had a great example staring me in the face: The O.J. Simpson fiasco. This worldwide event was actually the catalyst for "The Conversation" to begin with as the comments I mentioned earlier were about the Simpson case. So, yes, I was writing this novel while that trial was going on. If you go back and reread the "All Rise" chapter, you'll see a striking resemblance to the actual events—even the press conference after the verdict in the Simpson case.

A quick note on my personal history. I read the *The Autobiography of Malcolm X* when I was about thirty-three. Before then, I refused to read it because as far back as I can remember, all I ever heard about him was that Malcolm was a race hater and wanted a race riot. I believed those things as a child and refused to even consider reading it, looking only to Dr. Martin Luther King, Jr. as the true light for Black folk. As *fate* would have it, director Spike Lee released a biopic about Malcolm X. Prior to its release, there was serious buzz about the film. People were wearing X pants, shirts, jackets, and here in Toledo, Ohio, they even went so far as to sell chips with Malcolm X's picture on them.

I asked John Willis II, a coworker friend of mine, who I often discussed political, national, and world events with, about this phenomenon. I said, "Do you think these people even know who the man was?" Immediately, I was reminded that I didn't even know who the man was and had judged him based on what I was told. I wanted to talk about how foolish all of this was. But to do that factually, I had to read the book so I could feel justified in talking about the folly that was going on in my hometown.

Well, I read that book and it changed my thinking, not only on Malcolm X, but on life in America, period. And no, I didn't become a Muslim. I have never seen whites as devils or any such thing. Malcolm helped me see that part of America's race problem is that Blacks and Whites will not tell each other the truth as they see it. The truth, you see, is too scathing, and far too penetrating, and far too painful for either race. Malcolm X, as do I, advocated frank conversation between the black race and the white race. This conversation has yet to take place, except for inside the pages of this soul-stirring novel.

As the Bible says, "Ye shall know the truth and the truth shall set you free." The truth in this book is designed to bring to the surface that which is spoken openly in homes, at dinner tables, in country club locker rooms, and in office buildings throughout the land. Only in these places do people feel comfortable or free to voice their truth. Only in these places do whites say how they really feel about the politics of race. Only in these places do blacks say how they really feel about whites. Therefore, in these places, this novel can be discussed openly, but, hopefully with those to whom they should be speaking, without fear of death, physical, or by means of ostracism.

The inherent problem with truth, however, is that it angers people. Anger is often a necessary ingredient to get to the heart of any matter, race or otherwise. As a result of this anger, people are often murdered as I suspect I will be, figuratively speaking, for having the audacity to tell it like it is, not as people want it to be. I suspect my publisher, Zane, may have to take a hit or two for having the temerity and gumption to publish this work.

Another inherent problem with truth is its subjectivity. In other words, just because one believes something to be true, doesn't make it so. The problem therefore is people acting on so-called truths, or better still, people acting as if they know the truth when in fact they don't. But, because they believe they know, they act on said beliefs, and often find out later that they were wrong on a given matter. In the matter of race in America, this wrong belief can and often ends in disaster, death, and destruction.

For example, Susan Smith, who told the police that several black men took her car and her children. The children were later found dead in the stolen vehicle, submerged in a pond. Later, we learn the truth, that being that Susan Smith murdered her own children. Here's the question that no one asked—at least I never heard it asked. Why didn't Susan say white men did it? Wouldn't Americans still be outraged that men, any men, did this to a woman and defenseless, innocent children? Race would not have mattered, would it? Yet she said black men did it. Why? Probably because Susan believed whites would believe her. My question again is why would whites be so quick to believe this? Whatever the answer to these troubling questions is, it speaks volumes as to what people are quick to believe about their neighbors.

Surely someone will want to point to all the progress that has been made in the last twenty years. And I have no problem acknowledging this. However, recent events keep the subject matter alive. I am specifically referring to a November 2004 *Monday Night Football* introductory skit with Philadelphia wide receiver Terrell Owens (black) and Nicollette Sheridan (white) of ABC's *Desperate Housewives* series. Sheridan enters the Philadelphia Eagles locker room wearing nothing but a towel. In an attempt to seduce Owens, she drops the towel, supposedly baring all to the football player, then flings her naked body into Owens' arms, each leg flaring out to the side of his body, giving one the impression of an intercourse position.

People were up in arms, saying, "I don't wanna see that during *Monday Night Football*. Children are watching," as if ABC didn't know they would be. Later during that tumultuous week, certain members of the National

Football League admitted that this skit played into racial stereotypes. What racial stereotypes were they referring to? Soon O.J. Simpson and Kobe Bryant's names were thrown into the mix, causing more of a stir. Over what? Simulated sex between a black man and a white woman. Never mind that this is depicted in popular beer commercials these days during daylight hours.

Nevertheless, I wonder what kind of furor there would have been had New York Giants Tight End Jeremy Shockey (white) and Beyoncé Knowles of Destiny's Child, or Halle Berry, or Vivica A. Fox, or Serena Williams, or any other beautiful black woman had played the same roles as Owens and Sheridan. If the latter doesn't cause the same furor as the former, then we know a double standard still exists. If it does cause the same angst, then we know that America's race problem has much to do with the bedroom.

In telling this tale, I tried to make the characters speak the truth as they saw it, not as people want it to be. I'm sure lots of people are offended, but that's good. But do try to get past the offense and look beneath the surface, which is where the real story lies. What can you do to make America better? Stand up and be counted. Don't be a coward by allowing family members, friends, and coworkers to spew their racist comments in your presence. When you allow this to go on unchecked, you become a part of the problem. Instead, choose to be a part of the solution.

ABOUT THE AUTHOR

A native of Toledo, Ohio, Keith Lee Johnson began writing purely by accident when a literature professor unwittingly challenged his ability to tell a credible story in class one day. He picked up a pen that very day and has been writing ever since. Upon graduating from high school in June, Keith joined the United States Air Force the following September and attained a Top Secret security clearance. He served his country in Texas, Mississippi, Nevada, California, Turkey and various other places during his four years of service. Keith has written four books and is currently working on his fifth. He is the author of *Sugar & Spice*, *Pretenses* and *Little Black Girl Lost*. His next release will be *Scarecrow*. Visit the author at www.keithleejohnson.com.

ALSO AVAILABLE FROM
STREBOR BOOKS INTERNATIONAL

All titles are in stores now, unless otherwise noted.

Baptiste, Michael
Cracked Dreams 1-59309-035-8
Godchild 1-59309-044-7 (October 2005)

Bernard, D.V.
The Last Dream Before Dawn
0-9711953-2-3
God in the Image of Woman
1-59309-019-6

Billingsley, ReShonda Tate
Help! I've Turned Into My Mother
1-59309-050-1 (November 2005)

Brown, Laurinda D.
Fire & Brimstone 1-59309-015-3
UnderCover 1-59309-030-7
The Highest Price for Passion
1-59309-053-6 (December 2005)

Cheekes, Shonda
Another Man's Wife 1-59309-008-0
Blackgentlemen.com 0-9711953-8-2
In the Midst of it All 1-59309-038-2

Cooper, William Fredrick
Six Days in January 1-59309-017-X
Sistergirls.com 1-59309-004-8

Crockett, Mark
Turkeystuffer 0-9711953-3-1

Daniels, J and Bacon, Shonell
*Luvalwayz: The Opposite Sex and
Relationships* 0-9711953-1-5
Draw Me With Your Love
1-59309-000-5

Darden, J. Marie
Enemy Fields 1-59309-023-4
Finding Dignity 1-59309-051-X
(November 2005)

De Leon, Michelle
Missed Conceptions 1-59309-010-2
Love to the Third 1-59309-016-1
Once Upon a Family Tree
1-59309-028-5

Faye, Cheryl
Be Careful What You Wish For
1-59309-034-X

Halima, Shelley
Azucar Moreno 1-59309-032-3
Los Morenos 1-59309-049-8
(November 2005)

Handfield, Laurel
My Diet Starts Tomorrow
1-59309-005-6
Mirror Mirror 1-59309-014-5

Hayes, Lee
Passion Marks 1-59309-006-4
A Deeper Blue: Passion Marks II
1-59309-047-1 (October 2005)

Hobbs, Allison
Pandora's Box 1-59309-011-0
Insatiable 1-59309-031-5
Dangerously in Love 1-59309-048-X
(November 2005)

Hurd, Jimmy
Turnaround 1-59309-045-5
(October 2005)

Jenkins, Nikki
Playing With the Hand I Was Dealt
1-59309-046-3 (December 2005)

Johnson, Keith Lee
Sugar & Spice 1-59309-013-7
Pretenses 1-59309-018-8
Fate's Redemption 1-59309-018-8

Johnson, Rique
Love & Justice 1-59309-002-1
Whispers from a Troubled Heart
1-59309-020-X
Every Woman's Man 1-59309-036-6
Sistergirls.com 1-59309-004-8
A Dangerous Return 1-59309-043-9
(July 2005)

Lee, Darrien
All That and a Bag of Chips
0-9711953-0-7
Been There, Done That
1-59309-001-3
What Goes Around Comes Around
1-59309-024-2
When Hell Freezes Over 1-59309-042-0
(July 2005)

Luckett, Jonathan
Jasminium 1-59309-007-2
How Ya Livin' 1-59309-025-0
Dissolve 1-59309-041-2 (June 2005)

McKinney, Tina Brooks
All That Drama 1-59309-033-1
Lawd Mo Drama 1-59309-052-8
(December 2005)

Pinnock, Janice
The Last Good Kiss 1-59309-055-2
(December 2005)

Quartay, Nane
Feenin 0-9711953-7-4
The Badness 1-59309-037-4

Rivers, V. Anthony
Daughter by Spirit 0-9674601-4-X
Everybody Got Issues 1-59309-003-X
Sistergirls.com 1-59309-004-8

Roberts, J. Deotis
Roots of a Black Future 0-9674601-6-6
Christian Beliefs 0-9674601-5-8

Stephens, Sylvester
Our Time Has Come 1-59309-026-9

Turley II, Harold L.
Love's Game 1-59309-029-3
Confessions of a Lonely Soul
1-59309-054-4 (December 2005)

Valentine, Michelle
Nyagra's Falls 0-9711953-4-X

White, A.J.
Ballad of a Ghetto Poet
1-59309-009-9

White, Franklin
Money for Good 1-59309-012-9
Potentially Yours 1-59309-027-7

Zane (Editor)
Breaking the Cycle 1-59309-021-8
Blackgentlemen.com 0-9711953-8-2
Sistergirls.com 1-59309-004-8